FALLING

LUCINDA BRANT BOOKS

— Falling Series —
FALLING IN
FALLING UP
FALLING OUT

— Roxton Foundation Series —
NOBLE SATYR
HIS DUCHESS
HER DUKE
THEIR GRACES

— Roxton Family Saga —
NOBLE SATYR
MIDNIGHT MARRIAGE
AUTUMN DUCHESS
DAIR DEVIL
PROUD MARY
SATYR'S SON
ETERNALLY YOURS
FOREVER REMAIN

— Alec Halsey Mysteries —
DEADLY ENGAGEMENT
DEADLY AFFAIR
DEADLY PERIL
DEADLY KIN
DEADLY DESIRE

— Salt Hendon Books —
SALT BRIDE
SALT REDUX

'*Quizzing glass and quill, into my sedan chair and away —— the 1700s rock!*'

A *New York Times*, *USA Today*, *Amazon*, and *Audible* bestselling author of award-winning Georgian historical romances and mysteries, Lucinda's books are renowned for their wit, heart-felt drama and a happily ever-after. She has degrees in history and political science from the Australian National University and a postgraduate degree in education from Bond University, where she was awarded the Frank Surman Medal. *Noble Satyr*, Lucinda's first novel, was awarded the $10,000 *Random House/Woman's Day* Romantic Fiction Prize, and she has twice been a finalist for the Romance Writers' of Australia Romantic Book of the Year. Her novels have garnered multiple awards and become worldwide genre bestsellers. Lucinda lives a stone's throw from the beach, in a writing hut with wall-to-wall books on all aspects of the Eighteenth Century, collected over 40 years—Heaven. She loves to hear from readers (and she'll write back!).

lucindabrant@gmail.com | lucindabrant.com
pinterest.com/lucindabrant | x.com/lucindabrant
facebook.com/lucindabrantbooks | youtube.com/lucindabrantauthor

FALLING UP

An Enchanting Georgian Fairytale Romance...
of sorts...Regarding a Beautiful Beast
and His Penniless Redeemer

Lucinda Brant

A Sprigleaf Book
Published by Sprigleaf Pty. Ltd.

*Falling UP: An Enchanting Georgian Fairytale Romance…of sorts…
Regarding a Beautiful Beast and His Penniless Redeemer.*

A YA retelling of *Satyr's Son: A Georgian Historical Romance,*
available as Book 5 in the Roxton Family Saga.
*Back cover reviews are for the *Satyr's Son* edition of this book.

Typeset in EB Garamond.

ISBN 978-1-922985-27-9

10 9 8 7 6 5 4 3 2 1
Perfect Bound Paperback Edition. (i) I.

PART I

THE CITY

ONE

THE BOROUGH OF WESTMINSTER
LONDON

IT WAS A short walk to Leicester Square from Warner's Dispensary in Gerrard Street, where Miss Lisa Crisp resided with Dr. and Mrs. Warner. She hoped the errand would see her returned before she was missed; it was a needless worry. It was Wednesday afternoon. Any other day of the week, when she assisted in the dispensary, her absence would be noted. But not on a Wednesday. On a Wednesday she could do as she pleased. But as she was poor and friendless, she had no one to visit and nowhere to go.

But this particular Wednesday would prove to be the exception...

It was a fine summer's day, and as neither Dr. or Mrs. Warner would wonder at her whereabouts, Lisa did not feel obliged to tell them, or the household servants, where she was headed. Though she did raise servant eyebrows when Cook, in conversation with the housekeeper, paused mid-sentence to watch her pass through the kitchen and leave via the servant entrance, wearing her sensible half-boots, a wide-peaked bonnet, and cotton mittens.

Outside she was met in the small service area below street level by one Becky Bannister, seamstress and haberdasher's assistant. Becky served behind the counter of her great-aunt's shop, Humphreys' Haberdashers, on the corner of Gerrard and Princes Street, and when called upon, visited clients in their homes. A well-built girl with dark hair and rosy cheeks, she bobbed a respectful curtsy and prepared to pick up the basket at her feet, eager to be off. But Lisa was not ready just yet to ascend the steps into the noise and heat of town.

Spying empty flour sacks airing atop a stack of crates, Lisa took two and neatly placed them across the second-to-last step to save their petticoats from grime, and invited Becky to sit beside her.

"Before we visit Lord Westby's residence," Lisa said with a kind smile, "you had best tell me again what happened, and what it is you took."

"Miss, I done told ye," Becky explained. "The book fell into me work basket—"

"—and you decided to borrow it. Yes. You've already told me so, but I need to know precisely what happened if we are to prevail upon His Lordship not to press charges against you for theft." When the girl's bottom lip quivered, Lisa smiled reassuringly and placed a hand on Becky's bare forearm. "If you say the book was dropped into your basket, I believe you. Please, Becky. Tell me everything, and from the beginning. I said I would help you, and I will."

Becky sniffed and nodded, and some of her apprehension eased. Yesterday, when she had picked up her basket full of notions knowing the book was there, her only thought was that she might be able to exchange it for the shilling owed her by Peggy Markham, Lord Westby's mistress. But upon a night's reflection, her confidence in such a scheme fled, which was why, when Miss Crisp had come into the shop to purchase thread, she'd appealed to her for help.

Though they were both nineteen years of age, Becky regarded Miss Crisp—as did those with cause to visit Warner's Dispensary—as someone to be trusted; someone good in a crisis. After all, Miss Crisp was the dispensary's resident amanuensis, writing letters home for those who could not write themselves. Which was most of London, for while the majority of Londoners prided themselves on being able to read, few had been taught to write.

Often these were letters home to family in far off counties, filled with details about their new lives in the capital. Sometimes they were letters seeking employment or patronage. All were deeply personal and relied on Miss Crisp's discretion. Whatever the contents of these letters, the author always felt satisfied and better within themselves seeing Miss Crisp inscribe their words in ink.

Thus Becky knew that whatever she confided in Miss Crisp it would be treated with respect and in confidence. But as much as she tried to keep the panic from her voice, it was there, just bubbling under the surface, as she recounted her visit to the Leicester Square townhouse inhabited by one Lord Westby, and where also resided his mistress, the celebrated actress of Shakespearean tragedies, Mrs. Peggy Markham.

"Mrs. Markham did took three ribbons! She then refused to own she had 'em. She said I'd made a mistake in me reckonin'," Becky explained. "Which I never does 'cause Aunt gives m'ears a good box if I were to lose coin on any of our trimmin's. I know 'ow many ribbons I has before I leave the shop. And I count 'em again when puttin' everythin' back into me basket when I'm at a clientele's house."

"And this time...?" Lisa prompted when Becky clenched her teeth in an angry huff.

"She stole a pair o' garters. Pink silk with painted flowers. Worth a lot more than three ribbons, and I ain't told m'aunt them are now missin', too!"

"And Mrs. Markham refused to own she had the garters?"

"She did. I said I'd add them to the account, along with the three ribbons from the time before, and that made her mad—"

"I imagine it would," Lisa murmured.

"—and she called me a pert miss and threw up her 'ands. Said 'ow dare I question 'er word. She told me to gather me trimmin's and pointed to the door, in that dramatic way actresses 'ave about 'em. But I stood me ground."

"That was brave."

Becky glanced slyly at Lisa and confessed. "Not so brave as you think, Miss. I wanted to scramble out o' there faster than a fox in huntin' season, but me legs wouldn't work on account of 'im who was there."

Lisa frowned, trying to make sense of Becky's story. "There was someone—there was a gentleman—Lord Westby—with Mrs. Markham?"

Becky shook her head. "Not 'im. 'is Lordship was there, sittin' in a corner, lookin' like thunder and not sayin' a word. It was his friend, the other gent who was with 'em, he made me forget m'manners and stare."

"Oh? May I ask why you could not help staring at this gentleman?"

"You'll think me feverish, but 'e's bewitchin' 'andsome."

"Oh, Becky! Be*witching*?" Lisa giggled. "Truly?"

Becky huffed. "I ain't given to exaggeratin'!"

"Of course not," Lisa replied, contrite, and pressed her lips together to stifle any further incredulous mirth.

"You'd think the same if you saw 'im. Eyes and 'air blacker than a coal pit. His nose is a bit of a beak, but his mouth more than makes up for that. Too pretty for a gent." She grinned and confessed, "I just wanted to take 'is face between me 'ands and kiss it all over!"

When Lisa gasped, Becky's brow darkened.

"Just 'cause I wanted to don't mean I ever would. I know me place, and I know a gent like that wouldn't look twice at Becky Bannister, or, for that matter, at you, Miss. For the likes of you and me, 'e might as well live on the moon. Though a girl can dream, can't she?"

"No offence taken," Lisa replied with an understanding smile. "I agree. I daydream, too. My surprise had more to do with your description of the gentleman than any disapproval of your wish to kiss him. He sounds perfectly god-like, that he could very well have a place on Mount Olympus. Which is practically the moon, isn't it?"

"I don't know nothin' about Mount Oly-what's-it-called, but you're right. 'E only 'ad to speak for Mrs. Markham to go all doe-eyed. Which I reckon was why Lord Westby looked as dark as a thunder cloud. Jealous of 'is friend's good looks, is my guess, and his voice—"

"Voice?"

"Aye, miss. 'E 'as a voice that's rich and smooth, like the way hot chocolate slides down the back of y'throat."

"A voice like hot chocolate? Dear me, Becky, you have a lovely turn of phrase," Lisa complimented, clearing her throat.

"Aunt Humphreys says it's 'cause I daydream—*a lot*. But I wasn't daydreamin'. That gent was no phantom of me imagination! And I remember 'e said 'e only tolerated theatrics on a stage. And for Mrs. Markham to show 'im where she'd hid 'is book. 'E'd an auction to-to—*attend*." She nodded, satisfied she had relayed what the handsome gentleman had said, adding for emphasis because Miss Crisp was now staring at her with lips parted, "Auction. That's what 'e said. 'E was goin' to an *auction*."

"And he lost this book that's now in your basket at Lord Westby's residence?"

Becky nodded. "'E did. And Lord Westby wasn't offerin' to help 'im find it neither on account of bein' in a sulk. I never noticed the book at first 'cause I was busy lookin' at 'im. But then I went back to scoopin' up the ribbons and as I was puttin' 'em away Mrs. Markham gets off 'er chair, and there it is! The book! She'd been hidin' it under her skirts all along!"

"And she was hiding it from him?" When Becky nodded, Lisa added with a cock of her head, "I wonder why..."

"That's when I caught a glimpse of me pink garters. They were keepin' her stockin's up!" Becky ground her teeth, adding darkly, "She took 'em all right!"

"And the book?" Lisa interrupted.

"Mrs. Markham dropped it into me basket as soon as the gentleman who was lookin' for it turned his back and went into the next room to continue 'is search elsewhere."

Quickly shaking her thoughts clear of Mrs. Markham and her nameless but thoroughly handsome visitor, Lisa returned to the business at hand and asked Becky if she could take a look at this book that held so much interest for the gentleman with the velvety voice.

It was large and heavy, and the frontispiece told her almost everything she needed to know. It was a catalog worth the princely sum of five shillings and contained a listing of the entire contents of the Portland Museum, once owned by the Dowager Duchess of Portland, and which now, upon her death, was being sold by auctioneers Skinner and Co.

Lisa had read reports of the month-long auction in Dr. Warner's copy of *The Gentleman's Magazine*. The Dowager Duchess had been a great patroness of Natural History, and a voracious collector of all things associated with the science, from corals to all manner of shells, animals, insects, petrifications, plants, minerals, and related paraphernalia.

Flicking through the catalog's pages, she noticed annotations in the margins beside items for sale, and returning to the frontispiece she saw inscribed in the same elegant fist the initials H-A, separated by a hyphen.

What immediately crossed Lisa's mind and made her heart beat faster was twofold: That this H-A needed the catalog to be admitted to the auction, and as he had marked particular items not yet come up for sale, he would most certainly still be looking for his missing catalog. Secondly, and most disturbing, as the catalog was worth more than a shilling, its theft would be considered grand larceny, and a guilty verdict meant a sentence of death by hanging.

None of this Becky needed to know at that precise moment, so Lisa smiled bravely, hoping not to give away her fears, and returned the catalog to her.

"Is there anything else you should tell me about your visit to Lord Westby's? Or about this catalog before we head off?" When Becky shook her head, Lisa stood, adding in a tone she hoped exuded confidence, "Very well. Then when we arrive at Lord Westby's, you had best let me do the talking."

Becky nodded and smiled, picked up her basket, put it over her arm, and gave a huge sigh of relief.

"Thank you, Miss. I knew that if anyone can get that book back inside without me bein' dropped into a 'ot vat o' trouble, it'd be you!" She cocked her head in thought. "D'you think you could get Mrs. Markham to put 'er mark to 'er account, too?"

"One small miracle at a time, Becky," Lisa said with false buoyancy, and went up the steps to street level.

TWO

Lisa and Becky walked as one, arm in arm, down Gerrard Street and up Princes Street towards the river. The racket and bustle precluded conversation, so they stayed silent, the basket up front between them, and kept on the lookout for pickpockets amongst the crisscross of pedestrians and vocal street vendors.

Soon the narrow streets opened out and they were on the corner of a spacious cobbled square, fronted with rows of elegant townhouses, the grand mansion of Leicester House, once home to various members of the Royal Family and now occupied by Sir Ashton Lever's Museum of Natural History, forming the square's northern border. Central to this wide expanse was a sizeable quadrangle of grass with gravel crosswalks dominated by a gilt statue of the first King George. Here, within the confines of an iron fence, privileged residents took idle walks, and nursemaids supervised children in leading strings and those little lords and ladies running about in the summer sunshine with their hoops or kites. A crossing sweep worked every corner, and there was enough space for carriages, sedan chairs, riders on horseback, and pedestrians to pass one another with ease.

Leicester Square had once been the center of Polite Society, but the city and its industry had sufficiently encroached on its elegance that several of the townhouses were now occupied by shops and manufactories, a sign of the changing times. Persons of title, wealth, and influence had moved out a decade or more earlier and those who remained, whether through lack of funds or foresight, and whose townhouses were squeezed in amongst industry, did their best to ignore their changed surroundings and their mercantile neighbors.

Lord Westby was one such resident. Heir to the Duke of Oborne, His Lordship occupied a tall, narrow townhouse squashed between a carpet manufactory and the Dowager Marchioness of Fittleworth's residence. Whenever His Lordship stepped out into the square he made a habit of looking north to her abode, and never south to his mercantile neighbor.

Lisa, who had never had reason to visit Leicester Square, was fascinated by it all. In her preoccupation with the variety of pedestrians and the continual parade of carriages and sedan chairs going to and fro, she almost forgot why she was there. That is until Becky stopped in front of Lord Westby's residence.

"The servant door is back down the lane and—"

"Oh no, Becky," Lisa said, holding fast to the girl's arm. "We enter by the front door, or not at all."

Becky's eyes went wide and she swallowed. She had never entered a house by the front door, ever.

Lisa went up the shallow steps and lifted the silver knocker, only for the door to be wrenched open before she could knock, as if someone had been at the window peering out into the street in anticipation of their arrival. Startled, Lisa stumbled back to stand on the cobbles.

A short squat man with bulging eyes and a grizzled wig appeared out of the blackness.

"You're late!" he hissed and opened the door wider. "Come in! Come in! Quickly! Quickly!"

THE PORTER moved aside to let them enter, but when Lisa and Becky just stood there, recovering from the shock of such a reception, he stomped out onto the footpath, darted behind them, and fluttered his hands low, at his bended knees, as if driving a flock of geese.

"Go in! Go in! Don't stand about! Go in!"

The girls shuffled forward, looking over their shoulders to see what the little man was up to. And once they were in the vestibule, he slammed shut the door, which made them jump. They clung ever tighter to one another and glanced about. But there was a decided lack of wax in the sconces, and after the bright sunlight of a summer's day outside, their eyes needed time to adjust to the darkness. This was denied them when out of the gloom pounced a tall, stick-thin man with a long chin and furrowed brow. He glared down at them from a great height before looking over their heads to demand imperiously,

"Where are the others?"

"O-o-others?" Lisa stuttered, a swift look up from under her peaked bonnet.

But he hadn't addressed her. He was talking to his squat associate.

"No carriage, Mr. Packer. These two came on foot."

"No carriage? *On foot*?"

The tall, imperious personage, who Lisa decided was the butler of this establishment, rolled his eyes and sighed, as if this were the worst possible news he had ever received. He stepped to one side of the staircase, giving Lisa no time to explain, flicked a bony finger in direction of the first landing, and said in voice heavy with the worries of the world upon his pointy shoulders, "You two will have to do—for now. Up you go. First landing. Second door on the left. No need to knock. Just go in."

"I beg your pardon, but there seems to be some misunder—"

"My dear girl. Don't beg my pardon. It isn't up to me or you or your cherry-cheeked friend to wonder at the whys and wherefores, or the how-tos, for that matter. You're here, aren't you? His Lordship and the Batoni Brotherhood don't make a habit of waiting—for anything. Now up you go."

"Bat—Batoni Brother*hood*?"

"You're an inquisitive one, I'll say that for you!" the butler snorted, rudely looking Lisa up and down. "Take my advice and keep your voice bottled. You're not here for your conversation."

Lisa balked to be so familiarly addressed and arched an eyebrow in disapproval.

"Am I not?"

"Hardly! Though to look at you—Well! You all come in different shapes and sizes so it's not for me to say—"

"—because you're not here for your conversation, either?" Lisa quipped, and accompanied this with a deceptively sweet smile.

"Ha! I suppose I deserved that," the butler replied good-naturedly. "If you're quick about it, you might even get to choose your quarry, before your friends arrive."

Lisa had no idea what he was talking about. She glanced up the stairs, which were as ill-lit as the vestibule, and then smiled reassuringly at Becky, who, if she had any confidence in this venture before they entered Lord Westby's townhouse, now had none. She had lost her rosy glow and her eyes were wary.

"Friends?"

The butler rolled his eyes again and gave a snort, a glance at Becky.

"If not friends, then your female brethren." He jerked a thumb at the staircase. "Now up you go! Quick! Quick!"

Lisa wasn't sure what decided her to take the course of action she did because her first impulse was to hand over the catalog to the talkative butler with the excuse she had found it in the street, then flee the scene with Becky without divulging who they were. But something compelled her to hold her ground—curiosity, stubbornness, impetuosity, she wasn't sure which. She decided that to ascend the stairs into the unknown without fear of the consequences might at least provide some light relief from the ordinariness of her present and predicted future, and prove an adventure worth taking.

It was this same adventurous—the headmistress of Blacklands called it *impetuous*—streak that had seen her abscond from the school grounds to meet a friend at the Chelsea Bun House. It was the third such visit and the one reported to the headmistress, and it was her undoing. She was expelled just six months shy of her graduation. The Chelsea Bun House incident had forever tarnished her in the eyes of her school and her family. But when she reflected upon her actions— and she'd had two years in which to do so—she was confident she would not have acted any differently. And with a reputation so tarnished it would never regain its luster, taking this risk would be of little consequence, surely?

But she had no wish to drag Becky into further misadventure, so she did her best to dissuade her from venturing upstairs.

"Give me the catalog, Becky," she whispered. "You may stay here while I—"

"No, Miss. I'm comin' with ye!"

"Please. I have no idea who or what we'll encounter upstairs. Possibly an angry lord and his mistress. And as they don't know me, I may be able to persuade them to accept the catalog without further explanation. So it would be better for you to remain—"

"No, Miss. Beggin' ye pardon. I done brought y' 'ere," Becky stated stubbornly and hugged the basket closer. "We go up together, or not at all. They're me terms."

"Very well. But promise me, if I decide we need to leave—for whatever reason—we will—immediately."

When Becky nodded, Lisa untied the ribbons of her bonnet and handed it to the butler. He held this article of feminine attire between thumb and forefinger, as if it were poisonous, and gave it to the porter. Lisa lightly patted the wisps of hair come free from her coiled braids, then smoothed her cotton mitts over her slim arms, as if steeling herself for the interview. Finally, without a second look at the butler, she nodded to Becky and they went up the stairs.

They followed the butler's directions, and at the first landing Lisa picked up a lighted taper in its holder from a corner table to light their way along the dark passage. At the second door on their left they stopped. Instinctively, Becky hung back, and Lisa gave her the taper. She did not knock to announce their presence, but opened the door and went straight in.

Not in her wildest imaginings could she have foreseen what awaited them.

THREE

SEVERAL HOURS EARLIER, members of the Batoni Brotherhood had gathered for their regular bi-monthly get-together at the townhouse of Lord Westby, whose turn it was to play host. The Brotherhood's membership consisted of four young gentlemen who had taken the Grand Tour together. Sent off by their noble parents with tutors, valets, and servants in tow, they had wandered through France, Switzerland, the Italian States, and Greece for three years. Returning home via the Mediterranean coastline and with a better appreciation of their classical education, they brought with them trunks laden with artworks, books, finely-tailored clothing, and anything else from antiquity that took their fancy.

While abroad, these sons from Polite Society's first families made a pact. Upon their return, they would meet up once every other month to reminisce, discuss their collections of *objets d'art*, to eat a splendid supper, and drink themselves under the table. These gatherings had been going on now for just over a year and were eagerly anticipated by all members of the Brotherhood.

But the Batoni Brotherhood was about to change forever. Sir John 'Jack' Cavendish was to be the first of the foursome to take the plunge into matrimony. No one wanted change, though they all respected Jack's wish to marry his childhood sweetheart. It was just a little bit depressing that this get-together would be the last time they would meet as bachelors. Which was why everyone was determined to enjoy it for Jack's sake.

What was needed to lift the mood was more wine and, hopefully, not too long away, females to entertain them. So it was fortuitous when Lord Westby's butler poked his long face around the door.

"More bottles, Packer!" Seb, Lord Westby demanded. "And be quick about it. And have this mess cleared away. Room smells like Billingsgate. Can't have the girls mistaking us for a bunch of salty sea dogs—"

"—or pirates, Seb," interrupted Mr. Randal 'Bully' Knatchbull. "They could mistake us for pirates."

"Pirates, Bully? Well, I wouldn't mind being mistaken for a pirate. Still. Don't want to stink like one."

"Most definitely not."

"Pirates stink of fish."

"And oysters. Fish and oysters and-and—*seaweed*."

"A salty sea dog is a pirate," Lord Henri-Antoine 'Harry' Hesham cut in, bored. "Packer? Brandy would be appreciated."

The door was barely closed on the butler's back when Jack Cavendish lifted his chin off his chest and frowned across at his best friend. "Do you think that wise?" When Lord Henri-Antoine made no comment he hissed loudly, "Harry?! Harry?! Do you think—"

"I'm doing my best *not* to think."

"—you should have a brandy after so many bottles of claret?"

"You've been counting."

"No! Of course not!"

At this hot denial, Henri-Antoine opened an eye. The quick flush to his best friend's cheeks exposed the fib. He stared at Jack long enough to make him aware of his disapproval, then closed his accusatory eye.

"Oh, all right! I'll admit to it," Jack confessed, folding his legs back and sitting forward in the wingchair, a glance over at Seb and Bully, who were now huddled together on the sofa leafing through the pages of *Harris's List of Covent Garden Ladies*. Confident they were otherwise occupied, he added, "Perhaps you should have Michel fetched, to take you home—"

"And ruin this splendid gathering? Michel's not here. He's at the Portland auction, buying shells."

"Was that sensible?"

"Sensible? To trust Michel with the buying of shells?"

"Haha! No! Him there; you here."

At that Henri-Antoine opened both eyes with some effort. The thud to his temple was becoming unbearable. But he was determined to make it through the afternoon because it was his best friend's bachelor send-off, and that only happened once in a lifetime. Thus he made light of Jack's concern, so he would not worry, and to mask how he truly felt.

"I'm glad you're getting married. Time to put your worry to good use—about something, not nothing."

"You are not nothing, Harry. Never have been, never will be. You should've gone to the auction."

"I've been every day for three weeks. And seen enough shells, minerals, and dead things, to numb the most ardent collector. But Elsie will have her shells... There was one in particular... A nautilus... I hope I remembered correctly... I seem... I seem to have misplaced my catalog..."

Jack caught Henri-Antoine's grimace and was not fooled when his best friend made a quick recover by pretending to brush lint from the upturned cuff of his embroidered frock coat. Jack and Henri-Antoine had been best friends since they were nine years old, and Henri-Antoine's affliction remained an open family secret and was treated accordingly. Any medical specialist who professed to be an expert in the treatment of the falling sickness had been consulted, from London to Constantinople. But there was no cure. Yet, somehow, Henri-Antoine had convinced his mother and his brother that his malady had cured itself.

It was a lie. But Jack had bought into the lie because he knew how important it was to Henri-Antoine to be thought the same as every other fellow. And he understood Henri-Antoine's need for conceal-ment. The falling sickness carried great social stigma for sufferers and their families. Thus Henri-Antoine did everything his wealth could provide to ensure his affliction remained a closely-guarded secret.

But after a few drinks, Jack's anxiety increased tenfold, and he was prone to vocalizing his fears for Henri-Antoine's health, much to his best friend's chagrin.

"It's the smoke as well as the alcohol," Jack postulated, another furtive glance over at Seb and Bully. "Neither is good for you, and when combined—"

"This concern is touching, but unnecessary."

"Let me have a window opened, get you a flask of boiled lemon water—"

"For God's sake, Jack! Don't—don't—*fuss*."

Jack sat back but was undeterred, and persistent. "It's time you confided in your brother—"

"No."

"—because, as you rightly pointed out, once I'm married, I'll have other concerns—a wife, and hopefully in the not-too-distant future, children. That means I won't be around as much, and you need—"

"What I need is for you to—"

Henri-Antoine paused, willing himself to ignore the pain. He averted his face, giving Jack a view of his strong aquiline profile, and momentarily stared at the fireplace littered with the ash and discarded tips from half-a-dozen smoked India cheroots.

"What do you need me to do, Harry?"

"Keep your concern for those deserving of it," Henri-Antoine said with quiet menace, which was far more effective than had he shouted. "Live your life with your bride and brace of brats in the Cotswolds—wherever the hell that is—and never give me another thought. My life...my life shall—shall go on perfectly well without y—"

"But—Harry! I—"

"Ah! The brandy!" Henri-Antoine interrupted, ignoring Jack and tapping the table at his elbow for the footman to set down the silver tray holding decanter and glasses.

He bestirred himself to splash a generous drop of the amber fluid into each glass, then offered one to Jack. But when Jack hesitated, Henri-Antoine peered at him more closely and saw the flush to his face.

"Take it, Jack," he urged softly, and with a rare smile. "I want to toast our friendship."

Jack took the glass, swallowing down the lump in his throat. His voice was raw. "You can be vile at times, Harry. Do you know that?"

"I've never been anything less, dear fellow. Reason you are my only friend." Henri-Antoine raised his glass. "To Jack. Dependable.

Loyal. Responsible. Loving. Your bride is deserving of the very best, and you are the best, Jack."

Jack grinned sheepishly, losing his petulance, and the friends clinked glasses.

They savored the brandy.

"Thank you, Harry. You'll always be my best friend. It's just—It's just—"

"You've found your mate. More correctly, she found you. I am exceedingly happy for you both... I hope you are blessed with a brood."

"I wish—I wish you could be as happy as I am... That you, too, had found your mate."

Henri-Antoine pulled a face. "*Me?* And fairies are real! I grant I am excellent marriage mart material... But... What poor wretch would willingly take on the care and watering of such a pathetic creature?"

"I believe there is someone out there for you. I do," Jack said earnestly, eyes glassy again because this admission was the closest his friend had ever come to acknowledging his affliction. "You just haven't found her—and she hasn't found you—yet!"

"Oh, don't be forlorn," Henri-Antoine said dismissively. "I'm not you. I can't imagine restricting myself to a single female. What is it, Bully?" he drawled, catching sight of Randall Knatchbull waving Harris's List above his head in an effort to attract attention.

"Are there six or eight nymphs coming to entertain us, Harry?"

"Eight," Henri-Antoine replied. "Jack gets first pick—"

Jack's face burned. "Not me. Not ever again."

Henri-Antoine looked at the drop of brandy in his glass, then lifted his gaze and teased Jack mercilessly.

"Indeed?" he purred. "I seem to recall... Those were your exact words as we stumbled up the steps into Frau Dortman's. You made the same lame protest in the vestibule of Signora Lucia's, too. Your attempts to resist the charms of that pretty little redhead—"

"Shut up, Harry!" Jack demanded hotly and shot to his feet. "If you dare say another word—"

"Your wishes are noted. So is your prudery."

"I intend to be a devoted husband, and you know it."

"I do." Henri-Antoine sighed heavily. "Regrettably, uxoriousness is a family failing." He threw back the last drops of brandy. When

Jack continued to stand over him with hands clenched, he briefly closed his eyes. If Jack had one failing—no, two—it was that he was earnest to a fault, and that he rarely, if ever, appreciated Henri-Antoine's playful provocations. So he said to placate him, "I see I'm being vile again. I do beg your pardon."

"Jack? Don't tell me Harry is demanding first pick of the rosebuds?" Seb Westby called out, happy to witness a rare altercation between the best friends. "Are you surprised? After all, he paid for the bunch!"

Henri-Antoine waved a languid hand in Seb's direction without looking at him. "Take your pick, Westby. My treat."

"Harry?! Is this your mark beside the Jamaican beauty of Litchfield Street?" Bully enquired, unaware Henri-Antoine had turned from the conversation because his nose was back between the pages of the little book. "Says here she treads the Cyprian stage. Says she's got dark brown ringlets...I've always fancied dark brown ringlets, and it says here she—"

"But will she fancy *you*, Bully?" Seb interrupted with a snort of derision. "Sounds a bit exotic for your bland tastes. Best stick to the pap you know, and what they can stomach."

This cutting remark, made in an attempt to have the others laugh at Bully's expense, caused Henri-Antoine to rally and fix his derisory gaze on Lord Westby.

"Had you bothered to read Miss Wilson's excellent précis, Westby, you'd have kept your mouth shut."

"Why would I need to do that, eh?" Seb demanded, suddenly hot in the face. He stabbed a finger in Henri-Antoine's direction. "Are you daring to malign me, Hesham? Are you? Eh?"

"Seb! Don't be a complete zany," hissed Bully, grabbing at Westby's shirt sleeve in an attempt to pull him back down onto the sofa. "Seb! You're drunk! Harry meant nothing by it! And you know you never win with Harry!"

"Shut your porthole!" Seb snapped, and yanked his shirtsleeve free of Bully's fingers, attention wholly fixed on Henri-Antoine. "Why don't you stand up and face me like a man, Hesham. Get up I say!"

Henri-Antoine turned his head and looked Seb up and down with a slight lift of his brows and drawled, "And make a show of your glaring inadequacies? I think not. Sit down, Westby. You're making a fool of yourself."

"Why you-you—How dare you tell me what to do in my own house," Seb raged, face burning brighter. He scrambled over the low table to get to his quarry. "I'm going to mash your beak all over your face. Stand up I say!"

He launched himself at Henri-Antoine as if he were jumping off a jetty to board a boat, both legs in the air, and arms swinging wide.

Jack intercepted him, stepping in front of Seb just as he landed by Henri-Antoine's chair. They were both knocked sideways in the collision.

In one fluid movement, Henri-Antoine brought himself to his full height and dominated the space. His penchant for elaborately embroidered waistcoats and frock coats cloaked his athleticism. So even his friends were often surprised by the width in his shoulders, and to find he was the tallest in the room. But such physicality was all for nought when he was in the grip of his affliction. And he knew, as Seb came at him, that the onset of a seizure was imminent.

"Oi! Harry? Are you all right?" Bully demanded, when Henri-Antoine closed his eyes and swayed. He nudged Jack in the ribs. "Jack! Harry's turned as white as fresh snow."

At this pronouncement Jack forgot about controlling a furious Seb and turned to his best friend. "Let's sit you down, Ha—"

"*Not here,*" Henri-Antoine said through his teeth.

"I'll have the lads fetched."

"Do—*that… Mon Dieu,*" Henri-Antoine muttered, and strode from the room to Seb's growling protests that Jack and Bully unhand him so he could have a proper go at rearranging Henri-Antoine's neck cloth.

HENRI-ANTOINE had left it too late.

He no longer had a headache. That was bad—*very bad.*

He must not panic. He must keep his wits about him.

He must find a safe place…

An intense cold penetrated his left hand. It was as if it had been plunged into a pail of icy water. And his tongue was tingling. Sometimes it swelled. He was never certain. All he knew was that soon he wouldn't be able to talk at all, least make anyone understand what he was saying. He clamped his teeth shut.

He wouldn't call out. He mustn't make a sound. Not here. Not in front of others.

He had managed to make it to twenty-three without being a public disgrace. He wasn't about to let it happen now.

Where was Jack? He needed him to fetch the lads.

Why was the room full of bright light?

He was such a fool for drinking the brandy, for not listening to Jack. Jack had been right. Dear Jack…

He staggered to the door, or did he limp? He had no idea.

He had to get away from the light. He squinted.

The walls had begun to move.

The icy coldness had now reached his shoulder. He no longer had a left arm. It felt as if it were hanging loose and useless at his side, but in truth he knew it looked very different from how it felt. The muscles contracted, forcing the elbow to bend and his arm to adhere to his side and against his chest. His hand twisted at the wrist; the fingers pulling inwards. The muscles down one side of his neck did the same, tugging his head to the left, while his mouth became slack, and he drooled.

He had no idea how long the seizure would last because he always blacked out, always spiraled away into nothingness, and was left to the mercy of others. And while it lasted he was a distorted mess—a freak of nature—and a monstrous form of his true self. And he knew as dawn followed night he would be a slave to his affliction for the rest of his days.

He saw the door. It was open. *Thank God.*

Now to get out of the room.

But he could not leave.

Someone blocked his path. No. Not someone. A female. Or was it an angel? Diffuse light glowed around her hair like a halo. She had big blue eyes in a perfect oval face and she was staring at him in unblinking recognition, or was that fear? Did he know her? No! He was hallucinating. *She* was an hallucination. His befuddled, knotted, pulsating brain was confusing this girl with the Renaissance paintings he had so admired in the Italian states. Glorious Botticelli females with striking features and flowing hair.

If she were a Botticelli angel conjured by his seizure, then he reasoned he could simply walk through her. But he bumped up against her. She was flesh and blood after all. Not an ethereal being then. She crumpled against him—fainted with fright, he did not doubt it. She made an instant recover and pulled away. But she still blocked his escape. So he stuck his face in hers and demanded she get out of his way. What he snarled was something else entirely.

"J'ai désespérément besoin de faire pipi!—I desperately need to pee!"

Botticelli's angel instantly backed out of the room and disappeared into the blackness.

Henri-Antoine followed and promptly collapsed at her feet.

FOUR

W ITH BECKY at her back holding aloft the single taper, Lisa had entered a drawing room filled with the haze of tobacco smoke as thick as a winter morning's fog. Her eyes instantly watered, and her nose twitched. She thought she would sneeze. There was a lot of noise, shouting and scuffling, and furniture being bumped about. She managed a cursory glance at the chaotic state of the room, saw a group of young men over by the fireplace in the midst of an affray, and decided the best course of action was to leave the catalog on the nearest chair and flee.

But she wasn't given the opportunity because one of the young men turned away from his fellows and lumbered towards her.

Unaware she was blocking the exit, Lisa did not think to move aside. She was staring at the man coming towards her. Not at him precisely, because it was impolite to stare a stranger in the face, but at his waistcoat and matching frock coat in lilac silk with metallic thread embroidery. She had never seen such exquisite embroidery before nor such a soft-hued silk on a male. Faceted crystal gems covered the buckles of his polished black leather shoes, which she was sure had to be diamonds. He was the embodiment of aristocratic anecdote.

And then this resplendently-dressed gentleman was in front of her. Lisa had no time and nowhere to move.

He lurched.

Becky squealed with fright, dropped her basket and fled.

Instinctively Lisa knew Becky had deserted her without the need to glance over a shoulder. But she did not want to flee. The stranger held all her attention.

She had a moment of panic, that perhaps he meant to do her a harm, but that vanished as quickly as the thought had popped into her head. She was not naturally timid, nor did she instantly think the worst of people. Assisting in the dispensary, she had encountered enough curious persons come in off the streets experiencing illness and distress to varying degrees that little surprised her these days, about the people or what ailed them. And if she had learned anything from Dr. Warner's patients, it was that illness made no distinction between the poorest souls dressed in rags, and gentlemen such as this, dressed in fine clothes and diamonds. All were deserving of her compassion, and to be treated with dignity.

Nor did she fear him. A cursory diagnosis told her he was incapable of doing harm to anyone other than himself. He was either drunk beyond reason, taken ill, or affected by lunacy. Whatever had caused his present unhappy state he was suffering for it. Torment was writ large across his features, in the contortions in his fingers, and the straining in his neck in its fine white linen stock. He needed medical attention, something to ease his suffering, and, she realized too late, standing as a statue in the doorway was no way to be of help to him.

Yet before she could move, he walked right up to her as if she was not there at all and stepped on her foot.

This was so unexpected that she fell against him, biting her lip to stifle a cry of pain, because any sudden sound might startle him, and cause him to become agitated. Dr. Warner had cautioned his medical students when treating those who were clearly not in possession of their full faculties that any sudden movements or noise could send lunatics into an even greater frenzy.

Then the stranger startled her, sticking his face in hers and barking out an order. She did not understand, his words were slurred and almost unintelligible. But she had a sudden revelation that he was not speaking in English, but in French and it opened wide her eyes. He said he needed to urinate, and at once. That had Lisa tripping over her own petticoats to get out of his way. Yet no sooner had she backed out into the corridor, he staggering after her, than he crumpled at her feet.

WHEN HE HIT the floor with a thud, Lisa stared down at him, stunned.

It took Becky rushing over and tugging at her arm to break the spell.

"Come on, Miss!" she hissed. "Here's our chance! I'll get me basket and we'll flee—"

Lisa pulled her arm free and dropped to her knees beside the stranger.

"Bring the taper closer. I need to see if he's injured himself."

"Don't touch 'im, Miss! You dunno what 'es got!"

"He's unwell and needs our help," Lisa assured her, squinting up into the glow of the candle which was now just inches from her face. "Shine it over there so I can see if he's split his head or done himself any other injury."

Becky reluctantly did as she was told, the light from the taper flickering in her trembling hand. "By the looks of 'im, 'e ain't in 'is right mind!"

Lisa gently brushed back his mop of wavy black hair so she could see his face, wondering if the fall to the ground had knocked him unconscious. But his eyes were wide open, the pupils dilated, and he seemed to be staring without seeing. He certainly did not react to her touch or the closeness of her, so he did not know she was there. He trembled, but unlike Becky who did so from fright, these were not gentle tremors but a series of jerky actions in his limbs and torso, for which he seemed to have no control. The muscles in his neck remained strained, his head pulled to one side. She wished she could unravel his cravat—but where to start on the complicated knot in the soft folds of linen?

He had fallen on his right side, his frock coat bunching up under him, the skirts falling away from his black breeches. He was not at all relaxed, which she'd have expected had he knocked himself out. His left arm remained bent and adhered to his chest, his fingers gnarled and clinging to a couple of the covered buttons of his waistcoat.

Lisa wondered from these contortions if he were in pain. Yet, he hardly made a sound. She leaned in, beckoning Becky to bring the light closer. His mouth was twisted, pulled to one side like the rest of his body, with the lips slightly parted from which issued forth a low gurgling, but no intelligible words.

She sat back on her haunches, pondering what to do, and was distracted by the voices coming from the drawing room, where the door was still wide. At least the gentlemen were no longer shouting at one another or disturbing the furniture.

Instinctively, she knew the last thing this gentleman would want was for his friends to see him in such a reduced and vulnerable state. No doubt that was the reason he had tried to leave the room in such a hurry. So she had Becky quietly shut the door, hoping the gentlemen were too caught up in themselves to even notice that one of their number was no longer with them.

And as he continued to convulse, Lisa was reminded of young Joe, son of a local laundress, and a patient of Dr. Warner. Joe's mother was convinced her son's fits were the work of the devil, punishment for bearing a bastard. Dr. Warner told her most stridently not to be so foolish. Joe was not possessed of a demon. He suffered with the falling sickness, many children did, and it was not her fault or his. On one of Joe's many visits, Lisa had witnessed him have a fit; it had come on without warning, his thin little body wracked with sudden violent spasms, contorting his limbs and his face. It had ended just as abruptly, leaving Joe limp and exhausted, as if the life force had been sucked from him. She had never seen an adult have such an attack and had wrongly presumed the falling sickness a childhood ailment. Yet, here was this gentleman, a young man who seemed healthy in every other particular, in much the same reduced state as poor Joe. So he was not drunk, or mad, but a fellow sufferer...

Decided, she looked up at Becky, a hand to the stranger's shoulder, hoping touch might offer reassurance that he was not alone, just as she had done with Joe—though she had no reason to believe, that just like Joe, he was aware of her presence.

"Becky, find the butler. I need a coverlet. Also a basin of warm water and a clean cloth."

Becky stared down at Lisa as if she were as mad as the gentleman writhing on the floor.

"But—Miss! That's 'im!" she hissed. "That's the gent who was lookin' for the book. I'd know that nose anywhere. So we can't stay 'ere'—"

Lisa hid her astonishment, saying calmly, "I will not abandon him. He needs help. And I mean to stay until—"

"Miss, how can you 'elp? Best leave 'im to whatever devil 'as possessed 'is soul. Poor sot. And we don't want to get caught up in—"

"He's ill, not mad," Lisa interrupted stridently. "Now please do as I ask and then you may leave, if that is your wish. I'll be perfectly all right. Put the catalog on the table on the landing where it will be found. Make haste, Becky. Go!"

No sooner had Becky disappeared down the passageway, to offload the book then find the butler, than the drawing room door was wrenched open. A gentleman with a head of untidy copper curls bounded out of the smoke-filled drawing room, eyes wild and searching. He did not see Lisa just inches from his feet by the wall. His gaze remained over her head, looking down the darkened corridor one way, and then the other. There was something in his kind face that spoke to her—an inherent goodness—that here was a decent man, and that he was not being inquisitive for its own sake, or to be mischievous, but because he cared.

"Sir, your friend is down here with me," she said quietly.

The gentleman jumped, spun about and almost tripped over his feet. This provided Lisa with a moment's levity, and then he was on his knees, leaning over his friend, who continued to writhe and twist and make unintelligible mutterings in the muted light of the candle.

"Harry? Harry? It's Jack. Jack is here," he said gently. "You're safe. There's no one else. Just us and—" He glanced at Lisa and then thought better of mentioning her. "I'll go fetch the lads."

Yet he continued to kneel over his friend, stricken with such a mixture of distressing emotions that Lisa was compelled to offer him reassurance, even though she was unsure if this would help or hinder him in his distress.

They spoke in hushed tones.

"Sir, I've sent for a coverlet. He needs to be kept warm, and I thought it would also help—to keep him from prying eyes." When Jack nodded distractedly, she added, "Do you know how long his seizures last?"

Jack shook his head. "No..." He looked at Lisa then, a frown between his brows. "You are not repulsed by his convulsions?"

"Pardon, sir, but why would I be repulsed by another's suffering—?"

"I didn't mean—I hope you were not offended by my remark. It's just that most persons go out of their way to avoid those that are-are —*suffering*."

"You do not. Nor do I. But I confess to being less worried, seeing that you are not at all panicked by your friend's condition. So I can presume this is not an irregular occurrence—that he suffers from such seizures often?"

"From time to time. Not often, but enough..." Jack answered evasively before confessing with a sheepish smile, "Truth is, I knew he still had attacks but I'd no notion they were still severe. I've not seen him this way since—since we were boys..."

"He's had the falling sickness since a child?"

"Yes, from birth." Jack looked at Lisa wonderingly. "You know the name of his condition? Yes, it is indeed the falling sickness."

"This is not the first attack I have witnessed."

"It isn't? Is one of your Corinthians a sufferer?"

Lisa frowned. "Corinthians?"

"Customer. Patron. Regular. It's all the same thing."

Lisa blinked at him. "It is?"

Jack baulked, realizing she had no idea what he was talking about. He swallowed hard and took a good look at her. Natural hair. Unblemished skin. A high cut *décolletage* with a modesty fichu for good measure. Clear, confident diction. Not a hint of the coquette about her. Definitely not one of Harris's ladies. And young. If he were to hazard a further guess, not a servant either. Then who was she?

"You're not from Harris's, are you?" he blurted out.

"I've no idea what or who that is, so that should answer your question. But I can assure you that at Warner's Dispensary where I assist, I am not panicked at all by the ill or the injured and their suffering. Nor do I have a disgust of their ailments or of-of—their bodily fluids. I would be of no use to Dr. Warner or his patients if I did. Sir, I tell you this so your mind will be at ease in leaving your friend in the care of a female stranger—me—while you fetch the-the —*lads*?"

"The lads! Yes! Thank you! I must get them. That much I can do for Harry." He scrambled to his feet and closed the drawing room door then came back and looked down at Lisa. "If any gentleman should come out of that room and find you here—"

"I shall shepherd them back inside with some excuse I will do my best to invent while you are gone."

Jack sighed his relief. "Thank you, Miss-Miss—"

"Lisa. My name is Lisa," she said firmly, not wanting to give out her surname because she should not be at Lord Westby's townhouse in the first instance, and secondly she did not want her name or Becky's attached to the missing catalog, should inquiries be made at a later date. She smiled up at him, wanting to ask his name. Instead she said, "The lads, sir…?"

JACK FOLLOWED the same route Becky had taken and passed a footman coming up the stairs with a coverlet, and behind him, a rosy-cheeked girl with a porcelain basin. He did not stop, and when he returned with two big burly brutes, Henri-Antoine was tucked up under the coverlet. His head was propped up off the floor and resting on Lisa's thigh, and she was gently wiping his face with a damp cloth, her rosy-cheeked friend beside her, basin at the ready.

"The tremors have stopped and he's sleeping," Lisa advised Jack in a low voice when he knelt on the other side of her. She glanced up at the two men who were as wide as they were tall—she wouldn't have been surprised to learn their previous employment had been lifting felled trees onto drays. "He uttered a few words—Is your friend a Frenchman?"

"Did you have any trouble?" he asked, avoiding the question, a jerk in the direction of the drawing room door.

Lisa shook her head, gaze never leaving her patient.

"He became agitated when the seizures eased, and then stopped, which is when he spoke in French," she explained diffidently. "But he settled again and seemed to fall almost immediately into a deep sleep when I reassured him all was well and-and—" She paused, throat suddenly dry, and confessed, "—took to lightly stroking his hair, in the same way I did for Joe—a boy I know who also suffers with the falling sickness. He calms considerably if his hair is stroked."

"Ah. Does he? That's good to know, but what I meant was, did my friends in the drawing room bother you at all?"

"Oh! Oh! No. No, they have remained in the room." She suppressed a smile. "But that was because half-a-dozen most interesting and joyous females joined your friends not long after you went to fetch the lads. One of their number confided they were invited to help celebrate a gentleman's last weeks of freedom before his marriage—"

"Anyone would think I was being locked up!" Jack interrupted with an embarrassed huff, suddenly hot in the face. "And it wasn't my idea to invite them!"

Lisa made no comment, adding when Jack continued to look self-conscious, "They were in such high spirits they barely noticed me. And they certainly did not notice your friend because he was already under the coverlet."

Jack let out a sigh, gaze on the drawing room door. The crescendo of female laughter and chatter was audible, so, too, Seb and Bully's drunken bravado. No doubt those two were in seventh heaven to have eight of Harris's ladies all to themselves. He ignored what was going on in there and leaned over to take another look at Henri-Antoine. He was sleeping peacefully, face turned away, head resting comfortably on the girl's petticoats, as if she were his own feather pillow.

Jack remembered that after an attack Henri-Antoine was left exhausted and dazed, and depending on its severity could sleep for hours and hours. When he woke he would be sluggish, irritable, and uncommunicative. Nothing new in the latter, he thought with a wry smile. However, the smile faded at the thought that his best friend would, more than anything else, be upset at knowing he was the focus of an unwanted audience. He certainly would not appreciate having strangers attending on him, even if the female washing his face and stroking his hair was out of the common way. So with that in mind, he said to Lisa, a glance up at Becky,

"The lads can look after him now, Miss. That's what they're

trained to do. They'll take him away from here, make him comfortable, and watch over him until he is more himself. You and your friend may go about your business. Thank you for coming to his assistance. He would be most grateful and tell you so himself were he able."

Lisa smiled and nodded. She was not sure she believed him about his friend being grateful. That he had minders to care for him in such situations would suggest they were employed to prevent strangers interfering or bearing witness to an attack. She could not fault him for that, and he was fortunate indeed to have such a caring friend, and the means by which to make his situation as comfortable and as bearable as possible.

There was nothing left for her to say or do, so she carefully extracted herself from being his pillow, Jack quickly coming to her assistance, and got to her feet. And as she shook the creases from her petticoats she could not resist a last look at her patient in the muted candlelight.

He no longer had any muscle tightness. Gone were the strain to his neck, the clamp to the jaw, and the pull to his mouth. The handsome features with the strong nose were now in repose, the square chin nestling softly in the folds of a fine linen cravat she had dared to unknot and loosen. And the shock of black hair she had gently brushed back out of his eyes and stroked while offering him reassurance, now fell unrestrained to his shoulders. She could see that he also possessed high cheekbones, but it was at his mouth her gaze lingered longest. The lips were beautifully formed. Becky was right. It was a perfectly kissable mouth, and he was inordinately handsome.

She doubted she would ever see the likes of him again, wishing only that she'd had the opportunity to hear his voice when he was not agitated. She was sure he was possessed of a smooth, deep burr as Becky suggested. As to whether he sounded like hot chocolate tasted—full, velvety, and just a tiny bit wicked—that, too, she doubted she would be privileged to discover for herself.

Little could she know that she would indeed make these discoveries, in the most surprising of ways, and before the week was out.

FIVE

Lisa returned to Gerrard Street to the uncommon circumstance of the entire household being aware of her absence.

She came through the servants' entrance to a delicious mingling of aromas, the kitchen maids in the midst of a cooking frenzy, with biscuits being turned out of a hot oven, several fowls rotating on the spit, and various pots on the boil.

Cook was barking orders from the kitchen bench, but as soon as she saw Lisa, she quickly wiped her floured hands on her apron and pounced with the news the mistress had asked for her, and that was an hour or more ago. She warned that Lisa best have a good story to tell, adding that the mistress's mood had not improved with the arrival of Mrs. Warner's younger sister, Mrs. Cobban, visiting for the first time since returning from her bridal trip to Paris.

With a thank-you, Lisa quickly went up to her room. She exchanged her half-boots for house slippers, tidied her hair in the looking glass she kept in a drawer of the small desk by the window, and brushed down her petticoats.

Mrs. Warner's much-put-upon maid answered her scratch at the door, and let it be known with a significant lift of her eyes to the ceiling that all was not harmony with the mistress. Lisa smiled at her kindly and went through to the boudoir, and there hovered in the doorway, waiting to be noticed.

"Don't loiter, Lisa! We might think you were eavesdropping," Minette Warner ordered, beckoning her forward with the wave of a lace-bordered handkerchief. She held it up for her inspection. "Aren't these little squares divine? Henriette tells me all the best people are using square handkerchiefs in Paris these days. She's bought me a dozen."

"It is lovely. And they're square because King Louis made it law—"

"Law? What law? About *handkerchiefs*?"

"Yes. King Louis had it written into law just last year that all handkerchiefs made in France must be square," Lisa replied simply as she picked her way across the carpet strewn with opened gift boxes, careful not to step on lids, ribbons, and torn tissue paper. "I'm glad you're safe home, Henriette. Did you and Mr. Cobban enjoy your stay in Paris?"

"La! You are full of the most absurd knowledge," Minette said without heat, and dropped the handkerchief into its box and tossed it onto the table. "Of course Henriette enjoyed Paris. Who doesn't?"

"Mr. Cobban is the most attentive and generous of husbands," Henriette cooed. "I've come home with a carriage load of new dresses and necessaries that will take my maid at least a week to unpack."

"But where have you been, Lisa?" Minette complained. "We've been waiting to speak with you this past hour. It's not one of your days at the dispensary, so the poor aren't lining up for you to write for them about God-knows-what-nonsense, are they?"

"Is she still making a nuisance of herself in that way?" Henriette asked, surprised, not a look at Lisa, and reverting to French—the sisters' first language.

"Oh, she's not a nuisance," Minette countered. "Dear Dr. Warner has only good things to say about our cousin's assistance. He says she is useful and reliable, and has taken it upon herself to scent the rooms free of miasma, which is all I care about. Oh! And she keeps the the poor *orderly*." She shrugged. "Someone has to do it and it might as well be Lisa. It's not as if she has anything else to do with her time, and it does give her occupation."

"It will have to stop," Henriette stated. "And at once. It's bad enough her fingers are ink-stained—nothing a good scrubbing with soap and a pumice won't take care of—but what if the poor were to give her a hideous fever, or a rash?"

"I'd not thought of that... I dare say you're right..."

"Mama would not be pleased."

"Would she not?" Minette wondered aloud. "I'd have thought that if Lisa were struck down with flu or something more potent, poor Mama could then breathe a sigh of relief and refuse the invitation she has accepted on her behalf with a clear conscience."

Henriette's eyes lit up. "Oh yes! That would work in our favor!"

"But there is no point to be hopeful on that score. Lisa has never been ill a day in her life. Have you, Lisa?" Minette added loudly, reverting to English, and enunciating each word as if her cousin were incapable of understanding her. "You've never been ill a day in your life, have you?"

"No, Cousin Minette. I am blessed with good health, and good hearing."

"You see? As healthy as a milkmaid and the cow she milks," Minette complained in French to her sister.

"What a shame," Henriette mused. "Declining the invitation due to ill health would solve all our problems."

"It would. But as that is not about to happen, we must do as poor Mama has bid us. We owe it to her, and to our noble patroness."

"Invitation? May I know what invitation Aunt de Crespigny has accepted on my behalf?" Lisa interrupted politely, and in French, and with just a hint of a wry smile at their tactic of excluding her from a conversation they knew well enough she could understand.

The sisters turned their heads to regard Lisa with mild hostility, that she dared to intrude into their conversation and do so in French. Speaking in English to her, while they spoke in French between themselves, was just one of the many ways in which they imposed their authority over her—the poor relation who would forever be an embarrassment and a burden on the family. Just as they deliberately kept her standing in the middle of the carpet, knowing she could not sit until given permission to do so.

"Lisa, you seem to have forgotten that you live here because dear Dr. Warner and I have taken you in when no one else would have you. And as you are not of age, I must bestir myself from time to time to ensure you live within the proper restrictions for your youth and station in life. At nineteen, you are not permitted to leave the house, least of all go gallivanting about the town, without my permission. Which you did not obtain, and most assuredly should have done so."

"I am sorry I did not seek your permission, Cousin Minette," Lisa replied contritely. "But I did not wish to disturb you, and I did not think—"

"You most certainly did not think!" Henriette threw at her, itching to contribute to this chastisement.

"—you would mind if I ran an errand with Becky Bannister."

"Becky—*Bannister*? Do I know this personage?"

"Yes, Cousin. Becky is the niece and haberdasher's assistant to Widow Humphreys at Humphreys' Haberdashery. She has been here several times with her trimmings and—"

Henriette goggled at her, horrified. "You were seen out in the company of a—of a—haberdasher's *assistant*?" She looked at her sister and reverted to French. "How are we to correct such social ineptitude, and in a fortnight? It is impossible! *Impossible*."

"I dare say her social blindness can be attributed to the time she spends in the dispensary," Minette replied begrudgingly. "Dear Dr. Warner says that disease is the great leveler—that no matter what our social status, illness visits us all—"

"Minette! Forget about the poor and your dear doctor's dictates for the moment, this is far more important," Henriette hissed. "Poor Mama's reputation—*our reputation*—is at stake. And if Lulu had lived, we wouldn't be facing this dilemma, now would we?"

Minette sighed heavily. "There is no use making ourselves ill with sadness thinking of the past. We must deal with what is in front of us and do the best we can."

At that, the sisters turned again and this time they looked Lisa up and down, both with the same thought: If their younger sister Louise —affectionately known as Lulu—had not died of scarlet fever, their poor cousin Lisa Crisp would never have been sent in Lulu's place to Blacklands boarding school for young ladies. And had Lisa not attended Blacklands, where she had mixed with girls far above her social station, who were the daughters and sisters of politicians, merchant princes, and the like, she would never have received an invitation to what would most likely turn out to be the society wedding of the year.

"Sit. We have something of great importance to explain to you," Minette said in English, indicating a chair piled with emptied gift boxes and ribbons. She waited until Lisa had perched on the edge of a cushion and drew in a breath, as if the task ahead was going to be fatiguing in the extreme. "While Henriette was in Paris, she visited Mama—and before you ask it—Mama, Papa, and Toinette are enjoying their stay immensely. I do believe Toinette wrote you a letter. Is that so, Henriette?"

"I gave it—or did I leave it on the table? No matter. Once your girl clears everything away it will be found. It's not important. Full of childish chatter, no doubt," Henriette said dismissively of her twelve-year-old sister Toinette.

"She was so excited to be calling upon her French cousins for the first time," Lisa said with a smile. But she also remembered how fearful Toinette was about returning to England, because upon coming home, she was being sent to Blacklands for the first time.

Lisa vividly remembered her first days at Blacklands. She had arrived at the school in the middle of term, when all the girls were known to one another and she knew no one, and with only two plain gowns and a pair of scuffed half-boots to her name. She had then endured the sly looks and whispered jeers of her classmates for several weeks until her Uncle de Crespigny agreed to pay the expense of outfitting her with clothing suitable for a Blacklands schoolgirl. At least Toinette would have a better start to her school year...

"...So you see you must understand why it is you cannot blame Mama for withholding such letters," Minette was saying. "She thought it for the best not to raise your expectations that anything could come of such a friendship."

Lisa nodded absently. She had not heard the first part of her cousin's sentence and so was unsure what Minette was talking about, though she sensed by their defensive posturing—their chins had most certainly lifted—that her cousins were expecting her to react in a way that required them to justify what it was their mother had done on her behalf, and without her knowledge.

But at Minette's mention of letters she was so surprised she blurted out, "Aunt de Crespigny has letters—letters *for me?*"

"Do open your ears and pay attention!" Henriette retorted. "How are you to go into society, to make yourself pleasant and interested in what is taking place around you, and be able to make polite conversation, if you do not listen to your betters?"

"Mama withheld the letters for your own good, and ours," Minette explained. "Given the shocking nature of your expulsion from Blacklands, it was thought best that you leave those days—and any associations with the school—behind you for good."

Lisa looked from one sister to the other and addressed both.

"I do not understand. Someone from-from *Blacklands* has written to-to—*me*?"

"We were just as surprised as you," Minette confessed, "that any girl would want to know you after you departed the school under such a dark cloud. But you only have yourself to blame for that outcome, do you not? And if you had but given up the name of the boy whom you allowed to take liberties with your person behind the Chelsea Bun House, the headmistress had been prepared to let you stay on—"

"*Liberties?*" Lisa burst out before she could stop herself, adding in a more subdued voice, "It was just a kiss. That was all it was. One kiss."

"Just a kiss? *Just a kiss?* Have you no *shame?*" Henriette breathed indignantly. "That kiss ended your schooling, and your chances of ever marrying a good and decent man."

"Blacklands was your only chance of making something of yourself," Minette added with a heavy sigh. "What a pity you could not see that at the time. But you must see, *now*, that your shameful conduct was not only thoughtless but also selfish."

"Yes. Yes. You are right," Lisa replied, shoulders sagging. "It was thoughtless, and it was selfish." Then she sat up and said brightly, "But I have not lost hope that there is a gentleman out there who could love me for myself—"

"Don't be absurd and-and *naïve!*" Henriette blustered and gave an unladylike snort of derision. "Even if such a man existed, and he did forgive your wicked behavior, what have you got to recommend you other than your youth? Face facts: You have no dowry. You are penniless and thus have nothing to offer a prospective husband."

"But if this gentleman loved me for myself, surely my pecuniary situation would be of little consequence to him...?"

Minette and Henriette glanced at one another and then burst into a fit of the giggles at such an outrageous expectation.

While they had been at liberty to choose their husbands, both sisters had done so with the hard-headed pragmatism that comes from making a match with a man who could offer, first and foremost, financial security and a comfortable living; love was a secondary consideration. And while both were pretty, they had dowries of two thousand pounds apiece, which meant they had easily found husbands. The thought that their impoverished cousin would find a man to marry who would not only provide her with a comfortable living but fall in love with her was ludicrous in the extreme, hence their incredulous amusement.

"More fool you for thinking so," Henriette announced, dabbing the mirth from her eyes and losing her smile. "We are not here to listen to your daydreaming fantasies. If it were up to the family, you would never have been permitted to accept the invitation extended to you. Mama dearly wanted to refuse it but—"

"—she was *prevailed upon*—that is to say Mama was *ordered* by our noble patroness the Duchess of Roxton and Kinross to give an assurance you would attend," Minette explained. "And so Mama's wishes were overruled and there is nothing we could do about it."

Lisa's eyes went round at the mention of the Duchess of Roxton and Kinross. Her aunt had been chief lady-in-waiting to this aristocratic lady before her marriage to M'sieur de Crespigny. And Lisa knew all about her aunt's time in service from her holidays spent at the de Crespigny household at Christmastime. After supper, with tea and cake in the drawing room, her aunt told such wonderful stories of when she had lived in a palace full of servants and rooms lit with enough candles to turn night into day.

Her Aunt de Crespigny's tales were of magnificent mansions made of marble, velvet-lined carriages pulled by Arabian horses, and fragrant gardens dotted with fountains and follies. There were brilliantly-lit chandeliers in cavernous ballrooms where the great and titled danced until dawn, gilded drawing rooms for musical recitals, masquerade balls attended by hundreds, and endless summer picnics by a lake. And at the center of everything, a beautiful elfin queen—

the Duchess—and right behind her, Lisa's aunt, part of this fairy tale world inhabited by dukes and duchesses, kings and princes, noblemen and their ladies; all dressed in sumptuous silks and glittering diamond finery.

"I would never do anything to jeopardize my aunt's place in the Duchess's affections," Lisa assured her cousins. "You must believe me, Minette, Henriette. I know how much your mother treasures her years in service. What I do not understand is why you think I could—"

"If you *dare* say or-or do *anything* that diminishes the special bond between Mama and the Duchess, we will *hate* you for the rest of your days!" Henriette spat out. "Do you understand?"

Lisa nodded, taken aback by her cousin's vitriol.

"If you cause Mama the slightest aggravation, or worse, if you do something that offends the Duchess or a member of her family, we will disown you," Minette lectured. "You were almost sent away after your expulsion from Blacklands, but we thought better of it, given your tender years. But Papa had no compunction about ostracizing your father. Toussaint de Crespigny was a thief and a drunk. He stole from his family, drank his inheritance away, and left you and your mother to rot in a poorhouse. The only commendable thing he ever did was change his name to Crisp."

"Our parents saved you from the poorhouse. You owe it to them—and most particularly to Mama—not to disgrace yourself before the Duchess of Roxton and Kinross and her family." Henriette adding in a hiss, "Do—you—understand?"

Lisa nodded vigorously, sick to her stomach and trembling to be so reviled. She saw Henriette's fury and Minette's displeasure, but she could not understand why their anger was tinged with resentment and bitterness.

"I must—I must be thick-headed today because I-I still do not understand why you think—How you could think—I could cause your parents such-such distress... Please. I do not wish to-to upset anyone. Tell me what I must do so I can—I can ease your worries."

"You cannot ease them. It is out of our hands now," Minette explained. "All we can do is what has been asked of us, then send you off. Of course we will pray each and every day you are away that you acquit yourself without incident. But you have this knack of getting yourself into trouble and thus noticed—But not this time, Lisa. Understand me?" Before Lisa could respond, Minette looked to her sister. "Give her the invitation and the letters, Henriette, and let's be done with this."

Henriette snatched up off the table a bundle of letters tied up with ribbon and waved it in Lisa's face.

"You have been invited to spend a fortnight at Treat. That sentence alone would send most girls—no! any other girl—into an ecstasy of excitement, but you haven't the least notion of the great honor being bestowed upon you! You—"

"Oh, but I do know what Treat is, Henriette," Lisa assured her. "Treat is the ancestral home of the Dukes of Roxton. Aunt de Crespigny mentioned it many times. It is the largest privately-owned house in all of England, and has so many rooms, even those that live there can get lost if they take a wrong turn. And there is a lake, and acres and acres of gardens and avenues of white roses planted by the old Duke for the Duchess—"

"Yes! Yes! We've all heard Mama's stories," Henriette interrupted dismissively. "Your task is to get through the fortnight without being noticed. A fortnight will pass like that," she said with the snap of her fingers. "Your visit to Treat is fleeting. Nothing more than a heartbeat in time. And when it is over, you will have to take your head out of the clouds and return to your life here. Never forget, Lisa: You are poor. You have nowhere else to go, and we are the only family you have. Your life is here in Gerrard Street. The best you can hope for from life is to be of some use to the beggarly poor with your scribbles and helping in the dispensary. Do you understand?"

Lisa nodded obediently, gaze riveted to the packet of letters still held by Henriette. She wanted to snatch them, run up to the privacy of her room, and there tug off the black ribbon and read each letter quickly, and then again as slowly as possible. Though she had not been told the identity of her correspondent, or why she had received such a startling invitation, she had an inkling. And then Minette enlightened her.

"Not all your school friends have forsaken you it seems. And the one that did not just happens to have great and powerful relatives. And they do not come any more powerful than the Duke of Roxton, who is Miss Cavendish's uncle."

"How fortunate for you to be invited to her wedding," Henriette added bitterly. "Here's the invitation." She tossed it with the packet of letters onto Lisa's lap. "Now go away and leave us in peace."

Miss Theodora 'Teddy' Cavendish, Lisa's school friend from her Blacklands days, had not only written to her, but invited Lisa to her wedding.

"Teddy! Oh Teddy!" Lisa burst out breathlessly, and such was her overwhelming excitement that she rushed out of the room without waiting to be excused, the packet pressed to her bosom.

Teddy was getting married.

Teddy had invited her to the wedding.

Teddy had not forsaken her after all.

Lisa burst into tears.

SIX

LISA WAS IN her room, back up against the closed door, with no recollection of how she got there. She took a moment to compose herself, to quickly wipe her cheeks dry with the back of a shaking hand, and to take a few deep breaths, packet of letters still pressed to her heaving chest. And then she could wait no longer.

Kicking off her slippers and picking up her petticoats, she scrambled up onto her narrow bed. Here she sat, cross-legged. With trembling fingers she untied the black ribbon keeping the invitation and the collection of letters bundled together. With only a cursory glance at the invitation, she set it aside, eager to read the letters first. Seeing her name and her former address—Fournier Street, Spitalfields— written in her school friend's sloping script she gave a watery chuckle, and lovingly caressed those inked letters in a wonderment of recognition, that the letters were indeed from Teddy. And with recognition came remembrances of school days long past...

HOW MANY HOURS had they spent sitting side by side, practicing in their copybooks to write in the round hand cursive script of a Blacklands schoolgirl? How many formal letters had they copied out in this script, in English and in French, again all for practice, for when the day came when they were married ladies, and had the leisure to write letters to family and friends from their wallpapered boudoirs?

Teddy grumbled good-naturedly at the wasting of time over such pointless penmanship, because when she married she wouldn't be sitting in a drawing room letter-writing, but would be out riding up hill and down dale in the fresh air. Teddy's script was made all the more laborious because she wrote with her left hand, which was an extraordinary sight in itself. All girls wrote with their right hands, and those who did not had their left hand tied behind their backs so that they did. Not Teddy. She had permission to use her left hand, as long as she could copy the script as it was written and did not trail her hand in the drying ink.

Lisa had wondered aloud why Teddy was permitted to use her left hand, and Teddy told her, though she had surmised the answer. *Oh, it must be because I have powerful relatives who love me, Lisa*, she had whispered and then giggled, hunching her shoulders. But she had not said this with any degree of smugness, or a sense of superiority, just as fact. And one day she confided in Lisa just how powerful they were. One uncle was a duke, another an earl. Her closest cousin was a double duchess, and her mama was a lady, daughter of an earl. Lisa was awe struck. Teddy's relatives were not just powerful, they were from the aristocracy, and at the apex of their class. Teddy made her promise to keep this a secret. She did not want the other girls to think any differently of her. Lisa promised and then asked why, if her relatives were nobles, she had been sent to Blacklands, and not had a governess, or been sent to a seminary for the daughters of noblemen.

Teddy had screwed up her freckled nose in thought, then shrugged, saying her parents wanted her to be comfortable, to learn to speak French like a native—all her mama's family did—but most of all they wanted her to be happy. They thought she would be happiest at Blacklands. And Teddy was happy. Lisa marveled at her best friend's exuberance for life, her confidence, and her sunny disposition.

Though, for a short while, when she had first arrived at Blacklands, Teddy was miserable, pining for home, and Lisa had comforted her.

Lisa had already been at the school for four years, and being an orphan who spent only the Christmas holidays with her cousins,

Blacklands was her home. Whereas, Teddy had never been away from her family before, and never from her mother. And although Blacklands was in Chelsea, on the outskirts of the fashionable streets of Westminster, so was practically the country, it was *not* the country. It never would be as far as Teddy was concerned, whose home was in the Cotswolds in far-off Gloucestershire.

Lisa listened for hours to Teddy's stories about her ramblings through the countryside. She wished she could visit such a wondrous place. Lisa had never been further from the city than Blacklands, ever. Teddy promised that one day Lisa would indeed visit her and meet her family, and when she married Jack and took up residence at Abbeywood farm, Lisa could come to stay for as long as she wished.

"Jack?" Lisa had asked, surprised to learn Teddy knew whom she was to marry.

They were both thirteen years old, and Lisa had not even thought of boys, least of all knew one she would one day wish to marry.

"I'm going to marry Jack on my eighteenth birthday. But I promised Mama I would attend Blacklands for a few years first. That was one of the conditions," Teddy confided. "Because Mama wants me to be a lady, and to learn a little of the world, which she says will help me be a better wife to Jack."

Lisa was intrigued. She had turned her head on the pillow to look at Teddy in the moonlight that streamed in through the undraped window and across the narrow bed where they were snuggled up under the coverlet, to keep each other warm, and where they could have a whispered conversation without disturbing the night nurse.

Teddy had said this with such certainty that Lisa wondered if her marriage to Jack was an arranged union. Lisa had heard of such marriages for people who had powerful relatives. Teddy's response was to shake her head and press her lips hard together to stop herself from giggling. Lisa saw the laughter in her eyes, and smiled. She was glad Teddy wasn't being forced into a marriage. Even as a thirteen-year-old she was a romantic.

"Does Jack know you are going to marry him?"

"Naturally."

"And when did you know—know that you wanted to marry Jack?"

"When I was ten."

"*Ten?* Ten years old?"

Teddy nodded. "And I told him when I was twelve."

Lisa's eyes went round. "When you were twelve you told him you were going to marry him? Was he surprised? What did he say?"

"He was. But he said he would like to marry me, though it was usual for boys to do the asking. And if I was sincere, I was to ask him again when I was older. He said I might change my mind."

"Do you think you will—change your mind?"

Teddy shook her head on the pillow. "No. Never."

"When will you ask him again?"

"When I turn eighteen. I am determined."

When Lisa remained silent, Teddy mistook her fascination for incredulity, so she offered further explanation.

"And while I'm here at Blacklands, Jack is going on a Grand Journey—no! It's not called that... Oh! He's going on the *Grand Tour*. Yes. That's what it's called. Which is what boys do when they leave Oxford—that's university. Mama says the boys go in groups and wander about old palaces and ruins and spend a lot of their time pondering old paintings."

"Couldn't he do that here? There must be old paintings to ponder and plenty of ruins to wander about in England."

"Mama says young men need to go abroad to ponder, to see the old world. She says it's good for them, because when they come home they are no longer boys, and they will want to settle."

"Settle...?"

"Marry, silly."

"Oh! How long will he be away on this tour?"

"Mama says he'll be away for years—"

"*Years*?" Lisa was so surprised she forgot to whisper. Then added in a hiss, "What if he forgets you while he's away?"

"Forget?" Teddy sat up on an elbow and frowned through a tangle of hair. "He won't forget me. He's promised not to. Besides," she added with a cheeky grin, "I gave him a lock of my hair so he won't."

"Teddy!" Lisa gasped, now also up on an elbow. "Oh, but how wonderful of you!"

Teddy nodded, well pleased with herself, and then they both quickly lay back down and snuggled in under the coverlet because there was footfall and low voices. They smiled at each other and remained still and quiet and waited. They waited a long time for it to be quiet again, too excited to sleep. There was so much more Lisa wanted to know about Teddy's family and Jack, and the wondrous things boys could do once they had left Oxford and went abroad to ponder. They popped their heads out from under the coverlet and stared up at the ceiling illuminated by moonlight.

"Will you miss him while he's away?" Lisa finally asked, watching Teddy who was still staring at the ceiling.

"I will—a little. Mama says I mustn't. That I'm not to—*fret*. That Jack being away will give me plenty of time to grow up, too. And she says I'm not to worry about him, because he's going on this tour with his best friend, Harry, and they'll keep each other company and be too preoccupied to be thinking of home."

"Their parents are not worried they are going to be away from home for so long?"

"Worried? Why would they? Mama says going on the tour is a much better use of a wealthy young man's time than spending it in gentlemen's clubs, gambling, smoking, and drinking their days away—"

"Your mama said that to you?" Lisa's eyes were wide.

"No. Not to me. I overheard her say it to Papa. He agreed with her. She also said that there was little possibility of them getting into too much trouble, when they are journeying with a-a *yeomanry of attendants.*"

"What is—what is a *yeomanry of attendants?*"

"They are the persons who are part of their traveling party."

"Servants who carry their belongings?"

"Oh no. Of course they do have servants with them to do such tasks as carry their trunks, and to look after the carriages and horses, and to keep them safe while traveling about. But the yeomanry are people *attending* on them while they are away. Not servants in the strictest sense, so Mama says. Jack and Harry will have their own physician traveling with them, and two tutors, a major domo who looks after all the arrangements for their travel and accommodations, and of course they need their valets to dress them. Oh! And I nearly forgot, two of their school friends are also going with them, too, and they'll have their own yeomanry."

Lisa's eyes could not grow any rounder. She was envious of such travel arrangements and wished she had been born male and wealthy, so she, too, could be part of such a grand adventure.

"Imagine Jack and Harry and their friends and all those men in carriages, and on horseback, riding about the countryside and through towns," Lisa whispered with excitement. "The local people would be sure to stop and stare, and their children wave and jump up and down, to see such an astonishing procession! Don't you wish you could be part of it? To visit old towns, see old paintings, and meet the people?"

Teddy shrugged and was less than enthusiastic.

"I'm happy here—not *here*—but home. When Jack comes home and we marry, we'll never leave the Cotswolds again."

"*Never*?"

"Except when Jack comes to London for Parliament. My uncle Roxton is making him a Parliamentarian when he returns from abroad, so Jack says he must spend a few months of the year in London doing whatever it is Parliamentarians do. Which is why Mama says I need to learn to be a lady, so I can be a helpmate to Jack," Teddy confided. "I don't know how I am to help him by being here at school, but I will try. Mama says if I busy myself with my schooling I won't think about Jack being away, and the time will pass very quickly. But even if I do what she says, and I try my hardest, I still can't stop thinking of my family... I miss Mama every day, and Papa, and—Do you have any brothers and sisters, Lisa?"

Lisa sought out Teddy's hand and held it because she could see her friend was on the verge of tears.

"I don't. And both my parents are dead. I do have cousins... But they have each other... And I know if I had a mama like yours, and a family like yours, I would miss them too. Will you tell me about your family? I want to know *everything*. Don't leave *anything* out. I want to know *all* about them."

Teddy blinked the tears away and smiled and snuggled in, hand comfortably in Lisa's hold.

"I have two brothers. They are just babies. They are my *half*-brothers on account of Mama starting a second family. My father died when I was eight, and then Mama married again so I have a second papa. My big baby brother is named David and he's two. He has red hair just like mine.

Granny Kate calls him her cheeky monkey. My little baby brother is just six months old and his name is Luke. He has black hair like my Uncle Dair, Mama's brother. But he's still too small for us to know if he'll be as cheeky as David. But he does laugh a lot and is a happy baby, so Granny Kate and I think he could well be just as cheeky. I don't have a sister—yet. I asked Mama if her next baby could be a girl, and she said she would try her best—Lisa! I've had the most wonderful thought… *We* can be sisters! Would you? Would you like to have me as your sister Lisa?"

SEVEN

"OH, TEDDY, I've missed you so very *very* much," Lisa uttered on a whispered sob, Teddy's handwriting bringing to life the vivid recollection of girlhood confidences shared with her best friend.

Such wonderful memories, such happy days... Bittersweet tears spilled on to her cheeks and her heart swelled with warmth as she briefly closed her eyes, still dazed to think that not only did she have letters from her school friend, but an invitation to her wedding, and best of all, she would soon be reunited with Teddy.

For now, she lay on her bed and read and re-read Teddy's letters, all six of them written over the two-year period since Lisa had left Blacklands. She then stared at the invitation for the longest time with the biggest smile. So Teddy was finally marrying *her Jack*—more correctly Sir John George Cavendish Bt.—just as she said she would, but not on her eighteenth birthday, but closer to her nineteenth, which was what her parents had wanted, so Teddy had written in her final letter. She also gave Lisa the surprising news that her Mama had finally, after all these years, given her a sister—Sophie-Kate. Teddy had written her letter to Lisa just a week after the infant's birth in the early spring. And with this welcome announcement, Teddy added a postscript that she had enlisted the help of her mother's cousin, the Duchess of Roxton and Kinross, to ensure Lisa received this letter and invitation. She was determined to have her Blacklands sister at her wedding. And the Duchess had promised to do her very best to make this happen.

Lisa was in such awe to think Teddy had co-opted a duchess to help find her, that it bordered on fantasy. But in two weeks' time she would be off to Hampshire to be reunited with Teddy, meet her family, and be part of her wedding celebrations.

Two weeks could not go quickly enough for Lisa. But there was still much to do between now and then, not least of which was to be fitted into her cousin's cast-off gowns and shoes. And she could not neglect her duties at the dispensary, so Minette Warner lectured her the following Monday morning at breakfast.

LISA WAS SURPRISED to find Cousin Minette in the breakfast room. And by her gown and application of cosmetics and arranged coiffure, her cousin was dressed to leave the house.

Minette Warner informed her she was off to Fournier Street to spend the day with her parents, to welcome them home from Paris, and to give her mother an account of preparations for Lisa's stay in Hampshire. Her mother needed reassuring that everything had been done that could be done to make certain Lisa was a credit to the de Crespigny family. As to how she conducted herself while in such illustrious company, that was out of their control, and entirely in Lisa's hands. Did she understand?

"I do, Cousin," Lisa replied gravely and instinctively straightened her already straight back.

Since Lisa had received the invitation to Teddy's wedding, her cousin never missed an opportunity to repeat her mantra that she be on her best behavior, to never put herself forward, nor was she to get herself noticed. If she did not conduct herself with circumspection and humility, if she were singled out for any social infraction, her aunt would be mortified, and the family never forgive her.

Lisa took her cousin's monologues on correct conduct and conse-quences in good part, and was careful to temper her enthusiasm and happiness, saying with a smile,

"Please pass on my best wishes to my aunt and uncle, and to Toinette, for their safe return. And you will tell my aunt we have economized on employing a maid because Becky Bannister has agreed to accompany me to—"

"Yes. Yes. I will tell them," Minette interrupted, as if it was the most arduous task of her long day, and it not yet begun.

"At least this Becky Bannister is expert with a needle and thread, which has saved me employing my seamstress. I will grant, that was a stroke of luck—Oh! And while I'm away today, on no account are you to step outside the house. Heaven forbid something should befall you with less than a sennight until your journey, after the expense and effort we've incurred."

"Lisa will be fully occupied in the dispensary all day, dear heart, if the huddle of persons already at the door is any indication," Dr. Warner assured his wife with only one ear to the conversation, looking up over his wire rims from a letter that was consuming all his thoughts. He had left off his usual morning perusal of the newssheets.

"Good news I trust?" Mrs. Warner asked, sipping at her tea, gaze dropping to the letter in his hand.

"Good news? No. Confound it," Dr. Warner replied with uncustomary harshness. "It is not good news, my dear. It is the worst possible news!"

"Oh dear," Mrs. Warner pouted. "I do so dislike to see you so put out, Robert. It makes my head ache."

"Forgive me, my dear. But I'm afraid my mood has little chance of altering in the next little while—"

"Then it is as well I am going out for the day."

Lisa looked from Mrs. Warner, who had dropped her gaze to her teacup, to Dr. Warner, who had returned his attention to the letter, and asked in the silence,

"Would you care to share your news, as disappointing as it is, sir?"

Mrs. Warner could have kicked her cousin's shin for asking, but she forced a smile, said nothing, and picked up a slice of bread smothered in jam. And as Lisa had leaned in and continued to look at him expectantly, it was all the encouragement the physician needed to vocalize his frustration. So he told them.

The letter he waved about and then dropped on top of the pile of newssheets was from the Fournier Foundation. At this, both Lisa's and Mrs. Warner's ears pricked, because Fournier Street was where the de Crespigny family home was located, and where Mrs. Warner was bound after breakfast. The very same, said her husband. The foundation's head of trustees, an elderly physician by the name of Bailey, lived in Fournier Street.

The Foundation provided grants to medical professionals attending on the sick poor, and more importantly, to physicians engaged in anatomical research. There were strict criteria to meet. The foundation's trustees visited an applicant's premises, conducted interviews with the principals, and assessed the merit of the establishment and the research being carried out. And because the money was ongoing for three years, with yearly reviews and goals to be met, every physician in London and beyond submitted a funding application.

"The work of this foundation is—" Lisa began and had her sentence completed for her by Mrs. Warner; with a word she was not thinking of at all.

"—costly."

"—enormously worthwhile," Lisa finished, her enthusiasm causing her to interrupt her cousin. "Surely providing bright young men with the funds they need to focus on their anatomical investigations without their mind being clouded with the mundane worries of debt—whether to spend their meager allowance on books or bread— must give better focus to their studies?"

"That is true," Dr. Warner agreed with a smile, Lisa's keen interest lifting some of the gloom from his shoulders about the letter's depressing outcome.

"This Dr. Bailey must be a very wealthy gentleman indeed," Mrs. Warner added, focused on monetary considerations. "Such scholarships and funding as required by the dispensaries must run into the hundreds of pounds, if not more than a thousand in any given year."

"Dr. Bailey is the foundation's figurehead, my dear," Dr. Warner explained. "And while it is the board of trustees which approves and allocates the funds, where those initial funds originated, and who created the Fournier Foundation, remains a mystery. The gentleman who has generously donated his largesse to this beneficial enterprise wishes to remain in the shadows. It is not even certain if Dr. Bailey knows the benefactor's identity. But you are quite right, my dear, the foundation's charitable assistance must run into the hundreds of pounds, if not a thousand per annum."

"And you wrote to this foundation and requested funding for your endeavors," Mrs. Warner said with a bright smile.

"I did," he replied but with less enthusiasm than she was exhibiting on the expectation of a favorable outcome. "I requested monies to provide for an anatomical instructor and a morbid anatomist. The former would ease my teaching load, and the latter I could set to work making the wax models of specimens necessary for instruction. There is a new technique using various colored waxes of differing injection sizes. But it is necessary for the injection to be heated to a liquid, but not boiled, or that is likely to destroy the texture of the vessels to be filled..."

This was when the dear doctor lost the full attention of his wife, who now had only one ear to the conversation, daydreaming about the mysterious benefactor of the Fournier Foundation, wondering if he was a bachelor, married, a merchant who had made his money in any number of trade ventures, or perhaps he was a benevolent ancient nobleman with no children whose inheritance was not entailed and could be used to good purpose elsewhere other than his estate...

And because she was daydreaming, Mrs. Warner did not make immediate comment when her dear doctor revealed with a down-turn to his mouth that his application had been rejected on the grounds that the foundation had met its quota for the year. It was politely suggested that Dr. Warner apply again next funding cycle, which was an entire year from now. Valuable time and opportunity to acquire unique anatomical resources—by which Lisa knew the physician was referring to human specimens—would be lost between now and then. And as this was the second application which had been rejected, and for the same reason, Dr. Warner had his suspicions that his applications were not being put under the right noses.

"Do you mean Dr. Bailey's nose, sir?" Lisa asked, who had been all rapt attention while the physician described in superfluous detail the method of mixing the dyes for the purpose of injecting the different anatomical specimens.

Dr. Warner hit the side of the table with his palm, which jolted his inattentive wife from her private reveries. He smiled across at Lisa. "Precisely! That is indeed the nose I am talking about."

"Dear me, Dr. Warner! You gave me such a fright just now," Mrs. Warner complained, and to mask her inattentiveness added with a girlish pout, "I do believe it has upset my digestion."

"I do beg your pardon, my dear," the physician replied sheepishly, and pushed aside his plate of unfinished egg and toast.

"Perhaps if you were to invite Dr. Bailey to dinner, sir, he would see it as a gesture of goodwill. That you bear him no ill will despite the rejection of your application?" Lisa suggested, quickly putting aside her mug of hot chocolate and her napkin and scraping back her chair when her cousin rose from the table. "You could then find an opportunity to show him the dissecting room and your anatomical work?"

Dr. Warner, also up on his feet, beamed at Lisa. "By Jove, that is exactly what he will see it as! That has decided me. I shall write to Dr. Bailey tonight."

Minette Warner looked at Lisa and smiled thinly.

"And here was I thinking breakfast was a dull affair for you... Not so, it seems. Something to be reconsidered when you return from Hampshire. Now off you go; you must have a hundred and one tasks to do for the good doctor before he sees his first patient of the morning."

Lisa obediently bobbed a curtsy and departed, leaving behind a half-finished mug of hot chocolate. She collected up her writing box with its quills, ink, and paper and made her way across the passageway and through to the dispensary, which occupied the front rooms of the lower level of the double-fronted townhouse. Here she deposited her writing box in her usual corner, where she offered her services as amanuensis, took her apron off its peg, and quickly put it on over her gown. A check of the pins holding the lace cap to the crown of her head, and she bustled about performing her duties— seeing to the scent bottles and tussie mussies, that water jugs were filled, and soap, pumice, and towels provided in each of the curtained treatment cubicles—and all this accomplished without getting in the way of the medical assistants who were preparing for the first influx of patients.

And as the door to the dispensary was unlocked to admit the first patients of the day, Lisa's thoughts were all about the week after next. In a week's time she would be on her way to see Teddy, and to a place so vastly different from this that she found it difficult to imagine it at all.

NOT FIVE MINUTES after the dispensary doors were unlocked, the waiting crowd shuffling forwards on the pavement was made to part to allow two oversized men to enter the waiting room ahead of everyone else.

They were so out of place that Lisa blinked, and then she gave a start of recognition. They were *the lads*, the two servants sent for to assist the gentleman she had helped at Lord Westby's residence. She wondered what they were doing in such a place as this, and knew they were there for her when, after a quick look about the already crowded waiting room, their gaze locked on hers. There was the same spark of recognition in their eyes.

There was nothing for Lisa to do but stand her ground and let them come to her.

Wide-shouldered and a good head taller than those around them, they were also healthy, upright, and mobile, which was in marked contrast to the persons gathering at their backs. Their size and vigor might ensure everyone got out of their way, but it was their clothing that made people stare. They were dressed in suits of livery—fine black cloth with elaborate silver lacings and silver buttons—which was a proclamation of the wealth and importance of their master, and it gave them right-of-way to do and say as they pleased, their height and the size of their meaty fists merely reinforcing this.

The two lads came straight up to Lisa. And when they were in front of her they did not speak but stood aside to allow a gentleman to step up to her and make her a bow. She held her breath and her heart gave the oddest little leap, hoping for a moment it might be the handsome gentleman she had assisted at Lord Westby's. And then her pulse quickened, and not in a good way, wondering if he had come in search of her and Becky over his misplaced catalog to the Portland auction. And then the gentleman removed the perfumed handkerchief he was holding up to his nose to ward off the miasma of the sick, and she breathed a sigh of relief mixed with disappointment. She did not know this man at all.

The stranger gave an imperious lift of his brows, and asked, "Are you Lisa?"

She nodded and bobbed a polite curtsy. Then added, because he continued to regard her as if he required more from her, "Lisa Crisp, sir."

He inclined his head in thanks for this information, then said before turning on a heel and expecting her to obey, "Follow me, Miss Crisp. My master is desirous of a word, in private, in his carriage."

EIGHT

"S HE—*REFUSES*?"

"Yes, my lord."

Lord Henri-Antoine stared at his major domo framed in the carriage window as if the man were speaking any language but one he understood, and he understood at least six. He waited for further explanation.

"Miss Crisp is unable to leave the premises."

"Unable?"

"Yes, my lord."

"Is she recently crippled?"

"Not crippled."

"Then she is not unable, she is *unwilling*."

Michel Gallet dared to smile. "I did point out that difference. However, she will not budge."

"Then have her carried out here."

"Kicking and screaming—"

"She's not the screaming sort."

"Is she not, my lord...?"

Henri-Antoine was not fooled by his major domo's light tone of inquiry. He set his teeth and waited for the man's smile, and his gaze, to drop.

"Apologies, my lord... What would you have me do?"

Henri-Antoine glanced over his major domo's left shoulder to the crowd gathered by the steps up to the entrance of Warner's Dispensary. They were a ragged lot, with dirty faces and tired expressions, their interest in the shiny black lacquered *Berlin* with its matching four grays mingled with a wariness, no doubt as to the reason why such an impressive vehicle was here, and at this early hour, too.

He rarely ventured into this part of London—he had no need to, and when he did, it was only to visit Seb Westby. And he never came by carriage, but had burly chairmen in his employ take him up in his private sedan chair. His townhouse in Park Street was less than thirty minutes west by such a conveyance. Yet Warner's Dispensary here in Gerrard Street was a world away from the elegant houses, wide streets, and orderly, well-dressed pedestrians who inhabited the rarefied Westminster address where he lived. But such transportation would not do for a private word with Miss Lisa Crisp. It never entered his head that it was the four liveried postillions, the wide-shouldered lads, and most importantly his esteemed self, that were attracting more attention than his elegant town carriage.

He set his shoulders against the velvet upholstery with an annoyed sigh and had half a mind to tap the headboard with his gloved knuckle and be off. What was he doing here anyway? He was under no obligation to Miss Lisa Crisp. And if she didn't possess the good manners to come outside so he could have a civil word with her —after all he was the one who had called upon her—he need not exert himself further. He wouldn't. The act of coming here was more than enough of an acknowledgement of her good deed on his behalf.

And yet there was something—he could not put his finger on precisely *what*, but it greatly unsettled him—that made him resist giving the signal to his driver. Part of it was chivalry, instilled in him from the cradle, to do the right thing, to behave as a gentleman ought, and thank her in person. Part of it was curiosity, to want to put a face to the name Jack had given him of the girl who had come to his assistance when he had been at his most deplorable. And, if Jack were to be believed, Miss Lisa Crisp was a rare female indeed—calm, capable, cheerful, and not at all repulsed by his condition. That she worked amongst the sick poor no doubt accounted for that. Still. He wanted to see her for himself. He wanted to know if she equated to the Botticelli angel who had appeared out of his epileptic delirium as he staggered from West-by's drawing room. But most of all he wanted this feeling of disquiet and restlessness, a feeling that left him anxious for no apparent reason, to go away forthwith. And for some unfathomable reason this feeling had everything to do with the unflappable Miss Crisp.

He sat forward, his major domo still up on the carriage step at the window patiently waiting further instructions.

"I'm not going in there!" he blurted out, which said more about his troubled thoughts than his present predicament.

"A sensible decision, my lord. The place is jammed with all manner of diseased riff-raff, and the air is fetid."

"And yet Miss Crisp is in there amongst this riff-raff? Is she fetid, Michel?" he asked, hopeful of an affirmative response; it would give him the excuse he needed to leave at once.

"No, my lord. Quite the opposite. She is the spring flower blooming amongst the rotting refuse."

"Of course she is," Henri-Antoine muttered.

"Shall I try again to make her see reason...?"

Henri-Antoine nodded, a frown between his dark brows, gaze on the dispensary's front door which was being opened and closed with alarming regularity. "Do that." Adding in a complete reversal, "And you had best try your damndest, because if you can't persuade her, and she still refuses to come out, I will have to go to her."

"Is that wise, my lord? The level of miasma in such a place as a dispensary must be beyond what any healthy man can tolerate who is not used to being surrounded by illness. And for you to breathe such air would surely severely compromise your health, and thus I must counsel against putting yourself in a most dangerous situation."

There was that damned word again—*wise*—Jack, his servants, everyone around him, used it too often. If he were wise he'd not have got himself drunk and smoked enough cheroots to burn his throat. If he were wise he'd have left Westby's drawing room well before the onset of an attack. If he were wise he wouldn't be here now, outside a London *hôtel-Dieu*.

"Then you had best be at your most persuasive," he stated, and pulled the blind on his major-domo and the crowd of curious onlookers.

MICHEL GALLET returned to the carriage with the welcome news Miss Crisp could give His Lordship a few minutes of her time. She understood his master's reluctance to breath a miasma that could well cause him harm, but she could not come out to the carriage, of that she was adamant. She did, however, offer a solution to the dilemma. Dr. Warner had a private consulting room across the hall from the dispensary where their meeting could take place. The consulting room could be entered via a door that led onto the street, and was for the use of private patients only. M'sieur Gallet's master could come and go via this door, without coming into contact with the miasma that lingered in the dispensary.

However, she would first need to prepare herself, because Dr. Warner had rules which he himself, his medical attendants, his student physicians, and Lisa, were all required to follow when leaving the confines of the dispensary. Aprons and sleeves were to be removed, hands washed and nails scrubbed clean with soap, to remove all traces of the smell of the ill and the dying. A few drops of Warner's patented scent were then sprinkled on the skin to aid this process.

Perhaps one of the lads could wait by the private entrance, and when she was ready, Miss Crisp would unlock the consulting door and he could then inform his master?

"Such elaborate preparations, and all for a two-minute conversation," Henri-Antoine drawled, head back against the upholstery, eyes closed. He had a sudden thought and opened one eye and looked at Michel, who was still at the carriage window.

"You were careful not to mention me by name."

"I did not tell her, and she did not ask, my lord."

LISA WAS STANDING by the desk of the consulting room, the door that opened out onto the hallway left wide, so there was a clear view of the base of the stairs that led up to the private quarters where she resided with Dr. and Mrs. Warner. Past the staircase, further across the hall, was a closed door painted with the word *Dispensary* on the top rail. Beside this door sat Joseph, an elderly servant who had been in the physician's employ for decades, and now acted as porter, when he wasn't dozing in his chair.

She had left the consulting room door open so Joseph could see in and she could see him, because young ladies did not receive male callers who were not direct relatives or guardians, alone. Though the very idea this gentleman had come to call on her was so ludicrous as to be laughable. And although she had told one of the dispensary assistants where she would be and that she would return within the half-hour, she knew Cousin Minette would not be at all pleased she had agreed to this meeting, without Dr. Warner's knowledge or approval.

Yet she was not nervous in the same way as she had been when she and Becky had entered Lord Westby's residence. This was a different sort of nervousness. It was one of heart-pounding anticipation. She found herself worrying about her hair, and the sit of her lace cap, and the fact she was wearing a plain gown of serviceable linen, and her sensible half-boots that were scuffed at heel and toe. And it didn't matter how hard or for how long she scrubbed her hands, the ink stains from the hours spent as an amanuensis for the poor could not be scrubbed away. None of this had ever bothered her in the past. It shouldn't have bothered her now. But it did.

She felt inadequate, insignificant, ordinary. And then the door opened and none of that mattered.

NINE

FIRST TO STEP into the room was one of the beefy liveried lads. He took a sweeping look about him then opened the door wider to admit his master, who came in followed by the other beefy lad. This lad closed the door and stayed by it, while his twin went and stood by the open door that gave access to the hallway. Both exits were now blocked, leaving Lisa trapped with her visitor. Not that she felt trapped. Slightly unnerved by the presence of such hulks, yes, but her attention was quickly diverted from them to her visitor, who was taking a slow turn about the small room.

He stopped in front of her, close enough that all he need do to look her over was move his eyes, and without effort. He then planted the end of his walking stick to the floor by the toe of his shoe and let it lean outward, held in place by one gloved hand about its ivory handle with its diamond encrusted top. The knuckles of his right hand he put to his hip. With his chin parallel to the floor, and gaze direct, he thus presented himself, and waited, as was his right, to receive her due acknowledgment.

Lisa did not move. She could not. She was too much affected to do more than gawp at him as if he were a theater performer. Not that she had ever been to the theater or the opera, but she had read reports, and listened to her cousins talk on and on about whom they had seen in the boxes at Drury Lane, the performance of secondary importance to the illustrious personages in attendance.

Oh, but he was splendid!

He was everything she imagined he would be, if she ever had the opportunity to see him as he wished to be seen by others. Tall, lean, and angular, with a tousle of thick black hair pulled back off his face, his strong nose was just as aquiline and straight as she remembered it. And his mouth...as kissable as ever. The small horizontal crease in his square chin was a surprise and something she had not noticed when she had stroked his hair in the hopes it would soothe his suffering. It was also heavier, or perhaps that was because it now nestled in the folds of a white linen cravat tied off in a neat bow.

And where he had been dressed in lilac silk at Lord Westby's, this ensemble of waistcoat, frock coat and breeches was a pale sky-blue linen, the front panels of waistcoat and frock coat finely embroidered with a tangle of vine and flowers, with matching covered buttons. She supposed the jewels encrusted on the buckles in his black leather shoes were diamonds...

But as she had already dared to linger longer than was polite on such heady masculinity presented in such sumptuous finery, she reluctantly pulled her appreciative gaze up from his shoe buckles to his face, and with an expression she hoped did not reveal her thoughts.

A pair of black orbs stared at her with unblinking directness. She suddenly found her throat unaccountably dry. Pressing her lips together she swallowed and forced herself to breathe. With that stare he could beckon forth any female he fancied, and no doubt did, frequently; show displeasure without the need to say a word, and did; and he could appraise a female from face to feet without revealing his thoughts.

And he was doing just that—*to her.*

She wondered why. Possibly he was trying to recall if he remembered her from their brief encounter in the passageway of Lord Westby's townhouse, or was it because he had never before had to bother with noticing those beneath him in consequence. And then she happened to catch the facial tick that lifted the corner of his top lip. It was an infinitesimal movement, and one perhaps he was unaware of himself. But she did not doubt its significance. His stare might not give away his thoughts, but that facial tick most certainly did. He was aware that she had just been admiring him, and it amused him.

She was so startled to be discovered that she unconsciously put a hand flat to the desk, as if needing to support herself in case her knees buckled. Was it suddenly hot in this room? But there was no fire in the grate, only on Tuesdays when Dr. Warner saw private patients.

And then she castigated herself for her naïveté. Receiving the admiring glances and come-hither looks of females was a matter of course for him, as natural as breathing. All part of the social transactions within his world. But she was not of his world, and he was most definitely out of his milieu in Gerrard Street. And so perhaps it amused him to find himself admired by a social inferior. So why was he here, and why did he wish to see her? The Portland catalog came to mind but if he did indeed think she and Becky had anything to do with its disappearance, then surely he would have sent the bailiffs around, not come in person to accuse her of stealing his property?

Suddenly, she realized he had spoken to her, and while she did not catch the question, she guessed it, thankful to still have a hand to the desk. For if his person had made her knees unstable, his voice—that voice that was indeed as rich and as smooth as hot chocolate—was worthy of a dead faint onto a chaise longue. But as the nearest chaise was in her cousin's boudoir she remained upright and, she hoped, indifferent enough to answer him in a clear voice.

"Lisa Crisp, sir," she stated, and came away from the desk to finally find her manners and bob a curtsy, gaze respectfully lowered to the embroidered front of his waistcoat.

"I know your name, Miss Crisp. I asked for your age."

This brought her eyes up to his face, puzzled. "Why would you want to know my age, sir?"

He was taken aback she would question him. "Why would you not want to tell me?"

"I've no particular reason for withholding it from you. It's just— It's a rather mundane question—coming from you."

"Mundane? *Coming from me*? What question were you expecting me to ask?"

She smiled at his frown and relaxed a little. Gone was the fixed stare, replaced by a look of puzzlement which made him appear far more approachable.

"I'd no particular question in mind," she responded, and unable to stop herself because she had flustered him, added teasingly, "Perhaps you'll think of one before you leave."

"Think of one…?"

Her directness disconcerted him. He had wanted this interview to be short. He had gone to considerable trouble to find her with the limited information Jack had given him, and now he wished to thank her for her help in his hour of need then be on his way. But the short speech of thanks that was on the tip of his tongue vanished like a popped soap bubble the moment he entered the room and saw her standing by the desk. Instead, he had asked her for her age. Why in God's name? And she had the impertinence to withhold it from him. He needed to regain the initiative at once, before she startled him again. He should not have been surprised when she again overthrew his intent, but he was.

"Miss Crisp, I had hoped to conduct this conversation in my carriage, so as not to attract any undue attention to either of us."

"But that must be an impossible task for you, surely?"

"Impossible? Why?"

Lisa blinked at him and such was her surprise that she took a step closer, wondering if he was being ironic. She had to ask the question.

"Are you funning with me, sir?"

Now he was not only disconcerted but uncomfortable. He set his jaw and the stare returned.

"I assure you, Miss Crisp, that I do not *fun*—with anyone."

"Do you not? Not at all?"

Irritated, he wondered if she were simple. But one look in her blue eyes and he knew she was sincere in her incredulity. He did not know whether to be annoyed or flattered.

"Tell me, Miss Crisp," he purred. "Why would I find it an impossible task not to attract attention?"

Lisa gulped. "You want me to tell you?"

"I do."

"Very well. If I must. But I do not doubt for a moment you know the answer."

"I do not. And I hope your answer, unlike my question, will not be mundane."

Lisa's blue eyes sparked and she smiled.

"Well?" he demanded when she did not give him an immediate response.

"Oh! So you truly do want me to tell you?"

When his gaze shot to the bare ceiling and then back at her and he remained silent and expectant, she lost her smile and felt the heat rise in her throat. There was nothing for it. She would have to tell him.

"Because you are exceedingly handsome, so it stands to reason you attract an audience wherever you go."

The silence stretched between them and then he nodded gravely. The only sign that he was in any way embarrassed by her honest appraisal was the sudden color in his lean cheeks.

"So I am told. But I come from a family of exceptional beauty. I am its thorn."

Lisa gasped and then giggled, thinking his response absurd. Not that she disbelieved him, she just did not believe he could be a thorn in any family. She quickly put a hand to her mouth for her impolite response, but could not stop her shoulders from shaking.

"I beg your pardon, Miss Crisp," he drawled, affronted. "I was being perfectly candid."

Lisa nodded, quickly wiped her moist eyes dry and pressed her lips together before taking a breath and saying with a tremble, "I meant no disrespect, sir. It's just that you are no thorn, however beautiful the rest of your family members."

He threw up a gloved hand in dismissal of her frank appraisal.

"You might think so. No doubt in these heady environs, anyone with two working eyes and a straight back is considered a rose worthy of oils."

Lisa lost her smile, and her blue eyes clouded, all humor extinguished at his jibe. Perhaps he had meant it as a throwaway comment to hide his embarrassment at being complimented for his good looks. Regardless, that gave him no excuse to be disparaging of others, and his barb stung.

"Perhaps I was wrong," she said quietly but firmly. "Perhaps you are a thorn. True beauty does not wear a mask. It shines bright from the heart—and regardless of where that heart resides on any given compass point." She bobbed a curtsy. "I am relieved to see you looking so well after your recent seizure, sir. Now you must excuse me. I am wanted elsewhere."

TEN

Lord Henri-Antoine flushed scarlet.

She had rebuked *him*, then dismissed him as if he were a lackey. A girl in a plain gown and scuffed shoes, whose fingers were ink stained, the nails short to the quick, skin rough from work, and whose family were possibly one step up from the gutter, had dared to reproach *him*, the son of a duke and a double duchess, and brother of the most powerful duke in the kingdom.

He was outraged. He clenched his teeth to stop himself vocalizing his anger. Hard gripping his walking stick he counted to five to prevent himself turning on a heel and striding from the room. But then, just as quickly, the anger cooled, emotion giving way to reason as he recalled, as he always did when a situation demanded it, his father's words of wisdom: Always control your emotions when in the public gaze. Love and laughter are reserved for the privileged few. Arrogance is a nobleman's prerogative; but a true gentleman chooses to be humble when the circumstance calls for it. Never forget you are my son; others won't.

He deserved her rebuke.

He had permitted hubris to cloud good judgment and been ill mannered. He had highlighted their disparate circumstances by making light of her surroundings and its people, and he a guest in her home. He had been ungentlemanly, his response that of a conceited jackanapes. His father would be appalled. And for all his ducal arrogance, M'sieur le Duc d'Roxton would never have said what he did in the first place. He must make amends for such a social solecism.

Jack said he owed this girl, if not his life, then the hold on his dignity. She had taken care of him, shielded him from prying eyes, soothed him, even washed his face, for God's sake... He must've been a sorry sight... And Jack said she had not flinched or failed him.

He had wanted to disbelieve Jack, though he knew he spoke the truth, thinking this girl had to be too good to be true. And then he'd discovered where she resided, and that she volunteered her time at a dispensary, and it reinforced everything Jack had told him. And there was something else, something that had occurred immediately after he had come out of his seizure, that he knew Jack had not been party to, but this girl had. It was so deeply personal he wished with every drop of blood in his veins he'd been alone, that she had not been there with him. But she had, and she knew, and there was no point wishing it were otherwise, because there was nothing he could do about that now.

That knowledge, and his distasteful display of arrogance, only strengthened his resolve to make amends. And the sooner the better. He could then return to Park Street and consign this girl, and whatever uneasiness he was experiencing because of her, to yesterday. His life would return to its daily controlled rhythm; the façade he maintained that he was seizure-free firmly back in place, no one the wiser.

But where Miss Crisp was concerned, he was soon to learn, best laid plans were destined to go awry.

"Miss Crisp—A moment, if you please," he requested in an appeasing tone.

Lisa turned back into the room. Not that she could leave even if she wanted to. The beefy servant blocked her exit and was not about to step aside to let her pass until he was given the order to do so. But she stood her ground. And so Henri-Antoine came over to her. He made her a bow.

"Accept my humble apology for my bad manners. My comment about this place and its people was inexcusable. You are correct. I do wear a mask, and you—you have seen behind it."

"You refer to your affliction."

"I do." Adding lightly, the facial tick resurfacing, "I am still a thorn, with or without my mask. I have a prickly temperament. My family will tell you so. But what they cannot tell you is what is behind the mask, because they do not know."

Lisa took a step closer, head tilted in curiosity. "But how can they not? You have had the falling sickness since birth. So your friend confided."

Henri-Antoine's reflex was to curse Jack for his easy-going confidences, throw up a hand and brush off her question. He resisted. For coming to his aid she deserved his honesty. He wanted to be open with her, and he was never open with anyone.

"I prefer not to concern my family with my condition. And so I go to great lengths to make certain, as best I can, that they not interfere, and that the world remains ignorant."

"You can be assured of my discretion, sir," Lisa told him earnestly. Adding with a wry smile, "Though I have no notion of who your family are, nor do they know me. Regardless, I would never break your confidence."

"Thank you. You did not mention the—um—incident to the doctor with whom you reside?"

"No, sir. To no one. Though I do not understand why you would not want the support of your family."

"Believe me, Miss Crisp," he drawled. "I had enough support as a child to last me a dozen lifetimes."

She smiled in understanding.

"Children like to be coddled. Men do not—That is," she confided with a bashful smile, "not directly."

"Coddled, yes. Suffocated, no," he quipped, and then her acute observation penetrated his consciousness and he looked at her keenly, a frown between his black brows. "How old did you say you were?"

Her smile widened and she lifted her chin. There was a playful light in her blue eyes. "I did not say, sir."

"This unwillingness to tell me your age is tiresome," he complained. "Though it is unnecessary for me to know your age to deduce you did not grow up here in Gerrard Street."

Her eyes went round with surprise.

"That is true. I did not. From the age of nine I attended a boarding school for young ladies in Chelsea. But how did you know?"

"A boarding school for young ladies in Chelsea?" he repeated with a detached interest that hid his surprise. "Of course you did," he muttered.

He did not like this revelation at all because it would've been much easier on his conscience to dismiss her had she not been educated and carefully nurtured in the way of girls who are expected to marry and spend their lives as wives and mothers in comfort, if not in wealth. But something told him as soon as he set eyes on her that she was no mere servant of the physician Warner. There was nothing servile or coquettish in the way she conducted herself. She had a confident air and a polite, if rather direct, approach. He doubted she knew how to flirt, and arrogantly he was glad of it. He did not like the idea of her flirting—with anyone.

He wondered why she had been sent off to a boarding school at such a young age. He knew all about boarding school. He had hated every minute of his time at Eton. Not that he had let his feelings be known because it wasn't manly to blubber at being away from his parents, and he wanted so much to be thought of as just one of the boys. His falling sickness precluded that and forever set him apart. Yet it was only while he was at Eton that he'd considered his seizures a blessing. One too many attacks in a month, and his personal physician, who followed him everywhere, sent for his father. And M'sieur le Duc d'Roxton would arrive in state in his big black carriage with six fine horses to take him home. And all the boys and masters would be in awe of this ancient aristocrat who was king of his own dominion. And then one day his father told him he would not be returning to Eton. He and Jack would complete their education at home. It had been one of the happiest days of his life, and also one of the saddest. It was the day he had come upon his mother sobbing until she could not breathe, his father's physicians gathered around her, delivering her the devastating and life-altering news that there was no hope; M'sieur le Duc, her husband and his father, was dying...

"Sir? How did you know I did not grow up on Gerrard Street?" Lisa repeated, taking another step closer when he did not answer her immediately.

"How...?" he asked, dragging his thoughts out of the past to focus on her, which was a much more pleasant and soothing experience than reliving the painful memories of his boyhood.

She had a lovely smile and her deep blue eyes were bright and open. He doubted she had a deceitful bone in her body. A body that was too thin, but that did not detract from her beauty. Her pleasing oval face, slender limbs, and graceful neck, and the way she carried herself, were most attractive. And while she was not beautiful in a breathtaking sense, she was enough above the ordinary to be memorable.

He wondered if she was too thin because she tended to the sick. Who could eat well, if at all, after spending the day amongst the poorest of poor wretches, with all their attendant ailments, diseases, and complaints. He was intrigued she had managed to remain healthy and so full of life, given her daily routine.

"Tell me, Miss Crisp," he demanded more harshly than he intended because he did not like the idea of such a bright young female wasting her days in a dispensary heady with miasma. "For how long have you been working in the dispensary?"

It took her a moment to respond because she had been expecting an answer to her question about not growing up on Gerrard Street. And his sudden anger surprised her.

"Two years, perhaps a little longer—"

"Two *years?*" He was flabbergasted. When she nodded he asked, "And in those two years how often have you been struck down with an illness, or been infected by these people?"

"Never. I've never—"

"*Never?* Not a cold, or a fever, or the slightest chill *ever?*"

"No, sir."

"What about smallpox, consumption, puerile fever, any contagion whatsoever?"

Lisa shook her head. "No, sir. I've never been ill a day in my life."

It was Henri-Antoine's turn to take a step closer, and he allowed his gaze to sweep over her with uncustomary openness. With her glowing unblemished skin, shiny hair, and white smile, he believed her to be the healthiest person he had ever had the privilege of meeting. Yet he was incredulous, because it was as if he could not quite believe he had come across such a rare find in this most unlikely of places.

"*Fascinating.*"

Lisa took a step away mistaking his wonder for skepticism.

"It is the truth, sir. Dr Warner will attest to it. He says I am worthy of further study."

He nodded, and before he could stop himself muttered, "You are worthy indeed, Miss Crisp."

"I am?" She still wasn't sure if she should be flattered or alarmed. And because he was regarding her in a manner she found unnerving, added to fill the silence, "Dr. Warner is never ill either. And he spends many more hours than I do, shut up with his patients, and in the garret where he has his dissecting room."

Mention of a dissecting room piqued Henri-Antoine's interest and brought him out of his abstraction.

"There is a dissecting room upstairs?"

"And an anatomy theater, and a preparation room, too."

"Dr. Warner is well equipped. Do your duties extend outside the dispensary to assist the physician in these areas as well?"

Lisa smiled as if he had said something highly amusing. "Only the medical students and teaching staff *assist* Dr. Warner. And as you are well aware, they are all men."

"But you do go up there?"

"To change out the scent fabrics and tussie mussies. Bring new candles and soap, and make certain the soiled garments are collected up for laundering. They are all part of my duties in the dispensary and upstairs as well."

He raised an eyebrow. "Dear me, what a strong constitution you have, Miss Crisp. I'm sure the stench alone must be frightful, not to mention the sight of such grisly offerings being inspected, dissected, and injected by our medical marvels. Though you must sorely test their powers of concentration as you flit amongst the cadavers with your fragrance and your flowers."

Lisa's back stiffened and she clasped her hands in front of her.

"I assure you, sir, that I take my duties very seriously. Dr. Warner is a fine physician. He is also a brilliant teacher, and his research is second to none. I do not *flit* and I would never seek to distract—"

He held up a gloved hand. "Miss Crisp, I do not doubt it. I was not casting aspersions on your dedication, or the good doctor's expertise. I was merely—how did you put it?—*funning* with you."

"Oh? Oh! Yes, I see. So you were." Her smile was shy, but her eyes held a twinkle of mischief. "A good first attempt, but you need to practice if you wish to make others smile."

Later he wasn't sure what made him say it, the shy smile or the twinkle, when he spoke his thoughts.

"Making others smile does not interest me. Whereas, you do."

"I do?"

"And in answer to your previous question," he continued smoothly, waking from his trance, a glance at the pearl face of his gold pocket watch, which he had taken from a waistcoat pocket to give him pause to regain his equilibrium. He then met her gaze again with no idea of the hour or the minute. "I know you did not grow up here in Gerrard Street because you do not have the same cadence as your fellows. There is little, if any, dialect in your speech. It is a learned way of speaking. From your school days, perhaps? You do it very well, and most persons would not notice. I hear it because I have an excellent linguistic ear; comes from spending my boyhood lying on a sofa, listening."

"How intriguing. I am somewhat of a linguist myself. I learned Italian at school, and French, not English, was my first language when I was a small child, which may account for my learned way of speaking in English without any dialect. My family are French émigrés. Did you learn to be fluent in the French tongue while lying on a sofa?"

She was merely responding to him by making polite conversation. That's what he told himself. But when she mentioned her first language was French, his whole manner changed. He wondered if she had told him this as a veiled reference to the deeply personal incident that had occurred when she had tended to him at Westby's residence. He hoped, but could not be certain, it was an innocent conversational remark with no further meaning. Either way, it was a timely reminder of why he had come to Warner's Dispensary in the first place: Not to exchange pleasantries or to know more than was necessary about this girl, but to thank her for coming to his aid. And having done his duty, he would leave and never think about that embarrassing incident, or her, again.

And so he ignored her question, though when he bowed to her and looked into her eyes, he could not ignore the sensation of tight-ness in his chest, as if his cravat was bound too tightly about his throat and had cut off his breathing. He needed to end this interview and leave now, before he got caught up in something not of his own making, and which was taken wholly out of his control.

"Thank you for coming to my aid," he stated formally, and lifted his walking stick a fraction—a signal of his readiness to depart, and which saw the two lads move to stand together by the entrance door. "That you were witness to the twisted tremors of my broken, ill-made self was an unfortunate circumstance which I—"

"Please, sir, you need not apologize," Lisa interrupted. "The falling sickness is not new to me, and if it will ease your mind, I have seen far worse suffering and disease here at the dispensary than perhaps you can possibly imagine."

"My dear girl, I was not about to apologize," he retorted. "Had you not trespassed into Lord Westby's residence and put yourself in harm's way, you and your friend would not have had to deal with my-my—with what was, quite frankly, none of your business. What you were doing there and at that hour, I hate to hazard a guess. At least your interference in my collapse—"

Lisa gasped. "*Interference?*"

"—saved you from a state of affairs that was most certainly well beyond your purview of expertise."

"I beg your pardon, sir, but I do not understand. What did I say to anger you? What—"

"Good day, Miss Crisp... Let me out of here!" he growled at his minders as he turned on a heel, the short skirts of his frock coat swishing about his thighs, the walking stick snatched up and the diamond-studded handle pointed at the door.

Lisa went after him, but he was out the door, a servant before him, and one following up behind, and she stopped on the doorstep, a silent witness to his abrupt departure.

He crossed the short distance to his waiting carriage. The liveried postilions were keeping the crowd well back, and his major domo was on the pavement by the fold-down steps waiting for him.

"Not a word!"

Michel Gallet inclined his head and silently followed his master up into the carriage.

Lord Henri-Antoine leaned back against the padded headboard and closed his eyes. The feeling of disquiet and restlessness, the feeling that had left him anxious for no apparent reason since his seizure at Westby's, the feeling he hoped would vanish once he had met and thanked Miss Lisa Crisp, had not gone away at all. If anything, that feeling was now ten times worse. And with his eyes closed, the same vision remained in his mind's eye—that of a Botticelli beauty.

Only now the beauty had a name.

ELEVEN

Henri-Antoine had stormed out of the dispensary, determined that was an end to his obligation to Miss Crisp, and he need never think of her again. And yet, by some whim of lunacy, when the carriage set to, he peered out the window and at the precise moment it slowly passed by the open door. And there she was, framed in the doorway. That vision of her burned itself into his brain: Slender arms at right angles and hands clasped under her neat bosom. Her feet together, the scuffed toes of her half-boots just peeking out from under the hem of her plain gown. The curl of hair that had come loose from its pins tucked behind an ear out of the way and tickling her slender throat. Confusion was writ large on her lovely face. But all that was minor detail compared with what came next.

Her blue eyes sparked with recognition. Her smile lit up her whole face. She glowed. Egad but she was beautiful. He had wished at that moment those blue eyes and that smile were for him and him alone. And his wish was granted. Locked in the moment, it did not occur to him that she was looking directly at him, but she was.

What was his response? He did not give a curt nod in acknowledgement and then slowly pull the blind. Which would have been the polite thing to do, and the only response he need give her. No. He had not done that. He had reacted in a most uncharacteristic and cowardly manner. He threw himself back against the upholstery, into the shadows of the carriage interior, back where she could not see him. Heart racing and face hot, he felt as if he'd been caught out committing a heinous act; he felt peculiar and ridiculous.

He forgot to breathe.

He reasoned it was not his fault, and that he owed her nothing.

She was not his concern and there was nothing he could do to help her, not that she had asked for or wanted his help. She took pride in her efforts to help the sick poor. Yet for some unfathomable reason he felt compelled to do something, anything, to make her situation better. She had been educated and had all the hallmarks of a female who had a right to expect to live a life far removed from the one she was living now, down amongst the diseased and downtrodden. Why? Why did he feel this way? All because she had helped him? Or was there another reason? One he had no wish to acknowledge or explore. He told himself he would not be drawn in to something from which he was certain he could not extricate himself without great personal and emotional cost. What was she to him anyway? She was not his responsibility.

And yet every night after that cowardly action of hiding himself away in the shadows of his carriage, he tried to convince himself that when next he saw Miss Lisa Crisp, as he knew he would when the Fournier Foundation trustees visited Warner's Dispensary, he would see her as she appeared to others: A girl of no particular family, so far beneath him on the social ladder that he need not acknowledge her at all.

He failed miserably on all counts.

THE WARNER household had been in turmoil since the arrival of a letter from the Fournier Foundation informing Dr. Warner that the foundation's director Dr. Bailey would indeed take up his offer of a dinner engagement. Not only that but the trustees would all attend, and visit his dispensary and anatomy school before the end of the week. No special arrangements were necessary. The only stipulation was that the visit be conducted on a day the dispensary was closed to the sick poor; this was deliberate. Without patients, the trustees would have the ease of movement required to inspect the facilities, and uninterrupted time to conduct interviews with Dr. Warner and his staff.

Dr. Warner sent a reply within the hour, agreeing to all the terms stipulated.

Maids were set to dusting, scrubbing, polishing, and perfuming every surface in both the dispensary and the living quarters, from floorboards to the silver soup tureen, while Mrs. Warner and the housekeeper devised a menu of several courses fit for such distinguished guests. Cook sent her subordinates out to market at dawn to procure the freshest produce, and on the night before the visit there was a great deal of baking, basting, and roasting.

As these domestic arrangements continued apace, the physician and his medical staff set to organizing the anatomy theater and the preparation rooms. Various specimens, medical instruments, and scientific apparatus used in his student lectures were set out for display. Also a number of his research log books and patient case studies were opened and ready for the trustees' perusal. All of this Dr. Warner hoped would provide enough material to impress the visitors.

The good doctor and his wife were also keenly aware of making a favorable impression at dinner, and to this end, the couple were fastidious in dressing for the occasion.

"I'm still at a loss to know how I am to address these gentlemen," Minette Warner complained as she took one last critical appraisal of herself in the looking glass in a corner of her dressing room. She plucked at the lace at her elbows to even out the folds. "The director and two of the trustees—"

"—are medical men. Dr. Willan is a physician at the Fever Hospital, and Dr. Blizard is a consultant surgeon at the London Hospital."

"Yes. But the other gentlemen—the three trustees who wish to remain anonymous for the duration of their visit, even when they dine with us—how then am I to address *them*, Robert? It is most irregular and unsettling not to know the social standing of men at my own table."

"Most irregular, dear heart," Dr. Warner agreed. "But if I wish for their consideration, we must abide by their rules of inspection. We are to address the nameless trustees as 'sir' and are not to enquire into their names, occupations, or stations in life. That Dr. Bailey and the trustees have agreed to remain to dinner is an honor indeed. Though I'm afraid it will be a dull affair for you, my dear," he added with what he hoped was disappointment. "There will be little or no opportunity to take the conversation in any direction other than the one they wish to take it in. I would not blame you if you did not wish to join us."

"Not join you?" Minette Warner was affronted. "When have I not presided over a dinner at my own table? When have I not supported you in all your endeavors?"

"Dear heart, I know that, and you are a wonderful helpmate to me, but I at least can talk with them on a medical level."

"I suspect the anonymous gentlemen are not medical men at all," Minette Warner said, stating her wishful thinking aloud as she collected her fan from the dressing table. "Which is more reason for me to take my usual place at our table, to do my very best to appear most interested in anything they say—for you, dear Robert."

Dr. Warner smiled away any misgivings he had that his young wife would find the conversation unfathomable, and opened the door for her. "Thank you, dear heart. That is all I can ask of you."

The couple went downstairs to await their guests in the comfort of the drawing room, nervous, but confident in their own minds they were as prepared as they would ever be for the visit of the Fournier Foundation trustees. And while the household continued to be busy around them, from the kitchen to the nursery, the only person not tasked to provide assistance in any capacity was Lisa. She had been ordered by her cousin to remain in her room for the duration, and not to come out until told to do so, or unless the house was burning down around her ears.

So it came as a shock to the couple, and most particularly to Mrs. Warner, when upon their arrival, and just after introductions were made, one of the anonymous trustees asked the whereabouts of Miss Crisp.

LISA TOOK HER cousin's directive to remain in her room as she did everything else within the Warner household, placidly and with good grace. Besides, there was no reason for her to be present; what could she offer the trustees? And Becky was making minor adjustments to the length, fit, and fall of the gowns she was taking with her into Hampshire. These clothes would then be packed in the traveling trunk which lay open against the wall. Becky's small trunk was already stowed in a corner of the scullery, along with her coat and hat, as she was spending the night on a cot in Lisa's room.

"I've not seen you look prettier, Miss," Becky announced proudly as she got up off her knees and stepped back to inspect the line of the hem of Lisa's newly-fashioned Indienne cotton *robe à l'anglaise*. "A proper fittin' gown is what you needed, and in a pretty floral pattern, and now I reckon you'd turn the head of a duke, make no mistake."

Lisa playfully bobbed a curtsy. "Why, thank you. All credit to your expert needle, Becky. I would not have thought it possible to salvage enough fabric from such worn gowns, and then turn them into something that would fit me, least of all look *à la mode*."

Becky grinned at such praise. "There ain't much of you to fit, is there? So not much yardage was needed."

"That is very true," Lisa agreed with a smile and wished she had access to a looking glass to see for herself how the gown fitted. She certainly felt prettier for wearing such delicate and colorful fabrics, which were a welcome change from her serviceable linen gowns in dull browns and blues. She just hoped these outfits were suitable for her stay at Treat. But as she could do nothing about their suitability, she wasted no more time on needless worry. Teddy's relatives would have to take her as they found her.

Becky ran a critical eye over the gown and the fabric, determined to say her piece about the backhanded generosity of Lisa's cousins. "If you ask me, those gowns had seen better days, and weren't fit to be worn by the scullery, least of all you—"

"But I did not ask you," Lisa replied with the same smile. "And I am most grateful for any offering of clothing, and to you and Mrs. Humphreys for what you have done for me. Never forget that though I live in this house, I am poorer than Tina. At least the scullery is paid for her services."

Becky was about to speak when a knock on the door surprised them both, and a maid entered to inform Lisa she was wanted in the drawing room. The girl was asked to repeat this summons because of the specific instructions from her cousin to remain in her room.

"Madam wasn't the one who asked for you, Miss," said the maid. "It was one of the gentlemen who've come to look over the master's medical rooms."

"One of the members of the Fournier Foundation?" Lisa was mystified as to why she would be called to speak to one of the trustees.

"Aye, Miss. For they all came together. But when the others went through to the dispensary, this gent stayed behind. He did not give his name. Just asked for you, Miss. He be a fine looking gent with—"

"Thank you, Ann. I did not ask for your opinion of him, or his description," Lisa said, and turned away to say to Becky, "Make haste. I must change out of this gown and—"

"No, Miss," Becky said firmly. "Go to the drawin' room as you are. 'Bout time you got used to wearin' pretty things. And as you'll be in these clothes for the next two weeks, it's only right you see this visitor as you are."

And so it was that Lisa silently entered the drawing room, self-conscious in her newly-fashioned cotton gown, a lace-edged fichu tucked at her *décolletage*, and a small lace-edged cap pinned to the crown of her head. If there was anything amiss with her attire, it was her footwear. Not in anticipation of going outdoors, and having packed her new shoes in the traveling trunk, she only had her half-boots to hand, and they were beside the bed ready for the journey. She still wore her leather house mules on her stockinged feet, which, had she chanced to look down, were rather out of place paired with her cotton gown.

But her apprehension made her oblivious to her footwear, and, in fact, to how she presented in her new gown, for she was deep in thought wondering why she had been summoned by a member of the Fournier Foundation. Was something out of place in the dispensary that required her to explain herself? Perhaps it was the scent boxes, or had she not distributed enough tussie mussies to ward off the odors? But surely every surface had been scrubbed until it was odor free...? She hoped she had not caused Dr. Warner any embarrass-ment... Perhaps her worry was needless and they merely wished to ask her questions of a general nature...?

She was across the room before she realized it was occupied. But it was not the sense that there was someone else there, it was being addressed that brought her up short. She was so surprised, not so much to find herself spoken to, her private reverie cut short, but by the voice itself. She knew at once to whom it belonged. She was so happy he had returned to Gerrard Street—when he had stormed away she hardly expected to see him again—that it never occurred to her to make a pretense of being anything else. She turned to him with a beaming smile.

Henri-Antoine smiled back. He could not help himself.

Her unaffected delight was his undoing.

IN THOSE FEW minutes before he stepped out of his carriage to join the rest of the trustees who were milling about on the pavement outside Warner's Dispensary, Henri-Antoine hesitated, wondering what he was doing here once again. But he knew the answer, and he had brought it on himself.

He had orchestrated this meeting so he could see Lisa Crisp once more. He knew he should have left well enough alone—in plain terms, he should have left Miss Crisp alone. Dr. Warner would have submitted another funding application in due course, and perhaps the Foundation would have given his third submission their full attention, and they would have found themselves here anyway. But those submissions and those visits would have been a good six to eight months in the future.

So he had interfered. And Bailey was always obliging. He had to make certain the inspection happened before he and Jack quit London for Treat. He would be absent from town for a month, perhaps two. *What difference would two months make?* he wondered. Miss Crisp would still be here. Where else had she to go? But the real question was not would she still be here, it was why did he care?

Returning here made him doubt himself, and he never doubted himself about anything. Yet, here he was, and this time with a gift for her wrapped up in tissue paper and tied off with a large black bow. He placed the package on the sofa, only to move it to the low table, and then back again in the short interval while he waited for Miss Crisp to arrive.

The trustees had gone off to tour the vacant dispensary where Dr. Warner's medical associates waited to show them around. Mrs. Warner wanted to stay behind and await the gentlemen in the comfort of her drawing room. Henri-Antoine guessed from her manner, her dress, and her liberal use of cosmetics that she had rarely if ever been inside her husband's dispensary. A look to his major domo, and Michel knew what he wanted. Mrs. Warner was soon engaged in conversation. So engrossed did she become in whatever topic Michel had broached with her, that she went out of the room with him, following behind the trustees, the door closed, and Henri-Antoine was left alone with the package and its placement.

When Lisa came into the room the package was back on the low table, and Henri-Antoine was standing by the window looking out on the street and the crowd that had gathered, but which was now dispersing as his town carriage moved off, to return when he sent for it.

He turned as the door opened and watched Lisa cross the room with a purposeful but light tread, elbows in at her sides and hands clasped under her bosom in that way she must have been taught at boarding school and which was so ingrained it was habitual. He liked it, and he liked the way she carried herself. What surprised him was the effect she had on him dressed in a simple gown of Indienne cotton. But he gave himself no time to ruminate on this by addressing her so she knew he was in the room, because she seemed not to have noticed it was occupied.

And when she turned at the sound of his voice and smiled at him, he, for the first time in his life, felt his face split into a grin of its own accord. He was helpless to do anything about it, and felt utterly foolish. Only lunatics grinned. Sane people—*he*—did not. He was always in control of himself and his emotions because there were times— those times when he was victim to his affliction—when he had no control at all. And yet—and this was new to him, too—for the first time in his life, he did not care.

TWELVE

"OH!? HELLO." Lisa bobbed a curtsy of welcome. "Is your visit a coincidence, or are you truly a trustee of the Fournier Foundation?"

"I am—*truly*—a trustee."

As he seemed incapable of moving away from the window, and his walking stick was planted in the floor, she came over to him.

"Oh!? You are?" She was so surprised she blurted this out, then immediately apologized. "Forgive me. I don't know why I should be astonished. Of course you could be. Only, it seemed it was a coincidence—"

"—because you hoped I was here to see you?"

She smiled and blushed but she was not backward. "Yes. How did you guess?"

That made Henri-Antoine laugh. God! What was wrong with him? First he was grinning and now he was laughing out loud. The newness of this experience made him suddenly light-headed.

Lisa's blush deepened. He had a lovely white smile when he laughed. And it made her want to throw her arms around his neck and kiss him. She of course did not. She kept her elbows in at her sides and her hands together, dropped her chin and turned away to go over to the arrangement of sofa and chairs. She indicated the sofa, saying in what she hoped was an easiness of manner, when she was anything but calm, "Would you care to sit? Would you like me to ring for tea? Would you—"

"—like to tell me how it is you are a trustee of the Fournier Foundation? That is what you want to know, is it not, Miss Crisp?" he replied, joining her. He flicked out the skirts of his frock coat and sat at one end of the sofa, one foot slightly forward, and with his walking stick between his knees. He then indicated the rest of the sofa. "Please. Sit. And I will tell you."

She sat facing him. But not at the furthest end of the seat cushions but halfway along, so that they were in close proximity. Not close enough for her to appear forward, but not so far away that she would come across as a frigid miss. She then put her hands in her lap and waited.

"*Si vous êtes d'accord, je souhaite vous parler dans ma langue maternelle*— If you agree, I would like to speak to you in my native language."

She had a swift intake of breath and her blue eyes widened. "French is your first language, too?"

She should not have been surprised, but she was. It opened a Pandora's box of questions none of which she asked. Instead she smiled and replied in French.

"I wish very much for us to speak in French. Though you will have to forgive me because I am only permitted to speak English here in the house. So while I will understand what you say to me, I am out of practice with my speaking."

"*Tout ce dont vous avez besoin, c'est la pratique et la confiance. Plus nous conversons, j'espère que plus il deviendra facile pour vous. Oui?*—All you need is practice and confidence. The more we talk, I hope the easier it will become for you. Yes?"

She nodded and smiled but did not immediately reply. Not because she did not understand or because she could not answer, but because she needed a moment to compose herself. Listening and watching him as the French language rolled off his tongue with honeyed ease filled her with sensations she did not understand nor could she articulate them in any meaningful way had she been asked to do so. All she wanted to do was lie back on the cushions and close her eyes, and let him talk on and on so that his words washed over her, covering her in a warm coverlet of exquisite conversation. A word came to mind about this feeling—euphoria.

"That is true: The more I speak in French, the more confident I will become in speaking it—*with you*," she said, repeating back what he had said to her, her euphoria twisting itself inside out into foolishness. She clasped her fingers a little too tightly, as if this would stop her from descending further into some sort of ridiculous stupor. "What is it you wish to ask me? Oh! No! But you first," she added with a light laugh at her own slip. She leaned in a little. "You offered to tell me how it is you are a trustee of the Fournier Foundation."

He unconsciously mimicked her action and leaned into her and said, "I see that it pleases you I am."

She did not dissemble but was also filled with a mix of emotions: Surprised that he saw the pleasure writ large on her face; relieved he thought that pleasure derived from a mutual interest in the advancement of medical knowledge; and guilty that she was not thinking about the foundation at all, but was selfishly absorbed in how he made her feel.

"It does, sir. I am not surprised you have an interest in medicine, as anyone with your affliction must. Any investigations that unlock the secrets and wonders of the human body must give you, and others, some hope that one day physicians may be able to offer effective treatment, if not a cure."

"There will not be a cure for the falling sickness in my lifetime, Miss Crisp."

"Which makes your involvement in the foundation all the more admirable."

"It does? It could easily be seen as motivated by self-interest."

"How so?"

"It may appear that I am interested in the advancement of medical science for self-serving ends. Everyone else and their suffering—pardon me, but you will—can be damned to hell, for all I care."

Lisa was adamant in his defense. So much so it brought color to his lean cheeks.

"If that were the case then all a gentleman of your means need do is wait for medicine to advance, without you lifting a finger to help. After all, you are fortunate to be able to deal with your affliction in a most civilized manner and make yourself as comfortable as possible. You need not involve yourself personally in the medical field, and most particularly not in the running of a charitable fund that seeks to relieve the sick poor of their burden of illness, free of charge. Besides," she rattled on, warming further to her topic, and because his gaze remained fixed on her eyes, "a gentleman such as yourself need not show an interest in the sick poor at all. There are any number of charitable trusts to which you could give of your time and attention, and your wealth, that have nothing to do with poor relief, or medicine. And yet, here you are, a trustee of the Fournier Foundation. And so I do not believe you wish to consign anyone to hell, least of all the poor, sir."

"And I do not think you, Miss Crisp, have anything to concern yourself about your French language skills. With practice I could have you speaking like a native, so that not even my mother would guess you were from this side of the Channel, and not that."

"Oh? I don't? Could you? Is your mother French?" she asked in a rush, shy at his praise and because mention of his mother made their conversation that much more personal. And not least, because she had asked three successive questions. But she saw the absurd in her response and laughed behind her hand, confessing, "You may find me a poor pupil, sir, because I would prefer to listen to you."

"But ... Surely the poor pupil is the one who does not listen at all?"

When he continued to frown in thought, she blushed and said in a small voice before looking down at her hands, "I meant something else entirely..."

There followed such a long silence between them that she forced her gaze up to his face, and saw that he was looking at her intently, and she knew he understood the real meaning behind her confession. He smiled thinly, and something sparked in his dark eyes.

"Perhaps we should start an admiration society for French speakers—for two?"

She returned his smile, and said cheekily, "I will join. On condition you do all the talking."

He laughed and instantly put a fist to his mouth to stop himself.

"Will you tell me how you became interested in the Fournier Foundation?" she asked quietly, gaze following his hand up to his mouth and noticing for the first time that he had removed his gloves. His fingers were long and tapered, the nails manicured, and he wore a heavy gold signet ring on his pinky, which was set with a carnelian intaglio engraved with a coat of arms.

"At the risk of boring you—"

"I beg your pardon, but you cannot bore me," she interrupted without realizing it, attention still focused on his signet ring and the significance of that coat of arms. And when he moved his hand and let his arm lie across the length of the back of the sofa towards her, she rallied, saying seriously, which was at odds with the light in her eyes, "As we are now members of this newly-formed French speaking society, and I have joined on condition and expectation that you do all the talking, I must listen to whatever you have to say. So you see, I won't be bored. Besides," she continued, knowing she was prattling but unable to stop herself because he was looking at her in an odd sort of way that made her happy and nervous at one and the same time, "you have such a lovely voice, you could talk on any subject and I would listen, and in whatever language you cared to address me in. Though I am sure that is nothing new to you, to be complimented. And although I have only heard you speak in English and French, I am confident you must speak other tongues, too. You are too well spoken to have limited yourself to two. At Blacklands I also learned to read, write, and speak in Dante's language. But since coming to live with the Warners I have had even less practice speaking that language than I have French. But you—I could listen to you speak in French all day..."

Again the silence stretched, but this time she could not bring herself to look up to see his reaction, such was her embarrassment at allowing herself to blather. Yet it was easy to blather in French, to him. She doubted she would have been quite so effusive or as candid in English. She kept her gaze to the embroidered front of his linen waistcoat, with its sprays of lily of the valley and matching covered buttons, and waited for him to speak. After all, she had given him permission to talk without needing any contribution from her.

He took her up on her offer.

"I do not recall a time when I was not interested in medical science," he reflected. "Perhaps, initially, my interest was piqued because of my affliction, and being constantly surrounded by physicians, almost from birth. The closet off my bedchamber was a veritable pharmacopeia. I had a resident physician until my teens, and I have never gone anywhere or done anything without my shadows. I have three. The one that belongs to me, and the two belonging to the lads, a far more convivial name for the minders who follow me everywhere. And just like my shadow, I have learned to accept them as a matter of course. Their presence gives me a certain peculiarity amongst Society. Such a self-absorbed existence is as liberating as it is limiting.

"I am fortunate enough to have the means to be indulgent. Others —most others—will never have such freedom. But how the poor, debilitated by the falling sickness, and who carry its stigma for life, are able to function in our society with any sense of dignity, I cannot imagine... But the Foundation's *raison d'être* is to fund the advancement of medical science. It is a charitable trust for physicians, apothecaries, surgeons, and researchers, and their apprentices. I believe—the trustees believe—that the advancement of knowledge in the medical sciences is the only way forward to alleviating suffering, not only for the poor, but all mankind.

"But I fully appreciate my duties as a trustee are but a thimbleful's worth of effort when compared to those who dedicate their lives to treating the sick, and who spend their days toiling in the most barbaric of conditions, elbow-deep in human remains, all to improve our understanding. Nor can my efforts measure up against the comfort and reassurance you provide those wretches who visit the dispensary seeking relief, if not a cure, for their ills. One smile and a kind word must surely alleviate their pain, if only for that brief moment in time. And for many, that is more than enough to sustain them, to know they are thought of, and their ills believed, even if they are so self-absorbed, as indeed I was as a child, to take your smile and your kind word as a grand presumption."

"Sir, you are too kind—"

"I am never *too kind*, Miss Crisp. Nor should you be self-effacing. I give credit where it is due—well, I am much better at doing so nowadays... Now that I am no longer a petulant boy, spoiled beyond permission."

"Petulant? Never! Spoiled? Yes," she agreed, head cocked and smiling into his eyes. "I can well believe that even as a boy you had a distinct advantage over your fellows, which meant not only did your parents and your siblings spoil you, I am sure all those with whom you came in contact were only too willing to jump to do your bidding. Why, I would wager even your physician, your nurses, and your shadows were compliant to your boyish demands."

Henri-Antoine pulled a face, but he was not annoyed, despite the complaint in his tone. "Distinct advantage? Boyish demands? Dear me, Miss Crisp, whatever can you mean?"

"Oh, pray, sir! Surely you are funning with me. I have told you so already."

"I have not the slightest notion to what you are inferring," he said with a shrug, features schooled in what he hoped was an expression of neutrality. "And this despite being the proud owner of three full-length looking glasses, and five or more dressing mirrors." When Lisa giggled behind her hand, he added softly, leaning into her, "I demand that you give me a clearer explanation of your meaning."

His tone was playful but there was an intensity in his gaze that made her suddenly wary, and she shivered, swallowed and looked away.

"Please—please do not make me," she replied and in English.

That broke the spell.

He realized at once that their verbal sparring had gone too far for her; that she was, after all, quite young and innocent for all her worldly façade and maturity in dealing with the dispensary patients, and with him while in the throes of a seizure. For the second time in as many weeks he had lost his footing and overstepped the mark, which was unforgiveable; she with the power to unsettle him. He remembered that they were alone, and he a guest in her guardian's house. Had she been a young unmarried female of his own class, she would never have been left alone with him under any circumstances, and rightly so.

He sat back and let his arm drop to his knee, and remembered the package. But it did not seem appropriate to give it to her at that moment because she might misconstrue his intent. Thus he went to great pains to make conversation which he hoped would put her at her ease so she would be comfortable with him again. Following her lead, he reverted to English.

"My grandfather, my mother's father, was a physician, and a Parisian. Perhaps that is where I inherited my interest in medical science... It must be in the blood?" he mused, gaze on the diamond-studded top of his walking stick. "My grandfather the Chevalier was a gifted healer, and much to the horror of his noble parents he chose to study medicine, and not the law. Worse. Once he had graduated, he did not go into private practice to treat those of his own class, but used his healing gifts to help the poorest of the poor wretches in the hospital known as *La Salpêtrière*, where females of lowest repute, the insane, and those suffering from the falling sickness are incarcerated. Which is not surprising, given epileptics are thought by many to be one step away from madness—"

"That is unsupported prejudice. Dr. Warner will tell you so."

"Then he is one of our more enlightened medical men."

"He is, sir. But forgive me. I interrupted you telling me about your grandfather..."

"I will not tire you with the particulars of his medical career, as much as I know *you* would be fascinated by such detail. Suffice for me to tell you that my mother believes—thinking back on her childhood and instances where her father would shut himself away—that my grandfather was a fellow suffer, and spent his life hiding his affliction."

Lisa drew in a small breath and her blue eyes widened. "Your grandfather also suffered with the falling sickness?"

"That is my mother's postulation. Coincidentally, I bear one of his names... My parents could not have foreseen at my birth that I, too, would be a sufferer." Henri-Antoine was pensive, then said with a note of wonder, taking his gaze from his walking stick to look directly at Lisa, "I have not spoken about my grandfather in many years—with anyone... Nor have I behaved as a gentleman ought when I took my leave of you," he continued smoothly, seeing she was again comfortable in his company. "I ask that you accept this small token as my apology for my uncustomary discourtesy, and as a thank you for coming to my assistance at Lord Westby's townhouse."

He took the package from the low table and placed it between them on the sofa cushion.

"For-for *me*?"

"For you."

Lisa frowned at the package tied up with black ribbon.

"Please keep your frown for after you have opened it, if it is not to your liking."

Lisa's frown disappeared and she smiled into his eyes. "I am very sure I will like it because it is from you. May I unwrap it?"

Henri-Antoine waved a languid hand and sighed, though he was secretly pleased with her undisguised delight, and uncharacteristically apprehensive as to her reaction to his gift.

"Please do. It cannot unwrap itself."

"Very well then," she said, giving the bow a tug. "But I must warn you I am unused to receiving gifts—"

"It is a mere token."

"—of *any* kind. So I may shed a tear or two."

"Thank you for the warning. I will ready my handkerchief."

Lisa chuckled then gave her full attention to the package as the ribbon unraveled and the cloth fell open to reveal a rectangular wooden box. But it was so far from the ordinary as to be extraordinary. So much so that Lisa froze, speechless.

THIRTEEN

W HEN LISA did not move or say a word, Henri-Antoine leaned forward, frowning.

"Is it not to your taste, Miss Crisp...?"

Lisa shook her head and swallowed. She had never before seen such a beautiful object, and this one a writing box. This was her presumption given the diagonal cut to the lid and the drop handles at either side, though she had yet to be told or instructed on its function. She had seen a few finely-crafted boxes while at Blacklands, and envied those girls who were fortunate enough to own them. Her writing box had been made for her by one of the school's carpenters in payment for giving his son lessons in reading and writing. She still used it. A simple wooden box constructed from off-cuts, the writing slope covered with a piece of repurposed leather, and the hinges of a nondescript metal.

But this writing box on her cousin's sofa... It was a thing of beauty. As beautiful an object as it was functional. A work of art, carefully crafted to be seen as well as used. It belonged in a great lady's boudoir, and to be taken by her when she went traveling in her splendid carriage-and-four, perhaps with a livered footman employed for the precise purpose of carrying and caring for such a treasure.

Such was Lisa's reverence that she hesitantly and then gently caressed the lid, fingertips trailing over the gleaming red richness of the rosewood and the border of mother-of-pearl inlay, the fretting expertly cut and polished to represent foliage. The front face was similarly inlaid and here also was a polished brass lock. She wondered as to the whereabouts of the key because she itched to open it to see if it was as magnificent on the inside.

As if sensing Henri-Antoine held the key, she looked up through a mist of tears. He did indeed have it, but he put it aside to dig in a frock coat pocket for his handkerchief. This he held out to her.

"Th-Thank y-you," she muttered, swallowing hard. She patted her eyes and cheeks dry. "I-I am sorry. It-it is *very* beautiful, and cost you dearly, so I am a little overcome by it, and you, for gifting it to me. I never expected payment of any kind for assisting you in your distress—"

"And I would not insult you with payment, Miss Crisp. As to the cost, that is of little consequence to a man of my vulgar wealth. And this writing box was not the most expensive on offer, but it is the most tasteful. I hope you will pardon the presumption, I thought it perfect for you. But that is the least of my concerns. What does concern me is the rehabilitation of my reputation, which is beyond price," he drawled in a most superior manner. "Thus I must insist you accept this token so that I may feel better about myself."

His facial tick gave him away, and Lisa smiled and shook her head, not at all fooled by his haughtiness. She realized he was doing his best to make her feel at ease.

"Very well, sir. I should not like to be the cause of any further unease on your part. So I will accept your gift—pardon me, *your token* —with gratitude. Though I am mystified as to how you knew I am a keen letter writer. Or perhaps while you were investigating Dr. Warner's Dispensary for the foundation you discovered I am an amanuensis for the poor?"

"An amanuensis for the poor? Indeed! You never cease to surprise me, Miss Crisp. No. I did not know. And why do the poor require your services as a scribe?"

She told him, and she wasn't sure what surprised him more: That she provided such a service, or that while most of the persons who came through the dispensary doors could read, they could not write. He was such a willing ear, that she then went on to tell him about sitting in her corner with her writing box, and the poor lining up to take advantage of her services in dictating to her letters they could not write themselves.

"So you see, this beautiful writing box will be put to good use, and be cared for very well indeed," she told him happily, allowing her fingertips to again caress the box, as if needing the tangible to make certain it was there, and hers.

He could see his gift had made her happy, and that filled him with a sense of contentment, the unwanted apprehension he had been experiencing wondering if the box would please her vanishing as his gaze followed her fingers across the polished rosewood and mother-of-pearl inlay.

"It was your fingers," he confessed softly. "The ink stains... The ink stains to your fingers told me about your letter writing—No! You must not hide them away," he said more harshly than he intended when she snatched her hand away and made fists in her lap. "You should never be ashamed of the tell-tale signs caused by honest work. They are a badge of honor, are they not? And now that you have told me about your services as an amanuensis for the poor, I am more than ever delighted with myself at the appropriateness of my gift—pardon me, *my token.*"

"*Delighted with myself?*" she repeated with a gasp, and then giggled at the absurdity of his pronouncement. She asked sweetly, "How is it, sir, that you know just what to say to put me at my ease?"

Henri-Antoine shrugged, as if he had no idea. But his attempt at nonchalance failed because he could not stop himself from smiling at her undisguised happiness.

"Ah. This is when I *should* tell you I've spent years cultivating social insouciance. But I know that would not impress you—"

"You are right. It does not."

"—so I must confess I do not have an answer where you are concerned."

"You do not?"

Lisa pouted, unable to hide her disappointment, and again Henri-Antoine found himself grinning. Only this time he forgot to mentally castigate himself for his lax behavior, asking her in a light tone,

"Would you like me to show you the mechanics of your writing box, or do you wish to discover for yourself what—"

"Oh yes! Yes! Please show me—*everything*," she interrupted excitedly.

She hopped off the sofa, slipped off her mules so she could better sit on her haunches, and careful not to crush the skirts of her gown she sat on the carpet in front of him. Before he had time to even put aside his walking stick, she was settled, back straight, hands in her lap, with chin up and eyes bright, the keen student awaiting his instruction.

He held out the key. "Would you do the honors?"

Lisa nodded, and was up on her knees to turn the small but surprisingly heavy brass key in the lock. And as he folded back the lid until it lay flat on its polished brass hinges, she leaned ever forward, mouth at half-cock in amazement that what was revealed inside the writing box was even more luxurious than its outer casing.

With the two halves lying flat, the slope to the writing surface was evident. This was covered in a bright red leather bordered by a tooled frame stamped in gold. Here was the place to lay each sheet of paper and write in comfort, the red leather surface set within a framework of ebony facings inlaid with mother-of-pearl filigree work. At one end was a long, segmented storage compartment, one for quills, another for nibs and associated paraphernalia, and at either side a place for an inkwell. And there were two, of cut glass with silver stoppers.

Henri-Antoine removed one from its place to show Lisa how the mechanism worked in the silver lid to stop the ink from leaking, and how to unscrew it. He then gave it to her to try, which she did without any difficulty. But when he put out his hand to take the inkwell to put it back she hesitated, and looked up at him wonderingly. Her voice was barely above a whisper.

"You've had the lids engraved with my initials."

"Yes. Did you have someone else in mind...?"

She shook her head, too overcome to say more, and pushed the little bottle back into his hand.

Next he tugged gently on a small red leather tab in the center top edge of the writing surface and the entire half of the box lifted like a second lid to reveal a compartment underneath.

"A place to store your paper," he told her. "Let me astound you further—"

"Can you? I am more than a little tongue-tied as it is."

"I can tell," he quipped.

He put this lid back into position and pulled on a second tab at the end in front of the quill compartment and inkwells, and lifted back the writing surface as he had done before. This half also revealed a compartment. And he beckoned Lisa closer and to pay attention to what he was doing. He ran his fingers along the rose-wood panel below the compartment, and just as Lisa blinked, the panel came away in Henri-Antoine's fingers. Lisa took a breath, astonished when he removed the panel entirely and showed her the brass spring latch that held this panel in place. When pressure was applied to a particular spot, the catch released and the panel came away freely. She was about to ask why, when, having removed the panel, all was revealed.

"Three secret drawers with bone handle pulls, neatly concealed behind the wood panel. Tiny, but large enough to hold little notes, or keepsakes. And only you know they are there."

"And you," she said, smiling up at him. She reached in and slid open one of the drawers, and then tried the next, and finally she slid open the third. "Oh," she said, peering into each drawer with a feigned sigh of disappointment. "I thought... I thought perhaps you might have left me a note."

"A note? Did you? Is this writing box not enough—Oh! Ah! I see," he muttered, realizing too late when she clapped a hand to her mouth to hide her smile that she was teasing him. He made a quick recover, however, saying in a drawl, his tone at odds with the mirth in his dark eyes,

"If I'd not had those silver lids engraved, you ungrateful wretch, I'd think about returning this—"

"Oh no you don't!" she said fiercely, hands splayed covetously across the leather writing surface. But then she had a sudden thought and sat back on her haunches with her chin up, to say loftily, "By all means, sir. Take it. Though I warn you that in doing so you will lose any advantage you had, and you will no longer feel better about your-self. And—*and*," she stressed when he went to speak, continuing when he pressed his lips together, though it was obvious he was trying to suppress a grin, "I can draw but one conclusion from such petty retribution. That despite assurances to the contrary, you are as petulant and as indulged as you ever were as a boy. I am certain that is not how you wish to present yourself to me, is it?"

He shook his head obediently. Then in an about-face he nodded, which had her gasping and again sitting up, balancing on her knees, feigning affront. But her display fell flat when she became unbalanced and fell forward, only for him to catch her by the upper arm. And once he had her he did not instantly let her go. He stared into her flushed face, all humor extinguished.

"It is only fair I warn you, Miss Crisp," he said quietly. "Petulance and acting the pampered brat remain two of my better qualities."

She held his gaze. "I do not believe you."

He let her go and sat back, eyes anywhere but on her. She stayed silent and still, the feeling of his fingers about her arm lingering longer than was pleasant. And then she rallied, suddenly aware of the passage of time. They had been in the drawing room alone together for so long she was certain the trustees had had enough time to not only have a comprehensive tour of the dispensary, but must have ascended to inspect the anatomy theater and the preparation rooms. And he, whoever he was, because he had yet to confide in her his name, and she had never asked, was surely conspicuous by his absence.

The writing box was still open and pulled apart, and when she went to put it back together, he came to life and offered to help. His manner and tone gave nothing away of his thoughts. She asked to be shown how to work the spring-loaded catch so she would be able to remove the panel that concealed the secret drawers by herself. He obliged and she practiced several times until she was proficient. This interval gave them both the time and opportunity to return to the easy manner they found they enjoyed in each other's company. So much so that when the drawing room door opened to admit a trustee, Henri-Antoine and Lisa were so absorbed in the writing box and each other that they were oblivious to all else.

Lisa was up on her knees, head over the box, practicing one last time to release the hidden spring-loaded catch, while Henri-Antoine was so close he could count every dark lash framing her blue eyes. And while he was acutely aware of her he was sure she remained oblivious to him. Her concentration was on being able to use the catch to reveal the hidden drawers, and then be able to successfully replace the panel.

He quickly returned his thoughts to the task at hand and soon they had their heads together peering into the writing box's every nook and cranny, while he found himself giving her an account of his visit to *Toulmin and Gale* on New Bond Street, and how he had returned later that same night to retrieve the box once the silver lids of the inkwells had been engraved, the proprietor only too willing to keep his premises open well into the small hours to make certain the writing box was prepared to his client's satisfaction.

It was no surprise then that when the couple were addressed, they both jumped and turned as one to the doorway.

"APOLOGIES FOR the interruption, but we're wanted upstairs," Jack said chattily to Henri-Antoine.

He had waited until his best friend had finished recounting his visit to *Toulmin and Gale*, which also gave him the leisure to observe the girl kneeling on the carpet at Henri-Antoine's feet. He would not have recognized her from their brief meeting in the passageway at Westby's townhouse. He had been too distracted by Henri-Antoine's diminished health to notice much about her, except that she was young and pretty and far too self-possessed for a girl dealing with such a situation.

In the light of day, with her cheeks delicately tinged with color, and her eyes bright, dressed in a simple floral cotton gown, this girl was even prettier than he had first thought. And then she smiled at him in recognition, and her lovely smile lit up her features. He mentally corrected himself: She wasn't pretty, she was beautiful, as beautiful and as sunny as a spring day.

"Hello," she said, scrambling to her feet, allowing Henri-Antoine to help her up. She brushed down the skirts of her gown, looked about for her mules, slipped them on her stockinged feet and came across the room to drop a simple curtsy in greeting. "Today is full of surprises. Are you a trustee, too?"

Jack made her a bow, and could not help smiling. "I am. I'm only sorry that under the terms of our visit I cannot properly introduce myself, Miss—Miss—?"

"Miss Crisp. No matter. Your friend Harry hasn't introduced himself either—"

"What the devil—!" Henri-Antoine exploded, unable to contain his incredulity. He was utterly flummoxed. Jack's idiotic grin did not help his mood. He strode over to join them, and ignoring Jack demanded of Lisa, "How long have you known—"

"—your Christian name? Since my visit to Lord Westby's residence. Jack—" She looked at Jack. "That is your name, is it not, sir?" When he nodded, she continued. "Jack called you Harry that night, and so I presumed that to be your name."

For reasons he could not quite fathom he was not pleased to hear his name, and Jack's, tripping off her tongue with such familiarity. It was one thing to be at his ease with her when they were private—though thinking about this he was made uncomfortable by his social lapse—and he was annoyed with Jack for the interruption, and with her for compromising his judgment. And so he tried to restore order —the way his life ought to be conducted—and failed miserably.

"That is not my name," he enunciated coldly. "That is what *he* calls me. And Jack is not *his* name. That is what *I* call him. So remove your self-satisfied smile and no, you may not address us on such familiar terms—"

"Now hold on, Harry," Jack said, rushing to Lisa's defense. "Jack is what everyone calls me. And I'm not the only one who calls you Harry. Most of the family does, except your mother, and—"

"Keep out of this!" Henri-Antoine snapped, not taking his gaze from Lisa.

Jack threw up his hands and took two steps back. But he needn't have bothered to come to Lisa's defense because she was not upset in the least. In fact, if he had felt himself an intruder upon entering the room, he most certainly knew he was one watching these two verbally spar. But while she was enjoying every minute, Henri-Antoine was becoming increasingly uncomfortable as those seconds ticked by. If someone had recounted this scene to him, he would not have believed it possible, not of Henri-Antoine, whom he had always assumed he knew better than anyone—apparently not.

"You're irritated because you wanted to tell me your name your-self, and now you cannot," Lisa replied to Henri-Antoine. "Though why you wish to keep your name a secret... You cannot use the Fournier Foundation rules as an excuse. This is your second visit. And I was good enough to tell you my name on your first visit—"

"But not your age. You still haven't told me your age. Nor do I see that there is anything in that to make you smile," he grumbled. "I am being perfectly serious."

Lisa took a step closer so Jack would not overhear her. "Yes, I see that you are. And employing two of your *better qualities* to try and make me do your bidding will not work. I will not be coerced by such underhanded means."

Despite his best intentions to remain grave he was quickly real-izing he could not conjure any defense against her.

"You, Miss Crisp, are a shameless baggage," he drawled softly, looking down into her upturned smiling face. "Nor can you coerce *me*, with your sweetness and light. I have been burned once too often, and I am immune to such feminine wiles."

Lisa blinked at him. "I am not entirely certain I understand your meaning, sir."

He believed her. And he was likely to be burned by her if he remained in the orbit of her flame for much longer. He so wanted to take her in his arms and kiss her... That thought snapped him out of his reverie. And although he came to a sense of his surroundings and occasion, he was left feeling slightly inebriated. He wondered if he were experiencing the onset of an impending seizure, he was so whey-brained and disorientated. But this sensation was different from anything he had ever felt before, and that disturbed him most of all. So much so that he turned away and went over to the window, needing space and time to help him determine if he needed to excuse himself and send for the lads.

The drawing room door opened then to admit Minette Warner, and with her was Michel Gallet. She was fluttering her fan and saying something over her shoulder in response to the major domo. But when she turned into the room and was confronted with her cousin and two gentlemen, her smile fell away. She looked Lisa over, shot a glance at Jack, then one at Henri-Antoine, then fixed on the sofa and a pretty, filigree-worked wooden box sitting on a cloth and a length of black ribbon.

"How surprising to find you entertaining our guests in my absence, Lisa," Minette Warner said with a tight smile. "You may return to your room, where you were told to remain, and finish packing for your journey. And do make certain you remove that gown. You do not want it ruined before you have even arrived at your destination. The cotton is fragile, thin at best, given it has been worn many times before by Henriette. You could very well have put holes in the fabric already."

Lisa bobbed a curtsy, embarrassed to be caught out by her cousin, though she had done nothing wrong, and mortified to have the second-hand nature of her gown discussed openly, and before a gentleman who was always dressed with all the sartorial elegance of one attending a ball. Still, anything she said would sound petty, and it was her cousin's home and she a member of her household through the Warners' good graces. So she remained silent and went to collect her writing box off the sofa.

"Leave it. I'm certain it can't be yours—"

"Forgive the interruption, Madam," Henri-Antoine said with icy politeness. He wasn't sure what made his blood boil more: The condescending tone in which this woman spoke to a girl who lived under her roof, who was clearly not a servant, or watching the light go out of Lisa's eyes as she was being lectured to. "The writing box does indeed belong to Miss Crisp. No doubt she will put it to good use in her duties as amanuensis—"

Minette Warner was so surprised she forgot her manners and scoffed, "I hardly think writing letters for the poor requires such an expensive and ornamented writing equipage. And I am certain you will excuse me when I point out that, as Lisa is not of age, it is not her place to accept gifts from persons unknown to her guardian."

Henri-Antoine bowed his head with extreme politeness and smiled thinly. Jack did not like that smile at all, and he waited for his best friend to go in for the attack. And if he didn't he was certainly willing to do so to put this creature in her place.

"I agree—" Henri-Antoine began, and was rudely cut off.

"There, Lisa. Now run along."

"I agree that you cannot have thought through your response," Henri-Antoine stated, completing his sentence. "Nor do I excuse you for pointing out the obvious, or for making the inference there was anything improper in the gift-giving." And while Minette Warner was opening and closing her mouth to try and find the words to reply to such a set-down, he turned to Lisa and said smoothly, "And when you have put away your writing box, Miss Crisp, return here to join us in the dining room. The trustees may have questions regarding your duties in the dispensary."

Lisa stopped in front of him, the writing box hastily wrapped up and clutched to her chest.

"I am already in more strife than I can easily explain away in coming here to the drawing room," she whispered.

"The same strife you would've been in had you come out to my carriage when I called upon you that first time?"

Lisa nodded. "And you will only compound that by having me attend a dinner party to which I am not invited."

"I am invoking my right of request as a trustee. And if the good doctor and his dragon lady wife want the foundation to fund his enterprise, then they will not object to your presence at dinner."

Lisa stood her ground.

"Sir, this is one battle from which I ask you to retreat. Do not make me attend. There will be—consequences... And tomorrow I embark on my journey, which at least will give my cousin the time to forgive, if not forget, my infraction."

Henri-Antoine looked into her eyes. She did not blink or look away. "If that is your wish."

"It is."

"Then I will forgo your company... Are you away long?"

"A fortnight."

"Will it be a pleasant fortnight?"

Lisa's smile returned. "It will. I'm attending a friend's wedding."

"How coincidental. So am I." He jerked his head in Jack's direction. "He's getting leg-shackled."

Lisa turned to look at Jack—could this gentleman be Teddy's Jack? Surely not! But then she looked back at Henri-Antoine with wide eyes and lips slightly parted, her sudden thought too good to be true. Henri-Antoine's facial tick surfaced watching her. They looked at each other and Lisa knew then that he, too, was having a similar thought. Voicing it was unnecessary. The smile in their eyes was enough to communicate a most outlandish thought: Wouldn't it be the most wonderful coincidence imaginable if they happened to be attending the same wedding!

FOURTEEN

I T WAS STILL dark when Lisa and Becky were taken by hackney to the Bell Savage Inn at Ludgate Hill to board the Southampton stagecoach into Hampshire. Dr. Warner accompanied them, and it was he who gave the order to the *jarvie* to be off.

"My mind will be much easier if I see with my own eyes that you are put on the coach," he confessed. "That you secure an inside seat as was paid for, and that you have everything you need for a pleasant journey."

"Thank you, sir. That is kind," Lisa replied, stifling a yawn into her gloved fist, wondering how the physician could be so wide-awake, for surely he'd had little sleep after a full afternoon and dinner with the trustees of the Fournier Foundation. "Was the visit from the trustees and the dinner a success, sir? Do you think they were suitably impressed...?"

"Aye! I had a most productive discussion with my colleagues, Drs. Willan and Blizard, and I could see they were more than a little envious of the facilities I offer my anatomy students. Which bodes well for their report. And Dr. Bailey is a most distinguished physician, with the manners of a gentleman. And no wonder! He was once the personal physician to none other an exalted personage than the fifth Duke of Roxton, a most formidable old aristocrat—"

"—husband of the Duchess of Roxton and Kinross, to whom Aunt de Crespigny was lady-in-waiting?"

"The very same. You can imagine how well received this news was by Mrs. Warner. And despite Mrs. Warner's best efforts to have Dr. Bailey recount one or two small anecdotes about his years with the Duke, he could not be drawn on the subject."

"I am sure Cousin Minette did her best, sir," Lisa said with as much seriousness as she could put into her tone, all to stop herself rolling her eyes imagining her cousin's efforts at the dining table to entice Dr. Bailey to share gossip about his years as the physician of a duke, and not just any duke, but the one duke her cousin's mother had served.

Dr. Warner sat forward with a smile. "And I must share with you something about that estimable young gentleman who took it upon himself to speak with you in the drawing room, that I am sure will impress you as it did me."

"Yes, sir?" Lisa asked, again doing her best to appear grave. Only this time it was because she felt her face warm at the mention of he who had still to tell her his name, though she knew Jack called him Harry. She did not suppose Dr. Warner had discovered his name... "What did you learn?"

"Only that he has met *Dottore* Lazzaro Spallanzani himself!"

Lisa was deflated, and puzzled. "*Dottore*—Spallan—Spallanzani...?"

"The very man! Imagine!"

"I wish I could, sir. You will have to tell me more about him."

"Spallanzani is a most brilliant teacher and one of the greatest minds of our time. His theory of the spontaneous generation of microbes is most illuminating. But his greatest works are in the areas of fertilization and the processes of human digestion. He was made a Fellow of our Royal Society for his contributions to science."

"And a most worthy honor it would seem from his scientific labors," Lisa offered, not being able to contribute any scientific knowledge to the discussion. A glance at Becky, who had a look of disgust at the words *human digestion*, and she was forced to stifle a smile. "And one of the trustees had the honor of meeting him, you say?"

"Not one trustee but two. While on the Grand Tour, both young gentlemen took it upon themselves to visit the good *dottore*. Although it was the gentleman who spoke to you in the drawing room who was the catalyst for the visit. He has a keen interest in the scientific and the medical."

"Which is perhaps why he is a trustee of the Fournier Foundation...?"

"Indeed! Yes! No doubt," the physician replied buoyantly, only to become suddenly grave. He sat forward and asked conspiratorially, "He did not, by any chance, tell you his name?" When Lisa shook her head, he added with a nod, "I did not think so. But Mrs. Warner did wonder, and wished me to ask you. She noticed he wore a ring—"

"—set with a carnelian stone engraved with a coat of arms?"

"The very one! Mrs. Warner recognized the coat of arms immediately as belonging to the Hesham family, of which the Duke of Roxton is its head. She said she would know it anywhere, for she saw it painted on the side of the Duchess of Roxton's carriage when she visited her mother upon occasion."

"He is a member of the Duke of Roxton's family!?" Lisa blurted out before she could stop herself.

"That is the most likely explanation for him wearing such a ring. Who else but a family member would dare to do so otherwise? And if that is so, it would explain his connection to Dr. Bailey, and be a reason why he is a trustee—Ah! Here we are! Now, before you step outside, you must take this," he said and handed her a package that Lisa had not noticed but which had been beside him on the seat. "Your new writing box—"

"My-my new writing box?" Lisa repeated, mind still reeling with the knowledge about the owner of the carnelian-set gold ring, and wondering at the precise nature of his relationship to the Hesham family. "Pardon, sir, but Mrs. Warner said I had to leave it behind at Gerrard Street, it being too valuable—"

"She did. But I have countered her decision, for it was the wrong one. You must and will have your gift. It is a most beautiful writing aid, and this journey is the perfect opportunity for you to use it, too. I took the liberty of stocking it with a few sheets of paper, and your quills, and filled the inkwells—Ah! What is this! Dear me! Dear me! There is nothing to upset you, dearest girl," he said with a nervous laugh when Lisa threw her arms about his neck and hugged him, muffling her thanks into the upturned collar of his coat.

He patted her shoulder, sat back, dug in a pocket of his coat, and pressed into her gloved hand a small velvet pouch.

"You may have need of this for the journey. There are some fifteen shillings and a few pence. Tip the driver and the guard the going rate, a little more if they do you a kindness. Procure refreshment for you and Becky—"

"But, sir, Cook gave us apples and oranges, and we have bread, almond biscuits, and orange cake. Becky has it in her satchel. We won't need—"

"If you do not have need of it now, you may have need of it later."

Lisa blinked at him. There were tears in her eyes. "It is too much, sir."

He smiled and surprised her. "It is not nearly enough for all the hours you've spent in my dispensary aiding and comforting patients. Do not ever think I have been unaware of your efforts. In the dispensary and," he added with a chuckle, as the door to the hackney was wrenched open, "at breakfast when I am at my most loquacious! Now, let me see you both to the Southampton coach."

The noise in the yard of the Bell Savage was thunderous and jarring, the movement of animals, people, and vehicles hectic and frenetic. They had been set down in the middle of the inn's yard. Both girls immediately looked up at the tallness of the buildings with two floors of open galleries running along both sides. People were coming and going along their length, and guests were hanging over the balustrades watching the activity below, all under the honeyed glow of a hundred tapers.

Such was their preoccupation that the girls would have been lost had not Dr. Warner taken Lisa by the arm, and she in turn hooked her arm through Becky's. They then moved snake-like through the hustle and bustle of passengers and servants seemingly going in all directions, following four young boys carrying Lisa's and Becky's trunks between them, and making a path as they went, shouting at the top of their lungs to *Make way! Make way!*

Soon they were standing before a large coach with its roof strapped with luggage, and the outside passengers crowded about eager to climb aboard. The horses were being attended to, the coach-

man's box still without its driver, so there was still time for the girls
to be settled. Inside the coach were already seated three individuals, a
husband and wife, and between them a young boy.

The physician spoke to the head porter and that gentleman
glanced over at Lisa and Becky, nodded, and then Lisa saw Dr. Warner
press something into the palm of the man's hand—no doubt a coin
for his cooperation—and him smile and doff his cap in understanding. With their luggage carefully stowed, Lisa and Becky were invited
to board. Becky scrambled up inside. Lisa turned to give Dr. Warner
another hug of thanks.

"I'll write, so that you know we arrived safely."

"Do not waste your time in writing to us, my dear. Enjoy every
minute of your stay. It could be the one and only time you have the
opportunity to mix in such exalted circles. Remember everything you
see and do. Write that down. Share it with us when you return. Mrs.
Warner can hardly wait to hear all about it."

Lisa smiled and nodded, and with a quick glance over her shoulder, she climbed up into the coach. The door was shut on her back
before she was seated, and she set the writing box in its cloth bag on
the seat between her and Becky. She then looked out the window for
Dr. Warner, but he was already lost to the jostling crowd.

And so she snuggled into her corner of the interior, aware of the
racket and activity outside in the busy yard which slowly faded into a
homogeneous drone as the coach lurched forward, the driver maneu-
vering the horses into the line of carriages waiting to move off under
the archway. Once out into the street, the coaches would go their
separate ways out into the environs of a city that never slept. The
Southampton stagecoach would head southwest into a countryside
that was new to both girls, and eagerly anticipated.

Finally, Lisa and Becky were on their way.

WHEN LISA WOKE, the coach had left the city behind. She had no
idea for how long she had slept, though she had a vague awareness of
the carriage coming to a standstill upon several occasions, of thumps
above her head, and of people scrambling down and then up again.
But she had been too tired and drowsy with sleep to fully wake.

Becky was still asleep in her corner, but the couple across from them were wide-awake, though the boy leaning against his mother, who had her arm around him, had his eyes closed.

Lisa was still tired, but awake enough to take a peek out the window at the morning sky, which was streaked with clouds. Yet it was a lovely sunny day, with no hint of rain. This boded well for travel along dry roads, and for the passengers holding on above her head atop the roof, rain not adding to their woes of traveling in the open air.

The fresh green of summer was everywhere along the London to Portsmouth road, one of the busiest thoroughfares in the kingdom, in the hedgerows, the open spaces of rolling hills, and in the forests farther afield. The coach would remain on this route until Guildford, most of the travelers using this road on foot, headed towards the city. Many had walked all night. A few men on horseback trotted by. And then the coach overtook an open wagon being pulled slowly by eight horses, and which was full of carousing men.

"Sailors headed for their ships," the woman seated across from Lisa said in answer to her thoughtful frown when she sat back. "It will take a good three days before they see the harbor, and when they join their ships, they'll be at sea for months."

"Thank you. I see then why they are enjoying their time while on land…"

There was a long silence, but Lisa sensed the woman was still staring at her, as if trying to get her measure. She knew this was so when the woman asked,

"If you don't mind me making conversation, are you and your friend traveling all the way to Southampton?"

"No. We alight at Alston."

"Alston? Now there's a pretty village in a pretty part of Hampshire. Isn't that so, husband," she added in a loud voice, with little regard for her son or Becky, who were still asleep. If the husband had been dozing, he wasn't now. "Alston—it's a pretty village."

"Aye. The church with its set of bells is particularly worth a visit. And the town is not too distant from Treat, the Duke of Roxton's seat. I think *Paterson's* gives the exact mileage," the husband said, pulling from his pocket a copy of *Paterson's British Itinerary*. He leafed through the pages. "Treat is listed between the noble estates of Traine and Trebursey. And it's shown on the map, too." He then removed a folded piece of paper tucked in to hold a place at this particular page, and looked to his wife, and then said to Lisa, "But *Paterson's* don't give a good description of these fine noble establishments. Just where they are located. But this does, and so I kept it, thinking I'd like to take a tour of the grounds one day. For although we lived but a few miles from the estate, we never did make a visit. Did we, wife? We thought there'd be plenty of time… But then we had the boy, and he's not always at his best—"

"Sea air. That's what the doctor said he needed," interjected the wife. "One day he'll be as right as rain."

"—Which is why we moved to Southampton," the husband said, finishing his sentence. "We own a boarding establishment on Canute Road—"

"—which is in the fashionable part of town. It's always booked out for weeks ahead. A proper respectable establishment it is. With breakfast and dinner served every day, and a special dinner on Sundays."

"When it's warm enough, I take the boy into the sea baths," the husband continued. "I don't care too much for the salt water, but he loves it—"

"—and the smell of the salt," added his wife. "He'd leave the window open all night, even on a cold winter's day, if he had his way…"

Lisa regarded the boy with a soft smile. He looked to be asleep, which didn't surprise her, given their early start, but she wondered if he might be awake and listening, but preferred to stay snuggled up to his mother, who was warm and comforting, particularly when he was feeling poorly. The jolting of the carriage would not make him feel any better. The parents mistook her frown for one of concern for herself and were quick to reassure her.

"The physician says you can't catch what he's got."

"Now, Mother. That ain't strictly true. One of his doctors says you *can* catch it, and another says you can't because it's all in his head. Not that he imagines what he's got, but that it's his brain that's to blame. To tell you a truth, I don't think they know theirselves why he takes such turns. But he does. And what I can tell you is that we've never caught it off him. And none of our guests have ever complained of fainting spells and the like. Not that he's much around the guests..."

"If you don't mind me asking, does your son suffer with the falling sickness?"

Mother and father looked at one another and then at Lisa. Their startled and wary looks begged the question as to how she, who was not much more than a girl, knew about such things.

Lisa then felt compelled to tell them a little about Warner's Dispensary, and about Dr. Warner, adding with a reassuring smile, "So you see, I am not at all concerned for my health, or my companion's, either. And I would like very much to hear what that piece of paper has to say about the Duke of Roxton's estate."

"Yes! Yes! The paper," said the husband, taking his gaze from Lisa, whom he thought an extraordinarily confident young woman, and that it was a crying shame that such beauty was wasted tending to the sick poor. Still, if he'd been ill, he could think of nothing nicer than having this ministering angel tending to his woes. On that thought, he quickly cleared his throat and read aloud the description of the ancestral home of the dukes of Roxton:

"Treat. Seat of the dukes of Roxton. Five miles southwest of the village of Alston in the county of Hampshire. A substantial mansion fashioned in the Palladian style by architect William Kent. Said to be the largest privately-owned home in England. Originally an Elizabethan manor house. Much altered by Henry, fourth Duke of Roxton, the 'architect duke', at the turn of the century, and completed in all its glory by Renard, fifth Duke of Roxton. The Grand Gallery has an excellent selection of paintings by well-known artists from Holbein to Kneller, and grand portraits of the family abound. Of particular note is the full-length portrait of the fifth duchess by the French artist Jean-Honore Fragonard. The library is on two levels and said to have no equal in the kingdom. A grand ballroom with three chandeliers, a gilded music room, and several state reception rooms are open to the public on particular days.

"The grounds are much altered since Queen Anne's time. Gardens, lake, and immediate surrounding parkland are the work of Capability Brown. Many follies in various fanciful architectural styles can be found throughout the extensive grounds, and those not locked up against trespass may be viewed by the public. There is an artificial lake of considerable magnitude that can be crossed at various sites by one of three stone bridges. Small islands abound, with the largest, Swan Island, once home to a hermit and said to be haunted by his ghost. Worthy of note is the magnificent family mausoleum, final resting place of the dukes of Roxton and various Hesham family relatives. A grand domed roof set with a glass oculus, the mausoleum is built on the highest point on the estate. It is a beacon to travelers, for it can be seen from many miles. The interior is dominated by a life-like statue of the fifth duke. Not open to the public, except on foundation day.

"A small remuneration to the housekeeper for a tour of the public rooms within the house is expected. The grounds may be accessed when the family is not in residence by calling at the Gatehouse Lodge at the northern entrance. Crecy Hall, a restored Elizabethan manor, and its parkland, abuts the eastern shore of the lake, and was once part of the Roxton estate. It is presently the English residence of the Scots duke of Kinross, and is strictly off-limits all year round. No exceptions."

"Oh look!" exclaimed the wife, pointing out the window, before Lisa had time to thank or comment to the husband for reading out a most illuminating description of her destination. Her husband and Lisa followed her extended finger. "There! There, between the trees. Do you see it?"

And they did see it. A grand building with an equally grand portico held up by four fat columns. It stood proudly atop a hill of rolling lawn, much higher than the surrounding trees, so that it was easily visible from the road, and no doubt for miles around. The husband and wife enlightened Lisa about this particular mansion and its history as she kept her gaze out the window.

"That's Claremont—"

"—built by a rich nabob. What was his name…?"

"Clive. Lord Clive of India."

"Ah! That's right! Made his riches out on the subcontinent and brought it back here and built that house."

"It's said that from the top floor you can see as far back to London as St. Paul's—"

"All the way to St. Paul's?"

"All the way to St. Paul's, wife. But for all that, I don't believe

Clive's mansion can be matched against that belonging to His Grace of Roxton."

Lisa turned away from the window with a smile, the house now disappearing from view behind a clump of forest as the stagecoach rounded a bend.

"From the description you read me, I do not doubt you, sir. The Duke of Roxton's seat is beyond anything I can imagine."

"If you have the time and opportunity, and the coin to pay the housekeeper, I am certain it would surely be well worth the journey. You wouldn't regret it."

"Oh, I believe you, sir. And I will, and have no regrets."

PART II

THE COUNTRY

FIFTEEN

TREAT, ANCESTRAL HOME OF THE DUKES OF ROXTON
THE COUNTY OF HAMPSHIRE

LISA AND BECKY and their trunks were set down in front of the Swan Inn on the High Street of Alston, which was indeed a picturesque village. The girls said their farewells to the couple and their son, their leave-taking conducted in a rush. This suited Lisa because she would not have known how to respond had they asked her why she had not made it known that her destination was in fact Treat, when they had spoken to her about the Duke of Roxton's estate. For no sooner had Lisa and Becky said their farewells than they were approached by a gentleman in the somber attire of an upper servant, followed by two footmen in livery. The couple knew instantly to whom the livery belonged, and they stared at Lisa and Becky anew to see them greeted by none other than servants of the Duke of Roxton.

A carriage awaited the girls in the yard of the Swan Inn, ready to take them to Treat. They were surprised to find they were not the only occupants. A corner was occupied by a gentleman, the collar of his coat pulled up around his ears, and a felt hat pulled down over his eyes. With his chin on his chest, he appeared to be sleeping.

As the upper servant ignored this gentleman, whom Lisa suspected was another wedding guest, she and Becky did too, and obediently sat where directed, the upper servant introducing himself as assistant to His Grace of Roxton's secretary. He spoke to Lisa at length about her stay on the estate, and the upcoming nuptials of Miss Cavendish to Sir John. She must have glanced one too many times about the interior of the carriage, which was a compact vehicle but beautifully appointed throughout, with deep blue velvet cushions, satin buttons in the upholstery, and silk blinds with a delicate fringe, for the assistant secretary felt compelled to comment.

"This is Her Grace's estate carriage, used only to make short trips, to the village on fete days, special days at the local Alston school, of which Her Grace is patroness, and to visit such persons in the local environs as Her Grace deems worthy of her time."

"It has such a lovely interior," Lisa replied with a smile, gloved hands in her lap. "And it gives a most superior ride."

"This is a superior road," the stranger in the corner quipped without opening his eyes.

No one commented, though Lisa was startled to hear the stranger speak, and also amused by his quip, though she did her best to hide her smile.

The assistant secretary pretended deafness and gave Lisa a sealed packet which he said she did not need to open now, but it would be beneficial for her to read the entire contents and familiarize herself with the protocol sheet and the two maps, as soon as practicable upon her arrival at the Gatehouse Lodge, where she would be residing for the duration of her stay.

Lisa stared at the fat packet and at the wax seal, and then across at the assistant.

"Protocol sheet? Maps?" she enquired, requiring more information to understand what he was talking about. "Excuse me. It has been a long day, and I am a little tired."

The assistant coughed into his gloved hand and explained.

"A protocol sheet is a most necessary and instructive instrument if one is unfamiliar with the—um—*intricacies* of the customs, and the order of precedence, and the minutiae of the daily interactions of persons of position of a large estate, particularly the estate of a duke. I'm certain you, Miss Crisp, can appreciate, when the niece of a duke weds, the guest list is one long list of titled relatives and friends. All will be known to one another, and so it is helpful for those who have had little or no—*interaction*—with such exalted persons to know the difference say, when addressing an earl, and when addressing a viscount—"

"It would, but the examples you give are not good ones," interrupted the stranger, finally opening his eyes. "Both are addressed as 'my lord', whether they are the Earl of Big Breeches, or Viscount Hot Head. So how would she know? How would anyone unless they were related to the said Lord Big Breeches or Lord Hot Head?"

Lisa clapped a hand to her mouth to stop herself from laughing out loud. But she could not stop the twinkle in her eyes. The stranger, who was sitting across from her, smiled and winked before dropping his smile and saying to the affronted assistant secretary, "Please don't let me interfere in your instruction. Though I will add for the young lady's benefit, so that she may feel more comfortable knowing that as this is a family wedding, and the Duke of Roxton is a family man first and a nobleman second, he will not be standing on ceremony with any of his guests, the Earl of Big Breeches and Viscount Hot Head notwithstanding. If I know anything of the man, he values good manners and honesty above precedence and posturing."

"And you know His Grace well, do you, sir?" the assistant secretary asked stiffly, not expecting an answer.

"I should. Roxton and I are first cousins once removed."

The assistant secretary goggled at him, and then realizing his bad manners quickly looked away and down at his hands. There was a long silence, in which the stranger turned to stare out the window; then the assistant said diffidently to Lisa,

"There is a day-to-day itinerary included in the packet, with certain events organized in the lead-up to the wedding ceremony and wedding breakfast and the ball. Also included are two maps contained within the packet which I hope you will find most useful. One is of the estate's immediate landscaped environs, with various landmarks, follies, and such of interest inked in, which you may visit if you have the time during your stay. The second is a map of the big house showing the rooms which are open to guests, so that if you find yourself lost, or in difficulty navigating your way about, then the map will come in most useful."

The stranger leaned in and confided to Lisa, "Even family members get lost in such a monstrous place from time to time, so there's no shame in you having your map front and center."

He took a look out of the window, and surprised the occupants by knocking on the backboard above his head, signal for the driver to pull up the horses. He collected his satchel, and addressed Lisa.

"Up ahead the carriage will leave the avenue of trees and turn left to take you to the Gatehouse Lodge. If you look out to the right you will have an uninterrupted view across the lake to the big house. It is a breathtaking sight, and it never grows old. I envy you your first view of Treat. No matter what you have read, or been told, nothing can quite prepare you for the sheer scale of the place. It is simply beyond belief, and this from a man who has spent the last nine years living on the doorstep of the Chateau of Versailles. Ah, if Louis could but see how the Duke of Roxton lives!" He tugged the front of his hat. "Good day. I do not doubt we will meet again."

With that, the stranger exited the carriage and disappeared through the line of trees on the other side of the road. The assistant secretary knocked again for the driver to continue.

Lisa's gaze was still out the left window when Becky burst out on a gasp, sliding along the seat and then crossing to sit opposite Lisa so she too had an excellent view out the windows to the right, "Oh! Oh! Miss! Miss! Look! *Look*."

The two girls pressed their noses to the glass, mesmerized. It was just as the stranger described yet what he had said was still inadequate to the sight presented them. As the carriage veered left, leaving the avenue of trees, they trundled along a graveled drive which gave a clear view across rolling acres of lawn down to the wide blue waters of the lake. On the other side, the rolling lawns continued, sloping upwards to a hill, where sat perched a palace.

A grand central Palladian building, with enormous fat columns rose up three floors from a wide staircase that was almost the width of the building. A collection of buildings extended left and right from this imposing central structure, also three stories high, with rows and rows of windows that seemed to go on forever before turning a corner and continuing on, for how far, Lisa could not see. Her line of sight was broken by a second avenue of trees, now with only broken glimpses of the palace atop its hill seen between the green foliage.

Finally the carriage crossed a stone bridge and turned in through a set of gates and on up a circular drive that was lined with standards of white roses. It came to a stop in front of a quaint—everything else after glimpsing the palace of Treat could not be called anything else— Elizabethan two-story cottage with turned chimney pots and gargoyles atop the fanciful battlements.

THEIR CARRIAGE was not the only vehicle pulled up outside the entrance to the Gatehouse Lodge. An open buggy hitched to two horses, with a driver up front and two footmen in livery up back, was patiently awaiting its occupants.

Lisa and Becky were set down with their trunks behind this vehicle, and there they waited, watching their carriage depart, and it was almost at the entrance gates before there was any movement from within the manor. And then a great deal happened quickly, leaving the tired and mute Lisa and Becky fascinated spectators to a family leave-taking.

A boy with a mop of red curls dashed out of the house into the sunshine, and climbed up into the waiting buggy and slid along the seat to the end. A second, younger boy, with a head of black curls, was not half-a-dozen steps behind and scrambled to climb aboard. When he had difficulty in doing so, the older boy quickly slid back down the seat and stuck out his hand and hauled the younger boy up beside him. He made exaggerated groaning noises, to impress his brother. Both boys did not sit, but stood waiting, looking back to the house with eyes wide with excitement, as if their party was not complete for what was to be a grand adventure.

A servant appeared next with two small leather satchels which he put up behind the seat at the feet of the liveried footmen; another followed with a larger satchel, and this, too, went in with the others. Next out of the house strode a tall, well-built gentleman of middling years, dressed in a plain linen frock coat and top boots. He put up a hand to the two boys who jumped up and down with excitement and called out for Papa to hurry! Hur-*ry*!

But their papa did not immediately go to them. He turned to the house and waited to be joined by a small lady with an abundance of bright copper hair, who had an infant to her hip. He kissed the baby's rosy cheek and then one chubby hand that was held out to him, before gently kissing the lady's forehead. The gentleman then joined the two fidgeting boys in the buggy.

The sudden whoosh of a window being flung open with force had everyone looking to the house and up to the first floor. Hanging half out of an open window, her long red hair falling in tangled waves either side of her face, and her arms waving back and forth to get the attention of those below, was a young woman with bright eyes and an even brighter smile.

"Papa! David! Luke!" she shouted, and then shouted their names again so they all looked her way. "Have a wonderful, wonderful time! Don't sleep a wink! I love you! I'll miss you all!"

The two boys waved and shouted back. The gentleman blew her a kiss. Her baby sister giggled—she was watching her brothers making faces, and the little lady holding the baby took a deep breath and smiled but said nothing.

The buggy was gone off down the gravel drive and peace had descended once more on the Gatehouse Lodge, the girl with the long red hair remaining in the window, arms folded on the ledge, chin on her fist, gaze on the middle distance.

Lisa and Becky had gone unnoticed throughout the entire family leave-taking, backs up against the wall, trunks at their feet. But they were not invisible for long. For no sooner had David and Luke's mama turned to re-enter the house with her infant daughter than she noticed the two travel-weary girls. Lisa was staring up at the girl in the window. Becky was staring at the beautiful little lady in her floral-painted petticoats with the happy baby in her arms.

And then the girl in the window went to pull down the sash and happened to look below, and directly into the upturned smiling face of her best friend from Blacklands, and who was waving up at her. She couldn't believe her eyes. She pushed the sash back up and leaned out.

"Lisa! Lisa! Lisa! You're here at last! Mama! Mama! It's Lisa Crisp! It's Lisa! Wait! I'll be right there."

"OH DEAR. Have you been standing there awhile?" Lady Mary apologized, going forward to greet Lisa. She smiled. "So you are Lisa Crisp. Here at last. Did you have a pleasant journey?"

Lisa dropped a respectful curtsy, quick to realize when Teddy had shouted from the window that this fascinating little lady was her mother and, she remembered, the daughter of an earl; Becky followed her lead.

"Not long, my lady," Lisa replied. "And, yes, we had a pleasant journey. Thank you."

"Leave your trunks and your bag with your maid—she'll be taken care of by the housekeeper—and come inside."

"I beg your pardon, my lady," Lisa said politely but firmly, remaining beside Becky when the Lady Mary went to turn away. "Becky is not my maid. She is a seamstress who agreed to accompany me for my stay, and to-to—be of assistance to me."

"Oh? I see," replied Lady Mary, a glance at Becky. "Then we had best find a girl who can help Becky give you that assistance. Perhaps Becky can still remain with the trunks until the housekeeper comes, who will show her where everything is so she is comfortable and so she can be a help to you during your stay."

"I don't mind bein' Miss Crisp's maid for the duration," Becky stuck in, feeling she had to say something given Lisa had just made it plain she was not a servant. "It's all new to me and I'm just 'appy to be 'ere."

Lady Mary blinked, unaccustomed to being addressed by a social inferior whom she had not spoken to first, but managed to say evenly, "Yes, I see that you are..." Then said to Lisa as she shifted the baby in her arms, "I've heard a great deal about you, Miss Crisp."

"Have you, my lady?" Lisa replied politely, giving the cloth bag containing her writing box into Becky's safe keeping, and quickly falling into step beside the Lady Mary, who had turned to go inside.

"All of it from Teddy, of course, and most complimentary. My daughter says she would not have survived her time at Blacklands without your friendship. So for that alone, I am eternally grateful. She has always referred to you as her Blacklands sister."

"And now she does indeed have a sister."

"Yes! A surprise to us all, but quite the most wonderful surprise. This is Sophie-Kate, and she is five months old today."

"She is a beautiful baby, my lady."

"Yes… Yes, she is," Lady Mary said on a sigh of happiness and turned to the housekeeper who had come out under the portico, a male servant behind her. "Mrs. Rogers, here is Miss Crisp finally come at last. Her friend Becky is with her to act as her maid. If you would take Becky in hand and find one of the upstairs maids to chaperone her—perhaps Meg would do—so she knows what is to be done, and where everything is to be found, that would be a great help to us all."

Mrs. Rogers shot a glance at Lisa which swept over her from half-boots to small peaked bonnet, and then out across to Becky obediently standing by two trunks that had seen better days, and while she nodded to her mistress without a change in her expression, Lisa saw the disapproval in her gaze.

Her throat constricted to be summed up and then dismissed so summarily. But the uncomfortable feeling vanished the moment she entered the small vestibule behind the Lady Mary and to the sight of Teddy rushing down the winding staircase, so happy to see her that it brought tears to her eyes.

Teddy scooped Lisa up into her embrace and both girls hugged and cried and hugged some more to be reunited after a separation of two years. There was not a dry eye in the vestibule, the Lady Mary smiling through her tears to see her daughter so happy as she handed her baby daughter to her nurse, who also had a tear in her eye.

"May I take Lisa up to my room before supper, Mama?" Teddy asked, holding Lisa's hand. "We have so much to talk about, and I need to tell—"

"Perhaps allow Miss Crisp—"

"Lisa. Mama, you must call her Lisa, after all she is my Blacklands sister. Aren't you, Lisa?"

"Very well. Lisa has come a very long way in one day," Lady Mary replied patiently. "So you should do her the courtesy of allowing her to freshen up and perhaps take a dish of tea—"

"We can do all those things in my room—"

"As I was about to suggest, but—"

Teddy kissed her mother's cheek. "You are the most wonderful mama in all the world!"

"Thank you, my darling. But do not tire Lisa out on her first day. There will be plenty of time for the two of you to become reacquainted. And don't be late down for supper. You know how Granny Kate is one for punctuality, and how keen she is to meet your friend from your school days."

"Promise!" Teddy announced. She smiled at Lisa. "Come on, Blacklands sister! I have so much to tell you! But first," she added after she had led Lisa up the narrow winding staircase to the landing, and opened the immediate door to the right, which was her apartment, "I want to hear everything about what you've been doing since I last saw you. And I do mean *everything*."

SIXTEEN

LISA MANAGED to wash her face and hands and tidy her hair, and enjoy a cup of tea and a slice of seedy cake, while giving Teddy an account of her last two years living with the Warners in Gerrard Street. Teddy curled up on the window seat and listened attentively, and whatever her private thoughts about her best friend assisting in a dispensary for the sick poor, she showed most aversion for life in a great city, unable to fathom how anyone could live in a place where there were few open green spaces, so many people that one could not escape the hordes, and where there were more buildings than trees. She had found Chelsea too overrun with people, and could not wait to return to the peace and tranquility and pace of the Cotswolds.

It was Granny Kate who showed a keen interest in Lisa's duties within a medical dispensary, asking her all sorts of questions at supper, most impressed that she acted as an amanuensis for the poor. And Lisa could understand why, given Granny Kate was blind, and thus having someone to read out her letters and to write them was important to her. She told Lisa that she dictated all her letters to her companion, who also read the replies to her, Teddy often taking on this task whenever she was asked to do so.

"But I am only given letters to read out that Mama and Papa will allow me," Teddy revealed. "Which are all very interesting, but not as interesting as those from Granny's particular correspondents, who commit to paper an exchange of scandalous anecdotes from their youth, and are thus unfit for the eyes of a young lady; so Mama tells me."

"I don't know what surprises you more, Teddy," Granny Kate said with a laugh. "That I was once young, or that I could ever be involved in scandalous behavior."

Teddy squeezed the old lady's fingers, kissed her cheek, and whispered near her ear, "I believe both." She sat back and put aside her napkin. "And one day, after I am married, I won't take no for an answer and you will tell me *all* about it. May we be excused, Mama? Lisa has had such a day and is worn thin, and we still have much to talk about... I hope you don't mind sharing my bed," she asked Lisa when they were back upstairs in her bedchamber ready for bed.

A maid had warmed the bed sheets with the copper warming pan, a fire crackled in the grate despite it being the first month of summer, and a tray holding two mugs of hot milk had been placed on the window seat. Both girls were in their nightgowns and banyans, and Teddy stood before her dressing table, brushing her hair free of tangles.

"Why would I mind?" Lisa responded with a smile, sitting on the edge of the mattress of the four-poster bed watching Teddy brush and then braid her hair. "It will be like old times. Although this bed is far larger than the cots we slept in at school. But I am only sorry to put you to so much bother."

"It's no bother. It's just that this is such a small house—"

"Is it?"

"It's a gatekeeper's lodge. The entire structure would be swallowed up in one wing of Papa's house at home, and Abbeywood must be three times this size. But it's not the size that matters. It's that we can all stay here as a family, and I wanted you here with us. Which is why we are all sharing. The rest of the extended family and guests are over at the big house." Teddy gave a snort of laughter. "Big house! What a gigantic understatement! You must have thought so too when you first saw it. I am sure if I were to ascend in one of Signore Lunardi's balloons and look down upon the earth, Treat would be the most enormous structure to be seen for miles and miles! And I cannot wait for you to see inside Uncle Roxton's palace! You'll simply be dazzled blind by the twinkling lights from chandeliers in the ball-room alone."

"I am already dazzled and I have only seen the palace from across the lake. No doubt the ballroom will leave me speechless."

"Oh, it will. But you're not to feel too overwhelmed because I expect you to stand up and dance with every gentleman who asks you."

"That is kind of you to think I will be asked. But I am so out of practice—"

"Then we must make certain you are practiced by the time of the ball. I will not have you sitting in a corner, Lisa Crisp! Not when you are the cleverest and prettiest girl in the room. Your turn," she announced, tossing the hairbrush on the dressing table and pulling out the dressing stool for Lisa to sit upon. She patted the padded cushion. "Come along or our milk will grow cold. Oh! I have a better idea!" She brought the tray over to the dressing table. "We shall have it while I brush your hair."

When Lisa obediently sat before the looking glass, Teddy removed her friend's little lace cap, and then began taking out the multitude of pins that held up the coils of Lisa's waist-length hair. She suddenly paused and looked at Lisa's reflection. Her friend had lowered her gaze, so that her dark lashes covered her eyes.

"Do you not want me to brush your hair?" Teddy asked curiously.

Lisa shook her head, and then she could no longer hold back the pent-up emotion of this longed-for reunion. She put her face in her hands and cried. It was such a simple gesture—Teddy offering to brush her hair—and so evocative of their schoolgirl friendship that it meant the world to her. She sniffed and sat up and looked at Teddy through the looking glass and did her best to smile.

"I do," she said with a watery smile. "I do *very much*... It's only... No one has... No one since-since school, since *you*, and—forgive me," she apologized, dropping her gaze again. "I'm being foolish... I must be tired..."

Teddy put the hairbrush aside, dropped to her knees by the stool, and gathered Lisa into her arms and held her tightly. She kissed her and sat back and smiled.

"Never foolish, dearest Lisa. I remember you telling me once how you never did get hugs and kisses when you were a child."

"Not until I met you, and not since, my darling Teddy."

They stayed that way for a few moments longer, and after Lisa had dried her face with one of Teddy's handkerchiefs and they had both taken a few sips of hot milk, Teddy set to brushing Lisa's hair. And while her bristle brush went the length of Lisa's dark chestnut hair, in long even strokes, Teddy told Lisa how she had spent her time since leaving Blacklands some eighteen months earlier.

"My life is not half as exciting or as interesting as assisting a physician in his dispensary is it?" she said with a sigh. "And I thought I would marry Jack as soon I left school. I could see no reason for waiting. For what? Jack had returned from his years abroad, and was ready to settle—"

"After all those years pondering paintings?" Lisa asked airily with a cheeky knowing smile.

Teddy blinked and stopped mid-stroke on a gasp. And then she burst out laughing.

"Oh good grief! How like you to remember me telling you what Mama had told me! Were we such naïve little beings." She gave a snort of incredulity and resumed brushing. "If Jack did any pondering it wasn't in an art gallery!"

Both girls smiled and then giggled, and with Lisa's hair now plaited and tied off with a ribbon, they climbed into the big four-poster bed and snuggled in under the covers, a single silver chamber-stick on the bedside table and the fire in the grate providing light in the otherwise still, warm room. They were happy to lie there facing each other, reveling in their reunion and this renewal of a friendship that stretched back to when they were twelve years old.

"Are you at all worried about being married?" Lisa asked in the silence.

"Not worried. Nervous. Mama says I am not to worry if the first few months of being married doesn't go to plan. That if Jack and I are honest and gentle with each other it will all come together eventually. She says the first year of marriage is like the first time baking a cake."

"Baking a-a *cake*?"

"Yes. That even though you might have all the right ingredients and you follow the recipe for the most wondrous cake imaginable, it doesn't necessarily mean the cake will turn out precisely as you expect. And to not be disappointed with the result. It is still a cake.

And that to make a wondrous cake takes patience and practice. And then once you perfect the ingredients and the recipe, it will be a wondrous cake forever. She says the most important thing to remember is that Jack and I enjoy the making of the cake—making our marriage work—that we do it together."

Lisa thought about this for a moment, frowning, and then confessed, "I have no idea how to make a cake, or about being married for that matter, but I am confident your mother's advice is exceedingly wise. And from the little I saw of her with your step-papa when he and your brothers were off on their expedition in the woods, they love each other very much."

"Very much. And they have got their marriage recipe just right, because I now not only have two little brothers but also a baby sister."

The girls giggled, plumped their down-filled pillows and settled in again. There was a long silence, and then Teddy whispered,

"Are you still awake?"

"Yes."

"I'm not keeping you from sleeping, am I? I know you've had a long day—"

"I want to stay awake for as long as I can so we have as much time together as possible. Two weeks will go by too quickly otherwise."

"Do not worry about that for now," Teddy assured her. "I have something to tell you, but I need to talk it over with Jack first. And now Mama has met you she thinks it could work—"

"Plan? Work? About *me*?"

"Yes. I'm certain Jack will agree. He is so kind, and loving, and such a gentle soul."

"Are you not amazed that everything you told me when we were at school has turned out the way you said it would? You said you would marry Jack, and here you are about to marry him! I am so happy for you, Teddy. You know that, don't you?"

"Yes. You more than anyone else know how much I wanted this to all come true." Teddy put out her hand and she and Lisa interlocked fingers. "I was beyond grief-stricken when you were made to leave Blacklands. You do know I tried to find you after your departure?"

"I have all your letters now, and read them many times. Thank you for persisting. Thank you for finding me."

"How could I marry Jack without you here by my side, dearest Lisa? You are my closest friend, and you cared for me at school, and I would never have passed one exam if not for your tutoring. If girls were permitted to use their brains in the same way boys are, then you could have achieved anything. Did you know your friend Jamie Banks is about to head off to university to start his study to be a physician? I wish you could have gone and studied with him."

"I am very happy for him. And thank you for thinking me clever. But after assisting in the dispensary I do not think I could be a physician. A willing sympathetic ear to the problems of others, yes, but I do not possess the fortitude for anatomizing..."

There was a long silence before Teddy said, gently squeezing Lisa's fingers, "I do so want you to fall in love and marry, Lisa Crisp. For you to be as happy as me."

"I want that too. But I fear it is more wishful thinking than a likely outcome."

"Why do you say so? When you do fall in love and marry, we can confide in each other as we did at school, but as married women, about our husbands, about our babies, and—"

"I can wish about marrying one day, and that may come true. But I'm afraid I must leave the babies to you, dearest..."

"Has there been no change in you since school?" Teddy asked in a small voice.

"No change."

Another silence, and then Teddy sighed and said with a buoyancy she did not in the least feel, "In one way that makes you even more special—"

"And when you have babies I will be an aunt—of sorts," Lisa interrupted, trying to sound cheerful.

"Oh yes! And a godparent. I will have you for my baby's godmother."

"That would be lovely, and an honor. Thank you."

Lisa then rolled over onto her back and stared up at the pleated canopy, stifling a yawn, and closed her eyes. She was now too tired to share any more confidences that night, and just a little bit excited to start her magical two weeks in this magical place.

Soon she drifted off to sleep, dreaming not of palaces and ballrooms, but of a rosewood writing box, and the handsome gentleman with a pair of fine dark eyes who had given it to her. When he gazed upon her in a particular way, he made her happier than she ever thought possible. She hoped the Jack and Harry she had met at Lord Westby's townhouse and who had visited Gerrard Street were the very same Jack and Harry Teddy spoke of, and who would be here at Treat; Jack, the man Teddy was to marry, and Harry, his best friend, with his velvety voice and with whom Lisa was sure she was falling in love.

If only dreams could come true…

SEVENTEEN

LISA WOKE LATE. She had never slept so soundly, nor woken with the sun so high in the sky. She had a recollection of Teddy rising, and of water being splashed about, and women talking in hushed tones. And then, far off, doors were opened and closed, and there was movement outside on the gravel drive. A carriage arrived, and then it left. But that seemed to have happened hours ago.

When she padded through to the small dressing room, she found her clothes set out on the chaise: One of the floral gowns expertly altered by Becky, stays, petticoats, matching mittens, and her half-boots, which had been polished and set ready with a fresh pair of stockings. Also laid out were items new to her: A flimsy white apron of finest linen, a wide-brimmed straw hat, and a folding fan. She had never owned a fan before, though she had been instructed on how to use this most essential of feminine accoutrements while at school. Other girls had reveled in practicing how to flutter a fan like a lady. Lisa had thought it a great waste of her time. Now she was glad she had at least paid attention.

"You're up, Miss!" Becky announced buoyantly, coming through via the servant door carrying a brass can of hot water. She stepped aside to allow a girl in a mob cap, about the same age, and who carried a similar brass can, to come in after her. "This is Meg, and she's ever so 'elpful. There's a tub behind that screen at your back,

Miss, and once we 'ave you bathed and dressed, I'll fetch your breakfast, which you're to 'ave in your room, on account of the late 'our.
Miss Cavendish said you're not to worry 'bout sleepin' late. She
wanted you to. She's gone across to the big 'ouse with her mama and
granny to welcome some new arrivals. Now, let's get you ready.
You've a big day ahead o'you."

"ARE YOU CERTAIN Lady Mary said the pavilion?" Lisa asked
Becky, as they strolled up a leafy laneway that connected the Gatehouse Lodge with the Kinross estate of Crecy Hall.

"I am, Miss," Becky stated without hesitation. "I was told to
follow this path to its termination and we'd know the way from
there. Ain't this the prettiest walk?" she added with a sigh, looking
up and about at the tall avenue of beech trees. "I've never seen
anythin' like it. Then again, I've never seen anythin' like anythin' 'ere
before, anywhere."

"It is very pretty, and quite magical," Lisa agreed with a smile,
ignoring her nervousness at her first public engagement to enjoy the
moment.

It was a perfect summer's day, with a powder-blue sky where
drifted wisps of white cloud. And a slight breeze off the lake stirred
the bright green leaves on slender black branches of the beech that
provided a dappled shade from the hot sun.

She supposed she would have been less nervous had she not
discovered from Becky that when she and Meg had set to unpacking
her trunk late the night before, the Lady Mary's personal maid had
interrupted them, going through the entire contents before marching
off to inform her mistress of items found to be wanting.

Hence the straw hat, which was now tied over Lisa's freshly-
washed and braided hair, the flimsy apron covering the front of her
floral gown, and the fan that dangled from its cord about her wrist.
There were other items to come, and, according to Becky, the Lady
Mary's personal maid was most critical of the gown Lisa had hoped
to wear to the wedding and the ball. It would never do, and something would have to be done.

Lisa just hoped that she, unlike her wardrobe, did not prove a sad disappointment to Teddy's relatives and friends. But Becky's infectious wonderment soon had her putting these misgivings to the back of her mind, as they came to the end of the avenue and stepped into a wide-open space and the wondrous sight of an Elizabethan manor house, its rows of mullioned windows sparkling in the sun.

With its turned chimney pots and fanciful gargoyles at each corner, the manor was a much larger version of the Gatehouse Lodge, or more correctly, the lodge was a tinier version of this substantial mansion. Set atop a terraced fragrant garden that overlooked the lake, the approach from the tree-lined avenue from where Lisa and Becky emerged provided a view of endless green lawn rolling down to the water's edge, where rowing boats bobbed at a jetty.

Lisa and Becky stared at one another, as if needing confirmation from each other they were indeed seeing the same idyllic scene. And as they walked out from under the dappled shade and into the sunshine, their wonder increased as a pretty pavilion came into view. Atop a small hill, and overlooking the lake, the pavilion had a high domed roof supported by marble columns, and a set of wide steps open to the elements which gave access to its large interior.

"Don't be nervous, Miss," Becky said encouragingly when Lisa paused in the middle of the lawn, drew in a breath and squared her shoulders. "You look a picture. No one could say otherwise."

"Thank you, Becky. If we can get through this first day of introductions, I am confident we shall enjoy ourselves all the better. Let's see who awaits us..."

But when they arrived at the pavilion, they found it devoid of guests and family members. Servants were going about the business of decorating the marble columns with width lengths of silk ribbon, and setting chairs and tables in place. Lisa was left wondering at the whereabouts of the guests invited to nuncheon, and if they had arrived much too early for the event.

Before she could ask the question, Becky postulated, "Per'aps everyone is still up at the 'ouse?"

"Perhaps that's so. You stay here in the shade, while I take a walk across to the terrace. I may find some of the guests wandering about. If people begin to arrive, come find me. Otherwise, I shall return presently."

And while Becky gazed out across the lake, and watched swans gliding and ducks paddling in and around the jetty and the line of bobbing row boats, Lisa crossed to the terrace. Here she found winding stone steps leading up through the fragrant gardens to the house. But something made her turn away from the steps and walk further along the edge of the gardens until she came to a large oak tree halfway between the gardens and the lake. It was a majestic tree and ancient, and there, supported in its lower heavy branches, was a tree house fashioned to resemble the quarter deck of a sailing ship. She was so fascinated by this that she walked up under the oak's branches to take a better look, and finding her straw hat partially obstructed her view, she removed it, and let it dangle by its ribands at her side. She had walked halfway round the tree with her chin pointed skywards before she realized she was not alone.

A little girl was watching her. She was standing by a swing, holding one of two ropes tied either side of a damask-covered seat, the ropes rising high up into the branches of the oak, where they were affixed. She did not move or acknowledge Lisa in any way. In fact, her brow had furrowed, and her gaze was solemn. She was a beautiful child with large brown eyes that were slightly oblique, like a cat's, and a rosebud mouth in a heart-shaped face framed by dark honey ringlets threaded with fat silk ribbons. But for all her beauty, it was at her clothing Lisa stared.

The girl was dressed in a round gown of finest cotton, painted in vivid colorful detail with cherry blossoms and little songbirds. Underneath the gown were bright white cotton petticoats edged in delicate lace, and on her feet were slippers in the same cloth as the gown, secured with silk bows that matched her pink hair ribbons. She looked to be dressed for a grand occasion, but Lisa suspected that such exquisite clothing was everyday wear for the children who lived in such a magical place.

Lisa came over to her.

"Hello. My name is Lisa."

"Hello."

"What's your name?"

"Don't you know who I am?"

"No. But I should, shouldn't I."

"Everyone knows who I am."

"Do they? Everyone but me, it seems."

The little girl looked Lisa over. "Are you a lady's maid?"

"No. I'm a guest staying at the Gatehouse. I arrived yesterday for Miss Cavendish's wedding."

"I've never met anyone who doesn't know who I am."

"How fortunate for me to be the first stranger you have encountered," Lisa replied with a smile, doing her best to remain unnerved by the child's solemn questioning air.

But she had dealt with worse in the dispensary when children, ill or injured, wanted nothing to do with anyone who might make them feel more unwell than they already were. She wondered why the girl was alone, for surely a child possessed of such noble self-assurance and dressed in the expensive attire of the privileged few would be surrounded by a veritable army of nurses and maids.

"Do you wish to be here by yourself, or do you have friends coming to join you at the swing?" she asked.

The girl surprised her by choosing to answer her in French, and it made Lisa wonder if when she was petulant the girl spoke in the language that was second nature to her.

"I wanted to be alone because I am never alone! And so I ran away!"

Lisa was unperturbed by the girl's assertion that she had run away. In this idyll there did not seem to be anywhere to run off to where she would not be easily found.

"Then I will leave you to be alone," Lisa replied evenly in French, and turned towards the pavilion.

"*Attendez! Ne pars pas!*—Wait! Don't go!"

Lisa turned at the girl's order for her to stop but did not move, and waited.

"I would like you to stay—please." She regarded Lisa curiously and asked again, "Do you *honestly* not know who I am?"

"Honestly." Lisa smiled. "Unless of course you are a fairy princess who lives here under this oak. And as I have never been formally introduced to a fairy princess, I do not know if it is polite to curtsy, or should I kiss your hand, too?"

Something in what Lisa said made the girl giggle. She shook her head and then with her chin tilted up and a superior smile full of secrets said, "I don't live under a-a *tree*. I live over there in that house."

"Of course you do. It is a fine house. A fairy princess could live in such a house."

"But I am not a fairy princess. I'm a *marchioness*, and one day I will be a duchess."

Lisa hoped she did not appear as startled as she felt to discover a girl, who looked to be no more than seven or eight years old, to not only be ennobled, but who was also acutely aware of her status. Yet, there was nothing conceited in her declaration. It was said as a matter of fact. Just like her presumption that everyone should know who she was.

"How splendid," Lisa replied with a smile, masking her astonishment. She made a fuss of putting aside the wide-brimmed straw hat and fan, lifted her petticoats to her ankles so she could sink to sit on the grass. She looked up at the girl.

"Would you like to sit with me? Here, sit on my gown, so that your pretty petticoats are not ruined." Adding when the girl eagerly took her up on her offer, "I should think that as a marchioness who will one day be a duchess, you still must have a Christian name, yes? Perhaps you might like to share this with me, now we are no longer strangers to one another...?"

The girl considered this for a long moment, and such was the solemnity in her expression that Lisa was quick to stifle a smile, lest the child think her insincere or laughing at her. She could see the girl was weighing up whether she should trust this stranger with information that everyone else in her world knew as a matter of course. But once her mind was made up to put her trust in Lisa, there was no holding back her confidences. It was as if she needed to verbalize the explanation to make sense of it to herself. Lisa was certain the girl had never had to think deeply about her family connections before; those connections, like the existence of the sun and the moon, were just there, and everybody in her world knew it to be so. But now, thinking about them and trying to explain them to another, she realized her family ties were possibly beyond the comprehension of a stranger. So she gave it her best effort, and Lisa patiently listened, giving the convoluted explanation the gravity it was due. Surprisingly, in the end it all made perfect sense to them both.

"I have three Christian names," the girl stated. "Elspeth. Henrietta. Jane. Maman and Papa call me Elsie. And so do my big brothers. I have two. Roxton is much older than anyone. He's a duke. Henri-Antoine is my younger brother but he's old too. But not as old as Roxton. And I have a big sister, too, and her name is Sarah-Jane. She lives in France and has four children, three girls and a boy. Her husband is Cousin Charles. He's here for Teddy's wedding. But Sarah-Jane could not come because she is still nursing her baby. His name is Benjamin Franklin Fitzstuart and Papa says Baby Benjamin was named after a very important man called Benjamin Franklin. Papa says he is more important than him, even though my Papa is a duke, too. And everyone knows that after the king and his ministers, dukes are the most important men in the country."

She leaned into Lisa and said confidentially, "Maman told me she exchanges letters with Benjamin Franklin—not the baby, the old man. And that whatever Benjamin Franklin's greatness in the world, Papa will always be the most important man in the whole world to us."

"That is as it should be," Lisa replied earnestly, and said no more because she could see the girl had more to say.

"When we were in France in the spring, Maman and Papa and I lived in a house near Sarah-Jane and Charles, and every day we walked up the avenue to call on them. The houses there have blue shutters on the windows and high archways so the coach can pull right up at the door, which is not at the front of the house but at the side in the courtyard. The house was near the palace where the French King lives, and where Cousin Charles does important work for his new country. Maman once lived at the palace, but that was long ago when another king ruled France.

"And when Maman lived in the big house across the lake when my brothers were little like me, she was the Duchess of Roxton. But now she is the Duchess of Roxton and Kinross because she is married to my Papa, who is the Duke of Kinross, and so we live here in this house. Sometimes we live in London, and then there are times when we go to a big house with turrets that is on a lake called a loch far away in a country called Scotland. But it is still not as big as the big house that Roxton lives in. I like it here at this house the best, even though there are much better places to hide over in the big house. Henri-Antoine knows all the best hiding places, and so does Jack. You can call me Elsie, too, because we are no longer strangers. And because I would like you to be my friend... Would you like to be my friend...?"

"Thank you. I would like to be your friend very much, Elsie. And because we are friends you may call me Lisa. And thank you for telling me all about your family, which I found most interesting because I do not have a family of my own—"

"No family?" Elsie's eyes widened. She was intrigued. "None at all?"

"No brothers or sisters, and no mother or father."

"Do you have any cousins?"

"I have three female cousins. Two are married, and the youngest is twelve—"

"Julie is twelve, and she wants to be a duchess one day like me. Which is why she is sometimes not nice to me. Maman says that's because I will be a duchess regardless of who I marry, but Julie must find a duke to marry her. I think she will find a duke, because Julie is very pretty and she has a great look of my Maman; everyone says so."

"Then I am sure a duke will want to marry her."

"Are you sad not to have any brothers and sisters and parents?"

"I was sad when I was your age—"

"I am eight years and six months old."

"But I am not sad now because I keep myself occupied helping other people, and I have friends, and my best friend in the whole world is Miss Theodora Cavendish. I am sure you know her."

Elsie smiled and nodded. "I do! I like Teddy very much. She makes me laugh."

"Me too. She is always happy. So you see I am blessed to have such a good friend, and you are blessed to have a Maman and Papa, and two older brothers, and a sister, and many cousins. All of whom must love you very much. I cannot wait to meet them all."

And there was one member of Elsie's family in particular she was looking forward to meeting again, and who she was more than ever convinced had deliberately kept his nobility from her, and for reasons she could only speculate. Perhaps, like Elsie, he assumed she would know who he was without the need to inform her? Perhaps he did not feel the need to make himself known to one who was a social inferior. Perhaps he had just been amusing himself with her... But her intuition told her that these excuses did not ring true, that he did like her, and as much as she liked him, and so there had to be another reason he had made such an effort to remain anonymous. Whatever his reasoning, she would not speculate further and wait for him to tell her himself. She glanced at the swing.

"Now that we are friends, would you like me to push you on your swing?"

"I am not to swing by myself. Two of my maids and a footman must be here with me."

Lisa screwed up her mouth in response to such prescriptive coddling before she realized what she was doing. Elsie saw this and giggled.

"Henri-Antoine does that, too. So does Papa. But they do not let Maman see them do it because they do not wish to upset her. When they are with her they do as they are told—"

"And when they are not, sometimes they are naughty?"

Elsie put a finger to her lips and said in a loud whisper, "I am not to tell..." She grinned and nodded. "Very naughty."

"I do not know how much time is left to us before we are discovered... But perhaps we could be a little bit naughty together?" Lisa asked airily, a pointed sidelong glance at the swing.

Elsie was up off Lisa's petticoats, but instead of turning to the swing she rushed over to the base of the oak and scooped up two dolls which Lisa had failed to notice were propped against the trunk. Both were outfitted in court gowns of silk and embroidered with spangles that would have been the envy of any grown woman. One doll had black hair and was dressed in plum brocade, the other was blonde and wore a gown of ivory silk. Both were much loved.

"This is Mademoiselle Yvette," Elsie said, holding up the doll with the blonde hair. "And this," she said, holding up the doll with the black hair, "is Signorina Simonetta."

Lisa curtsied. "It is a pleasure to meet both your friends. Shall we sit them just over there in front of the swing so they can watch you, or shall they take turns with you?"

"They will take turns. Mademoiselle Yvette will be first, because she is my newest doll. Simonetta has had many swings."

"That is fair."

Elsie placed Signorina Simonetta sitting up a few paces from the front of the swing, arranging her dress to cover her stockinged legs, and placing the doll's hands in her lap. She then returned to Lisa, who was holding Mademoiselle Yvette. And when Lisa was sure Elsie was sitting securely on the swing's padded damask seat, and her hands were tight about the ribbon-covered rope, she put the doll beside Elsie, tucking it in securely with a quantity of the girl's cotton petticoats.

They had enough time for Signorina Simonetta and Mademoiselle Yvette to take turns on the swing with Elsie, and then on the third turn, both dolls watched on while Elsie went higher than she had ever been swung before. She was so excited that she was like any other child who enjoyed the wind in her hair and the thrill of going up in the air so that the toes of her slippers tipped the blue of the sky, heart racing and breath held, knowing that in the blink of an eye the swing would fall back again, and she would feel the drop in the pit of her stomach, and gasp every time.

Lisa came around to the front of the swing, letting it slow of its own accord, and sat cross-legged in the grass, with both dolls in her lap, watching Elsie enjoying her freedom. And because she was facing the swing, she was oblivious to the activity behind her.

If Elsie saw the small battalion of women headed her way, she chose to ignore them, intent on remaining on the swing for as long as possible, and doing her best with the movement of her stockinged legs to propel the ride herself to make it last as long as possible, now she was no longer being pushed.

Lisa was so engrossed in watching Elsie enjoying herself without a care in the world that she only became aware that they were no longer alone when a cloud moved in front of the sun at her back, or so it seemed, leaving her in shadow. In truth someone had come to stand directly behind her, blocking the sunlight. And then before she could turn to see who had cast her in shadow, a wave of women surged forward, either side of her, in a flap and rustle of petticoats and concerned chatter, all of it in French.

She scrambled to her feet, assisted by a firm hand about her upper arm. When she was let go she brushed down her petticoats, before turning about and coming face to face with the gentleman who consumed her dreams and who was never far from her thoughts.

EIGHTEEN

"HELLO," Henri-Antoine said in that velvety voice peculiar to him, and in something of the same cheeky manner in which Lisa had greeted him in Gerrard Street the day he had visited as a trustee of the Fournier Foundation. If he was surprised to see her here at his family home, he had made a herculean effort not to show it.

"Hello," Lisa echoed, also remaining calm and in control, mostly because she was not surprised at all to see him. Yet, being in his presence and in such close proximity she was unable to say anything further, and so allowed her gaze to flicker over him from linen stock to top boots.

She had admired his sartorial splendor of richly-embroidered frock coats and waistcoats in his urban setting, but out here in the country amongst the leafy greenery and fresh air, he looked relaxed, his lean face with a healthy glow. He was much in his element, and although dressed for comfort in buff breeches and a pale lemon-yellow linen waistcoat over a white shirt and plain stock, he was no less splendid. But it was his free-flowing dark hair which brought a warmth to her throat. Without pomade and ribbons, it fell loosely across his brow and down to his shoulders. On any other man such lack of restraint would have bordered on the effete, yet it suited him perfectly.

"Is this a fortuitous contrivance, Miss Crisp?" he drawled. "Or a spectacular coincidence? Are you a guest at the Cavendish wedding?"

"I am," she replied steadily, aware of his tease, hands behind her back, with chin up and smiling into his dark eyes. "And fate cannot be contrived, can it?"

He took a step closer. "Fate? I am inclined to think you are a practitioner of the dark arts, and are a witch."

"A witch? But you are the one who inhabits a magical world conjured by sorcery. Are you not then a sorcerer?"

"Touché. Tell me again: How old did you say you were...?"

Her smile widened. "And by what name did you say I should address you—my lord?"

He did not flinch. "If you know that," he murmured, "then you know the rest, *witch*."

Lisa suppressed a grin, lifting her brow in puzzlement, but there was no hiding the light of triumph in her blue eyes. "But it would be prudent to have the information that has been imparted to me confirmed. Though I am certain my source is impeccable."

His tone lost its playfulness. "I would have told you—eventually."

She continued to tease him. "Here? Or elsewhere? And when?"

"You're the witch, you tell me."

"Ah, but as a sorcerer you should have the answers."

His top lip twitched and her gaze dropped from his dark eyes to his mouth. She so wanted to kiss him. Her eyes lifted again to his and she drew in a breath. He was thinking the same thought as her. Instead of being shocked, she was elated.

"I did not know you would be here," he confessed. "But I dared to put my hope in wishful thinking."

"That is fate."

They took a step closer and were acutely aware they were within a hand span of each other, yet mindful they were in a public space. Their private reverie was intruded upon and they were dropped back into the here and now when Elsie broke from being fussed over by her nurses and maids. She pressed her dolls on a maid and rushed over to the couple and tucked her hand into her brother's fingers.

Touch made him look away from Lisa and down at his sister.

"Henri-Antoine, this is my new friend Lisa. I want her to be invited to Maman's picnic in the pavilion."

"As a guest, she already is, *ma petite chou*," he replied gently.

"Are you staying for the picnic?" she asked hopefully.

When the clutch of women took a step toward their charge, Henri-Antoine stopped them with a dark look, and they quickly retreated to the oak to await His Lordship's pleasure, and where two of his ever-present shadows lingered at a respectful distance. He went down on his haunches before his sister, not at all concerned Lisa was present and would hear every word of their discourse. He spoke to Elsie in French, their preferred language.

"Maman's picnic is a female-only affair for all of Teddy's friends and relatives, and of course that means you, too."

"But Maman would let you stay if you asked her. Papa is at home."

"So he is. But your papa will do as he is told and remain well away from the pavilion for the duration of the picnic. And I too must respect Maman's wishes. Remember what was threatened at breakfast?"

Elsie giggled

"Maman would never banish Papa to sleep in his dressing room, silly. There's no bed for him in there."

"I think it was an idle threat, too." He kissed the back of her hand. "I understand your wish to be alone better than any other, *ma petite chou*. But when you run off without telling anyone, and your ladies they cannot find you, Maman becomes frantic. I know the last thing you wish to do is upset her."

"I do not want Maman to be upset, and I do try to do as you say and ignore them all," she said, a glance over her shoulder at the half-dozen women obediently waiting by the tree. "But they fuss too much. I tell them not to, but they do not listen. So I run away to breathe. You must make Maman understand."

"She is trying her best to let you breathe, *ma chérie*. You are the most precious thing in the world to her and to your papa. She has no other daughter but you, and you are your papa's only legitimate heir. Which is why your women they are protective to the point of suffocation. But I will talk to Maman again, and to your papa, and perhaps we can contrive to make your breathing easier, *hein*? All Maman asks is that you tell her, or someone—anyone—when you wish to run away."

"But how is that running away if I tell someone? Did you tell Maman when you ran away and hid in the big house?"

Henri-Antoine could not help smiling. He shook his head.

"I did not. But I always had Jack with me, and so Maman she was not so worried. If anything were to happen to me, Jack could raise the alarm. If you go off by yourself, who is there to do that for you?"

"But you were an ill little boy, Henri-Antoine. That is what Maman told me. So she had cause to worry. I am not ill. Papa says I am a better swimmer than Sarah-Jane ever was. He says I have the heart of a tiger! But you do not even row on the lake without your bears at your back—"

"Bears?" He flicked her flushed cheek. "Is that what the lads look like to you?"

Elsie nodded and smiled. "But they do not dance like the bears I saw in Paris."

He winked. "They would if I told them to."

Elsie giggled, but then shook her head. "You would not make them. Maman says your lads help *her* to breathe."

"So they do. Which is one good reason I have them as my shadow."

"And if you were ever to fall ill again, yes?"

"Yes. If I were to fall ill again."

"I have never seen you without them except at table when they wait outside the door. I want you to have them because they look out for you, but do you not sometimes wish you could breathe without them?"

Henri-Antoine rose up to his full height on a sigh, gaze still on his sister.

"I wished for that every day when I was your age, *ma petite chou*. But I am old enough to be wise to the truth: I cannot breathe without them, and neither can our Maman. So I accept them, and do my best to ignore that they are there. But your life will be very different to mine. On my honor. One day you will be old enough to do as you please, and no one will be able to stop you from walking out from under the shadows of your women. For the present—for Maman and your Papa—you must strive to do your best to ignore your shadows, without being cruel or unkind in doing so, because they only have your best interests at heart, and do what they are told to do. If you accept this is the way life must be until you are older, then they will be gone, just like that," he said with a snap of his fingers. "As if by magic, you will no longer see them, even though they are still there. Can you understand that?"

Elsie cocked her head and squinted in thought. "You mean in the same way as the footmen who open all the doors, and the maids who clean out the grates before first light, and the laundresses who wash our clothes, whom I do not see at all but who are there every day, and who Maman says are most necessary to our comfort, and deserving of our gratitude."

Henri-Antoine lightly touched the tip of Elsie's little nose and wiggled it gently. "I see that you do understand."

Elsie smiled and grabbed her brother's hand and pressed it to her cheek. "I wish you were staying for the picnic."

Henri-Antoine glanced at Lisa but said to his sister, "I wish that too. But Jack and Freddie and the twins are waiting for me at the big house. We are having our own—er—picnic in the billiards room." He looked across at Elsie's maids and nodded, signal for them to approach. "But I shall see you in a day or two—I am sorry, *ma petite*, but Miss Crisp must remain here," he added when Elsie took hold of Lisa's hand, her ladies ready to return her to her mother. "I shall not keep her long. And then she will join you at the pavilion."

"Promise."

"Promise."

He watched Elsie take back her dolls from one of her maids, and go off across the lawn with her female entourage following close behind. He then signaled to the lads, who were still kicking their heels by the oak, to move on, which they did, to the stand of willows by the water's edge.

He and the lads had come by skiff across to Crecy Hall the day before, and would return to the big house the same way. His valet Kyte and his overnight bag had already done so via horseback. He knew not only Jack and his three nephews would be waiting him, but also Seb and Bully, but he had some unfinished business with Miss Crisp first, and they could wait; this could not.

"Come with me," he ordered.

Taking hold of Lisa's hand he strode off with her towards the oak.

"You do realize, my lord, that when Elsie lets it be known I am here, and that you are here, and that we are alone, questions will be asked. I could find myself in the awkward position of having to account for myself."

Undaunted, he walked on and around to the far side of the enormous tree, glancing about him, as if he had lost something, and still holding her hand.

"Getting yourself into an awkward situation did not seem to bother you when you took it upon yourself to enter Westby's house, did it?"

Lisa gaped at his back. Her mouth worked for several seconds and then she blurted out in a guilty rush, "I beg your pardon, my lord, but—"

"My lord? No, no, no, Miss Crisp. It will not do. I much preferred it when you called me sir—"

"—that was an entirely different circumstance—Oh? You do?"

"I do. But I would also prefer you not to call me sir, either. And you are right. Entering Westby's house was an entirely different circumstance. Your friend stole something of mine—"

"She did no such thing! Mrs. Markham dropped the catalog into Becky's basket in a bid to hide it from you, and no doubt to further infuriate Lord Westby. I offered to help Besty return it before she was wrongly accused of stealing—" Lisa blinked. "If I am not to call you my lord or sir, then how am I to address you?"

He let go of her hand, confident that they could not be seen, from the house, or by anyone approaching from the direction of the pavilion. He took a step toward her, and she backed away and came hard up against the tree trunk.

"Infuriate?" he asked with a frown of incomprehension. "Whatever can you mean, Miss Crisp?"

Lisa decided now was not the time for dissimulation. She met his gaze openly.

"From what Becky told me about the episode I have deduced that Mrs. Markham was hiding the catalog from you in an attempt to flirt with you, and in the process make Lord Westby jealous."

"Dear me, and you deduced this from—Becky?"

"I did."

"How astute of you. Yes, I do believe you are correct in that assumption."

"And further to what Becky told me, it would seem that Lord Westby was indeed jealous."

Henri-Antoine took a step closer. "Yes. Correct again."

"Is His Lordship in the habit of flirting with a friend's mistress to make that friend jealous?"

"She was attempting to flirt with me. Not the other way round."

"I do beg your pardon. I shall rephrase my question: Is His Lordship in the habit of allowing such flirtation to occur when it clearly upsets his friend?"

"If it shakes some sense into that friend to realize his affections are wasted on a second-rate actress, then yes."

"Oh? I see."

"I don't think that you do."

"I may be ignorant of many things, but I do know that gentlemen, married and unmarried, can and do allow their affections to be attached to a particular sort of woman. And I also know such matters are none of my business, my lor—sir—"

"Henri-Antoine. That is my name. And that is what I wish you to call me."

"I cannot call you by your Christian name!"

"Why? If when we are private I call you Lisa, then surely you can call me Henri-Antoine?"

Lisa unconsciously shook her head but then closed her eyes on a sigh for the briefest of moments hearing him say her name. She wished he would say it again so she knew it was real, that he had indeed said it and it wasn't because she was suddenly heady due to his closeness. He had his hand to the tree, gazed fixed on her through a tangle of hair that fell across his eyes. She was sure her heart was beating faster; that her blood was pumping too hard and drumming in her ears. Becky would say she was feverish. What had Becky called him—*bewitchin' 'andsome*? He was that, and much more. And if she didn't move away from his orbit that instant she was very sure she would do something she'd later regret. But at that moment she wasn't thinking about the future, or regrets, or consequences. She wasn't thinking logically at all. All she knew was that she wanted to kiss him.

In one last ditch effort to bring herself back from the brink of social ruin, she swallowed hard and asked curiously,

"What do you mean *I don't think that you do?*"

"I have no interest in flirting with Mrs. Markham or any other female for that matter. And since the day when you and your friend the haberdashery assistant turned up at Westby's with the catalog she did not steal—"

"Becky did not steal—Oh! You said that." She blinked up at him and resisted the urge to gently brush the hair out of his eyes. "Why—why are you telling me this?"

He moved closer. "Because you have caused me a great many sleepless nights, Lisa Crisp."

"I have?" She was nonplussed.

He nodded slowly, gaze fixed on hers. His upper lip twitched and his mouth parted slightly as he tried to suppress a grin at her complete lack of awareness as to his meaning. He tried to sound disconsolate, and gave a practiced sigh for good measure.

"Whatever am I to do with you?"

"Do? Do with *me?*"

She knew what she wanted to do with him, and that was kiss that perfect mouth, and the consequences could go hang. And then it happened. Thought succumbed to need, as if by magic—she a witch and he a sorcerer in this magical place.

In one fluid movement her arms slipped up about his neck and she leaned into him. On tiptoe, with her body pressed against his as if needing anchorage, she tilted her chin, closed her eyes, and let her mouth find his.

Surrender.

NINETEEN

H E WAS RARELY if ever surprised, but he was by her. And he had been since their first meeting at Gerrard Street. Now this. She had kissed him first!

He'd had every intention of kissing her. Reason he had brought her around to the far side of the oak, out of the potential prying gaze of guests and servants at the pavilion picnic. But intention had almost crippled him. He wanted their first kiss and everything about the moment to be perfect. It was to be a memory for them to cherish. And then she had stolen his initiative and kissed him!

Startled, he was slow to respond, not only because her kiss was unexpected, and thus the moment he had planned was lost, but because he had never been kissed in such a spontaneous, rather awkward manner which he supposed was how sweethearts shared a first kiss. It was a barely there, tentative touch of her lips to his, and it made him wonder if she had ever been kissed before, and presumed not. Which was why he had hesitated, and why he had planned the execution of this, their first kiss.

He not only wanted to kiss her, he needed to kiss her, and in the sort of reverential way that would allow her to gain some understanding of the depth of his feelings.

And then he surprised himself, for he realized he was being utterly selfish in wishing she had not stolen the initiative. It required great courage for her to be the one to kiss him first, to lay her feel-ings bare in that way. In doing so she gave him the choice to accept or reject her, and without consequence to himself, because she was not of his world. In his world, a girl did not find herself alone with a man, and she never permitted him to kiss her unless they were engaged, or, as in Jack and Teddy's case, an engagement had been on the horizon for years, and welcomed by both families, so there really was no going back from that.

But not for him. He was a free agent. He could kiss who he liked, and damn the consequences, particularly for a girl like Lisa, with no family, no pedigree, and nothing to offer him. She could not expect anything from him in return, certainly not marriage. His honor did not oblige him to offer her his name. Had she been of his world, there wasn't a girl who wouldn't want to marry the son of a duke, and not just any duke, and he not just any son. His brother was a duke, his nephew would be a duke, his stepfather was a duke, and his half-sister would be a duchess in her own right one day, and then there was his maman who was a double duchess. He was as steeped in aristocratic privilege as was possible, and he could, quite rightly, have any female he wanted, to bed, if she were a member of that fraternity who catered to men of his ilk, or to wed, if she were the daughter of the nobility with a pedigree that matched his own. But he didn't want just any female, and he didn't want to wed a noble-man's daughter. He had made up his mind. No one would do for him but Miss Lisa Crisp of Gerrard Street, Soho…

All this had raced through his mind as she let her arms fall away from his neck to take a step back only to find she had nowhere to go, with the oak behind her and him standing so close. He glimpsed the confusion and hurt in her blue eyes as she lowered her lashes and her chin, to say in a small voice, as her throat and cheeks stained with an embarrassing blush,

"The-the picnic… They must be wondering where I—"

"Lisa, your—"

"There is no need for you to-to say anything. I was the one who presumed—"

"Your kiss was perfectly lovely."

Her gaze flashed up to find him smiling down at her. It was a gentle smile which softened his whole face and made her heart give the oddest leap. Her brow cleared, and so did the hurt. She smiled hesitantly.

"Oh? It-it was?"

He nodded. "I'm the clumsy clod; I hesitated."

"Why?"

He huffed and grinned and then shook his head.

Her smile faded. "Should I not have asked? Is it impolite to do so? Forgive me for not knowing how precisely I should act, because I only arrived yesterday, and still have much to learn about—"

"Never second guess yourself. Like your kiss, you are perfectly lovely. I do not want you to be anything but yourself." He caressed her cheek. "Miss Crisp, presently of Gerrard Street, previously of the Blacklands School for young ladies, where I presume you became friends with Teddy…?"

When she gave a start and stated the obvious, he grinned.

"Yes. We are best friends."

"Naturally."

"But how did you—"

"—know? It did not take a mind the size of the moon to put the pieces together once you told me you went to a boarding school for young ladies in Chelsea. Only one boarding school—Blacklands—is appropriate. And only one girl who went to Blacklands who is about your age—which I have now calculated to be nineteen—is marrying in the county this week—Theodora Cavendish, the irrepressible Teddy."

"I am so relieved you know all about Blacklands, and my friendship with Teddy, because although my mind is not even the size of a-a balloon, least of all the moon, I did wonder if the Jack Teddy was marrying was the same Jack who is your best friend. You see, I do believe in fate, even if you think me a-a witch."

"You've bewitched me!"

"I have?"

Again he laughed, this time at the wonderment in her voice. He chucked her under the chin. "How could you think otherwise? Perhaps now you will tell me if I have indeed correctly calculated your age?"

She wrinkled her little nose. "Surely I do not need to, because as a sorcerer with a mind not quite the size of the moon, you already possess that information."

He inclined his head at her reasoning. "Very well then. Indulge my curiosity and set my mind at rest that you are nineteen, or closer to that age than you are eighteen."

"I do look younger than my years—

"What?!" He gave a theatrical start, hand to his chest, and pretended to be stricken. "Don't tell me! You're five and thirty!?"

Lisa gave an unladylike chortle and hung her head.

"This is not a laughing matter, Miss Crisp! You are a witch and have put me under your spell if you are in truth a middle-aged woman—"

"—with warty hands and a warty nose!" She became serious. "Teddy is nineteen and Jack must be your age—"

"I am eight-and-thirty. I just look younger than my years, too."

"Don't be ridiculous! If you were a sorcerer and you'd told me you were a hundred and thirty-eight, I would've believed you. Jack is four-and-twenty, so you must be too."

"Would it have bothered you had I been eight-and-thirty?" he asked with a frown, and then he shook his head and put up his hand. "You do not have to answer. I *am* being ridiculous."

"Because that was the age of your father when he fell in love and married your mother?"

He did not ask how she knew this, presuming Teddy had told her, but he did nod, and for some reason even this simple acknowledgment made his throat constrict with emotion. "He—he died too soon, and she—she was a widow much too early in her life..."

She saw him swallow hard, and sensed speaking about his parents, his father in particular, was not easy for him.

"What does age—what does any impediment—matter, when two people fall in love? All that matters is that they be together."

He stared at her hard and she was taken aback by the fierceness in his expression.

"A selfish expectation without thought to the consequences."

"They could not have predicted the future when they fell in love. All they had was the expectation—selfish or otherwise, though I do not think it selfish to surrender to fate—that their future happiness was dependent on each other."

He lost his harshness and pinched her chin. "There is that word again," he said with a sigh. "Fate." He peered at her. "So you are nineteen?"

When she rolled her eyes at his persistence he laughed out loud. She gave a practiced sigh of her own.

"If it will stop you pressing me further on the matter, then I will tell you I am indeed nineteen, but I am older than my years. Dr. Warner says I have an old head on young shoulders."

"Dear me," he drawled, taking a step back and allowing his gaze to sweep over her from boots to coiled braids. "If that is what an old head looks like, I am giddy with anticipation as to what awaits me— *Mon Dieu*. I said that out loud, didn't I?" he muttered in French, when she clapped a hand to her mouth in astonishment to hear him vocalize his yearning. He bit his lip as his face fired red. For the first time in his life he felt as gauche as a drunken sailor. "Forgive me—I should not have—"

"—said the truth?"

"—been an uncouth fiend."

"Is it uncouth to express your desire? For surely I may also do so, to you?" She smiled, adding shyly, "I think you are perfectly lovely— in every way."

"You do have an old head on those shoulders," he quipped, appeased that he had not shocked her. "I've never been called lovely before, and I accept your compliment because it is said with sincerity and without artifice."

"You did tell me to be myself," she teased. "So you will have to accept my compliments, too." She tilted her head and asked thoughtfully, "You will be yourself with me—always—won't you?"

He met her gaze openly. He knew her qualifier referred to his bouts of falling sickness. He also knew that as soon as he had taken her by the hand and led her behind the oak there was no going back, so he did not hesitate in his reply.

"I will do my best. It will take time, for I am by nature aloof. And I do my utmost to keep my seizures from my family, and have done so for years. To not do so—with you—will require *adjustment*. Curiously, I find I have no desire to hide anything from you."

She took a step closer again, and rested her palms lightly to the

front of his linen waistcoat. She was certain there were tears behind
her eyes.

"Thank you. Thank you for your honesty, and for trusting me.
That makes me very happy…"

He lifted her chin with the crook of one finger and stared into her
blue eyes rimmed with tears. "You, Lisa Crisp, make me happy. Are
those happy tears…?"

She nodded and smiled tremulously. "So why—why did you hesitate to kiss me?"

He leaned in and his breath tingled on her lips as he murmured,
"Because I wanted my kiss to be perfect."

"Perfect?" she echoed softly. "With such a kissable mouth, how
could it not be?"

"Kissable? Is it?" he muttered, taking her face gently between his
hands and lowering his mouth to hers. "Then let us see if I can live
up to your expectation…"

TWENTY

I F THEY WERE aware, it was not of time or place, but only of
each other. They remained sheltered and unseen by the ancient
oak's wide trunk, Lisa gathered up in Henri-Antoine's embrace, she
with her arms once more about his neck. And having enjoyed their
first tentative kiss, tenderness and hesitancy gave way to satisfying a
fervent longing that had simmered since his first visit to Gerrard
Street, and nothing and no one was going to stop them enjoying the
moment.

Kissing this most delectable creature in his arms was the first step
of many until she was his, body and soul. He had never met anyone
like her, and was certain he never would again. For in the space of a
few weeks his thoughts, and he was certain his heart, too, had been
conquered by a girl in a plain linen gown with ink-stained fingers.
She had managed to annoy, madden, bother, delight, charm, fascinate,
and finally invade his every waking moment. And he had the perfect
solution, one that would suit them both.

"If it were my choice, I would stay with you under this oak until
the stars appeared," he told her, touching his forehead to hers and
smiling into her eyes. "But for a little while longer, until Jack and
Teddy are wed, we must bow to the dictates of others. After that, our
time will be our own."

"Will it?" she asked sluggishly, forcing herself out of the daze of the most wonderful feeling she had ever experienced.

"It will," he assured her. "I've given your situation—"

"Situation?"

"—living in that house with those people, a great deal of thought. You won't mind giving that up will you?"

"Giving it up? What?" she asked, finally fully coming out of a delicious haze. She leaned against the tree, hands in the small of her back and took a deep breath. She mentally shook her brain to try and make sense of what he was telling her. "I—I don't understand."

"Helping in the dispensary. Being an amanuensis for the poor. You won't mind not doing that anymore."

"Why would I give it up? Yes, I would mind."

"I see..."

"I don't think that you do. Helping in the dispensary gives me purpose. Without it I have none. My education at Blacklands, if I am honest, was excellent for a girl who hoped to become the wife and helpmate of a merchant, or a-a banker. Or if my cousins had lowered their pride and permitted me to do so, to take up a post as governess. But fluency in the French and Italian languages is good for nothing when I am nothing—"

"Never say that," he cut in brusquely. "If you want to continue on with such projects then I will arrange it, but you will have to do so in a supervisory capacity, not in the day-to-day activities of a dispensary."

"Oh? Could I do that?"

"Certainly. Dispensaries with patients who need the services of a scribe are yet to be identified. After my—our—visit to Warner's Dispensary, the benefits of the sick poor having access to an amanuensis became evident. Dr. Warner sets great store on the power of the mind to aid in patient recovery. If the ill feel better within themselves, they are more likely to respond to treatment and heal that much the quicker."

"I agree. The sick poor can barely afford to eat, and they certainly can't pay for medical care, so how can they engage a scribe? But a letter home to a loved one, to family, and in their own words, does make them feel better. I have seen it time and again. It is a small service, but it means so much to them."

"Warner would not have thought it possible, or made his observations about the benefits of the power of the mind to help in the healing process, if not for you. And he readily admitted it at dinner."

Lisa showed her surprise. "He did?"

Henri-Antoine smiled. "He did. How could he not? He is dedicated to his vocation, and an excellent observationist."

"You give the sick poor a good deal of your thought, too."

"That surprises you. Because I am a nobleman?"

"I am not prejudiced. A selfish disregard for others is not the preserve of your class," she said with a cheeky smile, which cleared his brow in an instant. "My cousins are entirely self-absorbed. Minette married Dr. Warner, who has dedicated his life to the sick poor and their diseases, in spite of his chosen profession. He is wealthy and much respected, and she wanted a comfortable life."

"I do not condemn her for that. But I do for her spiteful behavior towards you."

"She is the nicer of my two cousins. She does try to temper her jealous spite. Henriette does not." She shook her thoughts free of her cousins, not wanting them to spoil her time in this magical place, and so said, "You can arrange for these scribes to be paid—"

"Through my—through the Fournier Foundation."

"And I could assist you—the foundation—with this endeavor?"

"Yes. There is much to be done and a great number of projects I—the trustees have under consideration which they wish to fund. I thought you might like to become involved...?"

"But if I am to no longer assist in Dr. Warner's Dispensary, how and where would I become involved in your—in the foundation's charitable works?"

"From Bath."

Lisa stood tall, stunned. "*Bath*? Why Bath?"

"I have a small estate on the outskirts of the town. A quaint Queen Anne house set in parkland. There is a stream at the bottom of a fragrant garden, and it is surrounded by woodland, and has several hectares of farming land attached to it, which is tenanted."

"It sounds delightful, but why would I need to go to Bath?"

He met her gaze openly and said flatly, "You could not remain in London. I won't have you subjected to gossip. That's not how I want you to live—"

"—to live?"

"—as my mistress."

And there it was, out in the open between them. Honesty showed her a future. What else had she expected from him? Marriage? Perhaps, for a fleeting second, she had hoped he might ask her to marry him. But she was level-headed enough to know that for a poor girl with no titled or influential relatives marriage to her was out of the question for him. Still, to hear him say it. To have him ask her to be his wife would have proven the depth of his feelings for her. Then again, in good conscience, she would have had to refuse him, and that would not have come easy, for her or for him.

She was thrilled and disappointed in the same breath, but ultimately she was happy, because his offer was as close to a declaration of love and commitment as an orphaned, penniless nobody of no family could ever expect from a wealthy eligible bachelor who was the second son of a duke from one of England's ancient families.

Paramount, she wanted to be with him, and if that meant being his mistress and living in a quaint Queen Anne House on the outskirts of Bath, then so be it. Her only worry was how to break the news to Teddy, and if, after Teddy was given this news, would she speak to her ever again? She did not doubt that Jack and Henri-Antoine would remain best friends, but could Lady Cavendish, niece of a duke, be friends with the mistress of her husband's best friend? The thought of losing Teddy when she had just found her again brought the tears back to her eyes. She quickly sniffed them away and tried to smile. This was not the time to think of Teddy, that dilemma could wait for another day, possibly after Teddy had married. She would not spoil Teddy and Jack's big day and the wedding celebrations with news of her imminent fall from grace. Henri-Antoine was no doubt expecting an answer to his offer, so she put a halt to her ruminations and looked up at him, and was startled.

The blood had gone from his face. He was chalk white. She wondered if he was experiencing the onset of a convulsion. But he seemed to be in control, too in control. His jaw was clamped shut and his dark eyes regarded her with an unblinking stare. It was as if he was forcing himself to remain calm when he was anything but. In fact, he looked terrified. A flash of insight provided her with the answer. He was petrified of what her answer would be, that she might refuse his offer... He did genuinely care for her, and deeply. It was writ large in his features.

She impulsively kissed his cheek.

"And you will visit me in this quaint house on the edge of town?" she asked buoyantly.

He heaved a sigh of relief and briefly closed his eyes. He nodded.

"I hope you mean to visit me often," she said in the silence, because he was still too affected to speak.

He drew her to him, the color returning to his face, and lightly kissed her forehead.

"So often it will be as if we are not living apart, but in the house together. I plan to stay for weeks at a time—"

"When you are not needed here, with your family, or required in London?"

"We will be a couple in every sense."

"In every sense?" she asked curiously.

"In every sense that matters."

"Oh! Yes, I see..."

He started to make plans for their future, saying aloud, "You will need pin money."

"Will I?"

"Yes. You must have an allowance, so you have money of your own."

"And you mean to give me this allowance—this pin money?"

"I do."

She would save as much of that as she could for the day when he no longer came. For a gentleman with a pedigree must marry, and marry well, and he would want a family of his own one day...

"And a dress allowance," he stated. "For as many dresses as you desire. I would like to see you in satin and silks."

"That would be lovely."

Good. She would save most of that money too. How many dresses would she need out in the country? Perhaps if she saved enough she could travel on the Continent? She'd always wanted to visit Constantinople, a wondrous city on the edge of the civilized world, and a place full of medical marvels and learning, according to Dr. Warner.

"And you must have a personal maid."

"I've never had a personal maid. Perhaps a female companion, too? For when you are not with me…"

"A companion. A personal maid. An upstairs maid. A butler. A housekeeper. A cook, and a footman. It will give me great pleasure to spend my wealth on you."

"You overwhelm me with your generosity…" She looked at him keenly. "But you do mean it—about assisting you with the work of the Fournier Foundation—because I cannot be idle in Bath, and I do have many ideas I wish to share with you, and with the Foundation, on how best to provide for the dispensaries and the physicians—"

"After receiving my offer, *every* girl I know would be calculating how best to spend my largesse on themselves, but not Miss Crisp," he interrupted, smiling at her note of hesitancy and look of uncertainty. He gently brushed the tip of his nose against hers and looked deep into her eyes. "She wonders how best she can serve my foundation, and help me go about distributing my wealth amongst the sick poor."

"Is that so wrong?" she asked, the note of hesitancy still in her voice because he was looking at her in a way she could not accurately interpret.

He shook his head. "No. Everything about it is right—Everything about *you* is right."

She smiled and kissed him, and he folded her into his embrace, and they shared a lingering kiss, to seal their bargain. He then let her go, and she took a few steps away from the oak, brushing down her flimsy apron and her petticoats and fussing with her hair. It was as if these mundane actions would calm her, for she had just made the most momentous decision of her young life. Perhaps in this magical place she was indeed a witch and he a sorcerer, for she could never have imagined while in London agreeing to such a scandalous proposal to become a nobleman's mistress.

But there was no thought of reneging. Not even when they parted, and Henri-Antoine headed off to the jetty, and she took the long way round to the pavilion via the terraced gardens. Every step closer to the pavilion and the sounds of female chatter was a step away from him, and she wished with all her heart she was still in his arms and they had remained under the oak until the stars appeared.

TWENTY-ONE

THE PRETTY PAVILION by the lake was festooned in a riot of silk ribbons in pastel shades of pinks, yellows, and blues. The fat marble columns were wrapped in sashes tied off in large bows, chairs were similarly adorned, and so too the large tubs bursting with color and the heavy scent of spring blooms.

Ladies in flowing gowns of painted cotton with layers of diaphanous petticoats and tiers of delicate lace cascading from elbow to wrists, had draped themselves on chairs, or on tapestry ottomans, and languidly fluttered fans to push the cool air coming off the lake across their unblemished *décolletages*, while engaging their nearest neighbor in conversation.

The low mahogany table was lost under the weight of baskets of seasonal fruits, pretty little cakes, macarons, and pastry delicacies contrived by the hand of a master pastry chef. And all served on plates of porcelain rimmed in gold and emblazoned with the ducal coat of arms of the dukes of Kinross.

A blanket spread on the lawn and scattered with cushions was in the shade at the base of the steps, occupied by Elsie and three little girls about the same age. They had with them their dolls, and child and doll were both dressed in their summer finery, their gowns and abundance of shiny hair a miniature mirror image of the clothes and coiffures of their mothers, aunts, and cousins up in the pavilion. They were enjoying a feast of their own, watched over by nurses, maids, and governesses who hovered at a discreet distance—not too close to their charges, but close enough to be called if needed.

And snaking in and around these pampered and privileged females, in the pavilion and on the lawn, were a small battalion of liveried footmen, in their distinctive peacock-green wool frock coats with silver braiding and buttons, offering trays of delicacies, tumblers of fruit punch, and flavored ices. They came and went with food and drink from the main house at the top of the terrace in a steady stream, much like ants coming and going from the nest.

Lisa encountered them as she came along the path of the second tier of the terrace between the hedgerows and tended garden beds, and she held back while several footmen rushed up the stone steps in pursuit of more ice from the icehouse. With the path clear, she took the stone steps down to the lawn, and there found several more footmen waiting for her to pass, carrying empty trays.

She kept her head down, thankful she was wearing the wide-brimmed straw hat. It covered her mussed hair, and shaded her face from the sun and the cursory sly glances of footmen and upper maids. She pressed her lips together, hoping to somehow hide her mouth and the telltale signs of her shameless behavior, which was a thoroughly idiotic notion and one that caused her to blush at her own naïveté. What was a passionate kiss behind a tree when she had agreed to an immoral relationship with Lord Henri-Antoine Hesham?

She was suddenly thirsty and hoped one of the army of footmen would offer her a tumbler of cool lemon water. She would then find somewhere to sit at the far end of the pavilion, where no one would notice her, and no one would engage her in conversation.

What she could not have foreseen was that the little girl whom she had befriended at the swing was waiting and watching for her arrival. The ramifications of being the new best friend of the most important little girl at the party, as well as the best friend of the bride to be, were soon apparent when she found herself the unwanted center of attention, and every conversation paused, and every pair of eyes looked her way.

As soon as Elsie saw Lisa, she put her dolls aside and jumped to her feet. She rushed across the lawn, brushing down her crumpled petticoats as she went and almost toppling face first into the grass, such was her excitement. Her three young relatives looked about to see what was the matter, and her chief lady-in-waiting sent two of her maids scurrying after her.

"I've waited a very long time for you to come," Elsie stated, standing before Lisa, with a concerned frown. "Were you lost?"

"Yes. A little," Lisa fibbed, and hoped her smile at least appeared genuine. "I'm sorry you had to wait. I must have turned right instead of left in the gardens. I never was good with my compass points."

Elsie accepted this explanation and taking hold of Lisa's hand walked with her across the lawn.

"We've had pistachio ices, and there's lots of cake. Julie ate two helpings of vanilla. Tina likes the lemon tarts best. She's eight. Harriet is six. She spilled strawberry punch on her gown and cried, because it is her best gown. Would you like a slice of chocolate cake, or do you like vanilla, like Julie?"

"Perhaps after I have something to drink. All that walking about the gardens in the sun has made me parched." She looked down at Elsie and said conspiratorially, with a quick hunch of her shoulders, "I may have a slice of each."

Lisa was startled by two footmen who suddenly materialized at her elbow. One held a tray of tumblers and a pitcher of fruit punch, and the other was there to pour out and hand her the tumbler. She was so thirsty she took a sip of fruit punch without really tasting it, and partially numbed her tongue and her lips, before looking into the tumbler and discovering shaved ice floating in her drink.

She had never had ice served in a drink before. In fact, she had never had a flavored ice or ice cream, so she savored this new experience, drinking the rest of her fruit punch slowly. It was delightfully refreshing, and just what she needed after the walk through the terraced gardens.

"Here you are!" Teddy announced. She had rushed down the steps and put her arms about Lisa. "We were about to send out a search party." She untied the ribbons holding Lisa's straw hat on and removed it, and quickly tidied Lisa's hair by re-pinning a few strands come loose from their pins. "We must have you looking your best to meet Cousin Duchess. And then I have another surprise for you." She turned and bobbed down and hugged Elsie to her and said kindly, "Thank you for letting me borrow your new friend for a little while. I want her to meet your mama. And perhaps when all the introductions are over with, you can come up into the pavilion and sit with us while we have our coffee?" And before Elsie had time to nod in agreement, Teddy kissed her swiftly on the cheek, and swept Lisa away, up the steps and into the pavilion to meet her female relatives.

All this was accomplished without giving Lisa time to think too deeply or prepare herself for meeting the one person who had made such a difference to her life. Not only had the Duchess of Roxton and Kinross sponsored her enrollment at Blacklands, but she had also gone to the effort of discovering her whereabouts, and ordered Lisa's aunt to give assurances of her attendance at Teddy's wedding. What did one say to such a wonderful woman? A simple thank-you seemed wholly inadequate. And if all this weren't enough to make Lisa anxious, there were the years of listening to her Aunt de Crespigny's stories about the fairy tale world she had inhabited as lady-in-waiting to this most beautiful, kind, and loving noblewoman, which had elevated Mme la Duchesse to mythical status within the de Crespigny household. And here was Lisa, who never expected she would ever know what such a mythical creature looked like, least of all be in her presence, and was about to be introduced to her.

"Here she is, Cousin Duchess!" Teddy announced brightly, bringing Lisa to stand before four women and a young girl, all sitting close together on an arrangement of comfortable chairs and a chaise longue.

Lisa managed to curtsy without faltering but did not know at which noblewoman she should direct her gaze. Her cousins' warning reverberated in her ears, and it effectively made her mute: *If you dare say or do anything that might interfere or diminish the special bond between Mama and Her Grace, we will hate you for the rest of your days.*

Teddy was about to speak on behalf of her tongue-tied friend, when the Duchess of Roxton and Kinross addressed Lisa in English with her decidedly French enunciation, "Was your journey a pleasant one, *chère fille?*"

Lisa's gaze was directed to a small woman with delicate features who reclined on cushions at the far end of the chaise in a cloud of cotton petticoats. Her mass of honey-blonde hair was generously streaked with silver, most notably at the temples, and she had a pair of fine green eyes that were reminiscent of Elsie's in shape if not in color. But it was to her mouth—at the cupid's bow—that Lisa was most drawn. Here was the feminine form of Henri-Antoine's very kissable mouth.

Banishing Henri-Antoine from her thoughts, she quickly looked up into the Duchess's eyes, and was surprised at the directness in the noblewoman's gaze.

Lisa knew then she was being acutely scrutinized and wondered if the Duchess had some knowledge of her son's interest in her. She would not have been surprised to learn that Elsie had told her mother she had left her brother in conversation with her newest friend. This increased Lisa's nervousness tenfold.

"Thank—Thank you, Mme la Duchesse, I had a-a most pleasant journey," Lisa replied haltingly though she did her best to suppress her unease, swallowing hard to clear her throat which made her voice more breathless than intended. She dropped another curtsy, gaze again flickering up to those steady green eyes, before politely lowering her lashes, the heat in her face having nothing to do with the warm summer weather.

"Teddy tells me you traveled down by the common stage. *Quelle? Cela ne peut pas l'être*—What? It cannot be!" Antonia demanded, reverting to her native tongue. "How is that so when I specifically instructed Gabrielle—your aunt—to have a diligence hired to convey you here?"

"I assure you, Mme la Duchesse, it was no inconvenience to take the stagecoach," Lisa replied diplomatically in French. "And to be fair to my aunt, I do not think she had any part in my travel plans."

"That I believe, *ma petite*. No doubt it was her daughters she entrusted with your voyage, yes?"

"Yes, Mme la Duchesse," Lisa replied, her nervousness evaporating at the Duchess's outrage on her behalf.

"It is a wonder those two they did not book you a seat on the outside of the stagecoach!"

Lisa suppressed a smile. "As thrilling as an outside seat atop the carriage would have been, for all of five minutes, the other thirteen hours would've been terrifying. So I am grateful to Dr. Warner, who secured us inside seats."

Antonia leaned forward, hands in the lap of the many layers of cotton petticoats, green eyes wide with horror. "*Thirteen* hours? *Mon Dieu!* But that is diabolical!"

Teddy giggled at her godmother's look of disgust.

"Mayhap to you, Cousin Duchess, because you have the most luxurious carriage in the kingdom." She confided to Lisa, "Mme la Duchesse's carriage has seats that can be turned into not one, but two beds! But I would *love* to travel on the roof of a coach, at least once. How thrilling to think that at any moment, and on any bend, the entire coach might overturn and we'd all end up in the shrubbery!"

"With broken bones, or a cracked skull, or no skull at all," Lady Mary stated with a shudder. She appealed to Lisa. "Is that not so, Miss Cr—Lisa?"

"It is, my lady," Lisa agreed. She grabbed Teddy's hand and turned her to face her. "Promise me, and your mama, your godmother, and your aunts, that you will never travel on a common stage, and *never* on the roof."

Teddy rolled her eyes and looked mulish, but then she smiled and kissed Lisa's cheek before turning to her most senior female relatives. She bobbed a curtsy. "I promise and double promise!"

The Duchess continued to stare at Lisa, and asked, "I hope you and your companion at least were not inconvenienced with having to share the inside of the coach with others?"

"There was only the one couple and their young son inside the carriage with us, Mme la Duchesse. They were returning to Southampton from London, where they had taken their son to visit with his physicians."

"That is quite a journey to undertake to seek out a physician."

"It is, Mme la Duchesse. But in my limited experience, devoted parents will do whatever it takes in the hopes a physician can offer them a cure for their child's affliction or, at the very least, provide some relief with medicinals—"

"Affliction?"

"The little boy suffers with the megrim," Lisa explained. "His physicians are not certain, but they theorize his headaches may be another manifestation of the falling sickness."

The Duchess sat up, fingers tight about the sticks of her fan.

"If it is the falling sickness, then me I pity them, because there is no cure," she stated bluntly. "One can go all the way to Constantinople, and the physicians there they have no clearer idea than they do here how to treat such a despicable illness."

Lisa met the Duchess's gaze openly, alerted to the possibility that this mother was well aware that her youngest son still suffered with seizures—this despite the precautions Henri-Antoine took to conceal his affliction from his family, particularly his mother. And thinking about this, why, as a loving mother, would the Duchess not know? The aristocracy lived with an army of servants catering to their every need and whim. It only required one servant to break the confidence of his master for his mother to remain informed. And if the Duchess did not allow her little daughter to breathe—as Elsie explained her mother's overprotective coddling—she certainly would be just as worried and protective of a son who suffered a life-long illness, albeit from a distance, now he was a young man with his own household.

Lisa decided to test her assumptions.

"I imagine it is heart-wrenching as a parent to watch your child suffer such seizures. And to remain a silent witness when that child chooses to suffer alone must be unbearably difficult..."

The Duchess's fan paused mid-flutter, green eyes fixed on Lisa. If she was taken aback by this indirect reference to her son's illness, she was even more surprised to discover Lisa had intimate knowledge of it. And yet, she forced herself to remain impassive. So when she spoke there was no change in the timbre of her voice, and she quickly and deftly took the conversation in another direction.

"That is very true. Your French tongue, it is very good. I had supposed Blacklands—it being a French boarding school—you would have excellent teachers in the language."

"We did, Mme la Duchesse," Lisa replied. "And may I say again how grateful I am to you for-for sponsoring me and-and—" She shuddered in a great breath and dashed tears away, "—for-for finding me..."

Antonia leaned forward with a smile. "I hope those are tears of happiness, *ma petite*. And now you must stop thanking me and enjoy your time here. *Ma chérie*," she said, turning to Teddy, who was holding her baby sister against her shoulder, "your school friends they must be eager to be reunited with Mlle Crisp, yes?"

"Oh, yes! Come, Lisa. I have such a surprise for you!" Teddy replied breathlessly, returning Sophie-Kate to their mother.

TWENTY-TWO

TEDDY TOOK Lisa by the hand and led her quickly through the crowd, weaving her way around ottomans and chairs and small clusters of guests, young and old, who were enjoying the plates of little cakes, sweetmeats, and ice-filled drinks, and who were seated further back in the pavilion, where it was cooler, and the breeze off the lake found its way between the fat columns. She finally came to a halt before a matron in an overlarge frilly cap, seated with two girls Teddy and Lisa's age.

It might be two years since they were at school together, but Lisa had not forgotten these two: The Honorable Violet Knatchbull, and the Honorable Margaret Medway. Known as *The Hons* at school, and privately by Lisa as *The Horribles*. She was not surprised they were guests at Teddy's wedding, though a small part of her hoped they would be unable to attend so as not to spoil her visit.

She did her best to hide her disappointment and displeasure, for if there were two girls at Blacklands who had caused her the most distress, it was Vi Knatchbull and Meg Medway. Both were daughters of career diplomats on postings abroad and had been placed at Blacklands because no other seminary for young ladies would have them. They were troublemakers and cousins, and did their utmost to hide their sour dispositions, and their dislike of Lisa, from Teddy. And because Teddy did not have a wicked bone in her body, she failed to see the true nature of *The Horribles*. And Lisa would be the last person to tell Teddy that Vi and Meg were the carry-tales who had informed the headmistress Lisa was seen kissing Jamie Banks, when an apothecary's apprentice, behind the Chelsea Bun House.

She supposed it was too much to ask that since she had left Blacklands, *The Horribles* may have changed for the better. Within a few minutes' conversation, Lisa knew this for wishful thinking. She did her best to ignore their snide remarks, determined they would not ruin her stay.

"What a surprise to see you again, Lisa. Teddy told us you'd been found," Vi Knatchbull said with a brittle smile. "Meg and I could hardly believe it! London is such a vast place, that you could have been living down any back alley, doing who knows what, never to be seen again. But here you are!"

"Not a back alley. A dispensary for the sick poor."

"Good—grief!?" Vi gave a start, a hand to her bosom in shock. "You've not got a contagion, have you?"

"What? Lisa ill?" Teddy scoffed. "She's never been ill, ever. No, silly. Lisa was assisting the physician at the dispensary."

Vi and Meg stared at Teddy, speechless, and then at Lisa, Vi finding her voice to say silkily, "Working with the poor hasn't done you any harm. You haven't changed at all, not even your clothes. I'm sure that gown was your Sunday best dress when we were at school, wasn't it?"

"You haven't changed either, Violet," Lisa commented with a straight face and a quick smile. "That gown is very pretty, and the perfect shade of green. Green always did suit you."

Meg stifled a laugh behind her fan at this backhanded compliment and nudged Vi before saying to her aunt, who was looking Lisa up and down through her quizzing glass,

"This is the poor girl I was telling you about, Aunt. She was at Blacklands with Vi and me, and Teddy. Miss Crisp was the cleverest girl in the school, which I suppose, when you think about it, being poor and with nothing better to do with her time than fill her head with the nonsense we were taught, she ought to have been—"

"Clever never got a girl anywhere worth getting," the matron announced stridently. She peered at Lisa through her quizzing glass, grotesquely magnifying one eye. "The wonder of it is—how do the poor enter such an esteemed institution?"

"The same way as everyone else," Lisa replied cheerfully. "Through the front gates."

The matron gave a start and drew in a breath and Vi and Meg held their breath too, hoping to see Miss Lisa Crisp get her comeuppance for her impertinent reply from such a stickler for form as the Dowager Marchioness of Fittleworth. But then her ladyship burst out laughing. It was such a genuine laugh full of good humor that Lisa decided the aunt, unlike her nieces, was genuine, too, and she liked her all the more for it.

"Hahahaha! Through the front gates! Hahahaha! I do approve of a gal with a sense of humor!"

Lisa smiled and dropped a curtsy to her ladyship, and having found the perfect excuse to quit the company of the matron's sour-faced nieces, said to Teddy, "Please excuse me, dearest. I spy Becky, and I must make certain she is being looked after..."

And off she went, back straight, through the crowd across the pavilion to where the maids, nurses, and footmen were congregated, waiting to serve and be of service.

Vi and Meg could hardly believe Lisa Crisp had quit their presence in preference for the company of servants. They both hoped the Dowager Marchioness was also making note of this social solecism, but to their frustration and angry embarrassment, their aunt had dropped her quizzing glass back on its riband and was talking to Teddy.

"You must not misconstrue me, my dear, for I do enjoy the occasional all-female gathering, but the decided lack of male company here today makes for a dull affair, particularly for my nieces. They need any and every opportunity put at their disposal to meet and make a favorable impression on a suitable suitor. They are pretty enough, but own waspish tongues, and to their great misfortune do not possess a defining feature—such as your glorious red locks, or Miss Crisp's beauty. Your friend might be poor but she has a face any painter would wish to immortalize with his brush. And I like her direct approach; men, no doubt, do too."

"Aunt! How unkind you are," Meg Medway whined, blushing. "Unlike Miss Crisp, who I am sure has never had an offer made to her, despite her-her *beauty*—for how can the poor be made offers when they have nothing to offer—I was made an offer just last week—"

"Which you should have accepted," Lady Fittleworth stated bluntly. "Knatchbull isn't the brightest candle in the sconce—after all he did offer for *you*—but he does have an income of a thousand a year and every expectation of inheriting his father's pile, even if it is badly in need of repair; the winds in Wales are brutal on man, beasts, and buildings!"

Meg pulled a face of disgust. "Marry Vi's brother? I can do better than Bully Knatchbull."

Vi glared at her friend. "You didn't tell me Bully had made you an offer. I'm glad you didn't take it. Bully can do better. Much better."

"Enough, wasps!" Lady Fittleworth demanded, lightly swatting each girl on the back of the hand with the closed sticks of her fan. She turned to Teddy with a roll of her eyes.

"How you tolerated these two at school, I shall never know! But do pity me because I have been instructed to have them married off before their parents return from abroad in the new year. So I hope Roxton and the other fathers and their cubs are now returned from their expedition into the woods, so that all the gentlemen may join the ladies for the rest of the week's activities before the wedding ceremony and the ball...?"

Teddy smiled at Vi and Meg who lost their disgruntled demeanors at the prospect of male company at future social gatherings, and reassured them and their aunt.

"This is the only all-female gathering, I assure you both. From tomorrow, all the men and boys will join us for the organized events, and as you are staying at the big house, you may even see them at the breakfast table, and most assuredly at all the dinners."

"I heard mention of a cricket match...?" Vi asked hopefully.

"Between the Duke's eleven and the guests' eleven," Teddy told them.

"Vi is hoping Lord Henri-Antoine will play."

"He does. With Jack, on the Duke's eleven," Teddy told Meg.

"Did you hear, Vi?" Meg taunted her with a snigger. "Lord Henri-Antoine will be playing at cricket. Perhaps he'll ask you to marry him after the match?"

Vi blushed, but embarrassment did not stop her retorting, "Perhaps he will! I have more chance of him making *me* an offer than him offering for *you!*"

"Westby said if Lord Henri-Antoine offers you anything not to take it because it will end with your ruin," Meg retorted. "And that it most assuredly won't end with him giving you his name—"

"Dear me, girls! Enough," Lady Fittleworth demanded. "Whatever Lord Henri-Antoine's unsavory proclivities, this is not the time nor the place to air them! You forget we are within earshot of his dear mama and his aunts, and Teddy is his cousin."

"Thank you for your consideration, my lady. But what Meg says is true," Teddy stated bluntly but without rancor. "Henri-Antoine isn't the marrying sort, and if he does eventually settle, it won't be until he is middle-aged, like his papa before him."

"I tried to warn you," Meg taunted Vi. "Roxton's brother offering for you is as likely as—oh! As likely as Lord Henri-Antoine offering marriage to any other female in England—Why, even poor Lisa Crisp has as much chance as you—"

"*Lisa Crisp as much chance as I?*" Vi was affronted and scoffed. "Sometimes, Meg, you make the most outrageous statements. Your brain is the size of a-a *peppercorn*. At least Lord Henri-Antoine is aware of who I am. Whereas he wouldn't know Lisa Crisp from a-a *hedgehog*! He certainly has no idea she exists."

Vi Knatchbull's emotive assertion was put to the test the very next evening when Henri-Antoine, Jack, and Lady Fittleworth were guests to dinner at the Gatehouse Lodge.

TWENTY-THREE

WITH THE RETURN of Teddy's step-papa, Mr. Bryce, and her two half-brothers from two days and nights spent out in the woods, the Gatehouse Lodge was no longer quiet and still. Servants, male and female, ran up and down stairs filling hip baths with soapy water. Nurses scrubbed clean the tired and aching bodies of their young charges, while their father found a few moments' respite soaking in a tub in his dressing room. In the kitchen, an Italian feast was being prepared, while footmen under the direction of the butler were trying their best to arrange the required number of chairs, and settings of china, silver, and glasses, around a dining room table that usually seated half that number.

Lisa and Teddy had spent the day in Teddy's bedchamber having Lisa pinned in and out of a selection of gowns that to Lisa seemed to have been conjured up as if by fairy dust, but which had in truth come from the wardrobes of Teddy's illustrious relatives that were of an approximate height to Lisa. The gowns were made from the sheerest cottons and the lightest silks in the most radiant array of colors she had ever seen, with delicate embroidery in spangles and metallic thread to sleeves, bodice, and hems. And there was such yardage in each gown that Lisa was certain three gowns could be cut from one in any other household. Accompanying these gowns were an assortment of matching under-petticoats, delicate white lace *engageantes*, stomachers covered in silk *eschelles*, as well as several chemises with lace edging worn to be seen at the *décolletage*.

Teddy was insistent Lisa choose three gowns, all to be altered to fit her slim frame. The most ornate, with spangles, would be reserved for the wedding and ball following the wedding breakfast, the second and most immediate gown to be worn that afternoon to dinner, a third of summery cotton would be perfect for the cricket match tomorrow. And once the gowns had been selected by Teddy and Lisa, Lady Mary and her personal maid were called to give their final approval. And then Becky was set to work with her pins, her needle and thread, and her expertise.

By the time Becky had finished altering and sewing the first gown, it was time to pin Lisa into it. Just as Becky had done with the cast-off gowns the cousins had given Lisa to use, this robe *à l'anglaise* of chocolate-brown silk fitted Lisa's lithe frame perfectly, the elbow-length sleeves molded to her long slim arms, and the bodice hugged her narrow back, the little white lace edge of the chemise just visible along the neckline against her unblemished skin. With the addition of tiered lace and blue silk bows at her elbows and a stomacher covered in matching bows, Lisa looked the part of best friend to the cousin of a duke.

She was nervous to be joining the family for their Italian feast. It would be her first formal dinner, and not eaten alone in the back parlor of Gerrard Street, since her days of communal dining at school. And it would be the first time gentlemen and guests would be present. She was particularly anxious at meeting Teddy's step-papa, having heard all about the dour Squire Bryce who had dared to reach up from his world to marry the daughter of an earl, because Teddy loved him as if he were indeed her true father. But what made her even more nervous was discovering that Jack and Henri-Antoine were coming to dinner. She wondered at the reception she would receive from the former, and how she was to conduct herself with the latter, and what he might think of her dressed in silks.

Sensing her nervousness, Teddy put her arm through Lisa's, and they entered the drawing room together. Lisa could not remember ever hearing the sound of adult laughter or such incessant chatter in a drawing room. Everyone was taking drinks before dinner and not speaking in English or French, but in the Italian language.

"Don't concern yourself, I can't speak the language as well as I ought, though I am much better at understanding what is being said," Teddy confessed near Lisa's ear. "As I recall, you used to practice your Italian language skills with the drawing master. Oh! And here's Jack. He'll speak in English with you. His Italian is inferior to mine, and having been on the Grand Tour, he has no excuse." Her smile died seeing the tiredness in her betrothed's eyes, and she said with a frown, stepping up to him, "You look green, Sir John."

He made her a bow then kissed her hand. "I am, Theodora, but I do not deserve any sympathy. Last night Harry, Seb, Bully, and the rest of the fellows succeeded in getting me as drunk as a sailor."

Teddy swiftly kissed his cheek. "Then you most certainly will not have any sympathy from me, or from Miss Crisp. And here she is." Teddy turned to Lisa, still holding Jack's hand. "You needn't worry that because we are formal you must be formal, also. It's just that everyone calls us Jack and Teddy, so we thought we'd call each other Sir John and Theodora. And as I won't allow anyone else to call me by that vile name, Jack saying it makes it very special. But as you are my best friend, and I am certain he will agree, you must call him Jack. And you," she added, turning back to Jack who was looking at Lisa with a smile, "my dear Sir John, will call her Lisa when you know each other better."

"Miss Crisp! How utterly delightful to see you here!" Jack announced with a bow. "When Harry told me that the Miss Crisp of Gerrard Street in Soho was the same Lisa Crisp who is my Theodora's best friend, well, I thought he was the drunk one! I can't tell you how happy I am for you both. And for you to be part of our wedding celebration."

"Likewise, Sir John," Lisa replied with a smile and bobbed a curtsy. "To be here with Teddy… To see her married to you… To share in your happiness… It is a dream come true for—"

"—all of us!" Teddy announced. "I hope you brought your viola with you?" she asked Jack. "We are to have dancing after dinner, and I do so want Lisa to hear you play. He is a splendid musician," she said to Lisa. "And has composed something just for me which I am not permitted to hear until our wedding day."

"How can it be a wedding gift if you hear it before the wedding?" Jack said with a grin. "And when don't I have my viola?" He looked at Lisa, a glance at Teddy, and spoke his thoughts aloud. "I hope you won't mind me saying this, Miss Crisp, but that shade of brown sets off your hair most becomingly. And the blue silk ribbons are a perfect match for your eyes."

Lisa thanked him for the compliment, brimming with happiness. It had been another wonderful day, just like the day before. Spending it with Teddy, being part of her family, seeing her and Jack so happy together, and now this gathering for dinner. She wasn't sure if it was the warm reception she had received, and the fact that Teddy was so loving and generous, or that it was this gown and the feel of the silk between her fingers, but suddenly she felt special, almost beautiful, and Jack's compliment made her heart swell. All that remained to make it perfect was to find herself seated next to Henri-Antoine during dinner.

"You see, Lisa!" Teddy exclaimed triumphantly. "I told you the brown and blue work well together on you. She does look divine in chocolate silk, does she not, Sir John."

"Divine," Jack agreed, then leaned into Teddy's ear to whisper, "Though, for me, nothing will ever surpass your ruby tresses and those freckles on your nose."

Teddy turned her head and looked up into his eyes. "Five more sleeps," she whispered. "Are you counting too?"

He nodded, and they would have kissed but for Lisa's unintentional interruption, which saw them move apart when she bobbed another curtsy and said merrily,

"Thank you, Sir John—"

"Jack. You must call me Jack," he interrupted, standing tall. He glanced around the room, looking for Henri-Antoine, then said to Lisa with a smile, "I insist. You are practically a member of the family, is she not, Theodora?"

"She is, but you must hush now on that score, or you will spoil the surprise," Teddy told him stridently, a finger to her lips and a significant glance at Lisa. But she need not have worried her best friend had overheard her caution, because her mother had approached with her stepfather and was introducing them.

Jack again looked about to see where Henri-Antoine had got to, because he had been at his side when the two girls had swept through the door, and then vanished. He had so wanted to see his reaction to Miss Crisp in her silk gown. She had been quite pretty in her floral petticoats when he had visited Gerrard Street as part of the Fournier Foundation, but this gown showed off her lovely form, and that she was not pretty at all, but breathtakingly lovely.

It was only when everyone had moved through to the dining hall and were being seated that Henri-Antoine reappeared, one of his lads following up behind, carrying a large parcel that looked to be the shape of a framed canvas, wrapped in cloth. This was leaned up against a wall by the sideboard, out of harm's way, and with no further comment, and Henri-Antoine was directed to sit on Lisa's right. Teddy and Jack sat opposite, with a chair left vacant on Lady Mary's right. Lisa was given no time to glance Henri-Antoine's way, for while everyone had taken their seats Jack remained standing and was waiting for conversations to cease. When he had their attention, he looked down the length of the table at Christopher Bryce, and receiving a nod from the squire, he addressed the gathering.

"I know we're all eager to taste Silvia's delectable dishes, so I will be brief," he said looking about the table. "Though I cannot be held accountable for the aftermath of this speech, and so I have apologized in advance to Silvia should we need a few moments to compose ourselves and regain our appetites. And I will also apologize on behalf of myself, Uncle Bryce, and Harry, because we know what you, my dear Aunt Mary, and you, dearest Theodora, and you Granny Kate, do not, and have kept from you for three nights. But I am assured that none of that will matter once the surprise is revealed."

"Surprise?" Teddy interrupted, eyes wide. "Oh, I do love surprises. Is it animal or vegetable? Do we all get to guess?"

"No guessing required, Teddy," her step-papa said quietly. "Though perhaps, Jack, you may care to ask her ladyship one simple question…?"

"Yes, sir." Jack turned to Lady Mary. "Aunt Mary, what have you been saying for months is the one thing missing that, if it could be obtained, would make our wedding celebration perfect in every way?"

Lady Mary looked down the length of the table at her husband, then across at her daughter, before looking up at Jack. She did not hesitate in her response.

"To have my brother—Teddy's Uncle Charles—here with us."

A hush came over the room. No one moved or spoke. Everyone, except the Lady Mary, was looking across her shoulder to the door behind her. At mention of her brother's name, a footman opened this door and into the room stepped a man of middling height, with a head of flaming hair that was a beacon to his familial connections. And with the same nose as his elder sister, there was no mistaking his kinship. Here was the stranger who had shared the carriage from Alston to Treat with Lisa.

"Mary?"

The Lady Mary's name was uttered just as Teddy jumped to her feet. But she did not go forward. This reunion was first and foremost between a brother and his sister, and no one wanted to spoil that moment.

Wide-eyed and shaking, the Lady Mary swiveled about on her chair at her name said by a beloved voice she had not heard in ten years, and never thought to hear again. She saw the gentleman standing just inside the door and froze. She was disbelieving. But when he smiled and took a step forward, she scrambled up so fast her chair fell back and hit the floor. She rushed up to him, threw herself into his arms, and was gathered up in her brother's loving embrace.

She sobbed and he submitted to her outpouring of joy and relief and disbelief, overcome by this reception. Christopher Bryce went forward and shook Charles's hand and offered his wife his handkerchief. The Lady Mary was still so overcome to see her youngest brother that she was only too happy to be comforted by her husband, as Teddy rushed forward to be introduced to the uncle she had heard so much about and had never met. And within a short interval of Charles Fitzstuart's surprise arrival at the Gatehouse Lodge, he was seated at his sister's left hand, dinner was upon the table, and everyone was enjoying Silvia's delectable dishes.

And while brother and sister became reacquainted, and exchanged news that had not made it into their correspondence over the years, or had yet to be written, they held hands. Lady Mary occasionally touched Charles's cheek, he squeezed her fingers or kissed the back of her hand, as if touch was needed as assurance that this was not a dream, that they were indeed reunited and in the same room together. They could not stop smiling.

They were left alone, everyone else getting on with eating, drinking, and chatting amongst themselves. And with footmen coming and going with covered dishes and topping up wine glasses, Henri-Antoine finally turned to Lisa and engaged her in conversation, silver knife and fork placed on his plate and pushed aside.

TWENTY-FOUR

LISA HAD BEEN just as caught up in the reunion between the siblings as the rest of the dinner guests, but with food and conversation came a return of her acute awareness that at her right shoulder sat Henri-Antoine. She pretended an interest in the food, but one sidelong glance at him and she lost her appetite for the mushroom-stuffed pasta. If the upturned cuffs of his lavender silk frock coat were any indication, then he was dressed resplendently. The silk was smothered in an intricate embroidery of honeysuckle, vine leaves, and tiny bees, and the white lace ruffle that covered his wrists was delicately paper-thin. So when she turned at her name, her lashes remained lowered, and she noted that the front panels and the buttons of his frock coat were similarly embroidered, the lace stock under his square chin matching the lace at his wrists. And how could she not fix on his mouth after he briefly touched a linen napkin to his lips.

"You are staring at me without blinking, Miss Crisp," he observed as he put aside the napkin. "Which makes me wonder—Do I have spinach caught between my teeth?"

Lisa's gaze flew up to his, startled, and then she clapped a hand to her mouth to stifle a giggle.

He smiled and winked. "That's better. I like it when you look me in the eye. It allows me to admire you. And now I see that your fine eyes do indeed match the blue of the silk bows to your gown. Which, by the way, is very pretty."

"Teddy and her mother have been most generous."

"And with the expertise of their seamstress, too. I'd no idea the small of your back was so narrow—"

"My lord! You can't say—"

"I just have. Now don't jump. Give me your hand."

He let his slide under the table and she followed his lead. And when they found each other's fingers and fumbled, then held on, neither could stifle a smile. And while he was searching out her hand, he made certain to look the other way, holding his glass for a footman to refill. He rested their entwined fingers on the skirts of his frock coat which covered his silken thigh, set the glass down after taking a sip, and turned to her with an expression that suggested they were the merest of acquaintances.

Before he could say a word she quipped, "That was expertly done. So expert in fact I suspect you've done this sort of thing before. Possibly with an actress or a mistress or two...?"

Taken aback, he almost spat his wine across the table, only managing to swallow it down hard at the last moment, then cough into his fist before taking a deep breath. He followed this up with another sip from his glass to calm himself. He squeezed her fingers, and when he could speak was curt.

"Don't be absurd! I've never—"

"Good. That is gratifying." She frowned and squeezed his fingers in return and regarded him with such a serious expression that he wondered what was the matter. "The thought of you holding hands with another makes me sad."

"Does it?" he drawled, schooling his features to remain neutral, though he could not stop the sudden onset of lightheadedness at her admission.

He wondered if he was still feeling the effects of the previous night, for though he had tempered his drinking and smoking to ensure his health remained robust, he had not fallen into bed until almost dawn, and then slept most of the day away. But then he realized this feeling had nothing to do with smoke-filled rooms and late nights and everything to do with Miss Lisa Crisp. When she continued to regard him with a frown, he said gently,

"I never want you to be sad. You do know that don't you?"

She nodded and her frown lifted. She took a swift glance about the table, saw that everyone was otherwise occupied, and said cheerfully, "Perhaps it is the wine making me sad, or happy, or both. I may have drunk a little too much, too quickly. It isn't the same as drinking tea or coffee or fruit punch, is it?"

"Were you not permitted wine in Gerrard Street?"

"There was no cause for me to drink it. I never dined in the dining room. And I suppose the Warners did not want me drinking wine on my own."

"You ate dinner alone?"

When she nodded it was his turn to frown, but like her, he did not let it linger. He was enjoying holding her hand too much to let his anger with the Warners and her life with them ruin their evening. He leaned sideways as he picked up his glass, hoping this action would mask his intent of confiding in her, and said while looking out across the table, and not at her,

"I missed your company today."

Her fingers shifted in his, which made him look at her. She smiled and confessed,

"And I missed you... I had hoped you would be at Crecy for nuncheon."

"That had been my intention. But my days are not my own while there are guests for the wedding. Elsie's disappointment at my absence was tempered by your presence. She likes you."

"I like her. And she loves you very much. You are a devoted brother."

"She is my sister. How could I not love her?"

Lisa looked down the table to where the Lady Mary and her brother were deep in conversation, heads together and peering at a miniature portrait in a gold frame. Three similar portraits were on the table before them. They were of Charles Fitzstuart's children home in France with their mother. She turned to Henri-Antoine with a smile.

"I have yet to meet your elder brother, but I suspect you and he are also close."

"In sentiment, if not in age. He is fifteen years my senior, and I am fifteen years older than Elsie. In many ways we grew up as you did."

"As I did?"

"As an only child."

"The gap in your ages allowed your mother to devote herself singularly to your infancies. But whatever the differences in years, you will always have each other."

"I visited Elsie before I came here tonight, to apologize for not being at nuncheon, and she could not wait to share with me your good deed."

"My good deed?"

"As scribe for Simone, her night nurse."

"That was to be a secret between Simone, Elsie, and me."

"My sister keeps no secrets from her parents, or her brothers."

Lisa inclined her head at this. "I did not expect she would, though I had hoped she might for Simone's sake. The poor girl is frightened out of her wits at losing her position within your mother's household and being sent back to France—"

"Why? All because she cannot form her letters? My mother would never be so callous. Simone should know this, as should all the servants in my mother's household."

"But Simone knows the importance your mother—and Elsie's papa—place on education, particularly the education of their daughter who is to be a duchess one day. She also knows Elsie is surrounded by persons who can benefit her upbringing. As someone who can read but not write, she feels inadequate."

"My mother and Kinross place great importance on education, that is true, but just as important to them is truthfulness, loyalty, and-and feelings. What is the worth of an education to a person if that person is a liar, a cheat, and has a heart of stone? But do not look so worried. Simone will be taught to form her letters, my mother will see to it, and then she will be able to write to her family, and feel more at ease." He sipped at his wine and then added, unable to hide his smile, "Elsie was particularly taken with your pretty writing box. Thank you for showing it to her. She now wants one of her own, and it must be as pretty and have as many secret drawers as the one owned by her friend Lisa."

"Perhaps she will receive one for her ninth birthday…? And why would she not want one of her own. It is the most beautiful writing box in all of England, and I shall cherish it always, and because it was a gift—"

"A mere token."

"—from you," she concluded and gave his fingers a harder squeeze than he anticipated, which made him flinch in surprise. She giggled. "Forgive me, but it is a gift, not a *mere* anything!"

"My dear Miss Crisp, you may have just damaged my fingers and tomorrow I am required to bowl at the cricket match—"

"You bowl with your left hand? Teddy is left-handed too."

"I see that is of more interest to you what hand is dominant than if you have bruised my fingers."

"Rot!" she retorted and pouted. "You have lovely hands, but your fingers are still much stronger than mine, so—"

"Lovely hands? As lovely as my kissable mouth…?"

Lisa felt her face grow hot under his steady gaze. So she showed him her profile, chin level with the table. "I will not feed your vanity, be you thorn or no!"

Far from taking offence, he laughed out loud before he could stop himself. He hissed in her ear. "Witch! The sooner I can get you to Bath the better!"

She turned her head at that and found him so close that their noses almost touched. They stared at one another, breath held, and she said in a whisper something that left him nonplussed and wondering.

"That may not be soon enough for—"

"Harry? Harry!"

It was Jack, and he wasn't the only one looking across the table at Henri-Antoine and Lisa Crisp in expectation of having their attention. Pudding had come and gone, and the table cleared of all but the coffee pot and cups and saucers. Hearing his name, the couple sprang apart, their entwined fingers pulling free, both keeping their hands under the table, as if by showing them there would be tell-tale signs of their illicit hand-holding.

"Uncle Bryce says you have an announcement to make," Jack said with a sheepish grin at the couple. "And now is as good a time as any to make it, because after coffee we'll all be moving back into the drawing room. Apparently there will be dancing, and I am required to practice the minuet—"

"—for the ball," Teddy interrupted. "Granny Kate and Papa have volunteered to be our orchestra. Although, I think—and Mama agrees—it would be an excellent notion if Papa and I were to dance the minuet first, so Jack can see how it is properly done."

"Indeed?! Am I such a bad dancer?" Jack asked indignant.

Henri-Antoine pushed back his chair and stood. "You are, Jack. You have two left feet. Mr. Bryce could offer you some pointers."

"Thank you! Thank you *very* much!" Jack said without heat, but his facial expression was one of such affront that it had everyone laughing at his expense.

"What have you there, Harry?" Teddy asked, intrigued, when Henri-Antoine picked up the large parcel wrapped in cloth one of his lads had earlier brought into the room; he propped it on a chair facing the table. "Is this another surprise?"

"Yes. Another surprise."

Jack's two left feet were instantly forgotten.

"But a small surprise. Nothing can compete with the appearance of Cousin Charles."

"That is true," Teddy agreed, and she leaned over and gave her uncle a swift kiss on the cheek. "Nothing will ever quite surprise us again, Uncle Charles. Will it, Mama?"

Lady Mary smiled and shook her head. "No. Nothing, my darling... But I feel for poor Harry—"

"Oh, don't you worry about *poor* Harry!" Jack scoffed. "Apparently *I'm* the one who cannot dance!"

There was general laughter which considerably lightened the mood, and all attention focused again on the wrapped parcel. Henri-Antoine looked to Teddy.

"This is for you both, but most particularly for you, Teddy. So I am confident Jack will allow you the honor of unwrapping it."

Teddy and Jack looked at one another and then at Henri-Antoine. It was Teddy who voiced what Jack was thinking too.

"But you have been generous to a fault, Harry. So much so that Jack and I can never ever thank you enough for what you have done for us, that this gift is surely too much."

"This is but a token—"

"His lordship only deals in tokens, not gifts," Lisa quipped.

Only after she had spoken and there was a heavy silence, all eyes shifting to look at her in surprise, did Lisa realize she had voiced her playful taunt out loud. So much for not drawing attention to herself and staying in the background as her cousins had instructed. What would Henri-Antoine think of her forwardness? What would Teddy's family think? She dared not look his way. Her face felt hot; mortified, she lowered her lashes and looked at her hands in her lap.

"That is very true, Miss Crisp," Jack agreed buoyantly, breaking the silence. And in an effort to make her feel comfortable again, and to relegate her outburst to the commonplace, he added with a grin, looking at his best friend, "Tokens or gifts, call them what you will, you have always been the most loyal and generous of men, Harry. And I raise my coffee cup to you."

Henri-Antoine gave a short bow. "Perhaps you should reserve judgment until you see what is under the cloth. Though, before you unwrap it, I have one stipulation: This is to hang in your Mount Street townhouse." He looked at Teddy, who had come to stand beside him. "Not to make you homesick, Teddy, but to make you more at home."

Everyone leaned forward in their chairs as Teddy, with Henri-Antoine's help, carefully removed the cord, and then peeled away the felt wrapping. What was revealed was a painting in a heavy gilt frame. It was a landscape, a morning scene, with a spectacular use of contrast between light and dark to capture the radiance of the dawn. Light filtered through trees and across the undulating hills of a Cotswold countryside in early spring, and drew the eye across the canvas to an Elizabethan manor house built from indigenous yellow stone that seemed to glow.

Granny Kate asked what those few at the table did not recognize, grumbling,

"Will someone enlighten this blind old lady what we are all looking at!"

Christopher Bryce quickly apologized to his mother, and in an under voice described the painting, while Teddy, after the initial shock of gazing at the most wonderful work of art she had ever seen, threw her arms around Henri-Antoine. Jack was out of his chair, and did likewise. Both had so many questions, as did the others around the table that Henri-Antoine was urged to tell them everything he knew about the painting. But then Teddy looked to her stepfather and then at her mother, and finally at Henri-Antoine, and said with a knowing laugh,

"Ha! That gentleman you told me was a surveyor come to check the boundaries wasn't a surveyor at all, was he?"

Christopher Bryce smiled, a glance at Lady Mary. "He was not. I did wonder when you might enquire why a surveyor in a flamboyant black felt hat and carrying about a sketch pad did not have his waywiser with him. And as I recall, you were rather rude to him when he set up his easel and paints."

"He wouldn't show me what he was about," Teddy countered with a pout. She looked to Henri-Antoine. "And it was you who sent this chap in the black hat to paint Abbeywood?"

"I commissioned Joseph Wright, yes," Henri-Antoine told her.

"Good—Lord! Joseph Derby? *The* Wright of Derby was at Abbeywood?" Jack exclaimed. "This is too much. Too, too much, Harry," he muttered, shaking his head as he continued to stare at the painting.

"It's done now. And turned out rather nicely," Henri-Antoine replied, points of color in his cheeks the only sign of his embarrassment at such an effusive response to his gift. "And Jack has the perfect place to hang it, Teddy. In the morning room, so you will see it at breakfast. The color palette is perfectly complemented by the curtains and wallpaper Jack chose."

"I do? It does? I chose?" And when his family laughed, well aware it was Harry and not Jack who would've had the greatest hand in decorating the Mount Street townhouse, he blustered, "Yes! Yes! Perfect spot! Perfect spot for this marvelous creation." He leaned into his best friend and said under his breath, "Now I know why you made me keep the space above the sideboard clear..."

Teddy did not hear this aside because she had gone over to Lisa, pulled her out of her chair, and brought her to stand with her before the painting, a hand about her waist and holding her close.

Everyone followed her lead, and now the entire family, except for Lady Fittlewood who chose to remain beside Granny Kate and drink tea and give her a running observation, now stood in a semi-circle admiring the painting.

"What do you think of our painting, Lisa?" Teddy asked.

Lisa gazed at the landscape in oils.

"It is wonderful, Teddy, and Mr. Wright is a gifted painter. I see in this painting why you love Abbeywood so much. It is just as magical a place as Treat, but in a different way—in an untamed way, as God intended."

"Well said, Miss Crisp," Christopher Bryce agreed.

Teddy put up her brows, and smiled at Lisa, a smile she knew well from their school days that indicated she was about to say or do something outrageous. It put Lisa on the alert, and she felt her smile widening in anticipation.

"Is this Wright of Derby a painter of significance?" Teddy asked with feigned wonder. "I can *see* that he is a superb craftsman, but I love Abbeywood, so anything to do with Abbeywood is wonderful to me, and I am the first to admit I know nothing of paintings, so I am not the best judge, am I?"

"Significant painter?" Jack repeated, almost shrilly. "Theodora! The man has exhibited at the Royal Academy. He painted *The Orrery* and *An Experiment on a Bird in the Air Pump* and—

Teddy shuddered. "Sounds frightful."

"—in my opinion," Jack added, warming to his topic, "is the greatest living exponent of *chiaroscuro* there is! Isn't that so, Harry."

"It is, Jack."

"Chiar—*oscuro*, Jack?" Teddy enquired, another mischievous side-long glance at Lisa. "Whatever is *chiaroscuro*?"

"It's a painting term for a technique on how an artist uses light and dark to highlight the subject matter of his work," Jack explained seriously, seemingly the only one who was unaware that Teddy was teasing him. Even Granny Kate heard the inflection in her voice, alerting her to Teddy's playfulness. "If you look here, at the way he has managed to capture the contrast between the light and the shadow on the stonework—"

"Dear me, Sir John Cavendish," Teddy interrupted. "I am stagger-ingly impressed. All those years wandering about abroad were good for something after all. You actually did ponder in front of paintings, when all the time I thought—"

"Teddy!" her mother cut in stridently.

"What? What did you think?" Jack demanded, face aglow at Teddy's spreading smile. He said to Henri-Antoine, "What did you write in your letters home?"

"My dear fellow," Henri-Antoine drawled, affronted, though his top lip twitched. "I have no idea what you or Teddy are talking about."

Teddy and Lisa burst into a fit of the giggles at Jack's red-faced embarrassment, and hugged each other. They could not help themselves. But no one minded. In fact everyone was all smiles to see these two friends so happy, and soon the girls had calmed, and were dabbing dry their eyes.

Christopher Bryce suggested they all remove to the drawing room, where the furniture had now been pushed to the walls and the carpet taken up in readiness for dancing.

Teddy grabbed Jack's hand.

"Let's tell her and everyone now, before the dancing."

Jack nodded and smiled. "If that is your wish."

"Jack and I have one last surprise for you," Teddy declared.

She waited for her family to fall silent and look her way, then grabbed Lisa's hand and drew her back beside her. She put her arm through Jack's, and after looking up at him with a smile, announced, sandwiched between her husband-to-be and her best friend,

"Jack and I have made this decision together, and it is one we want you all to embrace. We hope it won't come as a surprise to any of you, and we sincerely hope that after giving our decision due consideration, you will see that it is the best outcome for all of us." She smiled at Lisa and then again addressed her family. "Jack and I have decided to begin our married life by sharing it with another, one who is like a sister to me in all but blood. Lisa is to come live with us, and be part of our life, and share in everything we do. Not as a companion, or a servant, or a dependent, but as one of us." She looked at Jack and then impulsively kissed his cheek. "Of all the wedding presents Jack could possibly give me, this is the most wanted. We hope you think so too."

TWENTY-FIVE

I T WAS A gloriously sunny day without a cloud in the sky. The air was crisp. A light breeze rustled the tops of the trees. Swans glided along the surface of the lake. Children ran about playing and laughing on the gentle slope of the lawn, watched over by nurses and attendants, while their parents sat under marquees in the shade. Servants who had not drawn the short straw to be in attendance on their masters were at their leisure to enjoy a picnic lunch under their own marquee.

Everyone was focused on the cricket match in progress on the south lawn. The Duke's Eleven, captained by his son and heir, and comprising family members and household servants, were out in the field, while the Gentleman's Eleven, captained by Teddy's uncle Dair, Lord Strathsay, and made up of a team of noble guests, had won the toss and elected to bat.

Lunch was called, just as the best batsmen for the Gentleman's Eleven, Jamie Fitzstuart-Banks and Bully Knatchbull reached a fifty-run partnership. Both teams came off the field to great applause and joined the spectators for a well-earned feast and a welcome respite in the shade.

Lisa and Teddy, who were under the marquee closest to the field, were soon joined by members of the Gentleman's Eleven—Lord Westby, Bully Knatchbull, Jamie Fitzstuart-Banks, and several of their teammates. With Teddy's two school friends, Vi and Meg, sweeping up to do their best to monopolize the time of those gentlemen they considered worthy of their attention. Notably absent from this group were Jack and Henri-Antoine. Although they were part of the Duke's Eleven, Teddy had expected her betrothed to seek her out, and Lisa had hoped Henri-Antoine would do likewise, as she had not had a chance to speak with him since Teddy's shock announcement to her family the night before.

AT THE ANNOUNCEMENT, Lisa's astonishment had been profound. She had no words, for Teddy and Jack's generosity, for their family's ready acceptance of her to be part of their lives, but most of all she had no idea what to say to Henri-Antoine. But before she could even turn to look his way, everyone swarmed forward to welcome her into the family and he had disappeared out into the night.

She could not remember dancing with Mr. Bryce or Jack, but she had. And she had danced with Teddy's Uncle Charles, too. There was lots of laughter, and music, and everyone was so happy.

Later that night, when she and Teddy were drifting off to sleep, tucked up in Teddy's bed, her friend had been so full of excitement for a future which now included her in all her plans, that Lisa did not have the heart to deflate her enthusiasm. She was in such a state of emotional turmoil she hardly knew what her future held.

Her predicament left her at a loss to know what to do or say, for anything she said or did would surely be misconstrued.

She had hoped to clear her thoughts with a good night's sleep, which would allow her to be rational and formulate a plan. But the morning did not provide her with clarity or relief, and she was soon swept along in the wake of Teddy's happiness.

What could she say or do but join her and hope that an answer would present itself after the wedding ceremony, for she would not— for anything in the world—ruin Teddy and Jack's big day. Resolved, she did her best to be involved, and to remind herself just where she was and whom she was with. The day was cloudless, the aspect of the monolithic Palladian house as backdrop to this summer idyll magical, and, all things considered, she had never felt prettier in her new floral gown, or happier, in the company of people who cared for her.

She had just handed off her plate to a footman and accepted a tumbler of iced punch when she was mentally shaken from her musings by a tall young man with a broad chest and a head of coal-black curls that fell about his handsome angular face. He looked familiar... She gave a start. She knew who it was, but although he had been pointed out to her while he was out in the middle of the field batting, only now, with him standing before her, did she finally recognize the friend from her school days in Chelsea. She was so happy to see him.

"Mr. Banks! I hardly recognized you. How quickly boys grow into men."

Jamie Fitzstuart-Banks smiled and flushed. He made her a short bow.

"The pleasure is mine, Miss Crisp. You have not changed at all."

Lisa laughed. "Oh dear! Should I be worried?" she teased.

"I always thought you the prettiest girl to ever step outside the gates of Blacklands," he stated. "Most importantly for me, you were the cleverest."

As ever with him, he was frank, with no hint of flirtation in his words or manner. He treated her as he found her, and he had never defined her by her sex. She was someone he could talk to about his interests, which was possibly why she had always been comfortable in his company.

"Would you care to take a walk, Miss Crisp?"

She could see no harm in taking a stroll with him, now nuncheon was over, and Teddy was deep in conversation with *The Horribles* and a couple of other guests with whom Lisa was not yet acquainted. Besides, she wanted to hear all his news, and they could not talk freely while Vi and Meg had an ear to their conversation.

"I would like that very much. Let me fetch my hat."

They exited the marquee without another word or look at the others their own age congregated in the shade, Lisa with her wide-brimmed straw hat secured by a silk ribbon tied in a bow about her coil of braids at her nape. She held her tumbler of punch at her bodice, and Jamie walked beside her with his hands clasped behind his back, shirtsleeves rolled to the elbow, and waistcoat unbuttoned and hanging loose because he was still feeling the effects of the summer's day after his stint at the crease.

Soon they were so deep in conversation while strolling the perimeter of the cricket field, recalling their school days and visits to the Chelsea Bun House, that neither noticed how far they had strayed from the marquee, or that it was almost time for the game to resume. Nor were they aware of the attention they had attracted, not only from the marquee where their mutual friends were gossiping amongst themselves, but also from senior members of the Roxton family. And one member in particular, whose brooding silence was nothing new to his family, but whose preoccupation with Miss Lisa Crisp was being keenly monitored, not only by his brother and his mother, but by his best friend.

"I MUST CONFESS," Jamie said with a diffident smile, "that when Teddy wrote and told me your whereabouts had been discovered, I was overjoyed, for you both, but also for myself. You did not take your leave of me. In fact, you disappeared from Blacklands so thoroughly it was as if you had not been there at all."

Lisa was contrite. "I am sorry I was unable to say my farewells. I was not permitted to leave you a letter. I did think of writing to you at Banks House. I knew your family would pass on a letter from me but... I thought it best for you that I cut all ties."

He stopped in the shadows of a stand of shade trees and looked down at her. But as he could not see her face he bent his knees to peer under the brim of her hat.

"But—Miss Crisp—"

"Lisa. And I have called you Jamie since our school days. That should not change, surely, now we are older?"

"Yes, of course. Lisa. Why would cutting ties be best for me? We were good friends. No! We were the best of friends. I've never known a friend quite like you. Apart from my mother, who listens as only a mother can, you were the only other person who encouraged my wish to become a physician. Did you think your expulsion from Blacklands would change our friendship?"

She shook her head and tilted her chin up so he could stand straight and still see her face.

"No. But I knew that if you discovered why I had been expelled you would do something chivalrous, and that would be foolish. I could not allow you to jeopardize your schooling. You are by far the cleverest boy—excuse me—*young man*—I know. And you must fulfill your wish to be a physician. Tell me: You have now graduated from your Physic Garden apprenticeship, have you not?"

He smiled. "I have. And I know this will mean something to you —" His smile widened into a grin. "I was awarded the Hans Sloane medal for my efforts."

"Oh, Jamie! That is wonderful news! Such wonderful news." She impulsively gave his arm a squeeze. "I am so proud of you!"

He grabbed her hand and held it for a moment.

"I knew you would be pleased for me. Thank you."

"Your parents must be so proud, too."

"They are. I do believe I am the first person in my mother's family to gain a qualification. As for Papa... His Lordship laughed out loud. Not in a derogatory way, because he has always been supportive of my scientific endeavors, but because, as he said, if he had managed to sit still in a schoolroom for more than five minutes, his tutors would've given *him* a medal."

"And your stepfather, the botanist. He must be pleased to have another scientist in the family."

"He is. And two of my brothers have followed in my footsteps and are now apprenticed at the Physic Garden. But the person who showed the most enthusiasm, just like you, is my step-mama—"

"Lady Strathsay?"

Jamie nodded. "Do you remember me telling you about Her Lady-ship's cultivation of the pineapple? I think she secretly hoped I would further my studies in botany and perhaps take on the curation of her pinery."

"If only so you could be nearer to your father, and to be better known to your half-brothers and sister perhaps?"

Jamie's brow cleared. "I'd not thought of that... There may be some truth in it..."

"And now you have completed your apprenticeship, I hear you are still keen to pursue your medical studies?"

"My determination has not changed. And I am happy to report that I have been accepted to Glasgow University's medical school, and will depart for the north in the autumn."

"I am so happy for you. I know how much you wanted this. I trust your family are reconciled to your choice of vocation and are supportive?"

"They are. And although Papa was a military hero, he has no wish for any of his sons to go into the army. But I am not convinced he sees medicine as the ideal vocation for the son of a nobleman, regardless of my irregular birth. Law or the Church, or even the Foreign Office would be his preference. And he no doubt could've got me in the door with one word. But he is not against my choice, and has agreed to fund my studies."

"I am glad for you he has," Lisa assured him. "There is so much work to be done in every facet of medicine, that your scientific mind cannot be lost to any other sphere of knowledge," she added seriously, warming to her topic. "And I hope that with his son studying medicine, Lord Strathsay—and indeed your Roxton relatives—will take a greater interest in medical science. Much could be achieved if only those in positions of power and influence, and who have the means, chose to become patrons of such worthwhile medical endeavors."

"Well said, Miss—Lisa! You always were passionate about helping those less fortunate than ourselves."

"Oh, do forgive me if I am lecturing," Lisa apologized with a light laugh. "I suppose it is because I know from experience what it is to go without. And I have heard firsthand about the pitiable funding meted out to medical research from Dr. Warner's breakfast lectures."

"When Teddy confided you'd been helping in Warner's Dispensary for the sick poor, I admit I was not surprised. Your concern for the plight of the poor combined with your interest in my chosen vocation, I often wished if any one person could attend medical school with me, it was you."

"You will make a far better physician than I ever could. As I said to Teddy, I have no stomach for anatomizing, whereas, if I remember correctly, you took great delight in telling me how you investigated the internal organs of a cow your grandfather had just slaughtered—"

"A sheep. Ha! Yes! Your face went green, though you did make an effort to remain interested. I must have been a dead bore at times."

"Never a bore. Though I could have had less description on how you pulled out its entrails while they were still warm and moving to investigate the contents of its stomach."

They laughed, and in his joy at their renewed easy-going camaraderie, which he had missed since their school days, and because he had always considered her like a sister, he confided in her:

"You may decry the lack of patronage for medical science by our social superiors, but it should please you to know that there are those amongst my esteemed noble relatives who already do take a concerted interest in its advancement. I've been sworn to secrecy, but I will break my confidence for you because I know how much it will mean to you. I've been offered a position upon enrolment in my medical studies as a trustee of the Fournier Foundation, a foundation that—

"—provides funds to physicians who tend to the sick poor, and to anatomical schools. Yes, I am intimate with the foundation's work. Dr. Warner has applied for such funding, and I had the opportunity to meet a number of the trustees."

"Then you are aware the foundation is wholly financed by the Duke of Roxton's brother—"

"Lord Henri-Antoine?" Lisa interrupted, and hoped in her surprise her voice remained steady. "I had a suspicion... Though I was unaware it was his wealth alone that provided the means for the foundation to function."

"His Lordship was willed an enormous inheritance by his father, it is said because he knew his son would never be able to pursue the usual careers open to second sons due to his affliction. You are aware His Lordship suffers with the falling sickness—"

"I am."

"I assumed, as Teddy's friend, you would. It's the family's open secret. Everyone knows about it but no one ever mentions it. I remember as a boy asking why His Lordship is followed everywhere he goes by Goliath-like brutes, and why no one else noticed them lurking about in the shadows. I guess I thought I had conjured them up! Papa set me straight."

"And His Lordship has taken you into his confidence about the Fournier Foundation...?"

"He did. Only recently. Once he learned I was off to Glasgow. I suppose he wanted to be certain I was serious about pursuing a career in the medical profession."

"I'm so glad he did. Having a student physician on the board is an excellent idea. For how else can the trustees know the plight of medical students if not from a student himself?"

"Do you know, that's what he—what Lord Henri-Antoine said! He has this idea of offering scholarships to students identified as outstanding candidates to study as physicians but who are struggling to pay their way. And once they finish their studies, they would be bonded to a dispensary or a hospital for a number of years, as a way of repaying the foundation for its financial assistance. I already know of a couple of fellows who would greatly benefit from such a scheme."

"That is—that is such a worthwhile use of the foundation's funds... I am—I am so glad to hear it," Lisa replied, touched to learn Henri-Antoine was intent on implementing such a scheme. "I do hope he is able to find the funds to implement such scholarships."

"Oh, don't you worry about that!" Jamie said with a grin. "The interest alone from the capital he invested provides over two thousand pounds annually for the foundation's work. And that's without touching the interest from the principal he himself can draw on to live. So I should think Lord Henri-Antoine will be able to do whatever he wants without any hardship whatsoever, don't you?"

Lisa's eyes widened. She could barely comprehend such a staggering sum in interest, so she found herself incapable of calculating the principal, or even wanting to. She had surmised that Henri-Antoine was wealthy, but not to what extent. Somehow it seemed impolite and too personal to dwell on such particulars. But she did wonder how Jamie had come by such figures, and he told her without her even having to ask.

"My goodness!" she muttered. "I had no idea..."

"Not many do. He didn't tell me. Why would he? I overheard my father and his brother discussing the foundation, and of course my ears pricked up. But I know you would never break a confidence—"

"Never..." She looked up at him. "I think it for the best if you not mention to anyone that we discussed the foundation, or that you know anything about Lord Henri-Antoine's personal finances. For his sake, as much as your own."

He made her a small bow. "You have my word."

She nodded and smiled. "Perhaps we should head back…? Won't you be called soon to resume playing?"

"Yes! Yes! We must! I'd forgotten all about the match."

He picked up her empty tumbler, which she had placed at her feet to retie the ribbons of her hat, and kept hold of it so she would not have to carry it. They returned the way they had come, Jamie walking on Lisa's right to shield her from the sun.

"I cannot tell you how many times I went to the bun house in the hopes of seeing you there," he confessed. "I wished by some miracle of circumstance you might appear. I bought countless buns in the hopes you would."

"There were many times when I too wished to visit the Chelsea Bun House, just to see if you, too, were there. But you must believe me that it was for the best that I stayed away."

They walked on in companionable silence and when they were just a few feet from the shade of the marquee, Jamie turned to Lisa, back to the huddle of persons who were watching them intently.

"I wonder if you would do me the honor of allowing me to write to you from Glasgow?"

"I would like that very much."

"But you aren't going to tell me what happened that forced you to leave Blacklands, are you?"

Lisa removed her straw hat, saying with a smile up at him and a shake of her head, "It is unimportant. What is, is that we have found each other again, and we can continue our friendship."

"Oi! Banks!"

It was Bully Knatchbull, and he had stepped out of the shade of the marquee with a cricket bat under each arm. He made Lisa a quick bow of acknowledgment and then thrust one of the bats at Jamie.

"Come on! The game awaits, and our captain wants a word…"

TWENTY-SIX

Several of the female guests, Vi Knatchbull and Meg Medway among them, followed the players to the edge of the playing field where preparations were taking place in readiness to resume the match. And as they fluttered their fans in the summer sunshine, chatting amongst themselves and pretending a disinterest in the game, their admiring sidelong glances from under their straw hats were directed at both teams, who were in close proximity. The plethora of manly physiques were shown to advantage in knitted breeches and shirt fronts without cravats, and sleeves rolled to the elbow allowed for plenty of bare skin, increasing the tempo of fan-fluttering.

Bully Knatchbull and Jamie Fitzstuart-Banks were in conversation, while Jack, who had the ball, was talking with his captain, Freddy, Lord Alston. This left Lord Westby and Lord Henri-Antoine, who were preparing on the fringe of the group, to be pounced on by Vi and Meg. They were encouraged to come closer by Lord Westby, not because he was interested in flirting with either of them, but because he sought to use them to gain his revenge on Lord Henri-Antoine. He had waited this opportunity for a very long time, and he was certain he now had the means by which to cause his friend the kind of angst he had experienced when his mistress had flirted with Henri-Antoine, making him feel inadequate.

He had noticed Lisa from almost the moment she had appeared at the cricket match, and he made enquiries about the fetching little beauty. But it was what Vi and Meg confided about the girl to anyone who would listen, coupled with Henri-Antoine's interest—all through nuncheon he had sat in brooding silence watching Jamie Fitzstuart-Banks and Miss Crisp stroll the lawn's perimeter—that set him on his present course of action. He glanced at Henri-Antoine now, and sure enough, his gaze was fixed on the girl—if that wasn't infatuation, he didn't know what was!

Knowing Vi and Meg were within earshot, he asked in a loud, but noncommittal tone, "Jack! I say! Who's the pretty wisp of a thing talking to your bride?"

Jack looked up from inspecting the cricket ball, handed it to Freddy and came over to join Henri-Antoine and Seb Westby. He followed Westby's gaze across to Teddy and Lisa, but before he could ask him to repeat his question, Vi Knatchbull answered.

"I told you, Westby. She's the poor girl who was at Blacklands with us—"

"—and got herself expelled," stuck in Meg Medway with a snigger.

"However did she manage to do that?" Westby asked with feigned surprise, a glance at Henri-Antoine. "She don't look the type to get herself into trouble... And being a pauper, she couldn't afford to, could she? Whereas you, my dear Vi," he drawled and winked at Bully Knatchbull's sister, "are all sorts of trouble, you and Meg both. And no doubt cost your papas a pretty penny to get you out of trouble, too."

Both girls giggled and appeared bashful behind their fluttering fans.

"She's not worth your interest, Westby," Henri-Antoine stated flatly, tearing his gaze from Lisa and pretending to adjust the diamond-encrusted shirt buckle keeping his shirt front closed.

Westby put up his brows. "Is she not, Harry? And you would know this—*how*?"

"Jamie Fitzstuart-Banks certainly thinks she is," stuck in Meg with a smug smile, and yet when Henri-Antoine glared at her, dropped her smile and her gaze.

"Why would Banks think—" Westby began and was cut off.

"You're becoming a bore, Westby," Henri-Antoine enunciated coldly.

Jack looked from Henri-Antoine to Seb and back again, and hissed at his best friend's ear, "What's going on? What pauper? Who was expelled from what?"

"It doesn't matter," Henri-Antoine said through his teeth. "Drop it."

"I caught her kissing Jamie Banks behind the Chelsea Bun House!" Violet burst out in a much louder voice than she intended, and gave an involuntary nervous laugh.

"Did you indeed, Vi?" Westby purred, and with a lift of his brows encouraged her to continue.

"I was never more shocked, and neither was the headmistress. And did the proud little pauper deny it? Not her! She confessed to it. Bold as you please. And then refused to give *him* up to save herself. She'd have remained at Blacklands if only she'd named him. Little fool!"

"Dear me, Vi," Westby drawled with a heavy sigh of false sincerity. "Little fool indeed."

"I don't know whom you're telling tales about, but I don't like it one bit," Jack grumbled.

"And what's worse," Vi added in a loud breathless whisper, ignoring Jack's censure now that she had several pairs of male eyes fixed on her, including the unwavering gaze of Lord Henri-Antoine. "It happened more than once. We saw them behind the shop too many times to count. Isn't that the truth, Meg?!"

Meg looked about at the silent faces, and then at her friend who was glaring at her in a way that told her to agree to the lie or face the consequences of her displeasure later.

"Yes! Yes! It's all true. Every word," she agreed unconvincingly. Though she nodded, and nodded again, adding for good measure, with a contemptuous sniff, "And they weren't sharing a bun back behind the shop, if you get my meaning."

"*Well!*" Westby said with exaggerated emphasis, adding with tongue firmly planted in his cheek, and another sidelong glance at Henri-Antoine. "It looks as if our hero of the hour not only knows how to handle his bat, but his female admirers—"

"Shut up, Westby!" Henri-Antoine snapped, his gaze on Vi and Meg. "As for you two..."

Vi and Meg smiled saucily, huddling together and bobbing curtsies. Emboldened by Lord Westby's misplaced encouragement they were thrilled when England's wealthiest bachelor and the brother of the Duke of Roxton had finally turned his singular attention their way. They had misjudged his mood entirely, which made his blunt denunciation all the more devastating.

He stared at Meg. "You're a bitch. And you," he said with undisguised disgust, gaze transferring to Vi, "you're worse. You're a bitch and a snitch. A pox on you both!"

"Egad, Harry, that was uncalled for, surely?" Westby complained weakly with a sad shake of his head as Meg Medway and Vi Knatchbull burst into tears and fled, howling, up the slope of the lawn towards the marquees. Privately, he was enjoying every moment of his friend's discomfort. "Unless," he goaded, "you, like our hero Banks, has some —um—prior *experience* of Miss Crisp that you'd care to share—"

"That's it, Westby—" Henri-Antoine growled, taking a step toward Westby with fists clenched.

But at the mention of Lisa by name, Jack came to life, shouldered past Henri-Antoine and stood over Lord Westby.

"No one has anything to share about Miss Crisp," he seethed, glaring at Westby. He took a menacing sweep about him. "No one. Not now. Not ever. Or you'll answer to me. Got it?"

There was a deathly silence amongst the group, in marked contrast to the noise and activity surrounding them. And then, just as Teddy and Lisa announced their arrival with flushed cheeks and smiles, Henri-Antoine turned on Jack with a sneer, hands still clenched into fists.

"Got it? Oh yes, you've given us all a mind's eye full of just what you've got yourself, Jack Cavendish."

Jack blinked. He flushed scarlet at the inference. And when Henri-Antoine went to turn away, he grabbed his arm and pulled him back around.

"I don't like your tone!"

"I don't bloody well care!"

"Take back what you said! Take it back!"

Henri-Antoine pulled his arm free. "Go to hell!"

He stormed off. Jack would have followed, but Teddy caught at his arm and held on. It was Lisa who went after Henri-Antoine. She picked up her petticoats, and rushed across the lawn as he strode out towards the cricket pitch. She only managed to catch him up when he suddenly stopped, looked to the sky, closed his eyes, and took a deep breath. He stood there like that, as a statue, with his face warming in the sun, for several seconds before sensing someone was behind him. He dropped his chin and let out a breath.

"Go away! Damn you! Leave me in peace!"

TWENTY-SEVEN

"I WILL. If that's what you want. But first we need to talk."

Henri-Antoine swiveled about to face Lisa. But if he was surprised she was the one who had followed him, he did not show it. In fact, he stared at her, dark eyes expressionless, as if she were a stranger, and kept his lips pressed together. He wasn't going to be the one to start a conversation, not with her.

She swallowed down her nervousness and refused to cower. It was time to be brave. So she came closer, removed her fingers from her petticoats, straightened her spine, and held her hands close against her bodice. She hoped that by effecting a pretense of restraint she could remain in control and not allow her feelings to bubble up and overwhelm her. In a small way his aloofness helped; living with her cousins' intransigence meant she was resilient to offence and not easily overwhelmed.

"You left the dinner early. I hope it was not on my account, or because you were unwell."

He stared at her for so long she thought he was not about to reply. And when he did, his response sent her spirits plummeting, yet she would not let him see how much he upset her.

"I left because there was nothing to keep me there."

"Oh? The prospect of watching Jack dance with his two left feet, or standing up with me, was not inducement enough?"

"No."

"I wish you had stayed."

Again he said nothing, and again she waited. They stood a few feet apart, both with so much to say, and yet saying nothing. That they were now the actors in a deeply personal performance being played out in an open-air theater to a rapt audience did not occur to them. Everyone from the cricket players on the edge of the field, to the family and guests under the marquees on the hill, the handful of upper servants at the windows and those under their own marquee, to the gardeners resting in the shade, and the local tenant farmers and their families who had walked across to join in the day at the Duke's invitation, all eyes were on the Duke of Roxton's enigmatic younger brother and the poor girl from Soho.

It was Lisa who broke the silence.

"You're angry with me. I do not know why that is when I—"

"Spare me your indignation, Miss Crisp. I neither have the inclination or patience for your garbled excuses."

"My-my *garbled*—excuses? I have not the slightest notion what excuses, garbled or otherwise, you think I possess."

"Let's end this here and now. Put in simple terms: You accepted a better offer."

"Accepted a better...a better—*offer*?"

He rolled his eyes and clenched his jaw. "Are you intent on repeating everything I say?"

"I find that I must because I have no idea what you are talking about."

"So you have just said, Miss Crisp—"

"Am I no longer Lisa to you?"

His voice was cold. "You are no longer anything to me, Miss Crisp."

It was her turn to press her lips together, and to stifle a sob. She tried to hide that his words sliced deep, but she could not conceal the desolation in her eyes, which instantly filled with tears. She took a breath, and kept her gaze on his chest, on the small diamond-encrusted heart-shaped shirt buckle.

"His Lordship is-is—retracting his-his offer of a house in the country, pin money, and a companion?" she asked in what she hoped was a light tone, and with a watery sniff. "Does His Lordship forget he made such an offer and that I accepted it in-in good faith?"

He took a step closer. "Retracting? *Good faith*? You dare to imagine you are the injured party? Say it like it is. You received and accepted a better offer."

"No. I-I will not! You cannot make me say what is not—what is not true."

He threw up a hand in frustration. He was suddenly dry in the mouth, and the sun beating down on him was making his eyes ache and his temple throb. What was worse, she was upset. He hated himself for making her miserable. But the way he was feeling physically, and the unalterable fact she'd been taken from him, made him harsh.

"*Not true?* Oh, for God's sake! Are you pretending you didn't know? That you had no hint of what was to come last night. That Teddy's announcement was to you as a bolt of lightning that appears as if from nowhere? You cannot think me that buffle-headed!"

"It *was* as you say—a bolt of lightning, and it-it—*hit* me, as it must have you, suddenly and without warning. It was a-a shock. And it was *not* an offer. How can it be an offer when I was not given a choice?"

He grunted his disbelief.

"You made no protest to the contrary."

Her gaze flew up to his. Her voice was clear and strong and full of indignation.

"And how does His Lordship propose I was to do that? I was in shock. Nor was it the time or place to say anything to the contrary. Teddy and Jack were so happy, and so were their family. You must see that, surely?"

HE DID SEE IT, and she made perfect sense, but he did not want to see it, and nothing made sense to him anymore. He was in shock himself. Teddy's announcement had hit him as if he had been struck by lightning. One minute he saw a future, sharing his country manor house with Lisa, and the next, that future was taken from him, *she* was taken from him, and he left with nothing. He felt swindled.

The demon on his shoulder wanted him to believe that she could not be entirely blameless, that she must have known something of what Teddy proposed. After all, they had spent years at school together. They were best friends. Best friends shared confidences and kept secrets. Best friends remained true to one another. How could he compete with that—with Teddy?

He let the demon persuade him that she had led him on; she was just like the rest of the females from the lower orders who threw themselves at him. They wanted what they could get out of him. They did not want him for himself, and they certainly would not want him if they knew he was cursed with the falling sickness. And if he'd not had position and wealth, what was he, and how wanted would he be? But he was pragmatic. He'd wanted what they could give him, too, and that had suited him just fine at the time.

But Lisa... He had thought her different in every way...

Intuition. Common sense. His finer feelings. All warned him the demon was wrong. The demon was just making mischief. It wanted him to believe the worst of her because he believed the worst of himself. The demon was taking advantage of him because he was in shock. He was in shock because Teddy's pronouncement had made him realize just how much Miss Lisa Crisp meant to him, and how unworthy he was of her.

And then the demon reminded him about the salacious gossip he'd just been fed about Lisa and Jamie Banks. Gossip he would've considered baseless had he not spent a brooding half hour watching them strolling about the perimeter of the cricket field. And so he was inclined to think there was a grain of truth to it. They had walked so close together that there were several times when they had brushed arms, and they had talked and talked and not stopped for breath. Jamie had carried her tumbler for her, and he was a strapping young man just like his father, and just as handsome, and knowing their backgrounds, he was certain they shared a mutual interest in the medical sciences.

The deterioration in his health, Teddy's shock announcement at dinner, his feelings of inadequacy, and the mental image of Lisa in comfortable conversation with the physically robust Jamie Fitzstuart-Banks, all set him on the path to self-destruction.

He let the demon have its way.

"Bravo, Miss Crisp. I am almost convinced by your performance. As convinced as I was at the oak tree, when you led me to believe you had never kissed another. But there, too, I allowed myself to be taken in."

Lisa blinked at him, mortified.

"You think—You think I have-I have kiss-*kissed* another the way I kissed you?"

"Have you?"

"Need you ask me that?"

He put up his chin. "Need you hesitate? You either have or you have not."

She swallowed, sadness making her shoulders droop. Her voice was barely above a whisper.

"I have not, sir."

He put up his brows in arrogant surprise.

"Indeed? Perhaps not behind an oak tree, but behind the Chelsea Bun House...?"

"Behind the—" Her gaze flew up to his again and her throat constricted. "You hold against me one kiss between a girl and a boy who look upon each other as brother and sister?"

"Brother? And-and *sister*? I watched you taking a stroll with our batting hero—as did everyone else here today. I doubt anyone thought 'there goes a brother with his *sister*'!"

"I don't care what anyone else thinks—I care only what *you* think."

He scoffed. But far from her words appeasing his jealousy, which subconsciously he knew was ridiculous in the extreme, he was left even more wretched by his own outlandish assertions against her. *What was wrong with him? Why was he being such a facile reptile?* Being aware of his appalling behavior towards her did nothing to stop it continuing.

"Perhaps you should have thought about *me* before you went for a stroll with *him*."

"I was unaware I needed your permission to-to—do—Oh! To do anything at all! But I am glad this is out in the open between us, because I intend to continue my association with Jamie—and yes, I do call him Jamie and he calls me Lisa—because he is a dear friend—"

"Who you kissed behind the Chelsea Bun House. Some *friendship*."

"I was seventeen, and he the same age, and I kissed his cheek. He was—he still is—just a boy."

"If you are so determined I should know about the *friendship* between the two of you, tell me why you refused to give his name up to your headmistress at Blacklands."

Lisa sniffed but resisted the urge to pull the handkerchief from the pocket tied around her waist under her skirts.

"You infer I have something to be ashamed of. I do not. If I had given his name up, Jamie would most certainly have lost his apothecary's apprenticeship. Physic Garden apprentices and Blacklands girls were forbidden from socializing on any level. Which is why when we met on a Sunday at the Chelsea Bun House, we would take our bun to the lane at the back of the shop and there sit and share our bun and talk, oh! about all manner of topics, but mainly science."

Henri-Antoine frowned at her, incredulous.

"You willingly gave up your schooling—let yourself be expelled—all to save Jamie from expulsion?"

She flushed scarlet, not only at his disbelief, but because by his tone she sensed he thought her action, far from being noble, was foolhardy.

"I did. It was the right thing to do, and I stand by my decision. Jamie will one day be a brilliant physician. I have always thought so."

"I agree. He is also an exceedingly handsome young man."

Lisa resisted the urge to roll her eyes at his masculine persistence at stressing Jamie's physicality, and presumed this to be all part of his male reasoning as to why she would choose to be friends with Jamie. She thought about pointing out that when she had first met Jamie five years ago, he was thin-shouldered and spotty-faced. Instead, she did her best to cajole him out of his sullen moodiness, hoping that with playful teasing he would calm himself enough to finally see reason. For only with a cool head could they discuss what was to be done about the predicament in which they now found themselves, since Teddy's announcement of the night before.

"I do not disagree with you. But—" She regarded him with a tilt of her chin and a tremulous smile, "—I have no desire for him to kiss me in the way you kiss me... I wonder... As you now know who I have kissed, perhaps you would care to share with me the names of the females you have kissed?"

He stared at her, outraged, as if she possessed a second head.

"Don't be absurd!"

"Because you cannot tell me or will not?"

"I will not."

"But you do remember their names...?"

"I have never considered the act of kissing a commonplace thing. So of course I remember."

"I should imagine then that making love is even less commonplace, or I had hoped to find that out—with you. Though you have had many lovers, have you not?"

"If you expect me to name my lovers, you are to be vastly disappointed!"

"Oh? Because there are too few, or too many?"

When his jaw swung open, and he stared at her with outraged amazement that she could dare make such a suggestion, she felt the laughter bubble up in her throat, and she quickly put up a hand to smother her giggles.

TWENTY-EIGHT

Lisa's laughter was infectious and Henri-Antoine found himself smiling.

She had such a lovely laugh. And a lovely smile. And such beautiful eyes. She was clever and noble and all that was good with the world. He wanted to scoop her up and feel her in his arms and smother her with kisses.

And she had this gift, this way of taking his anger and his frustration and by turning it inside out, he saw how petulant and petty and thoroughly unreasonable he was being. All he wanted to do was laugh along with her.

But he needed to do something to alter this situation they were now in, convinced she was better off without him, and that Teddy's offer was the right one for her. Because despite his shock and anger, hurt and bitterness, at losing her, he had spent the previous night struggling to find a single reason why she should not live with Teddy and Jack. And because he had decided that this was the way her life should be, not the way he wanted it to be, he needed to do that something here and now, so she would walk away from him, knowing she had made the right choice. He could then stop feeling wretched, about himself, but most importantly so he could stop feeling anything at all for her.

And so he let the demon on his shoulder speak for him.

"It would seem that having a vast experience of women does not make a man immune to the wiles of a predatory female, particularly one who is pretty and lacking in experience," he drawled, and avoided looking at her. "Therein, no doubt, lay my downfall. I strayed from my usual preference, lost my head, and made an offer I would not have, had I been thinking with my brain."

Lisa's smile faded.

"I'm not entirely sure what you are talking about, but I sense you think I somehow tricked you into offering me a house in the country where I would live as your mistress?"

Her blunt summation made him sound absurd, and it was absurd, but he gave himself permission to allow bitterness to feed his demon. He inclined his head in agreement and then added to the absurdity with a sniff and a drawl of disdain.

"No doubt to someone like you my title, my pedigree, and my wealth were like shiny objects dangled before a kitten: Irresistible, and for the capturing."

"Someone like—someone like *me*...? Oh! You mean as an orphaned pauper living on the charity of her relations? As for irresistible and for the capturing..." She blushed scarlet, incensed by his outrageous assertion. "I do not know what saddens me more: That you think me so shallow of character that I agreed to be your mistress because I am dazzled by your wealth and privilege, or that you are so shallow of character that you must needs bolster your conceit by trumpeting your pedigree as son of a duke. As for your wealth... It is, quite frankly, unfathomable to me. I have all of fifteen shillings to my name, and that was given to me, most generously, by Dr. Warner. So in truth I do not have even one penny that is mine."

He contradicted himself by saying coldly, "When we first met I did not fling, or as you put it *trumpet*, my name or my consequence. In fact, you were clueless as to my identity."

"When we first met," she reminded him gently, "you were in no position to fling anything at me."

It was his turn to blush scarlet. She was right. Their first encounter had not been at Warner's Dispensary when she had refused to go out to his carriage, it was at Westby's townhouse when he was in the throes of a full-blown seizure. She deserved his thanks and his gratitude for taking care of him. But in his present destructive state of mind, and with the sun blazing in his eyes and his throat becoming drier by the minute, he allowed himself to hurtle back to a time before his father's death, when he was a sullen, petulant boy, full of resentment and self-consequence, who privately, desperately, wanted to be like every other boy. Most of all he wanted to be like his best friend Jack. Yet he knew with bitter certainty he never would be.

"Ah! Here it is! Voiced at last! I wondered when Miss Crisp, the dispensary assistant who has never been ill a day in her life, would find the moment to remind His Lordship that though he is a duke's son and wealthy beyond her comprehension, he is less than whole, and he certainly is not *wholesome*. He has frequent moments of monstrosity and madness which he cannot control, and never will be able to control, and he will spend the rest of his days a slave to his affliction. And were it not for his illustrious relations, he would have been committed and now be chained up with the lunatics in Bedlam, and there left to rot, an exhibit for curious paying visitors. Thank you, Miss Crisp. Thank you so much for your timely reminder. It can serve as your exit clause. You can sigh with relief knowing you have accepted the better offer. Your life with Teddy and Jack will be vastly different to the one I would have subjected you to, and you may live it without—"

"You are being self-pitying for its own sake, and I won't let you degrade yourself or me with such nonsense!"

Her sagacity made him want to laugh at his own irrationality, and her tears made him wretched. He wanted to fall to his knees and weep at her feet and beg forgiveness for such a ludicrous display of infantile behavior. He had no idea what had come over him to allow himself to display such raw and unfettered emotion. His conduct was not only childish and disgraceful, but it was also unforgiveable.

And here she was, behaving as she always did, with the utmost decorum and majesty. Perhaps he was mad. Perhaps he should be chained up in Bedlam. At the very least, locked away from family, friends, and good society. But most of all, far, far away from her. He didn't deserve her, and she certainly deserved better than him.

Having convinced himself that he had lost her forever, he set about satisfying his self-destruction, head pounding, eyes smarting, and welling up within him an unbridled panic that at any moment he would spiral out of control and black out.

"You should be flattered to have received two offers in two days. I have never offered any female what I offered you, and Teddy most certainly would never offer any female but you with what she and Jack are willing to provide."

"You cannot compare the two."

His gaze swept over her and fixed on the little lace edge of her chemise just peeking above the top of her bodice. He sneered and looked up into her eyes with undisguised lust.

"You're right. You wouldn't have to work on your back for Teddy."

His vulgar inference fell flat. Lisa had no idea as to what he was talking about.

"Work on my-my—*back*...?"

Oh Dear God. How had he descended into such crudity, and with her? He would never have been that coarse with any female, irrespective of her class or profession. He was a monster. He certainly was no gentleman. He felt ill and pitiful and utterly helpless. He sensed the latter feeling had less to do with her and everything to do with his physical deterioration. And with this awareness he did what his father had always told him to do when in the public gaze: Remain calm. Signal for help the way he had been shown. Breathe. Soon he would be in a safe place, out from under prying eyes, and out of harm's way.

From the corner of an eye he saw they had company, and his first thought was that it was the lads come to take him away. But he had yet to signal them.

And then his confrontation with Lisa was brought to an abrupt halt.

Suddenly, and without warning, Jack marched up to Henri-Antoine and grabbed him by the collar, then shoved him and walked him backwards, taking him as far from Lisa as he could manage without them both tripping and falling to the ground.

She followed and tried to offer an explanation, but Jack was in no mood to listen, even to her.

"That was a piece of filth I never thought I'd hear from the mouth of a gentleman," Jack snarled through his teeth near Henri-Antoine's ear. "You've outdone yourself this time, Harry! You've descended into the cesspit!"

TWENTY-NINE

Henri-Antoine twisted out of Jack's hold and pushed him off.

"If you hadn't stuck your nose in where it's not wanted you'd have been spared my cesspit tongue! Go away, Jack," Henri-Antoine complained, pulling at the points of his waistcoat and brushing down his sleeves. "I don't want you here. This is—*was*—between Miss Crisp and me, and none of your concern, so off you trot—"

"Be *damned* it's none of my concern!" Jack huffed. He came right up to Henri-Antoine and said in a low voice in the hopes Lisa would not overhear him, "You'd best tell me your intentions toward Miss Crisp."

"Intentions?" Henri-Antoine shrugged and pulled a face. "I have none."

"Good. Then stay away from her."

In an about-face, Henri-Antoine stared at Jack with astonishment.

"*You* are telling *me* to stay away from *her*?"

"You're damned right I am!"

Henri-Antoine glanced at Lisa, who stood some feet away, hugging her lithe frame in distress, and in a blinding moment of clarity he saw in Jack the means by which to bring about the annihilation of his own good character so all ties with Miss Lisa Crisp would be severed. She certainly would not want to have anything to do with him thereafter. She could then take up Teddy and Jack's offer to make her home with them with a clear conscience and wish him good riddance.

And so he turned on Jack, voice dripping with aristocratic condescension.

"It's a bit late in the day to be chivalrous where she's concerned," he goaded. "She's agreed to be my mistress. I'm setting her up in my house in Bath." He lightly punched Jack in the shoulder, winked and grinned, adding with a huff of laughter, "Interesting times ahead, eh, Jack?"

"Be damned you are!"

Henri-Antoine pulled a face and drawled, unconcerned, "Yes, I probably will be. But until then, I'll have a nice girl to come home to when I'm in the country."

"I won't let you do it!"

"What? Why? Oh do spare me your indignation. Wake up, Jack! She's a penniless orphan whose family were in service to mine. It's more than most servants can expect out of life. Don't worry. I'll look after her. Clothes. Fripperies. The occasional trip to town." He smirked. "As long as she does as she's told and continues to please me—"

"You're a self-centered muckworm. You know that?"

"Yes. I am. And you've always known it. So?"

"She's Teddy's best friend, for God's sake!"

"You are marrying Teddy. I am making Teddy's best friend my mistress. They are mutually exclusive propositions. If Teddy wants to write to her, I'll not object."

"I will!"

"And Teddy will do as you say?" Henri-Antoine snorted and rolled his eyes. "Best of luck with *that*."

When Henri-Antoine turned away and waved a hand, as if in dismissal, Jack took two strides, grabbed onto his shirt and spun him about. And before Henri-Antoine could pull out of his grasp, he snatched up a handful of his shirt front and jerked him up against his chest. The two young men were nose-to-nose and eye-to-eye.

Jack's voice was low and menacing and flat.

"If you think for one moment I will allow that girl into your bed all to satisfy your selfish needs, you do have ballocks for brains."

"It's not your decision, is it?"

"This isn't the Middle Ages. Just because she's poor and has no family, and her antecedents were vassals of the Dukes of Roxton, you look upon her as fit only to serve as your concubine? Shame on you! Shame. On. *You*."

"Have you done with the morality tale?" Henri-Antoine drawled, and for good measure sighed. He pretended an interest in his attire, and whined, "You've ruined the fibers of this shirt, and perhaps crushed the shirt buckle, which was a gift from the management of Burke's in appreciation of my *assiduous* patronage."

Jack's lip curled with repugnance. "You think such debauchery is something to boast about?! Well I'm done with you. And I don't know why we're arguing. The decision's been made. She's coming to live with Teddy and me. And there isn't a damn thing you can do about it. And unless you treat Miss Crisp with respect, and accept that she is now part of *my* family, you won't be welcome at Abbeywood. *Ever*."

And when Jack let him go with a contemptuous shove and opened wide his hand as if he no longer wanted the touch of him, Henri-Antoine smiled to himself, well satisfied he had destroyed not only his own good character but also all potential ties with Miss Lisa Crisp. He delivered the final verbal sword thrust to his own demise.

"Well. Well. Jack Cavendish," he purred. "You cunning fox! I doff my hat and bow most humbly to your libidinous dexterity. Not one, but *two* maidens to warm you up at night. Who's the debauchee—"

Jack planted his fist into his best friend's face.

With the best friends throwing punches and grappling with one another on the pitch, the cricket match was abandoned. Players rushed over to watch the spectacle. They were soon joined by guests and family who swarmed across the field. And while some of the ladies fell back so they would not have to witness the bestial behavior of two young men having a set-to, the gentlemen and boys flocked to join the cricket players who had formed a tight circle around the fight, shouting encouragement with every swing, thwack, and thump.

Forgotten on the sidelines was a horrified Lisa, who quickly averted her gaze the instant Jack landed the first sickening blow and blood began pouring from Henri-Antoine's nose.

Jack and Henri-Antoine were finally pulled off one another and held back on opposite sides of the circle, heaving in great breaths, Jack still combative, Henri-Antoine with head down and bleeding into the grass. The Duke instructed the disappointed cricketers, spectators, and relieved family members, to return to the marquees—afternoon tea was to be served before changing for dinner. And with the aid of the Duke's army of servants dispersing the crowd, as well as providing a barrier between onlookers and combatants, soon the guests and cricketers and family members drifted back across the field, chatter all about the astonishing events leading up to and including the set-to between the groom and his best man.

Everyone wondered what this would mean for the upcoming wedding.

When Teddy arrived, she took one look at Jack's bloodied shirt front and the split to his lip, and satisfied he was not seriously hurt, turned away in disgust to gather a distraught Lisa to her. From the comfort of Teddy's embrace, Lisa dared to glance over at Henri-Antoine. His shirt front was also spattered with blood, and blood glistened about his nostrils and mouth, which was strangely blue, and there was a gash to his top lip that looked to be swelling before her eyes.

Not one to faint at the sight of blood or injury or disease, and thought good in a crisis at Warner's Dispensary, an overwrought Lisa was oddly sensitive to seeing Henri-Antoine's blood spilt. She took one look at his busted lip and fainted, slipping through Teddy's arms to collapse in the grass.

Lord Strathsay, who was helping the Duke keep Henri-Antoine propped up, immediately crossed to assist Teddy with Lisa. Gathering the girl into his arms, and with his niece at his side, he strode off to the marquees, seeking shade and refreshment, and where he hoped to find his Countess, who was also known to be good in a crisis.

And while Lisa's faint caused the family alarm, it was a needed diversion for those guests still milling about. They turned their backs on Henri-Antoine to watch the girl be taken away and thus were unaware of His Lordship's collapse.

Henri-Antoine tried to reassure his distressed mother there was nothing to worry about, that he was not greatly hurt. But the Duchess did not believe him. She had arrived in a flurry of silken petticoats and greatly agitated, which meant she was talking in a rush of French no one but her sons could possibly understand. She demanded both boys be taken up to the big house immediately to be examined by Roxton's personal physician. Henri-Antoine was protesting this was unnecessary when suddenly his body stiffened. He blacked out and fell forward.

The Duke caught his brother before he fell flat on his face, and laid him in the grass at their mother's feet. She knelt beside him, a cool hand to his brow, and tried to soothe him. But while the Duke was able to stop his brother's fall, there was nothing he could do but watch on helplessly as Henri-Antoine succumbed to a full-blown seizure, his body convulsing and writhing before them. And when Antonia briefly looked up at her eldest son, her tears of anguish brought tears to his own eyes.

It was the first bout of falling sickness mother and her eldest son had witnessed in over a decade. The Duchess had thought herself prepared for such an eventuality. After all, she was aware that her younger son still suffered from bouts of his illness, though she allowed him the dignity of pretending ignorance. Discreet enquiries and regular secret reports from loyal servants kept her informed.

What mother would not keep a close eye on all her children, but most particularly on a son whom she had nursed from birth until his thirteenth year through so many attacks that if he went a week without one, she began entertaining fanciful notions he was cured. But he wasn't cured, and he never would be. And watching him as a young man surrender to such an uncontrollable illness, she realized she had forgotten just how frightening and horrid such an all-consuming attack was on the body and mind of the sufferer, and what a torment it was for his loved ones who could do nothing but be mere spectators to his suffering and indignity.

When four of Henri-Antoine's lads arrived to look after him, everyone from the Duke of Roxton to the Duke of Kinross and his duchess—Henri-Antoine's mother—to the footmen currently shielding His Lordship from prying eyes, were required to bow to their expertise and their master's wishes. So the family, however reluctantly, soon found themselves following the guests to return to the marquees, leaving Henri-Antoine in the care of his minders.

The day ended there, not only for Henri-Antoine and Jack, but for Teddy and Lisa too. Everyone thought it for the best if the girls were taken home to have an early night. They remained mute on the journey to the lodge, and later when they went up to Teddy's room. Neither wanted supper and so after their baths, they were put to bed, each with a mug of hot milk. The Lady Mary sat with her daughter and Lisa for a while. She brought Sophie-Kate with her, which offered Teddy some comfort because she loved to have cuddles with her baby sister. But despite the color returning to her face, and the bath helping to soothe her, Lisa was still so much affected by events that she fell asleep exhausted without saying her prayers or her good-nights.

THIRTY

Lisa's appetite had not returned the following morning when she went down to breakfast, the last of the family to do so, and where she found Teddy, who insisted she have a slice of toast and a cup of tea. Teddy told her that her papa had already left for the day with her eldest brother David, to go hawking with the other gentlemen and boys old enough to ride unassisted. The Duke and Duchess of Roxton had decided that the men would spend the day as far away from the big house as possible, while the ladies and girls would remain indoors occupying their time in more leisurely pursuits: Embroidering, dabbling in watercolors, walking the Long Gallery, enjoying a musical recital, and watching the children rehearse their dance steps and musical pieces to be performed at the wedding breakfast.

"And we are to spend our day here, doing whatever we please," Teddy said buoyantly. "Which will make for a nice change."

"You wish you were out hawking too, don't you?" Lisa said with a smile, nibbling on her toast.

Teddy grinned. "I do. But I also wish to spend the day with you, and Jack."

"He did not go hawking?"

"No. That pleasure was denied him. He must apologize to you for—"

"Oh, Teddy, no. Please," Lisa said with a self-conscious frown. "I could not bear it. It is I who should be apologizing to him."

"Nonsense! Besides, he wrote me the most wonderful apology letter." With a smug smile, Teddy held up a folded sheet of paper, its red seal broken. "It was delivered at first light, so he must have spent *all night* composing it. And this was after his scolding from the Duke, who summoned him to his library. It strikes dread into the hearts of those who must walk the length of that room with its hundreds and hundreds of books peering down from a great height as if they are persons in a courtroom, and with the judge—that's the Duke—seated behind his big desk, sour-faced and waiting to berate you for your infraction. So Jack says. And he has only ever had that happen to him once before, but he says the experience stays with you so you hope it never happens again!"

Lisa blinked. "But His Grace seems the most amiable of men, and Her Grace, too, is quite lovely. One does not have to be in their company long to see that they love each other very much, and adore all their children equally."

Teddy's eyes shone.

"There's lots of cake-making going on in that family that's certain!"

Lisa gasped, clapped a hand to her mouth and then could not help herself and giggled. When she found her breath, she said with a smile, "You are the wickedest girl I know! But also the most loving. Thank you for making me laugh."

Teddy poured them out a second cup of tea.

"You're very welcome. I do like to see you smile, Lisa. And you are not to concern yourself. None of what happened yesterday was your fault. Jack didn't tell me what Harry said to you to make him furious, but if you need to confide—"

"Thank you. I don't—I don't want to speak about—about that yet," Lisa confessed, losing her smile and putting her hand out across the table. When Teddy took hold of her fingers and smiled in understanding, she smiled back. "Let's have our tea first..."

She was relieved not to be made to speak openly about Henri-Antoine, because she was sure if she did she would barely be able to speak at all, or become a blubbering mess. And although she was desperate to know that he was not greatly harmed, and was safe, and how Jack had fared, she did not ask, again because it was still too raw. So instead she asked,

"I hope His Grace wasn't too harsh on Jack?"

"Jack accepted the rebuke, and once he had explained matters to the Duke they both agreed that while Jack should have shown more restraint and not hit Harry, he was provoked. And he explained everything, and I forgive him. In fact, I love him even more, if that is possible, for being so chivalrous."

"He did? He was? You do? He explained it all in his letter?"

"No, silly. His letter was about us. He gave me his explanation in person, as was proper. He's here. We had breakfast together before Papa and David set out for the big house. He's outdoors with Luke, who was most upset at being too young to go hawking with his big brother. So Jack and Luke are out playing in the wagon, Jack running it up the hill and then he and Luke getting in it and coming down at a speed, which I am very sure is sending Mama's lovely hair gray, however much she smiles and tries to appear as if she hasn't a care in the world."

"Do you know, Teddy, that as well as being beautiful, your mama is the most composed person I have ever met. I do not think anything or anyone ever ruffles her feathers."

Teddy stood and pushed in her chair. Lisa did likewise.

They linked arms and Teddy took Lisa to the back of the house, through the kitchen, out into the kitchen garden, and then on out the back gate, to the other side of the stone wall to an expanse of lawn at the base of a small hill. Here they joined Lady Mary, who had a hand up to the peak of her straw bonnet to further shade her eyes from the sun, and was standing by a haycock with two of the outdoor servants. Their attention was focused on Jack and four-year-old Luke who were seated in a wooden wagon that had large wheels at the rear and smaller wheels up front, all with a number of spokes missing. And by the messy state of the haycock, this wasn't their first or third run down the slope, and if they kept at it there was every chance of the wagon falling apart altogether.

Jack dug his boot heels into the grass and gave an almighty push so that the wagon sped forward with the weight of his body. Down the hill it rattled, its occupants holding on tight, the wind in Luke's face forcing the black ringlets out of his eyes, and Jack steering as best he could at speed and with little control, and only his feet as brakes.

It was luck rather than steering that kept the wagon on course, and once again it came to a thumping stop into the partially-destroyed haycock. Both occupants were left covered in straw and laughing, Luke with excitement, and Jack with relief to have survived another run. He breathed an audible sigh when the Lady Mary confirmed that was indeed the final wagon ride for today, ignoring Luke's repeated pleas for just one more run down the hill. His mother was firm. Luke needed to be cleaned up. Did he forget he was accompanying his mama and Sophie-Kate across to the big house where he was to play with the twins, who were the same age as he.

"I wonder if we'll have twins..." Jack mused, watching Luke run off ahead of his mother through the gate.

"Twins? I hope not!" Teddy said with a snort of incredulousness.

"Why not? The Duke and Duchess have two sets, and your Uncle Dair and Aunt Rory have a set, too."

Teddy carefully removed a hay stalk from Jack's hair, but then she gave him a playful shove.

"Just because we have aunts who've had twins, doesn't mean I will, or even want to. If you want twins, Sir John, *you* birth them!"

"If it meant you need not be in any pain or discomfort, I would!" Jack stated fiercely and grabbed her to him. He kissed her forehead, and then her mouth, both with an unusual tentativeness because his bottom lip had a small split and was swollen and was thus tender to the touch. "Unfortunately men are relegated to playing a bit part in that drama, and that is as a quivering jelly."

Teddy smiled up into Jack's eyes, one of which was showing signs of bruising. "But my quivering jelly..."

Suddenly, they came to a sense of their surroundings and Jack let Teddy go. It was not only because Lisa was there, but it was also the fact the situation yesterday still needed resolution, and a great deal had been left unsaid. The moment Jack had taken Teddy into his arms, Lisa had turned away and wandered a little way off pretending an interest in the haycock to give the couple some privacy. Now they came up to her, and sensing there was unease between them, Teddy said to Lisa,

"Don't be alarmed by the bruise or the cut to Sir John's lip. And on no account are you to offer him any sympathy. He brought it all on himself."

"Theodora is quite right," Jack replied good-naturedly. He bowed to Lisa with great courteousness. "But I do owe you an apology for my ungentlemanly conduct. The argument I had with Harry should never have come to blows, and never before an audience, and most definitely not before you, Miss Crisp. Can you forgive me?"

Lisa took the hand he held out to her, and looking down saw that his knuckles were grazed. She lightly covered his hand with hers and held it a little longer saying, after a hard swallow, and bravely meeting his troubled gaze, "You did what any man who professes to be a gentleman would do in coming to the aid of a female who is being verbally assaulted. As for the fight..." She let go of his hand and glanced at Teddy before saying with a sad smile, "How could you not have reacted in the way you did, when you were goaded to it?"

"Goaded to it?" Teddy repeated, puzzled, but was not given the chance to say more when Jack jumped in, eyes bright.

"That's what I said to Uncle Roxton! And I didn't say Harry provoked me to shift blame. I said that thinking about the fight and what started it, I'm convinced Harry made me as mad as hell fire so that it was impossible for me *not* to hit him!"

"I have thought about it, too," Lisa mused. "Over and over. All of it. And your physical response to his words was precisely what he wished for—"

"And I fell into his trap! More fool me!"

"Why would Harry *want* you to hit him?" Teddy asked, puzzled. "I know he is moody and exasperating, and there are times when I do not understand him at all, but he has never been so obnoxious that Sir John has ever wanted to hit him." She looked at Jack. "You said he made an ungentlemanly remark about Lisa, and that's what provoked you to strike out at him." She then looked at Lisa. "And it did seem to us up on the hill that the two of you were having an argument..." She looked from Lisa to Jack and back again, and put a hand to Lisa's arm and asked in a low voice, "Did he—did he make an improper advance? You were both very friendly at dinner, and perhaps he received the wrong impression altogether. He is a flirt, and you are exceedingly pretty, and—" She looked to Jack. "He did, didn't he?!"

But Jack wasn't looking at Teddy. He exchanged a look with Lisa which let her know he was well aware Harry's mood had everything to do with her, but he was not about to betray her. Instead, he threw up a hand and effected exasperation.

"I don't know precisely what was said," he lied. "I just didn't like his tone and manner. He can be intolerable at times, and struts about as only the son of a duke can! Miss Crisp ain't used to such overblown hubris, nor should she have to tolerate it. And Harry has this habit of doing the contrary thing for the simple pleasure of watching you squirm. Which is well and good for persons who know him, like me! And I've always tried to keep in mind that his affliction does play its part in his—"

"Illness cannot be used as an excuse to be rude," Lisa interrupted. "And so I have said many times to the patients at the dispensary. If they wish treatment and any sympathy at all, then they need to be mindful."

"I do not doubt you keep Warner's patients in check, Miss Crisp," Jack said with a smile, which dropped into a frown when he added, "But I should never have hit Harry. Never. I fear it brought on one of his attacks and—

"I do not think it helped, but it certainly did not bring on the attack," Lisa countered. "It is my considered opinion—and I am no expert, I can only go on instinct and observation—an attack was imminent. It was only a matter of *when*, not *if*. So you should not feel any guilt it was you who brought it on. I believe he knew it was coming. Having you hit him no doubt brought the episode forward, but it would have happened anyway. That he provoked you to hit him was shameful. That he had you hit him knowing he was experiencing the onset of a convulsion was unconscionable, but—and you know him much better than I, and so can correct me—such behavior was most uncharacteristic."

Jack nodded, and could not help a spreading smile, though he gave a little jump when his lip suddenly stung as a reminder of his foolhardiness. He agreed with everything she said because he knew, as she did, what had motivated his best friend to act in such an irrational and self-destructive manner. Teddy still did not, though she sensed there was something neither Jack nor Lisa was telling her.

"How clever you are, Lisa," she said wonderingly. "When you

make such observations, it disheartens me that females with intellect cannot pursue professional lives."

"Yes. For then I might have some hope of looking after myself, rather than needing to live off the charity of relatives who do not want me, and friends who do. Which brings me to your most generous and loving offer of having me live with you, and I am so pleased you are both here now for me to speak to you about—"

"We both arrived at the notion separately. Neither of us coerced the other. And we both want this outcome very much," Teddy assured her. "Is that not so, Sir John."

"It is."

Lisa nodded, but could not stop the tears welling up.

"I cannot tell you how much your offer means to me. When I was orphaned I became an unnecessary burden on my father's family. And there is some truth in that, isn't there? They did not know me, so why would they want me? So to have friends who want me to live with them, to be part of their family, means more than I can possibly tell you. But..." She went forward and took hold of Teddy's hands, and spoke to them both, "I hope you will understand that if I do accept your most wonderful offer, it is because I made the decision to do so, freely—"

"Of course! We never meant to compel you, Miss Crisp," Jack interrupted.

Lisa smiled. "I know you did not, Sir John. It was made with the best of intentions."

"Though perhaps we should have announced it more sensitively. Or not announced it at all, until we had spoken to you first...?" He glanced at Teddy, but said to Lisa, "I do believe Miss Crisp was not the only one who was startled by our announcement last night."

Lisa found herself blushing. "I see that you do understand."

Teddy looked from Lisa to Jack and back again. She was at a loss. "You do not want to be with us?"

"I do. It's that—"

"Miss Crisp must make that decision for herself," Jack explained and felt his face grow hot when he cautioned her. "Though I do hope... I trust that you will... That when you make your decision, you will not accept anything less than what you deserve, Miss Crisp."

Teddy presumed they were referring to Warner's Dispensary.

"Would you prefer to continue working with the poor to living with us?"

"I love you with all my heart, Teddy, and I have come to love your family, too. And you can be assured, both of you," she added, holding Jack's gaze, "that when I make my decision, it will be the right one for everyone." She smiled at Teddy. "But *my* future can wait until *your* future is well and truly secured by the wedding breakfast and ball. Of more immediate concern is putting matters to rights between you, Sir John, and His Lordship. And I believe I may be able to help. Though I will need you, Sir John, to take me to him."

"I wish I could, but I cannot. The only persons who know his whereabouts are his major domo, his valet, and the lads."

"Oh? He is not at the big house? I assumed he had an apartment..."

"He does. But he's not there. And even if he were, no one gets past Gallet, Kyte, and the lads until Harry gives the word. And I do mean *no* one," Jack apologized. "Not the Duke. Not his mother. And I never have in all the years I've known him. That lot are loyal to a fault and you can threaten all you want but they won't budge. Reminds me of the devotion of his father's servants. Given the choice, they'd rather crawl over hot coals then be disloyal to their master."

"I should still like to test the assertion. Will you take me to Mr. Gallet?"

"I can, but I'm afraid it won't do you any good. After one of his attacks it takes Harry a couple of days to come to his senses, and then we don't see him until—"

Teddy was aghast. "He doesn't—We don't—have a couple of days!"

"Then we must see what we can do to ensure he makes the ceremony," Lisa stated.

When both Teddy and Lisa stared at Jack expectantly, he threw up his hands and acquiesced. "Very well! I will take you to Gallet. But do not tell me you were not warned of the outcome."

"Then you'd best prepare the hot coals," Teddy said stridently.

She had no idea what it was Lisa thought she could do, or why she would want to go near a man who had subjected her to verbal abuse, but uppermost in her mind was her wedding. And if Lisa could get Harry to the church on time, then she was prepared for her best friend to do whatever it took to get him there alongside Jack.

"One way or the other, Gallet will tell Lisa of Harry's whereabouts, because I am getting married, with or without you, Sir John Cavendish!"

Jack didn't like to point out to his beloved she could not marry without him being present. Instead he did as he was told, and an hour later he and Lisa were in the marble vestibule of Lord Henri-Antoine's apartment in the north wing of the big house. Michel Gallet's stony face when a footman showed them into the drawing room told him he may just have to send for a bucket of hot coals.

THIRTY-ONE

I T WAS THE first time Lisa had been inside the Duke of Roxton's palace. So far all events had been held outside, or at Crecy Hall, and had matters not deteriorated at the cricket match, she would have had dinner in the state dining room. If the Palladian exterior was jaw-dropping, the interior was almost beyond comprehension. But her interest in her surroundings would have to wait. What she most wanted was to know Henri-Antoine's whereabouts, though she had an idea where he might be, but only his major domo could confirm it.

When a footman showed them into the drawing room of Lord Henri-Antoine's apartment they were met by a man dressed in marked contrast to his opulent surroundings. Wearing a plain blue suit, here was the man who, at Warner's Dispensary, had tried to cajole Lisa out into the street and into Lord Henri-Antoine's carriage. If he was surprised to see her, he did not show it. But she was surprised to see him and said in French before Jack had a chance to demand Harry's whereabouts,

"You have a twin at Crecy Hall, do you not, M'sieur?"

"I do, mademoiselle. My brother Marc he is major domo to *M'sieur le Duke et Mme la Duchesse d'Kinross.*"

"And you hold a similar position with her son. That is convenient."

"How so?"

"I wondered how *Mme la Duchesse* kept an eye on her son's health, and now I know. You are her eyes, are you not?"

"I cannot confirm or deny what mademoiselle says. What I can tell you is that as major domo to His Lordship, my prime objective is my master's welfare."

"Look here, Gallet," Jack stuck in, feeling he should contribute, "Miss Crisp needs a word with His Lordship. So if you'd be good enough to take her to him, we'll get out of your hair."

Michel Gallet bowed respectfully. "I regret to say, that is not possible, sir."

"You regret nothing. You just won't do it!"

"As you say, sir," Michel Gallet replied, and stood his ground.

Lisa dug in a pocket and pulled out the map of the estate she had been given on the carriage ride between Alston and Treat. This she showed to the major domo, who looked at it in some puzzlement, a glance at Jack, who was doing likewise.

"If you will indulge me for a moment, M'sieur Gallet. I made a study of this map, so that if I went for a walk, I might be able to do so without having to refer to it, though I kept it in my pocket should I need it. And do you know what surprised me most?"

The major domo shook his head. "No, mademoiselle. I do not."

"It was the number of follies and grottos within walking distance of the main house. Do you see how many there are? Perhaps there are more farther afield, but on this map alone there are eight. The one on Swan Island is not to be trespassed, but the others I presume are open to guests and visitors to the parkland alike?"

"I presume that to be the case, mademoiselle," agreed Michel Gallet.

"I was intrigued enough to enquire of the Lady Mary's brother, Mr. Fitzstuart, if he knew why there were so many, and he told me the ones within walking distance were all built by the fifth Duke. He remembered this particularly because he and his brother and sister spent their summers here, and these little outdoor buildings were constructed—"

"All great houses have follies and grottos. Some more than others," the major domo interrupted flatly. "I assure you, they are nothing to be surprised about."

"Aren't they?" Jack stuck in, suddenly on the alert because for the first time since entering the drawing room Michel Gallet appeared uncomfortable. He looked to Lisa. "Please continue, Miss Crisp. I'd like to hear what Cousin Charles had to say, because I spent my teens here, too, roaming the place with His Lordship, and there isn't a folly or grotto we haven't explored." He coughed into his fist. "Including Swan Island."

"That was my second thought while studying this map—that you, as His Lordship's best friend, would also know these follies and grottos well. Mr. Fitzstuart told me construction on these particular follies—the ones closest to the house—all began when the fifth Duke's second son was a small boy, and were all completed within a few years."

"Your second thought? Pray what was your first?" asked Jack.

Lisa answered with her gaze on the major domo. "That *M'sieur le Duc d'Roxton* was a nobleman of vision and compassion, and a most loving father…"

"He was, Miss Crisp. And you got this from looking at a map?" Jack asked with surprise.

"I did. For only a loving father who was thinking of his son's needs would have such little buildings placed within the landscape so that they were within easy reach. He had them situated so that his son could leave the safety of the house and explore farther afield knowing there was always somewhere for him to go where he could feel safe, and away from prying eyes. I do not doubt these places are interesting in themselves and are visited by family, guests, and visitors to the grounds. They are somewhere to sit and reflect on the landscape, to take a breath away from the sun and the heat, the rain and the wind. But their primary function was always to provide a safe haven for the Duke's second son. Is that not so, M'sieur Gallet?"

Jack stared at Lisa with something akin to stupefaction.

"By Jove, Miss Crisp! You've opened my eyes. I never gave them much thought. They were just places Harry and I explored. We even stayed overnight in a couple of them. Do I ever feel the ninny!"

Lisa smiled. "Oh, you need not feel the fool, Sir John. You said yourself, you have lived here most of your life, and thus you have never had to give any of this much thought. I, on the contrary, who have never been here, find everything fascinating, and it all requires a great deal of thought." She held up the map. "And you don't have one of these, do you?"

"I do not. Well?!" Jack said to the major domo. "How about it? Miss Crisp is right, isn't she? So in which one of these follies is your master holed up?"

Lisa indicated the Italian folly marked on the map. "I would hazard a guess it is this one, Sir John. The temple of Vejovis. Mr. Fitzstuart tells me Vejovis is the Roman God of healing. And this is the closest folly to where the cricket match was played." She glanced at the major domo, then back at the map. "And the cartographer was good enough to mark it as being part of this temple, Neptune's Grotto, which Mr. Fitzstuart tells me is a plunge pool."

"It is," Jack confirmed with a nod. "It's fed by the lake. The pool's heated now, but as boys we never swam there. Harry hated the place because one of his early treatments was being dunked in the damn thing, as if being submerged in freezing water would cure him! He said he almost drowned. Frightful business."

"Will you take me there?" Lisa asked.

"You think he's there?"

"I do. Bathing in warm water is considered beneficial in the treatment of many ills."

"Now that I come to think on it, he recently had a folly with a plunge bath built in the gardens of his house in Bath," Jack told her. "It has a cascading waterfall and is fed via a pump from the river. I thought it one of his extravagant affectations."

"Like his walking stick with its diamond-encrusted top...? Unnecessary but adding to his consequence?" She glanced at the major domo and saw that she had all his attention. "But have you thought that perhaps the walking stick is just as necessary as the plunge pool?"

"His walking stick?" Jack frowned. "And how is that, Miss Crisp?"

"As well as an aid to keeping him upright should he suddenly be overcome by symptoms of his affliction, he uses it to signal, without needing to say one word, to his minders—his lads as he calls them—and to you, M'sieur Gallet, should he need immediate assistance. Is that not so?"

"Egad! You *do* know him!" Jack announced with admiration. He addressed the major domo. "So, Gallet. If you don't take Miss Crisp to His Lordship, I will."

"I must point out that there is no guarantee His Lordship will see Miss Crisp. Or that the lads will admit her."

"Let's worry about that when we get there, shall we?"

Lisa held her breath hoping upon hope that her intuition had not failed her.

What she could not know was that the major domo was of the opinion that if there was one person whom his master would see, it was this girl standing before him. The first time he had visited Warner's Dispensary with his master, he had wondered what maggot had got into His Lordship's brain to want to visit such a health hell hole, and then there she was—Miss Lisa Crisp—sitting in her corner with her writing box, surrounded by the unwashed, ragged, and diseased poor, the sunshine in an otherwise bleak existence. And it wasn't only that she was arrestingly pretty, because she was, but he'd seen some rare beauties hanging off his master's arm, here in England and on the Continent. It was that Miss Crisp's beauty radiated from within. And as far as he was concerned that was the rarest form of beauty of all.

The major domo nodded his agreement, and Lisa breathed easily.

"But I take only Miss Crisp, Sir John."

Jack walked a few paces away from the major domo, signaling for Lisa to follow. And when she was standing before him, he said in a low voice, "If you go to the folly without my protection, and it is discovered that you went there alone, I cannot shield you from gossip —or from Harry. I say that with the deepest respect for both of you."

"I know you do. And I am deeply touched by your concern for my welfare. But you must know—you of all people, as Henri-Antoine's best friend—you must know our feelings for each other."

"I do now," he said with a huff of laughter, color in his cheeks, gingerly touching the cut to his lip. "What I do not know is what the future holds for either of you. What I wish for you may not be what eventuates, because Harry—"

"—is the Duke of Roxton's brother, and the son of a duke." Lisa smiled. "Do not concern yourself, Sir John. I may be young, and while I am not hard-hearted I am hard-headed. I know that to follow my heart, there will be consequences, and I accept that."

"All the same, Teddy and I would never abandon you. Remember that."

Lisa impulsively kissed his cheek. "Thank you. You are the kindest of men and I see why Teddy loves you. Now you must return to her, but please say nothing of this, yet. If I am to lose her good opinion, then let it be after you are married."

THIRTY-TWO

"**I** TOLD YOU. Tomorrow! Go away!"

It was the sudden brightness in an otherwise darkened room that had him awake. In his half-awake, half-asleep state Henri-Antoine was vaguely aware of the comings and goings on the floor below, and it gave him an odd sense of comfort. The lads brought food and clean drinking water, firewood to stoke the furnace, cleaned the place up, and emptied what needed to be emptied. And when they weren't moving about, Kyte came and went, taking away his clothing and replacing it with a clean set, which was just as well because he'd been left with only the shirt on his back. But as he was curled up in the big four poster bed, he didn't need anything else...

But for all the comings and goings below him, no one had trespassed into this room of the rotunda he used as a bedchamber since they had put him to bed.

The floor to ceiling windows that went all the way around—with views into the forest and out across the manicured gardens—had the curtains drawn to darken the room, but someone had uncovered one window and pulled up the sash to let in fresh air.

Unless there had been a death in the family, Henri-Antoine could think of no other reason for his servants' disobedience in bothering him. And it was this alarming thought that prompted him to roll onto his back. But he did not turn his head on the pillow to the undraped window, the light was too intense, but blinked up at the domed ceiling with its painting of a night sky full of twinkling stars. He lifted a hand mere inches off the coverlet, as signal the intruder had his permission to speak.

But when the silence stretched, he reluctantly squinted into the light, which made him wince, because of the bruising around his left eye. He was sure he must be running a fever. There in silhouette was a woman. He blinked. Surely he was hallucinating, but perhaps the apparition would at least be reasonable.

"The light hurts... Pull the curtain... Better. Now go away."

He dragged the bedsheet up over his head, turned away onto his side, and closed his eyes.

Lisa came over to the bed.

"I will wait downstairs. But I am not going away."

There was a flurry of activity under the bedsheet and then a hand was thrust out.

"No! Don't!"

"Don't wait downstairs, or don't go away?"

"Don't—don't go away." Fingertips patted the coverlet. "Stay."

She sat on the edge of the mattress and took hold of his hand. She was surprised at how cold it was. Then again, there was no fireplace, and with the sun shut out, there was nothing to warm the room. It was a gloriously sunny day outside, almost too hot, but this folly was back in amongst the shrubbery, on the edge of a coppice, and so received little direct sun.

She looked about for another coverlet, but could not see one by the bed. So she went to get up to search, but his fingers tightened about hers.

"Stay."

"I intend to. But you're cold and you need more covering. There might be something downstairs—"

"No," came the muffled response. He slowly lowered the bed sheet to his chin and squinted across at her. "I don't need... I just need... I just need—*you*... And to sleep."

She pressed her lips together, overcome by his admission, and nodded, giving his hand a squeeze before letting it go. It disappeared under the sheet and he turned on his side and resettled. Without another thought, she got up onto the bed and lay down on top of the coverlet beside him. She shifted sideways until she was pressed up against his back, plumped the pillow and lay back down again. And with a hand to his shoulder, her face at his neck, and her body curled around his, which was wrapped head to toe in the bedsheet, she closed her eyes. She lay there for a long while, content and happy, before drifting off into a deep sleep.

When she woke it was several hours later. If he had moved at all, he had not disturbed her. As she had hardly slept the night before, she was not surprised she'd had no difficulty falling asleep beside him. He was still wrapped in the bedsheet, but it was no longer up around his head. He had an arm out, on top of the coverlet, and his shoulder length black hair fell across his pillow in messy disarray. She rose up on an elbow to take a peek to see if he was still sleeping and was surprised, not by the dark stubble to his chin and jaw line, but by the bruising to his eye, and the cut to his lip, which was not as swollen as she expected.

She lay back down and shivered, realizing she was now cold, and that it was her fault for leaving the window ajar. She went to get up to close it, when her movement woke him.

"Get under the covers," he said drowsily. "Keep us both warm." When she hesitated that little bit too long, he woke enough to turn his head and say, "I am in no fit state to seduce you. I am weak…And when we finally do make love, I want—I want to be at my best—for you…"

Lisa smiled and blushed, but before removing her half boots she quickly went over and closed the window. In her stockinged feet she rearranged the bed linen, so she could freely slip under the coverlet, leaving the bedsheet between them. Settling, she gingerly pressed herself along his curved length and snuggled in.

He seemed to have drifted off to sleep again, for he was quiet a long time, and then he said, "I must rest, or the headache lingers."

"Then rest."

"You won't go away…?"

"I won't."

"It's not—It's not Jack's big day, is it?"

"No. The wedding is tomorrow."

"I thought…" He sighed. "Good. I don't want to miss it."

"He doesn't want you to miss it either."

"He forgives me?"

"He does."

"He is a dear man."

"He is. As are you."

"I am not," Henri-Antoine grumbled. He pulled her arm across his body, to bring her closer, and to find anchorage. "I am a scoundrel and an arrogant wantwit... I'm still furious with you."

Lisa stifled a smile into his back, fearing she might giggle. But she could not hide the laughter in her voice.

"Yes, I saw how furious you were with me when you goaded Jack into striking you."

"You don't care, do you?"

"That you provoked Jack to hit you and then you hit him back? I most certainly do!"

"Not that, *witch*. You don't care that I'm furious with you."

"Not a drop."

"I tried to warn you."

Lisa set her cheek between his shoulder blades.

"You did. Thank you."

There was a protracted silence before he said, "I'm sorry—sorry for everything... For what I said... I didn't mean any of it. It was despicable... I'm despicable... Staying with me will be your ruin."

"I am already ruined, my lord."

At that pronouncement, he unsettled them both by rolling over to face her and demanded she explain herself. Her response was to smile across at him and wonder how it was possible that even when he was unshaven and disheveled, with one black eye and a thunderous frown, he was still the most handsome man she knew. He might be overbearing, arrogant, uncompromising, and oft times inscrutable, but as she had discovered he was generous, compassionate, loyal, and loving, and all in all, the most complex person she had ever met, and she loved him. She was very sure she had fallen in love with him almost from their first meeting. She believed in fate, and had told him so. She also believed in being truthful, so she came right out and said it, and why not? She was here with him. She had agreed to be his mistress, and she could not wait for them to set up house together.

"Because I love you, Henri-Antoine."

He closed his eyes and turned his head on the pillow to stare unseeing at the stars sprinkling the ceiling, enjoying the few precious seconds to bathe in her declaration. And he found he was suddenly heady, as he had been when he had kissed her under the oak tree. He was so overcome with happiness, he grinned. But his grin made her frown and sit up on an elbow to stare down at him.

"I do beg your pardon if I have said something that makes you grin like a wantwit," she retaliated with a pout, feigning offence. "If this is how His Lordship responds to a declaration of love, then perhaps Jack did not hit you hard enough to knock the sense into you, as I had hoped!"

He chuckled, and reverted to his first language and said in French, "But *you* are the wantwit—*my* beautiful wantwit. You confess to loving a man who contrives to have his best friend hit him—to prove to you he is the last man with whom you should spend your life. You do this when he is as weak as a puppy and as woolly-headed as a lamb, thus he cannot respond as you deserve... And you wonder why I am smiling like a court fool?"

"If you expect me to feel sorry for your predicament—"

"Oh no! I feel sorry for yours!"

She gasped, and then laughed with him. And when she smiled down into his eyes he gently took her face between his long fingers, to draw her closer, and kissed her tenderly.

"You have made me very happy, Miss Lisa Crisp."

"And that makes me happy."

They snuggled in again, this time with his arm around her, content to remain still and silent, and for long enough that they drifted off into a state between sleeping and waking. When he spoke, Lisa wondered if they had been asleep at all.

"I want to stay here, with you, forever."

"We would then become an entry in one of those guidebooks about grand estates—"

"Guidebooks? About grand estates? Are there such things?"

"How else are ordinary persons to know about how their betters live?"

"I had no idea."

"That's because you live inside one."

"Inside a guidebook?"

"Yes."

"Why would we feature in such a compelling read?"

"Because if we stayed here forever we would eventually die—"

"How morbid you are."

"You did say forever."

"I did."

"And so if we did stay here forever our skeletons would eventually be discovered, lying together as we are now. And such a discovery would be worthy of an entry in any guidebook. Possibly as a cautionary tale about lovers—or in our case, soon to be lovers—that it is never wise to remain in bed forever—"

"Not wise? Hang that! Who wants to be wise when I can be in bed with you?"

Lisa sighed and smiled, and then suddenly became pensive. Perhaps it was the mention of death and dying. She wanted to know about his father. It was something he had said, and then done, when she had looked after him at Lord Westby's townhouse. It had remained unspoken between them but she wondered if now he might talk to her about it, and about his father, the illustrious fifth Duke.

"When you were ill as a child, was it your father who tended to you, because at Lord Westby's you—"

"Yes. I spent much of my boyhood recovering on a chaise longue in my father's libraries—"

"Libraries?"

"Here. London. Paris. Mostly here."

"And he would stroke your hair...?"

"No matter what he was doing, he would leave it all to sit with me after one of my attacks. He'd recount stories of his youth... His voice soothed me... I still hear it in my head... He had this way of speaking—It was compelling. He was compelling. And his voice... Hard to describe, but if you'd heard it you'd never forget it."

"Like your voice."

"Mine? Unforgettable?"

"No—"

"No? But you just said—"

"Your voice is-is—glorious."

He grinned. "Glorious?"

"You know it is! And I told you once before. Don't you remember? When you visited at Gerrard Street and gave me my most wondrous writing box. I said I could listen to you talk on and on in whatever language you chose." She smiled cheekily. "And Becky agrees with me. In fact she was the first to mention the hot chocolate—"

"Hot chocolate?"

"Your voice. That's what it sounds like. Your voice sounds like hot chocolate tastes: Smooth and delicious and-and just a tiny bit wicked."

"Hot chocolate? Wicked?"

He chuckled deep in his throat and then pulled a pillow over his face and held it there. Lisa wondered what was the matter until she felt his body convulsing, and knew he was shaking with laughter. She pulled the pillow away and he blinked up at her and she glared down at him, blushing.

"I was not exaggerating," she said earnestly. "Or-or trying to-to flatter you."

"Heaven forbid!" He winced at the pain behind his eyes and tugged the pillow out of her fingers. He playfully nudged her with it. "I was laughing with happiness, *witch*. You make me happy. Stop it!"

She smiled, and they both settled again.

He surprised her by confessing, "When you stroked my hair at Westby's I thought... For one blinding moment I believed it was my father—"

"*Ne vous arrêtez pas, mon cher papa. Dis m'en plus.*"

"Is that what I said: 'Do not stop, dearest papa. Tell me more.'?"

"You did, and now I understand why."

"I blubbered like an infant!"

"Because you realized I was not him. Sentiment is nothing of which to be ashamed. You loved your father immeasurably. It is only natural you still mourn him... And you were young when he died, were you not?"

"He became ill just after my ninth birthday. I was twelve when he died. I thought—as a boy I thought—I thought I had infected him with my illness."

"Oh no! I hope your mother, your brother, his physicians, assured you that was not so."

"I told no one... But why not think it? Many physicians—who my parents consulted about my illness, my father's personal physician, in fact—all warned that the falling sickness is contagious—"

"Rot! If that were the case your whole family, and all your servants, would have caught it and suffer from it. And no one else in your family has it, do they?"

"No."

"I rest my case! Oh, except your mother's father. But you did not catch it from him because he was dead well before you were born."

"Ah, but until it is disproved, there are physicians who will continue to believe we are infectious and demand our removal from society."

"And there are also physicians who think it is a manifestation of evil, a sign of madness. I know, because Dr. Warner told me in one of his lectures at the breakfast table. He is vehemently opposed to the postulation that the falling sickness is contagious or that it is a sign of evil—"

"Which is why I will fund his research, and his anatomy school."

"—but he does not discount the theory that when in the throes of a seizure, the sufferer is having a moment of madness."

"That could well be true. I do not know. I have no recollection." He turned his head on the pillow and met Lisa's gaze. "And because I do not know, who's to say that inside my head there isn't a monster—"

"I won't allow you to think that!" Lisa said fiercely, and kissed him to stop his words. She smiled when he winced. "Forgive me. I forgot about your split lip. But as you brought that on yourself, I have little sympathy. But for the boy, yes, I feel for him, deeply. The death of a parent, particularly one so loved as your father was loved, is a most harrowing experience. Though my own father's passing was a blessing in disguise. It may have left me an orphan but I no longer had to put up with his drunkenness. I preferred the poorhouse to living with him."

"I always wondered," Henri-Antoine mused, half in jest, a sidelong glance at Lisa, "if being sent to a poorhouse was like me being sent to Eton?"

"A school for the sons of the nobility like a-a poorhouse?" Lisa was aghast. "If you think that, then you do live in a fairy tale! You have no idea what life is like in a poorhouse."

"No. I don't. But you, my sweet girl, have no idea about life at Eton. Brutal place. Full of bullies. Boys locked up together in such places are little monsters... For this boy who thought himself a monster, I was scared witless. Never mind I was shadowed by a physician; he was bullied too. If not for Jack, I'd not have survived. My father finally rescued me. The experiment to see if I could be like other boys my age was a miserable failure."

"I cannot imagine you were ever like other boys, and I am not referring to your illness. Just as you are not like other men, particularly not those your equal. What other nobleman thinks about poorhouses, and dispensaries for the poor, and how best to advance medical science, or wholly sponsors a foundation that supports this work, and offers scholarships to poor but brilliant students—"

"*The worth of a great inheritance is measured not by how it is kept, but in how it is spent*. Words of wisdom my father left me in a letter the day I came into my inheritance on my twenty-first birthday... I have a thudding headache. I must sleep again. While I do, reflect on whether you wish to spend your life with a man who will forever be debilitated. When I wake and you are gone, I will accept your decision. I won't seek out Jack and punch his nose. If you stay—there will be no turning back, for either of us."

THIRTY-THREE

WHEN HENRI-ANTOINE came downstairs, it was midafternoon. He found the little table by one of the windows set for dinner. The French doors were wide. Just beyond the doors, where the path split left and right, the lads were seated on stools in the shade, playing at cards. He looked back at the table. It had two place settings. It gave him hope Lisa had decided to stay. But she was not at the folly. That the lads had positioned themselves at the fork in the path to stop trespassers, gave him the answer.

He pulled the hair out of his eyes and went outside in his shirt. The lads continued on with their card game as if he were not there. They were, after all, shadows, and he rarely needed to interact with them. Yet this time he came straight up to them, which had them instantly on their feet. He gestured for them to sit again and enquired, "You've kept the furnace stoked?"

"We have, my lord. Should've taken the chill off by now."

Henri-Antoine nodded and lingered. For the first time in his life he felt awkward and at a loss to know what to say to his lads, they who had been everywhere with him and knew his habits intimately. None of that had bothered him in the past. It did now, because of Lisa.

It was a relief when one of them said levelly, "Mr. Gallet will be here soon with nuncheon. But we were to tell Your Lordship that if we thought there was time, to send you to the grotto."

"And is there time?"

The lads looked at one another and then looked at Henri-Antoine and nodded. It was only when he strolled off down the path that wound its way through the coppice to Neptune's Grotto that they dared to grin at his back.

They returned to their card game.

HE SAW HER discarded clothing before he saw her. Each garment was neatly folded and the pile placed at the base of the white marble statue of a sea nymph. It was one of Neptune's daughters, seated at the edge of the plunge pool with a jug pouring water forth from its spout and into the pool. Lisa was partially hidden from view by this statue, submerged up to her chin, one hand holding onto the stone ledge. He wasn't sure if modesty had sent her into hiding, or if she was playing hide-and-go-seek. Or indeed if she realized he had seen her. He suspected not.

He stepped up onto the stone ledge where three steps descended into the water, wriggled his bare toes, and waited.

And just as he was about to step down into the water, she slowly waded out from behind the statue and came towards him. And when she was in front of him, she stood on the bottom step and rose up, the water rushing down her curves. Long wet strands of her hair plastered to her soaked chemise like tendrils of seaweed. To him she was the living personification of Botticelli's Venus, and her beauty left him speechless. And when she smiled shyly up at him and put out her hand in invitation, he did not hesitate to join her.

THE LADS REMAINED vigilant while Lisa and Henri-Antoine swam in the warmed waters of the plunge pool, making certain the couple's time remained uninterrupted by others. And there were others who tried to encroach. Several guests from the big house, either on foot or on horseback, were drawn to this section of the grounds by the smoke from the furnace's chimney. It was as if the white gray plume rising up into the blue of the sky beckoned all comers, a signal of invitation, much like the warmth of a fireplace fire on a chilly night.

Those guests hoping to visit the Temple of Vejovis rotunda, to see the view from the first floor, or to watch for themselves how the furnace heated the water of the pool to bathing temperature, were adamant they had permission from the Duke himself to go wherever they pleased. One couple even pleaded it was a medical necessity that they take a dip in the pool's warmed waters. Everyone was turned away.

The lads refused to be moved by any and all pleas, threats of prosecution, and even one threat of violence. Which was ludicrous, given their height and width, and the size of the muscles in their forearms and calves. All looked to have the strength to lift a sedan chair with occupant, on their own, and without any effort whatsoever.

And then along came a party of young gentlemen and ladies on horseback who could not be persuaded to leave. And when they were politely but firmly warned off, they protested by evoking ancient ancestors, their lineage, and connections to every powerfully political personage in the kingdom. The lads said not a word and remained unmoved.

And while the lads were being taunted, and thus distracted by this noble group, three of their number ducked around to the other side of the folly, through the shrubbery behind the privy. And by keeping low and moving by stealth, they progressed through the coppice, traversed a slope that took them below the level of the folly, to emerge unscathed and upright on a path that led straight to the entrance of the furnace, which was directly under the pool.

THE THREE congratulated each other on their success at getting past Henri-Antoine's monolithic lads, and finding themselves exactly where they hoped to be.

"Hear that?!" Bully Knatchbull hissed. "I *knew* it! Someone *is* splashing about in that pool!"

"Not someone, Bully. Harry. It's *Harry* with someone," Seb

Westby replied with a smug sneer. "Can't be anyone else. He doesn't go anywhere without those bears up behind him."

"Why does Harry need those bears? It's not as if an Englishman is likely to attack him, is it?" He gave a snort. "Oh, except Jack! Hahaha—"

"Forget about his bears, and concentrate on the matter in hand, Bully!"

"I don't see why he wouldn't want his Batoni Brotherhood to share in the fun of a splash in that pool. Seems only fair on a hot day."

"We told you why, Randal," his sister Violet whined, just as exasperated as Westby, and with a roll of her eyes in his direction. "He's with a female. And after what we witnessed at the cricket match we all know *her* name—"

"I don't like spying on a fellow when he's busy with a female," Bully complained. "Poor form. I'd rather march straight up to him and strike him with my glove and demand satisfaction—"

"This is the 80s, Bully. Not the 40s!" Westby countered. "Harry may look effete with his flowery clothes and his diamond-headed sticks and his bears, but he'd kill you in a duel. Look at what he did to Jack's face with his fists! Now unless you want to put up your fists—"

"And ruin this fine nose?" Bully said with a snort. "Not on my life!" When his sister gasped at his cowardice he added darkly, "Still. He's got to pay for what he said about Violet."

"So let's do this my way," Westby ordered. "We get eye-to-eye proof that the female he's with is the poor orphan, and then you leave the rest to me." He looked at Violet. "I promise you that by the end of the ball, you'll have your revenge, on him, and her, and so will I."

"You mean you'll have him apologize to Vi for what he said, don't you, Seb?" Bully asked, made nervous by the word *revenge*, which he did not like at all. "And I don't want any harm to come to that girl. She looks a nice sort. So I won't look over that wall if you intend to cause her a mischief!"

"She won't come to any more harm than she's already in. My word on it," assured Westby. "But Harry will get what's coming to him."

"Good. That's fair."

"Then it's settled. Can we get on with it before we're found out, or they're gone from here?" When Bully nodded, Seb turned to Violet. "You wanted to lead the way, so lead the way—"

"You're not looking over that wall!" Bully warned his sister.

"You are such a wet goose, Randal Knatchbull," Violet complained, and poked her tongue out at him. And with a hand to her straw hat, she ducked and went through the shrubbery, to climb the slope on the other side of the pool.

They emerged from the foliage directly behind a low privacy wall that screened bathers from the path used by servants bringing firewood to stoke the furnace. But as they were standing right up against the stacked stones, it was an easy thing to peer over it and into the pool. All three looked at one another, listened for any sounds coming from the other side of the wall, decided it was a good a time as any to pop their heads up, when they were startled by a voice at their backs.

"Lost your way?" drawled the voice.

Surprised, all three spun about and found themselves being scrutinized by none other than Henri-Antoine's much older brother, their host, His Grace the most Noble Duke of Roxton.

THIRTY-FOUR

As the Duke watched the trespassers leave, trudging up the path towards the folly, escorted by one of his brother's minders, an uneasy feeling formed in the pit of his stomach.

While all three of his younger brother's friends had attempted to offer him muddled explanations for their trespass, there was nothing they could say in defense of their prurient curiosity in wanting to take a peek over the wall into Neptune's Grotto, and they made no attempt to do so. And as the Duke did not mention it, it was as if it had never happened. He hoped his displeasure, and the fact Seb Westby's father had just arrived at the estate, would be enough to keep their mouths shut. The Duke of Oborne held the purse strings to his son's living and thus held great sway over him. One word from Roxton in Oborne's ear, and the threat of Seb Westby's debts not being paid might be enough to keep the young man's silence.

But there was already too much wild speculation and innuendo being exchanged behind fluttering fans and over communal snuff-boxes about the incident at the cricket match involving his brother. If any of it escaped the confines of the estate and found its way into the London scandal sheets, it would cause the sort of disgrace he abhorred. And he wasn't about to let his family be dragged down into the morass of common gossip by a girl whose family was one generation removed from servitude.

He would never have predicted his brother would lose his head over a girl of no family, no wealth, and no connections. And now he and this girl were showing a total disregard for him and his family, and their guests by swimming together in Neptune's grotto.

Something had to be done, and it had to be done at once.

Precisely what, he was not exactly certain. Buy her off and send her packing abroad came to mind, but that could wait. Paramount was getting Jack and Teddy married with the least fuss, and no scandal. The first order of business was having the girl returned to the Gatehouse Lodge and with the pretext she had spent the day at Treat with a fever, isolated within the house for fear of spreading contagion. His physician and a servant were in on the ploy.

Once the girl was back at the lodge, his brother could do his duty by Jack as his best man for the wedding tomorrow. With this in mind, he turned to his brother's major domo Michel Gallet—who had accompanied him to this secluded spot for the express purpose of keeping him informed of latest developments where his brother was concerned—and handed him a folded sheet of paper affixed with his ducal seal.

"Give this to him at once. And I don't care if you have to interrupt them. This must be done today. Best if she's removed under cover of darkness."

"If Your Grace insists."

"You foresee a problem? If so, I can send men to assist you."

"That won't be necessary, Your Grace. But..."

The Duke put up his brows and signaled for the major domo to speak his mind.

"She—Miss Crisp—she is not like all the others."

"She is not. The others knew their place. She does not because she has no place, and she certainly has no place being here. If there is nothing further—"

"There is, Your Grace." When the Duke said nothing but continued to stare at him, the major domo swallowed hard before speaking. "I have been in the employ of His Lordship for five years and thus I feel I have a measure of the man—"

"Gallet, Lord Henri-Antoine has been my brother for twenty-four, not five years. Whatever you feel you need to share with me, believe me, it is not needed or wanted. I appreciate your loyalty to him but—"

"Forgive the interruption, Your Grace, but my loyalty has and always has been to the family, your family, and thus to you both. And I would be doing you a disservice, as much as His Lordship, if I did not advise that to forcibly separate Miss Crisp from His Lordship will, in all probability, lead to an irreparable estrangement between you and His Lordship."

"Don't be absurd! Brothers don't fall out over a sly wench from the gutter!"

Michel Gallet straightened. "I beg your pardon, Your Grace, but I would advise you not to believe the common gossip being spread about Miss Crisp from malicious sources."

The Duke took a step toward the major domo, gloved hand clenched about his riding crop, and glowered down at him. "You—you *dare* to advise—*me* about-about this girl?"

"I do, Your Grace. Miss Crisp is poor, that is not in dispute. But she is, in my opinion, an estimable young woman—"

"Estimable? *Estimable?* Are you drunk or mad, Gallet? How can you defend her after what's—" The Duke waved his riding crop in the direction of Neptune's Grotto. "—after what's been going on over there? Estimable young females do not go swimming unchaperoned, and never with a man! Good God! Her behavior is-is—deplorable. The worst type of girl knows her place better than that trollop!"

"So it must seem to anyone who does not know Miss Crisp."

The Duke dropped his hand holding the crop. "And you know her, do you?"

"Better than those who seek to discredit her character."

"Ye Gods! She should have thought about her character before she embarked on this quest to entrap my brother—"

"She did nothing of the sort!" Michel Gallet retorted, and immediately felt his face grow hot at his social lapse. "Pardon, Your Grace. But that is far from the case."

"Are you certain you haven't fallen for a beautiful face?"

"No, Your Grace. Miss Crisp is a beauty but she is also a beautiful person."

The Duke wanted to laugh but as the major domo appeared

serious he resisted the urge. He said calmly, "Her actions would suggest otherwise."

"Her actions are those of a young woman in love. As such, the consequences are irrelevant."

"What a romantic you are, Gallet!"

"I merely offer you my observations as one who has come to know Miss Crisp, and who knows His Lordship intimately."

"Do you indeed, Gallet?"

"I do, Your Grace."

The Duke capitulated. There was no harm in asking. "What would you advise?"

The major domo did not hesitate in his response. "That Your Grace allow me to handle this state of affairs. I will ensure Miss Crisp is returned to the Gatehouse Lodge this afternoon, and that His Lordship returns to his apartment; no one the wiser."

"And if I do not let you handle it?"

Michel Gallet held out the sealed note the Duke had given him for his master.

"Then I am afraid, Your Grace, that there will follow an estrangement between you and His Lordship."

When the Duke took back his note and thrust it into his pocket, the major domo dared to breathe a small sigh of relief.

"So tell me, Gallet," said the Duke. "Why would my brother and I have a falling out over this girl from Soho?"

Michel Gallet held the Duke's gaze and his voice was steady and clear.

"Because, Your Grace, Lord Henri-Antoine and Miss Crisp are deeply in love."

<h1 style="text-align:center">THIRTY-FIVE</h1>

THE SUN HAD set by the time Lisa was ushered into the Gatehouse Lodge by a bleary-eyed maid. She tip-toed up the staircase and was on the landing when the Lady Mary appeared, holding a taper. She took one sweeping look at Lisa and while her expression did not change, Lisa became acutely aware that her attitude most certainly had. Gone was the warmth in her voice, and her manner was decidedly chilly.

"Is there to be a wedding tomorrow, Miss Crisp?"

Lisa bobbed a curtsy and kept her eyes lowered. "Yes, my lady."

"Then you had best get to bed. You have a big task ahead of you making certain my daughter has the happiest day of her life."

"Yes, my lady. My lady, I—"

"No. I do not want or care to know. Teddy's happiness is all that matters."

"Yes, my lady."

When Lisa finally slipped into bed beside Teddy, she lay there staring up at the canopy, not moving, hoping she had not woken her friend, and wondering what she knew and what to tell her. Michel Gallet had told her what to say, and she was mortified to think the Duke of Roxton had gone to the trouble of putting it about she had a fever and had been confined to the house until it passed. And so if he had done that, then he knew the rest. And if the Duke knew, then so did Henri-Antoine's mother... So much for staying in the background as her cousins had demanded of her. Still, she could not do anything to change their opinion of her now, nor did she want to if it meant never having spent time with Henri-Antoine at the folly. She had no regrets. What was required of her now was to get through the rest of her stay without causing a scandal, or doing anything that might interfere with Teddy's happiness.

"You've returned," a drowsy Teddy muttered, sliding across the bed to snuggle in beside Lisa. "Are you feeling better...?"

"Yes. Yes. Much better."

"I'm glad. Because I would have been sad had you not been able to be with me tomorrow."

"I would not miss your wedding for anything, Teddy. You are going to be a most beautiful bride..."

"And Sir John a handsome groom."

"Yes! The handsomest! Now sleep."

Lisa turned her head on the pillow and tried to sleep.

TEDDY'S WEDDING DRESS was of blue silk, the bodice and over-gown adorned with delicate white lace rushes, with *engageantes* at her elbows; the pearl choker about her throat had been presented to her at breakfast by her parents. Pearls strung on blue ribbons were threaded through the braids of her fiery hair, and diamond clasps and pearl-headed pins helped keep her coiffure in place.

Lisa wore a similar gown in shell pink silk, the fabric without lace embellishment, except at the elbows, the bodice cut low across her breasts. A sheer fichu was strategically crisscrossed over her *décolletage* and tied in a large bow in the small of her back. Matching pink ribbons adorned her hair, which was similarly styled to Teddy's, fat curls brought forward to cascade over one shoulder.

The girls and Teddy's step-father were the last to leave the Gate-house Lodge for the Treat Family chapel. And by the time their carriage arrived at the big house, family and guests were seated and waiting, the groom and his four male attendants the most anxious of all, Jack pacing up and down before the congregation, clenching and unclenching his fingers. Henri-Antoine, far from offering soothing words of reassurance, teased his best friend mercilessly, and the two were soon bantering back and forth in their usual manner that had everyone smiling and laughing along with them, none more pleased at this reconciliation than their immediate family.

And then there she was, Teddy as a beautiful bride escorted down the aisle on the arm of her proud step-papa. She could not stop smiling, and when Jack turned and saw her, he could not stop smiling either. And when she was brought to stand beside him before the Duke's chaplain, the couple gave a little joyous hunch of the shoulders, they were so happy. The bouquet was passed to Lisa to care for during the ceremony, once Christopher Bryce had done his part and given Teddy's hand to Jack.

And while the service celebrated the coming together of two young people clearly in love, it was not lost on the congregation that this was a highly desirable dynastic union. It joined two branches of the same family, further strengthening the Roxton family tree. Theodora Charlotte Cavendish, as the new Lady Cavendish, walked down the aisle on the arm of her husband, Sir John George Cavendish, without the inconvenience of ever having to change her surname.

The newly-married couple left the chapel showered in white rose petals, handfuls thrown from baskets held by the young girls of the family dressed in their best silks. Lisa followed the couple and behind her were the groomsmen, the Duke and Duchess of Roxton, and the mother and step-papa of the bride, and finally the rest of the congregation spilled out into the expansive black-and-white marble paved courtyard.

Bride and groom were surrounded by well-wishers offering their congratulations, while the younger children were finally able to run about, watched over by their nurses and maids, the army of liveried footmen with trays of drinks doing their best to avoid these small personages dressed in outfits that replicated those worn by their parents.

Finding herself jostled to the outer rim of this circle of feathers and finery, Lisa retreated to stand by one of the enormous marble urns planted with topiary that were placed around the perimeter of this courtyard. Here she remained a spectator to the comings and goings of the liveried footmen; the little boys weaving in and out amongst the adults, chasing each other; the little girls in a cluster on the other side, twirling about so that their silk gowns lifted to show their white stockings, while throwing the remainder of the rose petals above their heads, so that the petals fell into their hair. And then there were the small clusters of guests in non-stop conversation, laughing and chatting amongst themselves. In the center of it all, was a radiant Teddy and Jack, so happy to finally be able to begin their married life, and surrounded by their loving family and friends.

Lisa had never felt more alone in a crowd. London streets were friendlier than this. And while it was nonsense to think she was being deliberately ignored, it was an easy thing for her to feel she was being shunned. And all the while she stood alone by the urn, in her peripheral vision she was acutely aware of Henri-Antoine, one of a group of young gentlemen in conversation by a set of open French doors. He was dressed in a coral pink ensemble, the matching frock coat and waistcoat smothered in gold thread and spangles; a pink ribbon tied back his hair, and he leaned lightly on his diamond-topped walking stick. It had not escaped her notice that Jack had chosen to wear a similar outfit in blue silk so that he matched Teddy's color choice, just as Henri-Antoine matched hers. It was fanciful for her to believe this was deliberate, but the romantic in her liked to think so, and it made her smile.

Yet she dared not look his way for fear she would be unable to hide her feelings, and with the growing suspicion that perhaps their time at the folly, as secluded as that spot was on the estate, had not been kept as private as she had hoped. The last thing she wanted was to draw attention to him or to her, to *them*. Yet her suspicion was realized, when through the chatter and the laughter she heard her name mentioned on the other side of the urn, and by *The Horribles*. A cold dread seized her. And while she could pretend to deafness and continue to smile and watch the activity in the courtyard, she could not help overhearing snippets of a conversation she was certain was deliberately loud for her benefit: *Just another conquest...fortune hunting mopsqueezer...Chelsea Bun House all over again...Athanasian wench...Roxton to have her gone by morning...Banished once and for all...*

"Miss Crisp, I thought you might care for a glass of wine? I do beg your pardon, did I startle you?"

Lisa mentally shook herself and looked about to find Jamie Fitzstuart-Banks at her elbow. He held two glasses of wine, and she readily accepted one. Doing her best to ignore those on the other side of the urn, she turned her shoulder to them and smiled brightly.

"Thank you. Not at all. I was miles away. In London, in fact."

"Do you return to Gerrard Street soon?"

"Yes. Yes. I suspect in the next day or two. When a carriage can be arranged to take me to Alston for the stagecoach."

"I leave for Banks House in the morning. Perhaps you would care to journey up to London with me and my father's family?

"That is kind in you. But I have my companion with me—"

"There are two carriages, and Papa and I always ride. So plenty of room for you and your companion."

"Thank you, but I would not wish to inconvenience Lord and Lady Strathsay and their children, or you."

"It is no trouble at all. In fact, it was Papa who suggested it," Jamie admitted with a self-conscious smile and heightened color to his cheeks. "So you see," he said apologetically, "your travel plans are all arranged."

"I see that they are," Lisa replied placidly.

She made no further protest, though she felt heat in her face realizing her return to London must have been a topic of discussion within the family. Her departure arranged with the minimum of fuss or whiff of scandal attached to the family's good name. It was obvious her separation from Henri-Antoine could not come soon enough for all concerned.

"Please thank your parents," Lisa continued in a steady voice. "I will be sure to have our trunks packed tonight, if a servant could be sent to collect them and let us know the time for us to be ready in the morning, I would be most grateful."

Jamie bowed and soon excused himself, disappearing back into the crowd, his commission accomplished, and Lisa finished off her wine and looked about for a footman to collect her empty glass. She revised her earlier estimation that she had never felt more alone in a crowd; this was the moment, knowing she was considered an embarrassment, and unwanted by these almost mythical beings in their fairy land; she almost wished the Duchess of Roxton and Kinross had not made the effort to find her. But she quickly retracted that sentiment because she loved Teddy and it was wonderful to see her married to "her Jack" at last. Nor did she regret her time with Henri-Antoine. She would cherish those few precious hours spent with him forever. And just as tears welled behind her eyes and she was castigating herself for her self-pity, small fingers slipped into her hand. She turned to find Elsie looking up at her with a frown.

"Are you sad, Lisa?" the little girl asked gravely.

Lisa went down on her haunches and kissed Elsie's cheek.

"Thank you for rescuing me. I was feeling a little bit lonely. But now you are here I am much better." Lisa admired the girl's exquisitely-painted silk gown and the pearls threaded in her hair, and gently repinned a diamond pin that had come loose in her coiffure. "There. You won't lose that pretty pin. And you look beautiful in your gown, Elsie."

"You are too pretty to be sad, Lisa. I like your hair with ribbons in your braids. Henri-Antoine is wearing pink too. Did you see him? Would you like to sit at my table at the breakfast?"

"I would like that very much, but perhaps you have a special place at a special table?"

Elsie smiled and whispered in French behind her hand at Lisa's ear, "I do and your seat it is next to mine. Maman she promised me."

Lisa was genuinely surprised and delighted. "That makes me so happy. We shall have the most wondrous time together."

Elsie hunched her shoulders and held her hands close to her bodice, and she would have said more, except fingers placed lightly on her shoulder had her looking up and around. It was her eldest brother, and she said to him, "Julian, this is Lisa and she has a seat next to mine at the wedding breakfast. Maman promised."

"How delightful, *ma petite*. I wonder if you would allow Miss Crisp and me a few moments to talk?" the Duke of Roxton asked in French, and with a smile that softened his features, making him appear almost approachable. It was clear he loved his little sister very much. "You will see her again as we are all going into the State Dining Room soon. She will find you there. You may tell Maman that it is almost time. Would you do that for me, *ma soeur chérie*?" He waited until his little sister had skipped off into the crowd before turning to Lisa and saying conversationally, the warmth gone from his voice, "I am pleased you accepted the Strathsays' offer of a place in their carriage. Your return journey to London will be much more comfortable than the one coming here."

"Thank you for your consideration, Your Grace," Lisa replied levelly, hoping she sounded more confident than she felt. At least shaking knees did not make a noise. "And thank you for permitting me to attend Teddy's wedding. My stay here has provided me with a lifetime of memories."

The Duke arched a brow at this, but as Lisa's gaze remained steady and there was nothing in her manner to imply she was being insincere, he made no comment, inclined his head and walked off, just as Teddy, with Jack in tow, pounced on her.

She hugged Lisa to her, kissed her cheek and grabbing her hand said, "Sir John and I won't allow you to hide behind the topiary! Come! We're going indoors for the breakfast, and you must sit with us—"

"I would love to, but I promised Elsie—"

"Oh? Then you must not disappoint her. But promise me you will sit with us when the pudding arrives. I'm certain Elsie will let you go then. Doesn't Sir John's eye look much better today?"

"Much better. And Teddy…"

Teddy looked around at Lisa from kissing her new husband's cheek and frowned when she saw she was making her curtsy. "Lisa? No! You do not curtsy to me—"

"But I must make my curtsy to Lady Cavendish. Is that not so, Sir John?"

"It is a lovely gesture, and you are Lady Cavendish now, my love."

"Walnut pickle to that!" Teddy pouted. "I won't have my best friend curtsy to me!"

"Walnut—*walnut pickle*?" Jack was surprised. He had never heard that expression before.

Lisa laughed and quickly put a hand to her mouth before saying, "Oh Teddy! I haven't heard you say that since Blacklands."

"I haven't heard you say it ever," Jack grumbled, feeling left out of the joke.

Teddy's eyes shone and she let Lisa explain. "Teddy used the expression at school to signal her displeasure. It always made me giggle, for it is quite harmless, and our teachers did not know what to make of it."

"Papa loathes walnut pickle," Teddy explained. "He knows. You say it to him and see if he doesn't laugh too."

"I will," Jack stated emphatically. "I'll mention it casually during the speeches." He grabbed Teddy's hand because everyone was making for the French doors, and said to Lisa, "You will join us for cake, won't you, Miss Crisp—"

"She most certainly will not!" Teddy said with a snort, and dragged Jack away before he knew what was happening.

Lisa watched the crowd part to allow the bridal couple to pass through the doors before them, her spirits very much lifted with this brief interlude; Teddy always had the power to make her feel better about anything and everything. And just as she decided it was time for her to join the throng, there was an almost imperceptible touch to the middle of her back. She did not need to turn around to know who it was.

"I wish we were seated together. No matter. Come the ball, my duties will be over. I'll find you."

Lisa's smile remained fixed nor did she react but she did take a small step so that his fingers were firm against her back. A slight tilt of her chin to her right shoulder, and she said, "I have the great honor of sitting with your sister."

"Excellent. Elsie will look after you. And Roxton is mistaken. The Strathsays will be leaving tomorrow without you."

"It's been arranged—"

"Over my dead carcass it has! You and I—*we*—have other plans. Give Elsie a kiss from me..."

THIRTY-SIX

Tᴿᵁᴱ ᵀᴼ ᴴᴵˢ word, Henri-Antoine found Lisa in the ballroom not many minutes after the Duke's string ensemble had struck up the music for the first dance of the evening, the minuet. The bridal couple went through the intricate steps effortlessly, as a pair used to commanding a public space all their lives, and not, as Lisa knew, Teddy tucked away in the Cotswolds, a tomboy to the tips of her fingers.

Lisa had never danced in public, only at school, so when Henri-Antoine came up to her she had this terror he meant to have her dance with him. It must have been writ large on her features because he smiled and winked and leaned in to say at her ear, "The terrace is deserted."

"I thought you were about to ask me to dance," Lisa confessed with a laugh of relief when they were outside.

She had her hands to the balustrade and was looking up into a late afternoon sky. When he made no reply she turned to discover he had stepped away from her. He bowed and held out his hand. She shook her head.

"No. I cannot. I have not danced since school."

"No excuse. We can hear the musicians well enough, and should darkness descend, there is enough wax burning out here to illumi-nate St. Paul's. Come. Take my hand."

"I do not doubt you dance beautifully, but I am gauche and—

"You danced the other night with Cousin Charles and with Jack, did you not?"

"I did. But—"

"If you managed to dance with Jack's two left feet, you can dance with me."

"That was in the obscurity of a dining room. This—this is vastly different."

"I did not bring you out here to save you from public embarrassment. I want you all to myself."

"That is what I want too."

When she placed her hand in his he dared to raise it to his lips.

"Then ignore the world on the other side of those windows. Listen to the music and concentrate on me, as I will be on you."

She smiled tremulously. "I would like nothing better than to forget the world, and I can do that when we are alone together, and because—and because, aside from Teddy, whom I love as dearly as I would love a sister, you are all that matters to me. But you—you have family and obligation and duty, and the world watches and whispers and waits. I do not want to be the cause of any—*unpleasantness* between you and your brother, or be an embarrassment to your family."

He came up to her, still holding her hand, and his concern made his tone harsh. "Embarrassment? Was something said to you? Did Roxton—"

"No. No. He was most correct. I do not doubt he knows about us, but he refrained from being impolite. But there are others here who also know—"

"Let them!" he retorted. "My business is none of their affair."

She touched his cheek briefly. "It is one thing for us to share a house in Bath, away from the world, quite another for you to flaunt me under the noses of your peers at a ball. Not even the Prince of Wales dares to do that with Mrs. Fitzherbert, and it is rumored he's married to her."

"The Prince is an infantile idiot," Henri-Antoine said. He glared at her. "Is that how you think I see you? As a Mrs. Fitzherbert?"

"You? No. But I doubt even she has been called a-a *fortune hunting mopsqueezer*. As for an *Athanasian wench*, I have no idea what that is!"

Henri-Antoine went still. Lisa wondered if he had heard her, such was the faraway look in his eye. And then he spoke, and his voice was like ice. "Forgive me. You should never have been subjected to such filth. I will deal with that presently. For now..." He mentally shook himself free of his rage and smiled and bowed to her again. "The music beckons. Come. Let us treat ourselves to an allemande..."

She smiled and curtsied and gave him her hand again. With the formalities exchanged, he bowing to her, and she curtsying to him, they joined hands and were soon dancing up and down the terrace. He was exceptionally light on his feet and expert at guiding her through the intricate steps, so that while their first run through was fraught with missteps and mishandlings, at which they both smiled and laughed as they fumbled on, their second dance was much more fluid, Lisa gaining confidence with each turn and step. It was not long before they were both smiling and concentrating less on their steps and on each other as they took turns ducking under each other's raised arms, and then dancing back-to-back, then face-to-face, and all the while with their fingers entwined. It was as intimate as a couple could get upon a dance floor without actually kissing. And they were so in harmony with each other and enjoying themselves that it was not long before the small number of persons watching them through the window had swelled to a crowd.

It was only when they stopped to regain their breath, and Henri-Antoine went off to seek out a footman with a drinks tray, that the crowd at the windows reluctantly dispersed. Lisa retreated to the far end of the balustrade to await Henri-Antoine's return, her face flushed from dancing and cooled by the breeze coming in off the lake, its surface shimmering in summer's dusky light.

Dancing with Henri-Antoine had restored her confidence and her happiness, so that when she felt a tug on the bow at her back holding her fichu in place, she naturally assumed he had returned with glasses of refreshment, and was playfully alerting her to the fact.

When a second tug unraveled the bow, she turned around with a teasing scold, accusing him of undressing her, the fichu opening up from where it had been crisscrossed over her bodice, and now left hanging loose about her shoulders. But it was not Henri-Antoine. It was Lord Westby.

WESTBY WAS SO close Lisa could smell the spirits on his breath, and then he dared to come even closer. And when she went to tug the fichu from his fingers he closed them into a fist and whipped the thin white strip of gauze from her shoulders. She tried to quell a rising panic and kept her voice firm.

"My lord, I am cold. Please give me my fichu."

"Why? You don't need it. Everyone should see your bubbies. They're rather perfect." He lifted his gaze to her eyes. "Lucky Harry, and now lucky me..."

"I should warn you, Lord Henri-Antoine will be here at any moment—"

"I'm waiting for him. It's time he returned the favor—"

"Favor?" she asked, with what she hoped was genuine curiosity, reasoning that if she could not threaten him she needed to keep him talking and Henri-Antoine would arrive before Lord Westby had a chance to act upon whatever demons were driving him. "What favor is that, my lord?"

"It's only fair he share you with me."

"But I do not wish to be shared."

"It's not up to you, is it?" he drawled with a smug smile, and set his hands on the balustrade either side of her, trapping her. He leaned in and attempted a kiss, but when she quickly averted her face, he settled for sniffing her neck and whispering near her ear, "Whores get what whores deserve."

Lisa grimaced and felt herself heave when he kissed her ear. When she tried to swat him away, he grabbed her wrist and squeezed. Despite the pain and the fear of what he might do next, her voice was steady when she spat back bravely,

"I am not a whore, and even if I were, I'm not *your* whore! And you've no right to force yourself on any woman, whore or no!"

She tugged her hand free and pushed him with all her strength. Off his guard and wrong-footed, Westby stumbled but made a quick recover. He lunged for her. Before Lisa had taken more than a couple of steps he had pulled her into his arms.

"Let's strike a bargain. I'll forget Harry's flirtation with Peggy

Markham if you come with me into those bushes. And if you don't do what I want, I'll tell Harry you did it anyway. He'll believe a Batoni Brother before he—*Sweet Mary Mother of God!*" He yelped. "What the —*what the devil!*"

Instantly he staggered back and away, a hand to his ear and swearing profusely. It was obvious he was in considerable pain. Lisa could only stare, wondering what had happened, and breathed a huge sigh of relief.

Salvation had arrived in the form of a six-foot four-inch smoking giant.

THIRTY-SEVEN

W HEN HENRI-ANTOINE had stepped off the terrace back into the ballroom he found a footman with a drinks tray, absconded with two glasses of champagne, and was almost at the open French doors again when his brother stepped into his path. He blinked at him, wondering what was the matter. The Duke might look to be sailing on a calm sea, smiling serenely, jeweled snuff box in hand, but Henri-Antoine took one look into his eyes, eyes that were so like their mother's, and just like hers, could not hide his innermost feelings. He saw troubled waters. So he immediately thought something must be the matter with one of his nephews or nieces.

"Julian? What is it?"

The Duke took the glasses from his brother and offloaded them on the liveried footman at his elbow, then sent the servant away.

"Stay inside, Harry."

"Wh—why? What's happened?"

"More than enough. Your private performance has fed the flames, when I had almost put it out. Or did you think it would go unnoticed? Half my guests were at the windows."

At the word *performance*, Henri-Antoine's eyes went dull and his jaw tightened. He watched his brother shift his gaze out across the ballroom and smile benignly as he spoke. It was only when he finally looked at him again that Henri-Antoine deigned to reply.

"Keep your concerns to yourself, and stop interfering unnecessarily in my affairs."

"Interfere unnecessarily?" repeated the Duke. Henri-Antoine had his full attention. "Everything is my concern, Harry, most particularly my family—you, what goes on here at—"

"I'll be gone tomorrow, and she is coming with me. Concern yourself with that!"

Henri-Antoine went to step around his brother, but the Duke walked into his path again and they bumped chests. Henri-Antoine stepped back, but he did not step away.

"Out. Of. My. Way."

The Duke moved closer, doing his best to ensure their conversation was not overheard. He lowered his voice to a hissed whisper.

"You risk making an even greater fool of yoursel—"

"More fool you for not trusting in my judgment!"

The Duke huffed his disbelief. "*Judgment?*" He looked his brother over and drawled, "But it's not your brain that's doing the thinking, is it?"

Henri-Antoine's lip curled. "Envious I got to choose my favorite dish from the menu and you didn't?"

"How dare—*Mon Dieu*, how dare you speak to me—"

"This isn't about you. It is about choice."

"Choice?"

"Mine. To live as I please with whom I please."

"That's not choice. That's being selfish."

"Yes. I am. I can be." Henri-Antoine regarded his brother with some sympathy. "I'm sorry you didn't get to choose whom you were to marry, or how you wanted to live your life."

"Have I ever shirked my responsibilities? Have I ever disappointed Deb, our parents, my children, you? Have I not done the best that I can with the estate for Frederick, for posterity?"

"You have, Julian. You are an exemplary duke, a wonderful husband and papa, a good master, and a wise and circumspect politician. Everything you do is commendable. No one has ever said otherwise; I certainly sing your praises."

"Thank you. Which is why, as your brother, I concern myself in your aff—"

"Still, if it all went to the bottom of the sea tomorrow—your marriage, the estate, the respect and esteem in which the family, the children, *everyone* holds you—as an eldest son you could blame it all on *mon père*. Seb Westby blames his father for everything. He can. He's the eldest son. I cannot. My choices are mine to make. So are my mistakes."

The Duke took another sweeping look about at his guests, saw his duchess regarding him from across the room, smiled and rolled his eyes at her, then looked back at his brother. He smiled.

"No one is prouder of you than I, Harry. The inheritance *mon père* left you, you could've squandered the lot. But you haven't. You're putting it to good use. What the Fournier Foundation has already achieved in a few short years could change medical science forever."

"Yes. It will. You have never meddled in that aspect of my life, so refrain from interfering in my private life."

The Duke opened his mouth to speak, then felt a presence at his elbow and looked about to find his mother had swept up to them with a bright smile, fluttering a painted gouache fan at her *décolletage*.

"JULIAN, I require your immediate attention to a matter that has been troubling me for quite some time," the Duchess of Roxton and Kinross announced in French. "And it cannot wait. So please, to come with me." She put her arm through his and did the same with Henri-Antoine. "You too, *mon chou*. This problem that has arisen requires both my sons."

And without a word of protest, she swept her sons off to an anteroom a few feet behind them which had been set aside for guests who wished to rest somewhere away from the noise. Unsurprisingly it was deserted. Antonia had seen to that, and two footmen stood guard at the entrance to make certain it remained that way. With the door closed on the noise of orchestra competing with dancers and conversations, the Duke looked to his mother, nonplussed.

"Maman, you certainly know how to pick your moment. What is this problem—"

"You. You are the problem, Julian."

Roxton's face turned brick red. He had the expression of a guilty four-year-old caught with his fingers in the strawberry jam.

"Why am I the problem, when it is Harry who—"

"Do not blame your brother."

"But, Maman!" The Duke wiped a hand over his face, exasperated

Henri-Antoine gave a start. Had His Grace actually whined like a four-year-old? And then he looked at his mother, this tiny woman in heels who glared up in warning at her big, pouting forty-year-old son, that she was not to be trifled with, and his anger evaporated at the absurdity of this scene. The laughter bubbled up within him until his shoulders shook. Now his mother and brother were staring at him.

"It's not—it's not—*all* Julian's fault, Maman," he finally managed to say.

"Thank you, Harry," the Duke conceded, much mollified, by the concession and his brother's good humor.

"Most of it, but not all."

"Harry, if you had not—"

"Enough! Both of you!" Antonia demanded. She looked from one to the other, pointing her fan. "Why is it that these conversations they arise at the most inopportune times? Could this not have waited until tomorrow?"

"It seems not. Harry is leaving in the morning."

Antonia put up her brows in surprise and waited for her younger son to explain.

"To Bath."

"To Martin's house?"

"Yes. Though we should stop calling it that, now it has reverted to me."

"Yes. Of course."

"And more importantly, because Martin is here now, in his final resting place with *mon père*, where he belongs."

"He's taking that girl with him," the Duke stated sullenly.

"Lisa is not *that girl*, just as Martin was never *that servant*," Henri-Antoine corrected.

"You can't compare the two!"

"I can and will," Henri-Antoine stated. "Martin may have been *mon père's* valet for a time, but he was much more than just a servant, wasn't he? He was our parents' life-long friend. He was your godfather and confidant. He was a friend of this family. And most of all he was an estimable and honorable gentleman. An aristocrat in thought, word, and deed, if not in blood. And we all loved him."

"Yes. Yes, he was," Antonia agreed quietly. "And you said it very well, *mon fils chéri*. He was more honorable and noble than many of those born to it by blood. You do not have to look further than our own relatives to find those of noble blood who have not lived up to their potential: My uncle, the grandson of a king, was a scoundrel."

Roxton looked at his brother. "And this girl—this Miss Crisp... What is she to you, Harry?"

Henri-Antoine did not hesitate in his response. "Lisa is everything to me. In a word, she is priceless."

There was a stunned silence until the Duke found his voice.

"And you, Maman? What is your opinion of this g—of Miss Crisp?"

"Oh? Is someone finally asking me what I think?" the Duchess teased, a wink at Henri-Antoine, though the Duke continued to look uncomfortable and anxious. "If my son says she is priceless, then I believe it. So," she added, looking from one son to the other, "what is to be done with Mlle Crisp?"

THIRTY-EIGHT

Jonathon, Duke of Kinross, stuck his cheroot in the side of his mouth and scooped up Lisa's discarded fichu. He gave it a little shake and inspected it a moment, orientating it to its purpose, and then he smiled at Lisa and held it up.

"Let's tie this back on you," he said jovially. "And then we can have a little talk."

With her arms crossed over her low bodice, Lisa stared up at him. Here was the six-foot four-inch smoking giant in the form of Elsie's papa. At the wedding breakfast, when she had been seated beside Elsie, also at her end of the table was the Duke of Kinross and his wife, the double duchess Antonia, Duchess of Roxton and Kinross. Lisa had witnessed how father and daughter adored one another, as did the Duke and Duchess. And for her to be seated in their company was an honor indeed.

Though she was thankful she had Elsie to talk to, because she felt out of her depth in such exalted circles. Her de Crespigny cousins would definitely be envious, and possibly not believe her. Then again, there wasn't much she could tell them that they would believe about her stay.

And this latest episode—Lord Westby's attempted seduction—made her feel foolish and embarrassed. So much so that she burst into tears of relief when Elsie's papa placed a comforting arm about her shoulders and patted her arm.

"I'd cry, too, if an oaf like Westby had pawed me! Drunken dolt! Come. Let me arrange your fichu. I'm rather an expert in female attire, particularly those outfits belonging to Mademoiselle Yvette and Signorina Simonetta. Elsie can attest I'm the best personal maid those two have. That's better! You should laugh. You'd laugh even harder if you saw Elsie and her papa having afternoon tea and chattering away with her two dolls in French or Italian or both!"

"I would enjoy such an afternoon tea, Your Grace," Lisa assured him with a watery sniff.

She let him arrange the fichu about her shoulders and turn her this way and that, and finally, when he had tied the bow to his satisfaction she thanked him and would have said more, but he stepped away and disappeared back into the shadows, alerted by a series of moans and muttered threats. And when she heard another yelp, followed by pleas and assurances, she could hardly believe her ears, least of all her eyes, when Lord Westby stumbled out of the darkness and crossed in front of the windows, a silhouette of a man doubled over with a hand to his ear.

Kinross returned to Lisa, puffing on his cheroot and then exhaling smoke up into the night sky.

"He'll not be bothering you or Harry again. That nasty hole to his ear will be a nice reminder. Me threatening to geld him if he ever came near you again was the decider."

Lisa's eyes opened wide. "You burned him with the end of your cheroot?"

"I branded him with a good behavior mark. He'll look at it and he'll behave."

Lisa gasped and then giggled.

Kinross grinned. "That's better. You have a lovely laugh and it suits you. Are you feeling up to having that little talk?"

Lisa nodded. "I'm feeling much better, Your Grace. So yes. Though..." She looked over at the open French doors. "I had expected His Lordship to have returned by now... He went to fetch refreshment. I wonder what has detained him—or whom..."

"Whom" was right. Kinross knew. Before his attention was diverted by Westby coming out onto the terrace and bothering Lisa, he had been watching Henri-Antoine through the windows. He saw his Duchess sweep up to her sons, and all three disappear from view. He did not need an imagination to know what was being discussed—this girl standing before him. But he pretended ignorance, his smile just as friendly as before.

"Possibly detained by some fellow or other wanting a word. You know how it is at these types of functions—Come to think on it, you wouldn't know... Lucky you! But trust me. So many people want to bleat in m'ear about something." He lifted his cheroot and leaned into Lisa to whisper. "I gave these things up years ago, so don't tell my wife."

Lisa cocked her head. "Somehow I suspect *Mme la Duchesse* is aware of your ploy, and your habits, Your Grace."

"Ha! I knew you had a good brain the first time I saw you. It's written all over your face, and you have intelligent eyes, just like my wife. Besides, Elsie has taken a shine to you. My daughter may only be eight-and-a-half years old, but she has an old head on her shoulders. Far too grave for a little person, but later that will stand her in good stead, as it has you. Particularly..." His smile turned sentimental. "Particularly when it comes to choosing a mate."

Lisa's smile dropped and so did her gaze. She was thankful they were standing by the balustrade and not by a wall sconce or taper and thus in a blaze of candlelight, for she was sure her face had flushed with color.

"The thing about being loved by an intelligent woman," Kinross continued smoothly as if he were blind to Lisa's sudden awkwardness, "is that I know my wife loves me—*for me*. She fell in love with a plain-speaking, no-nonsense, bull-headed fellow who doesn't suffer fools, and sets more store by a man's courage and loyalty and friendship than he does the type of coronet he's got stuck on his head. I came late to my ermine, and I don't mind telling you that being a duke is more trouble than it's worth. And mine wasn't worth a groat until I brought to it my merchant fortune.

"But my wife was a duchess when I met her, and her son's a duke, and by all accounts the most powerful peer in the realm, who owns half of England. That means they have a lot of relatives and friends, and retainers, who are always surrounding them. I've bought into the family business, if you like. I trot myself out at functions, and play my part. And I let people bow and scrape to my dukedom when it suits me, or when I must. But I never lose sight of who I am, and neither does my wife."

Lisa wondered where he was taking this homily, and could have kicked herself for not realizing at his mention of a mate that his story was leading straight to Henri-Antoine. But she had forgotten her own predicament, fascinated by his story. So when he eventually mentioned Henri-Antoine in the same breath, she should not have been surprised, but she was, and again she felt herself blush. But this time she did not look away.

"And as you're an intelligent girl, you won't take this the wrong way or be missish when I tell you that when we are alone together we are simply Jonathon and Antonia, a man and a woman who love and respect each other and are the best of friends. The ermines and the titles and ancient lineages only mean something on public occasions, and that's where they belong, and where the earwigs and foot-lickers swarm like flies to carrion, feasting on our self-consequence. What's important as a couple is that you live as if those trappings don't exist; that you live honestly, and without the prejudice of family interference and expectation. Do you understand, m'dear?"

"I think that I do, though for me—"

"What am I saying? Of course you understand!" he declared, deliberately interrupting her because he had more to say, and because he was aware time was short. Henri-Antoine would return at any moment. He drew back on his cheroot and exhaled away from her. "Which brings me to the family I married into. I can tell you—I'm certain you'll understand because you're not one of them—it's not easy being part of this lot. You think I'm being flippant. After all I'm a duke. But my wife's first husband was the venerated fifth Duke— You've heard of him?"

"Yes, Your Grace. I have. My aunt was *Mme la Duchesse's* personal maid for many years—"

"That's right! Gabrielle! How could I forget that?! Wonderful woman. Couldn't have done without her at Elsie's birth. And she was there for the birth of the two boys, too." He smiled slyly. "I'll wager she has a story or ten about her time here—"

"Stories, yes. But nothing inappropriate or any confidences

broken. She is—has always been—most circumspect with her story-telling. And she guards her memories."

Kinross nodded as if this was a given, and returned to his line of thought. "The fifth Duke was very much his own man, Miss Crisp. And so am I. People take me as they find me, or not at all. And that pleases my wife, and the family know where I stand."

"I see that you are. And *Mme la Duchesse* would not have fallen in love with you and married you otherwise. I dare say she would also have been most disappointed had you changed just to please her or her family."

"Precisely! And that brings me to my step-son Henri-Antoine, though except for his mother, we all call him Harry. He's-he's—complicated," Kinross mused, gaze seemingly on his cheroot, but with a heightened awareness of Lisa and her reactions. "He not only looks like his father, but his mother tells me he has his temperament too. He's not one of these fellows who trumpets his feelings about, or easily shows emotion, even with family. His illness has left him self-absorbed. And I guess with good reason. It's a hell of a disadvantage to live with, not knowing from one day to the next if you'll be struck down with a seizure. Though we—his mother and I—suspect this last episode was of his own making—"

"Your Grace, I—"

"—and said more about his emotional state than it did his health. But apart from his aloofness with his fellows, and oft being inscrutable he is also—"

"—kind, generous, caring, shy, intensely private, and-and—loving," Lisa stated, and having had the courage to speak her mind she added for good measure, "And I-I love him with my whole heart."

"Yes, I rather thought that was the way of things."

She bravely looked up at him with a wan smile. "I'm afraid I have allowed my heart to rule this old head of mine..."

"May I offer you a piece of advice? It's what I've been wanting to say to you from the beginning."

"I welcome any advice you care to give me, Your Grace."

"Be yourself. Always. Don't second-guess. He either loves you as you are, or not at all. And I am confident he does love you, Miss Crisp. No man who dances with a woman the way Harry danced with you just now could not be in love! That you love each other is all that matters. Not his family. Not his mother. Most certainly not his brother. And the rest of it—ancient ancestors, this pile of stone, the relatives, society—it's irrelevant when all is said and done."

"To me and how I feel about him, most definitely. But what about my humble circumstances? I see no shame in being poor. It is not something I can alter about myself, other than do my best to find useful employment and try not to be a burden on my family. But I have no family connections, certainly no ancestors worth mentioning, and if we ever did have a pile of stone, there certainly wasn't enough of it to build anything useful. I wonder if that is irrelevant to him...?"

"Ha! I made my fortune on the subcontinent, and all I had when I started out was self-belief, a willingness to work hard, and a good business brain. Some things can't be measured in pounds and pence, or by examining a parchment to see what branch you sit on in the family tree. It is often intangibles that mean the most—they do to me. Things such as honor, integrity, intelligence, love, kindness, faithfulness, generosity, loyalty. I could go on. But I think I've put my case well enough, don't you?"

"Yes, Your Grace. And thank you."

He smiled and patted her shoulder, and at the sound of voices, straightened and stubbed his cheroot on the sole of his shoe. "Just you remember when the time comes what I said about being yourself."

And as he went off across the terrace to return to the ballroom, Lisa wondered what he meant by "when the time comes," but she certainly remembered his words, and they were to be a comfort and a strength when she needed them most. For now, Teddy and Jack had escaped their guests to join her on the terrace, and Henri-Antoine was a few steps behind them, and at his back a footman carrying a tray of drinks.

"Here you are!" Teddy announced, rushing up to Lisa in a whirlwind of silk petticoats and smiles. She gave Lisa a hug. "We were looking for you inside everywhere, were we not, Sir John?"

"Everywhere. Didn't think to look out here," Jack admitted. "Until Harry told us where you were. At least you had Kinross to keep you company." He frowned. "Thought I saw Seb slip out here, but Uncle Charles and I were deep in conversation about his plans once he gets to these new United States of America, so I couldn't get away. Must have been mistaken…"

Henri-Antoine distributed glasses of champagne, and held his up, a wink at Lisa.

"Before I toast the newlyweds, I first must implore your forgiveness for my asinine behavior at the cricket match, the results of which are still starkly evident—"

"No, Harry. No! Not tonight," Jack said firmly. "All's forgiven and forgotten. To point out fact, I'd forgotten all about it until Lady Fittleworth asked how I'd come by my purple eye."

"I was very helpful and said he'd run into a door," Teddy told them with a grin.

"A door!" Jack blustered, affronted. "Might as well have said I'd stuck myself in the eye with my viola bow!"

Everyone laughed, except Jack.

Teddy kissed her husband's cheek. "I'll remember that for next time."

"There won't be a next time. I've sworn off hitting best friends."

"So have I, Jack. Never again." Henri-Antoine raised his glass. "To Sir John and Lady Cavendish. Wishing you a long life, a happy marriage, and infants aplenty. The best friends this best friend could have."

The other three raised their glasses in reply and sipped.

"Thank you, Harry. And I should like to toast my best friend," Teddy said, raising her glass again and smiling at Lisa. "To Lisa Crisp. The best friend a girl could possibly have. I am so happy you are in my—our—lives."

They all sipped again.

"But you're not coming to live with us, are you?" Teddy added wistfully, gaze still on Lisa.

Lisa teared up and shook her head. "No, dearest. I am not. But— but I do hope you will allow me to visit you—both of you—"

"Most definitely! Whatever the circumstances," Jack stated emphatically, not a glance at Henri-Antoine. "Would never turn you away. Always welcome. Always. Isn't that so, Theodora?"

"Yes. Whatever the circumstances," Teddy replied forlornly, giving Lisa's arm a squeeze. "Always…"

As she, too, avoided looking at Henri-Antoine, Lisa wondered if

Jack had confided in his bride, and precisely what it was he had said to her. It did not bode well that Teddy was regarding her as if she were about to be sentenced to hanging. There followed a moment's awkward silence between the four, until Henri-Antoine coughed into his fist again and said quietly,

"This is your day, Teddy—Jack—so I do not wish to say anything further tonight. But tomorrow... Tomorrow I hope to have something to tell you both."

"We'll still be here tomorrow, won't we, Sir John?" Teddy replied, suddenly bright and eager again. "We aren't departing for Bath until the day after tomorrow. We have all day tomorrow."

Jack looked at Lisa and then at Henri-Antoine and noted they were going out of their way not to look at each other.

"Yes. That's right. All day tomorrow, and the night. We'll be here tomorrow night, too. And when we leave the day after tomorrow, it won't be until mid-morning. So plenty of time..."

Teddy and Jack hoped that Henri-Antoine's announcement was what they were both secretly wishing for and wanted to hear but had not voiced out loud for fear it might not come true. Lisa had no idea what that announcement could be.

THIRTY-NINE

Not long after the toasts on the terrace, Henri-Antoine dismissed his lads for the rest of the evening, and taking Lisa by the hand, slipped away from the ball to his apartment. He took her through a labyrinth of passageways, ill-lit back stairs, and rooms that seemed to go on forever. Most rooms had some form of lighting, or a fire in the grate, and if there wasn't either, there was always a manservant or a maid just around a corner, going about their duties, and who could offer His Lordship whatever he required.

At one stage Lisa asked, "Are we still in the same house or have we trespassed onto another's property? This place goes on forever!"

"If you do not know your way around, it does. I am taking the shortest route possible."

"So your apartment is closer to Paris than it is to London?"

"You may well be right. It is as far from everything as I could possibly make it. And it might as well be in France. It is staffed with my servants. I bring them down with me from the London house, even my cook."

"Of course you do," Lisa muttered and tried to quell her surprise. "Who else is to cook for you in your own kitchen, if not your own cook—"

"Precisely, and—" He frowned and flushed. "Is that your tongue I see planted in your cheek, Miss Crisp?"

"A trick of the light, my lord."

He said nothing further, though he gave her a sidelong glance so she knew he had noted her playful impudence, and then she made him stop again as they were about to pass through one room in particular that had her wondering if they had stumbled upon a smuggler's hoard.

The room glittered with gilding and gold metal thread in the furniture tapestries. One wall was covered floor to ceiling in the largest mirrors Lisa had ever seen. But it was what was reflected in the candlelight, as Henri-Antoine walked about with his taper, that opened wide Lisa's eyes: A treasure trove of trinkets, boxes, statues, paintings, furniture, fixtures, and oddments, all piled up and in a jumble, as if these items had been ransacked, not only from other houses, but previous centuries.

This monolith of a building had a surprise around every corner, and each surprise was more surprising than the last.

"This is the room the family calls the Ancestral Guilt Room," Henri-Antoine explained. "My nephew Freddy, who will one day—a day long into the future—be the seventh duke, has dubbed it the *What do we do with this lot because we don't want it, but it's been in the family for generations* room." He ran a finger around the rim of a marble pedestal that supported a cup made from polished seashell and silver. There was an inscription but he did not read it out. "Some of these pieces date back before Queen Bess's time. Some of it belongs to me. Most of it my brother inherited from our father, who inherited it from his. My mother has a few pieces here, willed to her by her grandmother, a nasty old witch of a woman. None of us want this-this—*stuff*, but we don't know what to do with it."

"If none of you want it, not even your nephew, then perhaps it could be put to better use?" Lisa suggested, trying to take in as much of the hoard as possible.

"Such as?"

"You could hold an auction—"

"Auction?" Henri-Antoine was surprised but Lisa had all his attention. "Go on."

"There may be other pieces your brother and your mother, and any other relatives, would like to contribute to the auction, and feel they are superfluous to their needs."

"That would include most of what's stuffed in this house," Henri-Antoine quipped. He smiled. "But go on."

"You could have a catalog printed, like the one advertising the Duchess of Portland's collection, and list all the items here in this room, and whatever else is contributed."

"I know Deb, my sister-in-law, would gladly contribute. She's been wanting to do something with this lot for years. But my brother is a sentimentalist. He would need convincing."

"It seems a waste to have all this sitting here being of no use, particularly when no one in the family wants it, when it could be used to better purpose, and for other's enjoyment. Lots of people bought objects from the Portland collection, and no doubt most of those items had been gathering dust for years."

"Such as Elsie's shell.

"Yes. Just like Elsie's shell. And perhaps your brother would be more agreeable to the idea if it was named the Roxton Catalog?"

"He might indeed."

"And if the proceeds were used for a worthwhile cause…?"

"That would certainly add weight to the argument for him, his duchess, and our mother."

"And what more worthwhile cause could there be than the one closest to your heart: The Fournier Foundation for medical research."

He grinned. "You are a mind reader."

"Oh? I thought I was a witch."

He stuck the taper on the nearest surface, grabbed her to him and gently took her face in his hands. He kissed her. "You're so clever. No wonder I love you. Come," he said and snatched up the taper, leading her by the hand. "My apartment is through this door and along the passageway."

Lisa followed, mute. She was dazed by his declaration. He had never said it before, so she wondered if she had misheard him. Particularly, as it was said in such an offhand manner. So she did not attach great importance to it. And by the time they entered his apartment she was distracted enough not to dwell on it. For there on the carpet by a sofa was her battered trunk, and sitting on the lid was her rosewood writing box in its cloth cover.

"Where's Becky?" she asked, looking about, as if the girl was to be found near her belongings.

"Returning to London with the Strathsays—"

"But—"

"If you want her back, you'll have to write to the Widow Humphreys offering her niece employment."

"Is that what she told you?"

"That is what she told my major domo."

Lisa was suddenly awkward. "Her aunt may not allow her to be employed by the likes of me."

"The likes of you?" Henri-Antoine was puzzled. "She should be so fortunate. Widow Humphreys can advertise to her clientele her niece is seamstress to Her Ladyship. Her business will treble overnight."

When he crossed to the rosewood writing box and set it in the middle of the sofa and beckoned her to join him, she had a flash of memory. Of him presenting the writing box to her in Gerrard Street, he dressed just as magnificently. But how formal he had been with her upon that occasion. And here he was, not that many weeks later, with the same box, in very different circumstances indeed. She wondered what he wanted with it at this hour. For her to write a letter, and to whom? She grinned.

"Does His Lordship require the services of an amanuensis in the middle of the night?"

"Droll. It's just that I won't be able to sleep until I have your answer," he replied, the writing box now between them on the sofa.

"You intend to dictate this answer and I am to write it down?" she asked cheekily.

He looked at her with one eyebrow raised over his blackened eye.

"There is more to this writing box than meets the eye, isn't there?"

She knew at once. Without further prompting she opened the lid, which was unlocked, and folded back the red leather writing surface to expose the compartment below, pressed on the panel that concealed the three little drawers, and removed it. She looked up at Henri-Antoine.

"You have left me a note?"

"Notes."

She gave a little gasp of pleasure.

"When? How? I don't recall you having access to my writing box since Gerrard Street."

He smiled thinly. "His Lordship works in mysterious ways. But I know you won't leave it there, so let me tell you. I wrote the notes. I had Michel conceal them. I was otherwise occupied at a wedding."

"They were put there tonight?"

"Today. Yes."

"And you wrote them—when?"

Henri-Antoine sat back against the sofa cushions.

"You're not a witch. You're a grand inquisitor!"

She giggled. The truth was she was excited and apprehensive, and these were her first secret notes. She took a deep breath and asked, "Which drawer should I open first?"

He threw up a hand. "It matters not. Only your answer matters."

She gave a tug on the little round horn pull of the left-hand drawer, and there inside the compartment was a tiny piece of folded paper. It read: *Try the third drawer along.* She folded the paper and put it back and slid the drawer closed, a look up under her lashes at Henri-Antoine who was grinning at her. So she did as the note instructed, and pulled open the right-hand drawer. Inside was another piece of paper, but this paper was wrapped around something. Lisa slowly unwrapped it, and what she saw made her stare at Henri-Antoine in astonishment.

"It's a ring!"

"Wonderful. Michel managed to place it there without it falling out of the paper. That would have required a treasure hunt to find it—"

"It is real? Is it old?"

"Do you mean are those diamonds and sapphires paste? No, they are not paste. Yes, they are real. Yes, the ring is old. It requires a good polish. The last to wear it was my grandmother, Madeleine-Julie Salvan Hesham, Marchioness of Alston, daughter of the Comte de Salvan, and my father's mother."

"Your father's mother?"

"Yes. She died over fifty years ago..."

Lisa held the ring between thumb and forefinger and inspected it closely, turning it this way and that in the candlelight.

"Your grandmother had slim fingers."

He smiled. Trust her to be interested in the anatomy of the wearer rather than the value of the stones, or, surprisingly, the significance of what the ring symbolized.

"She was five-and-forty when she died. Of course, there is the possibility her fingers were even slimmer when she married, and the ring has been altered since. She was just sixteen when she eloped with my grandfather."

"Eloped? How—How did you come by the ring?"

"I see the grand inquisitor has returned," he muttered. "My father left it to me, along with a letter," he explained patiently. "I opened the letter for the first time this morning. That ring was inside the packet."

"A letter from your father?" Lisa was intrigued. "He wrote you a letter to be opened *today*?"

"Not today precisely. The letter was for me to open when I had come to a particular decision about my life."

"Did he not also leave you a letter to be opened on your twenty-first birthday, too?"

"He did."

"How delightful and farsighted of him! He loved you very much." She frowned and leaned across and kissed him, before looking into his eyes. "I can imagine reading such a letter was emotional for you…"

He held her gaze. "The entire week has been like that."

She kissed him again, and lightly pressed her lips to his black eye. She then held out the ring shyly. "Will you put it on me?"

"Gladly. First, you should peek in the middle and final drawer, and give me your answer."

"Oh yes! Silly me forgot that drawer. Dazzled by precious stones!"

"Dazzled by the circumference of *grandmère's* ring finger."

Lisa laughed and was still smiling when she pulled open the tiny middle drawer of her writing box. She was not surprised to find tucked inside a third small piece of paper. She quickly pulled it out and unfolded it and was smiling up at Henri-Antoine before she even glanced at the note itself. And then she let her gaze drop to the paper

Drawn on the paper was a love heart, and inside the love heart were two words: *Marry me.*

She stared at the heart, and at the words, and drew a deep breath. She thought she might stop breathing from happiness. Finally, she exhaled, carefully folded the note with shaking fingers and sat there, head bent. And then the tears came. They dropped onto the folded paper with a splash. She could not stop them, nor did she try. She was indescribably happy that he loved her so much he wanted to marry her, and she was unutterably miserable because she loved him so much she had to refuse him.

When she was finally able to articulate her feelings, she enlightened him that she was crying from happiness, overwhelmed by the occasion and what it meant, but most of all because she could not give him the answer he was expecting. He was stunned. But he was not angry or sad, or even disappointed. Strangely, he was numb.

He believed her when she told him she loved him. He even believed her when she confidently assured him she had every intention of living with him as his mistress, and they would be a couple in every sense. But he did not believe her when she said he could not marry her. It interested him that she did not say she could not marry *him*, but that he could not marry *her*. What did that mean, precisely? What doubting bee was buzzing about in her head, and who had put it there? Two and two did not add up to four.

Perhaps a good night's sleep would bring perspective and some answers. With this in mind, he set the writing box aside, and put his grandmother's wedding band on the side table by a little silver handbell which he then rang. When his major domo appeared in the doorway, Henri-Antoine made Lisa a bow and wished her a goodnight. He was gone from the room before she looked up from her lap.

It took them both a long time to fall asleep. He on the chaise longue in his dressing room, she tucked up in his big four poster bed, both wondering what tomorrow would bring.

FORTY

LISA WOKE in the big bed thinking herself back in her narrow bed in Gerrard Street. But she was surrounded by plump pillows filled with the softest down, and covered by sheets of the finest linen, and the bed was enormous, the canopy and bed curtains of velvet. The curtains covering the windows had been drawn back, and light streamed across the carpet. Placed across the coverlet at the end of the bed was one of Henri-Antoine's banyans, of golden yellow silk damask, and with the sleeves rolled up.

Lisa threw back the covers, and wearing the banyan over her chemise, arms hugged about her body, she followed the light through to a spacious dressing room, furnished with chaise longue, chair, and curio cabinets. Stacks of books lined the window seat. A fire smoldered in the grate. And sitting on tiles before the fireplace was a large, linen-lined copper bath. Through an open doorway she could see into a closet, and hanging on pegs along the wall were sumptuous frock coats in silks, linens, and cottons, alongside matching waistcoats, and there was a row of mahogany clothes presses.

What surprised her most were the clothes laid out on the chaise longue under the windowsill. They were hers. A floral cotton caraco, petticoats to match, a flimsy apron, clean stockings, and a chemise. She was staring at this assortment when a thin-shouldered man dressed in black frock coat and breeches came through from the closet, and introduced himself as Kyte, His Lordship's valet. Two manservants carrying pails of hot water followed, and behind them a maidservant, who kept her eyes lowered to the parquetry.

"Good morning, ma'am," Kyte said cheerfully, as if it was an everyday occurrence for Lisa to be in his master's dressing room. He made her a small bow. "Rose will help you bathe and dress and arrange your hair the way you like it, while I make certain your breakfast has been set out in the alcove of the drawing room. I trust hot chocolate, toast, and an egg meets with your approval? After breakfast the lads will escort you to His Grace's library."

The thought of eating made her queasy. She might sip the hot chocolate. What made her lose her appetite altogether was mention of the library. And any awkwardness she had being in Henri-Antoine's apartment vanished, replaced with apprehension and dread; she had heard from Jack what it meant to be summoned to His Grace's library. But mention of Henri-Antoine's lads made her curious.

"The lads are to take me?"

"M'sieur Gallet is to take you. The lads will be your escort."

"Escort?" Lisa thought the word ominous.

"Yes, ma'am."

When Lisa continued to frown, Kyte thought it best to explain. He dumped a towel, hairbrush, and pins on the maid, and sent her across to the bathing area to supervise the placement of a privacy screen, then turned to Lisa with the same noncommittal smile.

"His Lordship has assigned two of his lads to you. For your protection—"

"Excuse me, Mr. Kyte—"

"Kyte, ma'am. Just Kyte."

"Oh? Excuse me, Kyte, but I do not understand why I need protection here in His Grace's house."

The valet's fixed smile slipped slightly. The girl was young and beautiful and he was not surprised his master was besotted. But there was nothing tawdry about her, or her relationship with his master. Michel Gallet had confided about the little notes, and the ring, left in the rosewood writing box. And as she carried herself with dignity and was devoid of artifice, he treated her with the respect he thought she deserved, and was polite.

"His Lordship considers it necessary for your well-being and his peace of mind that whenever you step outside the confines of his apartment, the lads be with you at all times. In this way you may move about freely, unconcerned at being approached by persons with whom you do not wish to have speech or contact. I assure you, all of His Lordship's servants are most discreet and loyal."

"I would never doubt it, Kyte."

The valet bowed and would have departed but Lisa had one further question, and that was the whereabouts of his master.

"His Lordship rose early with the intention of taking a morning ride. I dressed him for just such an outing. However, he did not inform me of his subsequent movements, but M'sieur Gallet may be able to provide you with the answer after your breakfast."

Later, when the major domo arrived to take her to the library, Lisa asked him the same question. He apologized for not being able to tell her His Lordship's present whereabouts. But he was able to elaborate on his master's early morning activities, and gave Lisa an entertaining account while she finished her hot chocolate.

"His Lordship did indeed go riding," Michel told her. "But first he attended to some unfinished business at the stables. It seems that last night he ordered a carriage to be made ready for departure at first light, and instructed that the trunks and belongings of a number of guests be packed and these guests and their personal servants be aboard the carriage by dawn. Unfortunately, His Lordship's directive was perceived as one of amusing himself at their expense and they were all disbelieving. Thus, while their servants had indeed done as instructed and had themselves and the trunks and belongings of their masters aboard the carriage as ordered, the guests were still abed when they should have been making their way to the stables. Undeterred by this circumstance, His Lordship had the guests rallied, and when they objected to the early hour, and what they considered gross mistreatment and refused to do what was ordered of them, His Lordship took the only option left to him."

"What—what did he do, M'sieur Gallet?" Lisa asked, chocolate cup paused between saucer and mouth.

"His Lordship had the lads manhandle them to the carriage in their nightshirts. And when the females objected most stridently, His

Lordship ordered the lads to swing them up over a shoulder and carry them, kicking and screaming if need be, to the waiting carriage—"

"There were women involved?" Lisa put aside her chocolate cup, and sat up straight.

"Two gentlemen and two females. A brother and his sister—the Knatchbulls—and Mr. Knatchbull's close friend Lord Westby, and Miss Knatchbull's friend, a Miss Medway. All four were subsequently bundled into the carriage, their various items of clothing thrown in after them, and the carriage, under escort of outriders, was ordered to take them to The Swan—"

"—at Alston?"

Mention of the local inn where she and Becky had been set down by the stagecoach gave Lisa a kernel of an idea as to why Henri-Antoine had sent the carriage to that particular location, and under escort.

"Yes, ma'am. A number of stagecoaches pass through the town, setting down and picking up passengers, mostly for travelers taking the London to Southampton road."

Lisa set aside her cup and patted her mouth with the linen napkin before asking calmly, "What happened at Alston, M'sieur Gallet?"

"While the Knatchbulls, Lord Westby, and Miss Medway were taking refreshment at The Swan, their carriage left for London without them—"

"To London—*without them?*"

"Yes, ma'am. Their personal servants and belongings were permitted to depart in the carriage provided by His Lordship, while their masters were detained under armed escort until the stagecoach arrived."

"Dear me. I fear they will not enjoy their journey on the common coach."

"They will not. Although, one of the lads confided Mr. Knatchbull was inclined to see the humor in the exploit and confessed that they were all deserving of His Lordship's justifiable ire. He was willing to take the inconvenience on the chin. Lord Westby was not so inclined and had to be restrained from lashing out at his friend, whom he blamed entirely. As for the two females... They burst into howls of self-pity and nothing the gentlemen said or did could silence them."

"I have sympathy for those unfortunate people having to share the carriage with them all the way to London."

"His Lordship's sympathy was also for the common traveler. He instructed the carriage carrying the servants and belongings to stop five miles up the road and wait for the stagecoach's arrival. Whereupon their masters were permitted to rejoin the carriage for the rest of the journey to their Westminster abodes... If you have finished your chocolate, ma'am, it is time for us to go. We do not want to keep His Grace waiting."

Lisa suddenly looked as if she were about to climb a scaffold. And as she followed Michel Gallet through a warren of passageways and rooms to what seemed the farthest reaches of this palatial collection of buildings, two of the lads at her back, she wondered if they were her escort to make certain she did not escape and dart off to hide. And as she failed to see any of the guests, she presumed she was being taken to the library via a route that deliberately avoided the public rooms.

Finally, they came to a set of inlaid double doors where two footmen stood as sentries. Here, M'sieur Gallet left her with a bow, and the two lads at her back went over to an alcove to wait. One of the sentries disappeared inside, and did not return for over a minute, and then with the unsurprising news His Grace was ready to receive her. Once inside, she was to walk the length of the room, and not to dawdle, and to do so in a straight line, and not to deviate. With those instructions, the door was held wide, she entered, and the door closed on her back before she had taken more than four steps.

She did not loiter, and kept to the central path, but she could not resist looking about her in fascination and awe. The room was on the same vast scale as the ballroom, with floor-to-ceiling bookcases on two levels, a narrow walkway with an ornate railing running around three sides and accessed via a spiral staircase. There were collections of chairs, tables covered in maps and large folios and rolled parchments, world and celestial globes on pedestals, statues and marble busts in alcoves, oriental rugs scattered across the parquetry, and along the entire length of one wall, windows divided one from the other by impressive paintings.

Lisa came right up to an enormous desk, where the Duke sat, and who rose up out of his chair on her approach. The thud of her heart was in her ears as she dropped a curtsy as he came to stand before her. He invited her to join him by a fireplace that was to one side of a second spiral staircase that lead up to the narrow walkways and more bookshelves. Here also was a collection of comfortable wing chairs and two high-backed settees back-to-back, one facing the fireplace, the other the spiral staircase. It was on the settee facing the fireplace that the Duke indicated Lisa sit.

She wondered why he did not sit opposite, and if he intended to deliver her a stern lecture on his feet. And then, as if from nowhere, the Duchess of Roxton and Kinross swept up to stand beside her son. And both mother and son stared at her without expression and in silence. Lisa instantly shot up off the settee and down into a curtsy in one motion, sick to her stomach and so nervous she thought she was about to be physically ill.

FORTY-ONE

A LITTLE WHILE earlier, while Lisa was taking her breakfast and before she was escorted through the labyrinth of passageways and rooms to the library, the Duke and his mother were already ensconced in there, grim-faced and concerned. They were discussing Miss Lisa Crisp and what they could do, if anything, about her.

"If this is to be done properly, then you must do as I ask," the Duke stated, watching his mother pace before him.

The Duchess threw up a hand and kept pacing. Roxton was tired and after the previous day, with the wedding celebration and then the ball, he had hoped to enjoy a morning of doing nothing more than sharing it with his wife. And now this... Watching his mother walk back and forth in front of his desk made him even more tired. Did she never weary?

"Maman—"

"Yes. Yes. Naturally we will do it the way you say, Julian. It is just —It is just—"

"—unpleasant. For everyone. But we must think of Harry—"

"He is all I am thinking about." She met her son's gaze. "Be gentle with her. She is young. And this—" She swept an arm in a wide arc. "—all of this it is overwhelming to our friends, so imagine how it must be to a girl from her background. Incomprehensible, yes?"

"I will strive to be as gentle as I can, given the circumstances."

The Duchess was unconvinced. "That is what worries me, Julian. The circumstances."

Roxton resisted the urge to roll his eyes.

"And what worries me, Maman, is that you will attempt to soften the blow. That will not work in this instance. Miss Crisp is not a stray kitten in need of a bowl of cream. She has—by all accounts—a brain, and I will call upon her to use it so that she understands the gravity of her situation. She must. For all our sakes."

Antonia wrung her hands, but when she nodded, Roxton sighed his relief.

"So you must resist interfering—"

"Interfering—?"

"—for Harry's sake. I know you. You are too kind, too emotional. You want everyone to be happy—"

"And there is something wrong with that?"

"Not in the least. I love you for it. But there are times when kindness won't work. Please, leave this to me."

"I do not know how it is you can be so-so—*indifferent*."

Roxton gave a bark of laughter and shook his head.

"And this from a woman who was married to the most inscrutable nobleman of his age!"

Antonia pouted. "But your father he was never like that with me."

"No. He was not. But just like him, it falls upon me as duke to put the planets of our world back into alignment. So. You will play your part and say not a word?"

"I will. For Henri-Antoine. It will be difficult, but I will do it."

"Good. That is all I ask. Then we are all agreed." Roxton looked over her head towards the fireplace. "I only hope you will thank me in the end…"

FORTY-TWO

"**P**LEASE SIT, Miss Crisp," the Duke ordered. He waited for his mother to take her place on the sofa, then flicked out the skirts of his frock coat and sat beside her. His gaze remained on Lisa. "Now that the wedding is over, and so, too, the ball, I wonder at your plans?"

"My plans, Your Grace?"

"I suspect you must be eager to get back to Gerrard Street and your duties there. I do not doubt Dr. Warner has missed your assistance. And his patients requiring the services of a scribe must be lining the footpath waiting for your return."

Lisa moved a little on the settee, but kept her back straight. She glanced at the Duchess, then looked to the Duke in some surprise.

"You know about-about my duties at the dispensary?"

"I do." The Duke smiled. It was not pleasant. "I know everything there is to know about you, Miss Crisp."

Lisa cocked her head in curiosity. "Then...surely...Your Grace does not need to ask me about my plans?"

Antonia's fan shot up to her mouth to cover a smile, and she cleared her throat to stop a laugh and quickly lowered her lashes. Roxton paid her no heed and did his best to ignore Lisa's question, though he did not think her being impudent.

"Indulge me, Miss Crisp."

"Very well, Your Grace," she replied calmly, though her fingers tightened in her lap; her only sign of nervousness. "Upon my arrival here, I had every intention of returning to Gerrard Street to resume my duties but-but my—*circumstances* changed—"

"—and so you no longer wish to assist the sick poor or continue writing letters for them...?"

"I do, but I hope to help many more than just those who attend Warner's Dispensary by assisting in the work of the Fournier Foundation—"

"—from Bath. To be precise, from a manor house on the outskirts of town?"

"Y-yes, Your Grace."

"My brother's house to be precise."

"Yes, Your Grace."

"Where you intend to live and assist in the work of the Fournier Foundation? And how precisely will you do that from Bath?"

"I-I do not know exactly, Your Grace. The-the particulars have yet to be worked through with His Lordship—"

"My brother with whom you intend to share this manor house on the outskirts of Bath?"

Lisa dared not look at Henri-Antonie's mother, but she bravely met the Duke's gaze.

"Yes, Your Grace."

"And you fully intend to live in sin with him."

"Your Grace, I-I... It may look to you as-as—"

The Duke sat forward. "I understand perfectly, Miss Crisp. I am a man of the world. And in the lofty circles I inhabit, it is commonplace. You've been made an offer of a far better life, and so you have made the hard-headed decision to change your vocation from dispensary assistant to prostitute."

Lisa could not have been more shocked had he struck her across the face. Her cheeks drained of color and then glowed pink.

"A-a *prostitute*? No! No! No, Your Grace. That is not how—"

"And why not?" the Duke continued smoothly, as if she had not spoken. "You're very pretty. Why would a taking little thing of beauty want to toil away helping the poor, the diseased, and the dying? That must be the fastest route to losing your looks. God knows what diseases you could catch from such a hell hole! And how could you ever hope to escape such a place if not through the—um—*patronage* of a wealthy gentleman? What luck you happened upon my brother—

"It wasn't like that. I am not like that."

"—whom I hear you tended with your own fine hands. He was grateful for your assistance, and of course when he saw you again, he could not help but notice your beauty. He is a mere male after all. Is that when you formulated your plan to ensnare him? Knowing you would be attending the same wedding? You must have thought all your Christmases had come to you at once."

"Excuse me, Your Grace, but I did no such thing as-as *ensnare* His Lordship. For the longest time I did not even know who he was. I only knew that—that it was—that it was *fate* that had brought us together—"

"Fate?" The Duke scoffed. "Come now, Miss Crisp! That is the stuff of fairy tales."

"Pardon, Your Grace, but Treat is the stuff of fairy tales for someone like me, and yet here I am."

The Duke's features hardened. "Yes. And here you are. How old are you, Miss Crisp?"

Lisa took a deep breath and was inclined to tell him that he knew the answer to that question, as he did all the other questions. But she suspected these questions—indeed this entire interview—was designed to humiliate her into thinking twice about being Henri-Antoine's mistress and to make her return to Gerrard Street. What the Duchess thought of this, and of her, she could only speculate. But she did not want to do that, because it would only make her sadder than she already was. Best to answer the questions, and hopefully she would then be able to flee the library as soon as possible.

"I am nineteen years old, Your Grace."

"Nineteen?" The Duke looked genuinely surprised, and then he pulled a face and dared to look her over as if she were a prize filly with an eye to purchase. "Nineteen... Then I'd say you've a few years to enjoy that fine house on the outskirts of Bath. But I wouldn't become complacent. If you want my advice, I'd trot off to town upon occasion, best when my brother is here or in London, so you can scout for potential suitors to replace him when—"

"Replace him? I have no intention of—"

"Your intentions are irrelevant, Miss Crisp. All I care about is my brother. He will tire of you, and he will move on to something younger and fresher, so you had best have your wits about you, and a new lover waiting for you in the wings. For I will not countenance him spending one penny more on you than is necessary." He smiled briefly. "I dare say, a pretty girl like you, who has had a smattering of education, will have no trouble in attracting a new lover—"

Lisa shot to her feet, furious. It was the phrase *smattering of education* that burst the dam of her tolerance and circumspection. She could not defend the indefensible. The Duke could call her prostitute if he so wished, under the circumstances. She had agreed to be Henri-Antoine's mistress. But she was proud of her education, and there had been nothing shoddy in her schooling. Besides, she would not have Blacklands maligned before the one person who had been instrumental in her gaining a good education.

"With respect, Your Grace, I did not have a-a *smattering of education*. I had an excellent education," Lisa stated confidently. "Blacklands was—*is*—a superior educational institution for young ladies, and I took full advantage of what was on offer." She dared to address Antonia. "Please believe me, *Mme la Duchesse*. I am forever grateful to you. I only wish—I only wish—matters had turned out differently—"

"Sit, Miss Crisp," the Duke demanded wearily. "It is rather late in the day for you to wish for an outcome that will not disappoint my mother, particularly when you have every intention of further wasting your education by becoming a nobleman's whore, regardless it is her son you are bedding—"

"I am not a-a whore," Lisa stated, putting up her chin. "I intend to be His Lordship's mistress, and there is a difference."

She resumed her seat on the settee, and returned her hands to her lap. But she could not bring herself to look at the Duke, and she dared not even glance at the Duchess. When the silence stretched she kept her chin tucked in, gaze on the flimsy apron covering her floral petticoats. Finally the Duke spoke, and she detected a note of regret which sent her to the brink of tears.

"And yet, Miss Crisp, you were offered so much more..."

This did bring Lisa's gaze back up to look at the Duke. She knew he was alluding to Henri-Antoine's marriage proposal, and she was surprised he knew about it so soon. Perhaps it was the Duke with whom Henri-Antoine had gone out riding earlier that morning, and no doubt confided in his brother. Knowing this did bring the tears spilling onto her cheeks. But she was quick to dash them away. She detected regret in his voice, and looking up into his eyes she saw it. Or was it wishful thinking on her part that he considered her acceptable as a wife for his brother? That indeed would have surprised her. No doubt it was because the Duke had his mother's eyes, and thus this gave a false sense of the compassion in him which was writ large in hers. She decided to pretend ignorance of his meaning.

"I beg your pardon, Your Grace?"

"You have refused my brother's offer of marriage."

"I have, Your Grace."

"May I—we—know why that is?"

"The offer was made under duress…"

"Duress? You mean he would not have asked you had you not forced his hand?"

"No, Your Grace. I did nothing of the sort. He should not have asked me, that is all."

"And yet, he did… Why do you think that is?"

Lisa shrugged, eyes on the flimsy apron. She plucked at a thread. She swallowed and looked up. "Because he-he is a gentleman. Because he is good and kind and loving and all that is honorable."

"I do not disagree with you. But that does not answer my question as to why you refused him."

Lisa looked from the Duke to the Duchess and back again, and smiled sadly. "Surely you know the answer, as you've known the answers to all the questions you have put to me."

"Ah, but the answer to this question I am not entirely convinced. I must hear you say it."

Lisa stared at him through a film of tears. "Because I love Henri-Antoine—too well—to marry him."

"I see… You refused his offer of marriage for his sake?"

Lisa nodded. She could not speak.

"But—if marriage to you is what he wants…?"

"It is not what he wants!" she said in a rush and sniffed. "He wants for us to live in his house in the country, where we will be husband and wife in all but name. And I am willing to do this because I love him, and it would suit us both. And when we come up to London, I will stay with him at his house. And it is from his house in London where I can be of assistance to him with the Fournier Foundation. I will visit dispensaries under cover of the foundation, and no one need know who I am, or my connection to His Lordship. Foundation trustees are anonymous after all. Besides, who amongst the poor and the sick will care about my morals, when they have larger problems to worry them, such as their next meal, or where to obtain enough pennies for their medications? And the physicians most certainly won't concern themselves with His Lordship's *domestic* arrangements—they certainly haven't up to now—I do beg your pardon," she added stiffly when there was a sudden snort of laughter. "I am sincere, Your Grace."

"No one would accuse you of anything less, Miss Crisp."

"I assure you that aside from the work of the Fournier Foundation, I will not be seen in public with him. I will be discreet and I will do everything I can not to be an embarrassment to him, or to you, or to your family. But I will live with him, support him, love him, and be his wife in every respect."

Finally, Antonia could no longer remain silent. It was her turn to sit forward. Her voice was soft and gentle.

"You could do all those things and more, *ma petite*, and not ruin yourself, by simply marrying my son."

"*Mme la Duchesse*, marriage has-has—*expectations*."

"Surely those expectations can only be to your benefit, Miss Crisp?" said the Duke. "And if you are concerned lest he take a mistress in the future, I can assure you that in my family the males are all uxorious to a fault. Once they find a mate, it is for life."

"Oh, I believe you, Your Grace. And I am confident of his fidelity."

"You are?"

"Yes. Because—" She smiled and blushed. "I do believe that he loves me as much as I love him. And I do not say that with conceit or as a wishful thinker. I believe it, with my whole heart."

The Duke stared at her with surprise, and then he surprised himself by smiling.

"And I believe you, Miss Crisp. Thus, here is my dilemma. If you love him, and he loves you, and you are willing to live with him as his mistress, in what is essentially a marriage, then why the fickleness?"

"Fickleness?"

"In not allowing my brother to give your union its spiritual and legal due?"

"I told you. I cannot marry him, for his sake."

"So you have said, again."

Lisa looked from mother to son and back to the Duchess, a frown between her brows.

"I thought perhaps Teddy—that Teddy may have confided in-in her mother at the very least, and that Lady Mary may have confided in you, *Mme la Duchesse*, and that you, Your Grace, would know the answer to this question, too... The simple truth is I cannot be a true wife to Henri-Antoine."

For the first time since Lisa had sat on the settee, mother and son looked at one another, and both were nonplussed. They waited for Lisa to provide further clarification, the Duke confessing, "No one has said a word to either of us. So we must assume Teddy has kept your confidence."

"I did not ask her to do so, nor have we discussed the matter in depth. But it is something she has known about me since we were at school together. She did enquire about it when I came here, which was only natural, because it was something which is not in the common way for most females once they progress past a certain age. And I did tell Teddy nothing has changed in me since we were at school. And since my time at the dispensary, and having consulted Dr. Warner, who would never break my confidence, I do know I am not unique. There are others, but Dr. Warner tells me these women are few."

The Duke tried to make sense of this but was completely baffled.

"Which is what, Miss Crisp?"

There was no other way to say it, so Lisa just came out and said it. She had not openly discussed this quirk about herself except with Dr. Warner, and it surprised her how much it affected her to say it out loud.

"I will not bear children, Your Grace. More correctly, I cannot conceive. I am barren, and will likely remain so for the rest of my life."

The Duke was so shocked that it was as if a great weight had just fallen on his head and fuddled his brain. He stared at Lisa as if he did not believe her, and she stared back at him with resignation and sadness. He was so affected that he felt the emotion well up within him and he had to look away. Lisa in turn saw that he was genuinely distressed, and she tried to reassure him, and it wasn't until she looked at the Duchess and saw that she, too, was on the verge of tears, that she faltered and had to resort to her handkerchief.

"You both must see now why I cannot marry Henri-Antoine. Your Grace, you of all men understand that such a defect disqualifies me from being his wife. Marrying your brother is out of the question. I could not do that to him—deny him fatherhood. And I was too over-come to confide in him when he asked me. But I will tell him. I promise you that."

"Are you certain?" asked the Duke. "I do not mean to pry. I just— Dear me. I do not know what to say. I am—"

"—sorry for me? Please, there is no need to be. I have come to terms with my failing, accepted it, almost welcomed it—"

"Welcomed it?"

Lisa glanced at the Duchess, who was smiling in understanding.

"Yes, Your Grace. On those particular days of the month when females have their menses and I do not—"

"Ah! I see! Yes. I understand—"

"Of course you do," Lisa interrupted to save him further embar-rassment. "What husband does not? And while there were girls at school who cursed their monthly courses, I was praying for them! But what I want and wish and pray for has not eventuated and so I fear it may never happen."

It was the Duchess who asked the question.

"Do you not think—as you are only nineteen—that matters they may change for you one day?"

"Perhaps, *Mme la Duchesse*. I can live in hope. But living in hope is no way for your son to live, for any husband to live, is it? Every husband has a right to expect children of a marriage. A barren marriage is not something I would wish on anyone. Surely that way leads to heartbreak? And you are wrong, Your Grace," she stated, looking back at the Duke. "I do not believe Henri-Antoine will cast me aside without providing for me. But if the day arrives when he decides he does want children, then I will accept his wishes. It will break my heart to lose him, but because I love him, I will encourage him to marry and have a family. I only hope that he will at least allow me to continue my work for his foundation, for I wholeheartedly believe in his cause. It is only through advances in medicine that people's lives will eventually change for the better." She smiled, remembering the Duke of Kinross's advice that when the time came she should be herself, and so added, "You may think my words the fanciful expectations of an idealist, but that is what I believe, how I feel, and what I am."

"Your convictions, they are not fanciful in the least, *ma petite*," the Duchess responded, getting up off the sofa, indication that as far as she was concerned, this interview was over.

The Duke stood, and so did Lisa, who smiled and blushed and bobbed a curtsy, before addressing them both.

"I do not know if I will have this opportunity to be in your company again, for Henri-Antoine has plans for us to travel on to Bath as soon as it can be arranged. So allow me to thank you both for having me to stay. I hope my presence did not cause you too much embarrassment or social discomfort. At least it will not happen in the future, for I shall, as I assured you earlier, be exceedingly discreet, as I am sure he will be, too."

The Duke looked over his shoulder and nodded to a footman who stood to attention halfway up the library towards the main entrance, and mother and son watched on silently as Lisa was escorted away, her back and shoulders as straight as when she had entered the library. They then stood there, not knowing what to say. The interview had not gone as they had anticipated, and yet it had gone beyond their expectations. And they were still in shock from Lisa's revelation. Both were wondering at Henri-Antoine's reaction to such news.

Finally, the Duke turned to the settee on which Lisa had been seated with her back to the spiral stairs.

"I'm sorry, Harry. I don't know what I can say that will give you any comfort."

Henri-Antoine came lightly down the spiral staircase. He had been there all along, out of sight, seated on the first landing, listening to the entire interview. It was he who had snorted laughter at Lisa's oblique reference that the sick poor and their physicians could care less about his philandering. That snort had almost given away his presence, but thankfully Lisa had assumed it was the Duke.

He kissed his mother's cheek then gave his brother a hug.

"No need for an apology," he said matter-of-factly and smiled. "Thank you both. What is done is done. By virtue of her honesty, Miss Crisp has sealed her fate, and mine."

FORTY-THREE

W HEN LISA DEPARTED the library and returned to Henri-Antoine's apartment, Michel Gallet gave her the news that His Lordship wished to see her at the family mausoleum. A carriage and two of the lads were waiting to take her there. When she arrived at the Palladian mausoleum with its domed roof and glass oculus, she did not go inside but sat on the bench in the shade and admired the view.

Henri-Antoine found her there fifteen minutes later.

"The view from here is enchanting," Lisa said conversationally when Henri-Antoine joined her at the bench. "You can see all the way to France! Or that's what I'd like to think that blue haze is off in the distance."

"At least you know what you're looking at," he replied in the same conversational tone. "We've had family members think that way lies London, looking for St. Paul's, and arguing about it."

He handed the reins of his mount to one of the two lads who had arrived on horseback with him, and they moved off down the path and disappeared behind the building to join their fellows in the shade. Removing his gloves and shoving them into a pocket of his riding frock coat, he kept an eye on Lisa, who was watching him from under her wide-brimmed straw hat.

This was the first they had seen of each other since she had refused his offer of marriage the night before.

He sat beside her and looked out at a view he had seen so many times since he was a small boy that he was certain he could draw a map of it from memory. But as this was the first time he had looked out on this landscape in Lisa's company, he gave the moment its due. And while they sat in companionable silence, he sought out her hand, and they silently held hands, both wanting to speak about the night before yet acutely aware that much still needed to be said, and soon.

A haze of heat blanketed the landscape, and a sweep of countryside with the big house dominating the foreground, and further afield, forests and a meandering river, and the gently undulating patchwork of farming lands.

It was such a delight to be still and to say and do nothing, fingers entwined. And they were happy in each other's company, despite the undercurrent of unease and uncertainty that still swirled about them.

"Shall I tell you about two of the happiest days of my life, and a third, which I hope will be today?" he said at last.

She nodded and smiled, but instead of saying yes, asked, "Why today?"

"Trust you to choose the more difficult alternative! No. Not that one first."

"Then tell me about the other two days."

He shifted to face her, legs crossed, and an arm over the back of the bench.

"The first happy day was the day my nephew Frederick—Freddy—was born. I was nine years old. It was the happiest day because it meant I was no longer my brother's heir. That if my father died, and so, too, did my brother, I would not be duke, Freddy would be. I cannot describe to you my relief."

"Because you felt unworthy of the title? You were, after all, only a little boy."

"There was that, of course. My father was in his middle years when Julian was born, and an old man when I finally arrived. There was a real fear he might not live to see my brother have children, and thus not know if his dukedom would live on after him. And there was I, the second son: Always sickly, always coddled, a constant worry to my parents, and second in line to inherit a dukedom... Then Freddy came along, which was a huge relief to everyone, particularly my father."

"And the second happy day?"

Henri-Antoine grinned. "That day was when Deb presented Julian with twin sons, two years after Freddy's entrance into the world. So with the heir to the dukedom producing three sons in two years, its future was secured beyond doubt, and this second son was set free from all obligation and expectation."

"But you would never have shirked your responsibilities and the obligation had it come your way."

"Thank you. I would not. But with three nephews, I was now free to live my life how I pleased to purpose it, not how others deemed I must, as my brother must. And having slid to the fourth notch on the branch of the family tree, I was able to breathe easier. I cannot prove, but I am certain that the births of my three nephews helped decrease the frequency, if not the severity, of my seizures."

"And the third happy day? Today, did you say...?"

"Ah, that depends on you," he replied as he untied the silk bow holding on her hat. He carefully laid it on the seat, stood and held out his hand. "I want to show you something—No! First must come introductions."

They walked hand in hand across to the mausoleum. The iron gates were unlocked and one of the heavy, brass-inlaid double doors was open in invitation. The vestibule was lit by two burning tapers in elaborate sconces, and fresh flowers spilled from urns either side of the entrance. There was a chair in the corner and beside it a mahogany box filled with candles.

Once inside the cavernous space of the main room, Lisa let go of Henri-Antoine's hand and walked on ahead, fascinated, and eager to look about. Not only was the Italian marble floor and much of the interior surprisingly well-lit from above by the summer sun streaming through the enormous glass oculus, but so too were the painted walls and marble monuments to long-dead ancestors. Tapers in sconces at intervals around the room had been lit by the caretaker in preparation for His Lordship's visit. That old gent came out of the shadows, bowed and quietly returned to his chair in the vestibule, where he would remain until needed, or until it was time to snuff the candles at sundown, when the doors were locked and the padlock clamped to the iron gates.

"The mausoleum is opened up each morning while my mother is in residence at Crecy Hall," Henri-Antoine told her. "She visits my father once a week, sometimes more often when she chooses. And there are times during the year when it is open to celebrate anniversaries, and of course on those days when it receives a new resident."

"It is a beautiful place... And welcoming..."

"I knew you would think so. I feel the same way. I've been coming here since my teens. At first it was not a happy place, for obvious reasons. But my mother finds great comfort in spending time with my father, who was taken away from her much too early in her life. She brings flowers, and Kinross often accompanies her. And when I'm in residence I will often stop in on one of my rides, to see my father, and now that Martin—he was my father's valet and then his best friend and my brother's godparent—now Martin has joined my father, I-I come to-to see him, too..."

"Are all the dukes of Roxton in residence?" Lisa asked conversationally, hearing the break in Henri-Antoine's voice at the mention of Martin, and so she hoped her question would help him make a recover.

She had wandered over to stand directly under the glass oculus, to bathe in the light, and then moved off to study the walls painted with classical figures in white robes and wreaths, and carrying musical instruments and dancing in a never-ending procession that remained unbroken around the interior. The procession weaved in and out of the alcoves set into the walls, each alcove flanked by a burning taper. A few of the alcoves were vacant, awaiting occupation, while others contained a marble statue of its resident, some of a man and a woman, reclining on polished granite platforms carved with names and dates, and under which was the stone casket that held the coffin containing the mortal remains of the ancestor immortalized in stone.

"They are all here," Henri-Antoine said at last, watching Lisa and through her eyes, enjoying this first visit to the last resting place of his ancestors. "Except my grandfather, my father's father. He died before he could become duke, and as he lived in France for most of his life and married a Frenchwoman, is buried alongside her in Paris."

"Madeleine Julie Salvan Hesham, the Marchioness of Alston, and whose ring you-you wanted me to have?"

"Yes. And all the duchesses are here," he continued. "And when her time comes my mother will be laid to rest here, too, beside my father. And like him, she will have a seat in the mausoleum—"

"Seat?"

"Come. I'll show you."

"What about the Duke of Kinross?" Lisa asked, staying put. She did not like the idea of Elsie's papa being left out of the family group.

Henri-Antoine came over to her, and smiled down at her frown. He understood at once.

"My father is the love of my mother's life, but in this life, the one she has now without him, Kinross is the love of her life. Fate has favored her with two great loves."

"She deserves nothing less."

"Yes. I think so too."

"And will he—will His Grace of Kinross have a place here with her?"

He heard her hesitancy, and his smile widened into a grin.

"What a romantic you are, Lisa Crisp!"

She pouted. "I am not ashamed to agree with you."

He flicked her cheek. "And I am not ashamed to say that I am glad you are."

She smiled. "So. Tell me. Will he have a place here with your mother?"

"He will. But not all of him."

Lisa gave a start, intrigued, as he knew she would be, by his cryptic reply. She leaned in and whispered. "Not all of him? Oh! Which parts? And what is happening to the rest of him?"

Henri-Antoine laughed out loud and shook his head. His laugh echoed and he put a hand to his mouth. "Dear me! Now look at what you have made me do!"

She pouted again, but could not hold back her smile. "You have no one to blame but yourself for that outburst. You baited me with that reply. Do not deny it! You knew I would ask just such a question. Surely you did not expect me to pretend to be revolted, or squeamish?"

"I am guilty as charged. And my father would be most impressed.

Come. I want you to meet him—Ah! But first, Kinross… His heart will be interred here, with my mother. The rest of his earthly remains must be buried on Leven Island, which is in the middle of a loch in Scotland, and is the last resting place of the chiefs of his clan, and the dukes of Kinross."

"How romantic," Lisa said on a sigh, satisfied with this outcome.

"I knew you would think so. Others recoil as soon as they hear the bit about the heart—"

"Why should they? It's not as if he's having it cut out while he is still alive! It is a wonderfully romantic gesture, and I understand why he would leave that part of himself here with your mother. I'm sure your father does not mind in the least, and approves, because His Grace of Kinross loves her just as deeply as he does."

"I'm sure he does, too. Come."

He took her hand and they walked across and sat on a marble bench set back from the wall and directly in front of one monument in particular. Vases of white roses had been placed on the floor and on the monument's lower heavy plinth of red marble a row of candles burned brightly.

Staring out at the world in white marble was a life-size statue of a nobleman seated on a high-backed chair. He was dressed in frock coat and breeches, had across his chest a ribbon—the Star and Garter— and about his shoulders was draped a ducal robe on which he sat and which pooled in folds at his buckled shoes.

Lisa knew immediately this nobleman's identity, and had no doubts the sculpture was to the life. Henri-Antoine was in this nobleman's image, from high forehead to cheekbones, to strong nose and square chin. The resemblance was uncanny. If there was a point of difference it was in the nobleman's mouth. The Duke possessed a thin-lipped sneer, whereas Henri-Antoine had that oh-so-kissable mouth. She kissed him now, and said with a cheeky smile,

"Your father is an exceedingly handsome man."

Henri-Antoine grabbed her hand and kissed her fingers, too over-come with emotion to speak. She wondered if she had offended him, and thought her bad-mannered for kissing him in front of his father's tomb, which was not giving the fifth duke or the occasion the proper veneration. After all, this was the last resting place of an ancient noble family, and he was the son of this duke who stared out at the world as if he owned it.

"Forgive me. I meant no disrespect. I was just so happy to finally meet him, and to see that you are indeed in his image. I've not yet seen the portraits in the Gallery. Teddy says there is one in particular of your parents, not long after they were married. She says the Duke is so like you, or should I say, you are so like him, that the hairs rise on her arms every time she looks at it... I do not doubt he would've been pleased at the resemblance, but he would have been prouder of how you conduct your life and what you have set out to achieve."

"There is no need to apologize," he muttered, still holding her hand. "He would have enjoyed meeting you very much..." He rallied and said in a clearer voice, "That his portrait sets the hairs up on the arms of young ladies he would've found amusing in the extreme. I do." He smiled then surprised Lisa by turning to address his father's effigy, and in French. "*Mon père*, this is Lisa, the girl you told me about in your letter. Is she not just as you described her to me? And more beautiful and cleverer than even you could have foreseen..."

Lisa stared up at the fifth duke in awe. Finally she found her voice.

"He told you about-about *me*—in a letter? But—but he has never met me! You were only a boy when he died. He could not have foreseen my existence. So how is it possible?"

"He did not need to meet you. In his letter he described the girl I would marry, and that girl is you."

"Perhaps—perhaps he told you about the girl who loves you and with whom you would share a house in the country. Is that not the same thing?"

"No. He left me a letter to be opened in the event I was contemplating marrying for love. Had I made a dynastic match, one not based on my feelings, then the letter would have remained unopened, and thus unread."

"And you read his letter yesterday before you had M'sieur Gallet put those little notes in my writing box?"

"I did."

"And inside this letter was your grandmother's ring."

"Her wedding band. Yes."

"But if you had never opened the letter, her wedding band would have been lost forever!"

"Not forever. No doubt a descendant would have eventually opened the letter and found the ring. But lost to me, yes."

"He-he must have been confident you would marry for love."

Henri-Antoine again kissed the back of her hand, and smiled. "So now you know. I not only resemble him in looks, but in temperament. He married for love, and for no other reason. And that is the only reason for me to marry. What about you?"

"Me? I-I never thought I would marry... I dreamed about it. What girl doesn't? And of course I dreamed of marrying for love. But I also dreamed of marrying a man who would—who would love me for me, for myself, and-and that is the stuff of dreams, isn't it?"

Henri-Antoine kept his features perfectly composed, though his top lip gave a twitch, when he asked, "Then, surely, last night, all your dreams came true...?"

Lisa nodded, so forlorn she failed to see that twitch, her eyes downcast and shoulders slumped. She sniffed.

"I never expected they would. I—I was caught off-guard. I was so dull I did not even suspect that ring was a wedding band." She looked up at him through her lashes. "I still want to live with you in your house in the country, even if it is in sin, and without a wedding band."

"But I do not want to live with you in sin. I cannot."

"No?" Lisa repeated in a small voice, though her eyes were wide. "Why not? I thought—I thought we had an agreement..." She glanced up at the fifth duke. "Is it because of the letter your father wrote? Would he not approve?"

"No. It is because I love you. I love you beyond words. I love you more than there are stars in the heavens. Lisa—" He smiled into her eyes and gently brushed a wisp of hair from her flushed cheek. "*I love you.* And I can say it a hundred different ways, and in several languages, until you are convinced, if that is what you need to hear to believe me. I brought you before my father, to show you the depth and sincerity of my feelings. And because I love you, I want to marry you, to make you my life's partner."

Lisa sighed and smiled into his eyes. Tears glistened on her lashes. "I love you beyond words, too. You must know that. Yes?"

"Yes. And you have told me, and with sincerity from the first. I am

the dull one. It took me a little longer to realize I had—as Jack calls it
—fallen off the cliff into love with you."

Lisa looked at their fingers entwined, and then up at him. "If we
love one another then surely we can live together in sin—"

"—until such time as I decide to marry someone else...?"

She sat up, hopeful. "Yes! That may never happen, and I hope it
never will, but if I were your mistress, you would still be free to
marry, and—"

"Don't be an infant, Lisa!" he demanded harshly. "I love you. I
want to marry you. I offer you my grandmother's wedding band, and
you throw it all back in my face with the notion that one day I will
leave you and marry someone else? Do you honestly believe me
capable of such a despicable act? If you do, then you also believe me
to be insincere, that I am fickle and a-a liar, and that I do not love you
at all! What type of man—nay, *monster*—do you think I am?"

"No! No! That is not true. I *do* believe you! I know that you love
me, that you truly do want to marry me. I know you would never
leave me! You are *not* a monster. It is me! I'm the monster because—
because I cannot give you what you have a right to expect as a
husband, and for that reason alone you cannot marry me."

"If you tell me you cannot marry me because you do not love me,
then I accept that. But if you are about to tell me you cannot marry
me because you believe yourself to be barren, that is not a reason I
accept. That makes no difference to me. I love you. I want to marry
you—as you are."

Lisa stared at him, shocked. "You-you—*know*?"

"I do. Such an impediment may have swayed another man, but I
am not like other men. And while I am sad for you, I am not greatly
troubled that our marriage will remain childless. I believe fate has
other plans for us." He smiled. "I have a much grander vision, and
with you at my side to help me, I hope to achieve great things, not for
a handful of children, but for thousands of children, and their children's children. That by harnessing the power of science we can
advance medicine, and in so doing we will improve the health of this
country's most vulnerable subjects." He shrugged. "And there is the
small detail that if you do not marry me I will not allow you to
help me."

"You are threatening me?"

He put up his chin. "I am. It is the only recourse I have left."

She glanced at the fifth duke's monument and smiled crookedly. "It must be. *He* doesn't scare me."

Henri-Antoine's mouth dropped open, and then he laughed heartily. "*Mon Dieu.* You are the girl for me!"

She giggled, then said seriously, "And your family, what will they think—"

"My mother and brother are at this minute waiting for us to join them for nuncheon so my brother can make a formal announcement to the family."

"*Announcement*? Your brother and-and your *mother*?"

"You've met my brother. How eager do you think he is for us to marry, when the alternative is us living in sin? And when I left them, my mother was having him draft a letter to Moore—he's the Archbishop of Canterbury—requesting a special license. All going well, we'll be married before the week is out."

Lisa was heady and happy and all at sea at one and the same time. She hardly knew what to say. So when Henri-Antoine dug in a pocket and held up his grandmother's ring she marveled at him. "You brought it with you."

"I did. And now I would like to slip *grandmère's* ring on your finger here, before my august parent, to seal our commitment. We can then toast our engagement with the family, and of course Teddy and Jack, who are also awaiting our news."

Lisa put out her hand, and he slipped the diamond and sapphire band on her finger, then kissed it. She then held up her hand and turned it this way and that, admiring the ring which fit her finger remarkably well.

"Does everyone know we are here, and am I the only one who is surprised by this?"

He leaned in and kissed her. "For someone who is exceedingly clever, and who is perceptive about the needs of others, you have been rather dull-witted about your own, my darling."

"What I need, my lord," she breathed, kissing him again, "is for you to kiss me properly to seal our bargain—and then I will believe this is not a dream but truly happening."

A little while later, when they came up for air, he stood, and helped her to do likewise. He went forward and briefly placed his hand across the bridge of his father's shoe, before stepping back and making him a quaint little bow. He then turned to Lisa with a smile and put out his hand.

"I have one last detail to show you before we return to the house."

They walked not half-a-dozen steps toward the double doors, when he stopped and turned to face an alcove, his back to the light streaming through the oculus. Lisa wondered why this particular alcove because it was empty of monuments and tombs to ancient ancestors.

"Do you remember, at the folly, telling me about guidebooks—"

"—to grand estates? The ones visitors and travelers use to know something about the families and homes of the nobility? Of course."

"And how you said that if we decided to remain in bed forever we would eventually become skeletons and be written up in one of these guidebooks as some sort of curiosity?"

Lisa giggled. "Oh dear. Did I?"

"You did. And you said such a discovery would be worthy of an entry in any guidebook."

"It would."

He indicated the alcove. "This is much better."

Lisa stared at the painted wall and the space, a niche large enough for a sizeable monument, two at a pinch, and she peered at Henri-Antoine with an inkling of an idea, but she could hardly believe it so let him explain further.

"Had you refused me, this was my final ploy—my wonderfully romantic gesture, one you at least would appreciate—to convince you of my sincerity in wanting to marry you. This will be my final resting place. When that time comes, hopefully far, far into the future, I will join the rest of my family here. And when your time comes," he added, drawing her closer and putting an arm around her waist and then kissing her temple, "you will join me. And Lord and Lady Henri-Antoine Hesham, those great medical philanthropists, will be written up in guidebooks, and not only will family come to pay their respects, but hopefully we will have done enough good work in our lifetimes that we'll have the odd visit from a grateful physician or two. In any case, we will be here together, our monument an earthly symbol to our eternal love for one another."

Lisa looked up at him through a film of tears and when he turned to her, she put her arms up about his neck. She was so happy.

"That is indeed a wonderfully romantic gesture, and I love you even more, if that is possible. I always thought fairy tales were just that, tales, but you have made my fairy tale come true."

"But of course," he drawled, and winked. "My mother is, after all, a renowned fairy godmother. Come. I cannot wait to introduce my future wife to the family…"

EPILOGUE

T HE SMART TOWN CARRIAGE with its four outriders pulled up in front of Warner's Dispensary and immediately attracted a crowd. Those walking the footpaths stopped to stare. Patients entering the dispensary alerted those inside to the arrival, and soon the ill and the not-so-ill were spilling out onto the street to discover just who was inside such an expensive town chariot.

A gentleman dressed all in black stepped down from the carriage. He went not to the entrance used by the sick poor, but to the one for the exclusive use of private patients. He did not need to knock. The door was open, and standing on the threshold was the Warners' butler, waiting to welcome the distinguished visitors on behalf of his master.

Inside the consulting room a group of persons had assembled to hear what they knew to be good news. Still, regardless of the funding the dispensary was to receive from the Fournier Foundation, everyone was nervous, and none more so than the dear doctor, who paced back and forth with his hands behind his back. Three of the doctor's assistants loitered in the corridor, hoping to catch a glimpse of the visitors, while in the room waiting to welcome them, along with Dr. Warner, were his two consultant physicians and the anatomy instructor, Mrs. Warner, and her sister Mrs. Cobban.

Less than two months had gone by since the dispensary had been visited by the trustees of the Fournier Foundation. And upon that occasion Dr. Warner was warned not to expect any word on the progress of his application until late autumn at the earliest. Yet, here it was the first days of August, and a letter had arrived with news that his application had been successful. Not only that, but the foundation's patrons, normally reticent to divulge their identities, were eager to visit his dispensary at their earliest convenience, due to their imminent departure abroad; the noble couple were setting off on their bridal trip.

Michel Gallet returned to the carriage with news everything was in readiness. And with the lads keeping the crowd back, Lord Henri-Antoine alighted from the carriage, diamond-headed walking stick in hand. He helped his wife to firm ground, and wrapped her arm around his to make the short walk to the consulting room. The crowd surged forward to take a better look. They were particularly interested in the beautiful young lady in her redingote robe of striped satin; a string of pearls about her white throat; and set at a rakish angle over her upswept curls, a black felt hat decorated with plumes and satin ribbons that matched her gown. More than a few could not believe their eyes, but it was true, and they recognized in this fashionable lady their amanuensis from her previous life. A cheer went up in greeting. And then another.

The noble couple paused. Her Ladyship stayed her husband while she thanked the residents of Gerrard Street and the patients to Warner's Dispensary for their good wishes. She smiled at the eager grubby faces of the wide-eyed children and the grinning adults, all happy to wish the couple many years of wedded bliss. A final cheer went up as Henri-Antoine and Lisa disappeared inside the building, the lads at their back staying vigil on the steps.

Inside, Dr. Warner greeted his esteemed guests with a bow and smiles, genuinely happy for the couple but most particularly for Lisa, whom he bashfully complimented as quite the loveliest bride he had ever seen. His Lordship's stare swept the room, and he noted with satisfaction the due acknowledgement of the de Crespigny sisters, Mrs. Warner and Mrs. Cobban, who eased themselves into an appropriately low curtsy with eyes respectfully downcast in recognition of their cousin's newly elevated status as wife of the second son of a duke, sister-in-law of the all-powerful Duke of Roxton, and daughter-in-law of their esteemed and beloved patroness the Duchess of Roxton and Kinross.

Henri-Antoine smiled, unable to hide his pride, when he announced to one and all, "Allow me to introduce my wife, the Lady Henri-Antoine Hesham, patroness of the Fournier Foundation..."

~ THE END ~

BONUS LETTER

From Lisa to her mother-in-law, the Duchess of Roxton and Kinross, sent from Constantinople while on her honeymoon.

Lady Henri-Antoine Hesham, the White House on Third Hill, Constantinople, to Her Grace the Most Noble Duchess of Kinross, Leven Castle via Kinross, Fife, Scotland.

[*Translated from the French.*]

The White House on Third Hill, Constantinople,
August 12, 1787

Dear Maman-Duchess,

I trust this letter finds you, Papa-Kinross, and Elsie in the best of good health.

Before I write anything else, I, we, thank you from the bottom of our hearts for the truly special and touching gift you sent to help us celebrate the first anniversary of our marriage. I can hardly believe it is thirteen months to the day since my life changed forever. The months have gone by too quickly, but each one has been more magical than the last, and you know from our letters how very happy we are.

Your gift arrived only two days ago, so it was indeed a wonderful surprise! Neither of us had any expectations of what it could be, though Henri-Antoine knew immediately he removed the wooden box from its crate and shed its wrappings. He set the box on the low table before us, and it was as well that we were seated on cushions and just inches from the ground because he swayed and grabbed the table edge. You can imagine I thought he was unwell, but he assured me he was not.

Before he opened the lid, he gently ran his fingers over the box's polished surface in the same manner I have seen him do when calming a frightened dog or petting a cat, as if the object had life and was a treasured pet. And when he slowly opened it out to reveal the inlaid interior and the playing pieces and cups within, there were tears in his eyes. He was so overcome that I remained silent yet could hardly wait for him to tell me the significance of this playing box, and most particularly its special significance for him.

When he told me that this was the very backgammon board you and his father played on every day of your married life, I, too, was overcome. He told me in a trembling voice how he would watch you both from the chaise longue, and how he often felt an intruder because when you played at backgammon you forgot everyone else, and it was as if it was just the two of you in the library. But he also told me that it was you who taught him how to play. And he recalled the day he won his first game from his father, and his father's look of incredulity that his eight-year-old son had beaten him at his own game. That memory had Henri-Antoine grinning. Though he then was incredulous himself that you had parted with this most treasured and loved item.

But I understand why you did, and you know, do you not, Maman-Duchess, that we will cherish this as you do, and always will. Henri-Antoine has already written to thank you, and no doubt he told you I am a complete novice at the game. Though I am certain you knew this was so. We have decided that we will honor your gift by playing each evening, while having our Turkish coffee.

I am very willing to learn, and Henri-Antoine is already proving a patient if exacting teacher. I have a plan to improve my game so that he will be more than a little surprised (and no doubt think it all down to his superior teaching skills). When he visits the coffee houses (which you know are denied to women) to smoke a hookah and play at backgammon with the local men, I intend to practice my game with Michel, who Henri-Antoine let slip is more than a tolerable opponent. In this way I hope to emulate his feat as an eight-year-old and beat him at his own game—one day!

Please thank Elsie for her recent letter enclosing her delightful watercolors of her dear little kitten Blanche, and of the loch, and the pretty purple flowers. I have placed these and her letters in a specially bound book which I keep in my boudoir and will show her when we return home. I will write to her separately of course, but direct that letter to Crecy, so she will have that waiting for her upon your return there at the end of the month.

Do you recall how in my previous letter I was on a mission to find a suitable companion for Elsie's dolls? Well I have finally found her! Mlle Yvette and Signorina Simonetta are to have a new friend. I have named her *Sevil*, which means 'to be loved' in Turkish. And I know she will be.

Sevil is the same size as Elsie's other companions, with caramel skin, dark hair, dark eyes, and a rosebud mouth. She is dressed in the costume of a female of the sultan's harem in pantaloons, long over-jacket, and has a turban atop her hair, all in vibrant silks. Her hair is free flowing and so thick it can be arranged in all manner of styles. I have asked Becky to fashion Sevil half a dozen similar outfits in different silks, and to make her several pairs of matching slippers. We found tiny silver bracelets for her wrists and ankles at the markets. And I commissioned one of the woodworkers to make her a special box for her to lie in, lined in velvet, and a small clothespress for her clothing and various accessories. She also has a most wondrous miniature stringed instrument called a Tambur (we have an adult-sized one to present to Jack) which can be tuned and played if one is dexterous enough to pluck delicately at the strings. I cannot wait for Elsie and her companions to meet Sevil. Henri-Antoine says, and he is quite right, that I am as excited as if the doll were mine, for I have indeed derived great pleasure in having Sevil dressed, and in commissioning the making of her accessories.

I had crated and shipped the second lot of silks and threads you requested, and Henri-Antoine has visited the carpet warehouse twice to see progress for himself. As the order is such a large one, he is greeted by the weavers as if their sultan has come amongst them, and as you can imagine he does not disappoint, and plays his part, as do the lads.

I found a Turkish coffee service and all its pieces like the one Henri-Antoine remembers you using and he drinking from the little cups when you stayed here. He says it is similar to the travel set His Grace has at Treat. I am hopeful it will please you and Papa-Kinross. I liked it so much I bought four complete sets: One for you, one for Jack and Teddy, one for the townhouse in Park Street, and one for the house in Bath. Henri-Antoine intends to fashion a room in both houses in the Ottoman style and has ordered what amounts to two entire rooms' worth of what is necessary to replicate our private sitting room here, everything from the silk cushions, hangings, wallpapers, carpets (you see why the weavers venerate him!), low stools, couches, and even two nargiles. I am told a nargile is the same thing with a different name as the hookah Papa-Kinross brought with him from the subcontinent. Henri-Antoine insists Papa-Kinross have one for use at Leven.

My dear husband tells me he was introduced to the pleasures of smoking from the water-pipe by His Grace in his teens, though perhaps that was not something he wished you to discover, so please do not take Papa-Kinross to task, Maman-Duchess. But such expertise as Henri-Antoine has in using a water-pipe has come in useful here. The physicians we have consulted have provided him with a special herbal tobacco, a substitute for the usual tobacco used in the water-pipe, which they assure us will help alleviate his symptoms, if not stop the onset of a seizure.

On that score, he had a most severe attack two weeks ago, which I believe was brought on by the lack of proper recuperation from a seizure the previous week. And it is all because he insisted on accompanying me to the textile markets during the heat of the day. I had arranged for my lady's maid and Becky to go with me, and as you know I never step out of our compound without two of the lads as escort.

I have gone alone in this manner to the markets on several occasions, but Henri-Antoine was determined and intractable that this time he would come with me. I knew his stubbornness was not only because he was still feeling unwell, but because it had become a point of male pride for him to be my escort. This was because Sir Jonas Wetherby (I told you about the scholar of Oriental languages attached to the embassy in a previous letter), dared to make an unguarded remark under the influence of strong spirits to Henri-Antoine at the Occidental Club, and before others.

Sir Jonas dared to suggest that His Lordship was cavalier in allowing such a beauty (me) to roam about Constantinople's streets without her husband's protection. That while I had my lady's maid and liveried servants with me, they were no substitute for a young bride having her husband's arm. That a husband was the best and only signal to the locals that here is a female who is not only carefully nurtured, and of the highest possible rank within her own society, but she is to be treated with the utmost respect, and not to be trifled with by the local men.

I do not know what angered Henri-Antoine the most: To be lectured to about his want of manners as a gentleman, his seeming neglect as a husband, or that Sir Jonas would have the impertinence to suggest the locals would ever dare 'trifle' with His Lordship's wife. All of these is my guess. No matter that Sir Jonas is quite a stupid man, for all his abilities as a translator. He may be good at his job, but he must lack basic comprehension skills, for anyone with a modicum of understanding would not make such an unguarded remark to a social superior, and never to a new husband, and most definitely not to His Lordship.

I have no idea what Henri-Antoine said by way of reply, only that the sting in Sir Jonas's words led to him getting out of bed well before he should have. A day spent enjoying the cool waters of our plunge pool and the use of the nargile would have served him better. But I realized there was no use offering up this suggestion when his male pride had taken a battering. And so he came with me.

To shorten a sorry story, this second attack was most severe and required that the lads spirit him away down a darkened alley, and there we remained until his sedan chair could be fetched to carry him home. He was put back to bed where he remained for four days.

It is the worst attack since our stay in Padua. And while I am all sympathy for his suffering, I did tell him it served him to rights for not staying abed until he was fully recovered. I also stated that I refuse to leave our compound again under any circumstance, barring invasion by the Russians, if he could not offer me the assurance he would rest until he was well. And if he did not understand me then perhaps I should call in Sir Jonas to translate my words into a language he not only understood, but which was simple enough for him to comprehend.

My dear husband informed me he had already ordered the servants to bar Sir Jonas from admittance to our house, so he would not have to suffer that fool again. He grumbled some more but soon apologized. His accompanying look of affected contrition (though I believe he was truly sorry) was such that I burst into giggles. This had him grinning in response, and all was forgiven, though he refused to forgive Sir Jonas. Which I said was reasonable, and we kissed and made up. Maman-Duchess this is the only disagreement we have had in our first year of marriage.

As to possible invasion by the Russians, I know the situation in the Crimea has been reported in the English newssheets, and you must be worried lest this war between the Turks and the Russians arrives here in Constantinople. Henri-Antoine says the coffee houses are full of nothing else but talk of war, that it will be soon, for the Sultan cannot allow Empress Catherine to take what does not belong to her.

This state of affairs, with the threat of war imminent and all that entails for a nation facing invasion, means we have already made arrangements to leave here and return home as soon as possible. All our belongings that are not absolutely necessary for our day-to-day existence have been crated, and these with the sedan chairs and carriages are already at the docks ready to be loaded aboard ship. We leave in a week's time, under sail, so that we return to England with all speed. It is not only the coming of war that motivates us but because we have been away long enough now, and because of Teddy's most wonderful and longed-for news!

We are both so thrilled and excited that Teddy and Jack are finally to become parents. We have been expecting this for some months now, and dared not to hope against hope it would be sooner rather than later. I know Teddy was grateful not to fall pregnant almost at once, but with the passing of months, a hint of apprehension had crept into her letters that she had not already done so. And just as I received her letter expressing this apprehension another arrived almost the very next day with news of her pregnancy and the baby due in the new year, around the time of her baby sister's second birthday, which would be a lovely double celebration for both families. We are so looking forward to being home for the birth, and to take on the role of doting godparents.

Which brings me to answer the question you asked in the letter previous to the one you just sent, about my health. Naturally Henri-Antoine is fully apprised, but you are the only other to whom I will confide. Perhaps one day I may tell Teddy, but at the present time she must focus on her own health and her baby.

I did allow myself to submit to a physical examination, and by one of the most learned and respected midwives in this city. She has delivered more babies than any male physician here. My interpreter assured me that even the women of the Sultan's harem trust her with their lives, and with their fertility. I would never have permitted a male, no matter how learned, to examine me in this most intimate of ways, but I felt exceedingly comfortable in her presence and with her manner. And while I know Henri-Antoine is not at all bothered at the prospect of us remaining childless, and says so with such conviction that I believe him, he also says, and I know you will take this in the right manner, that my barren state is a blessing in disguise, because he has no wish to bring a child into the world who suffers his affliction. And I would be lying to you if I said I did not agree with him. Yet there are times, not very often, when I allow my reasoning to scatter and I daydream of possibilities. So with this in mind, and to have peace of mind, I permitted the midwife to examine me.

The outcome was not as I expected. The examination itself was more discomforting to my dignity than anything else, and when she had finished she was smiling, so I took that as a good sign. Through the interpreter she told me I was indeed female, which made me wonder if something was lost in the translation because how could I be anything else, until it was explained to me (and perhaps you are aware of this, but I most certainly was not) that there are women in this world—and this shocked me, though I do not disbelieve her—who may have every outward appearance of being a female, but who are devoid of the reproductive organs necessary to conceive and bear children. I would be lying if I told you this did not greatly unsettle me. Yet, after the examination she was able to assure me that I am indeed in possession of a womb. So in theory at least, I can grow a child within me. But she did add that my womb is small for a female my age and even for one who has never had children. She said this may account for my lack of menses. And it is her learned opinion that for me conception may just be a matter of time. She said as I am young I have many years, indeed decades, of hope left to me.

To be frank, Maman-Duchess, we do not want to spend decades in hope, and so we will put this new-found knowledge aside and return to living our lives. I mean to live each day as I have every other day since my marriage, and that is as a loving wife, companion, and help-mate to your son, whom you know, as surely as the sun rises every morning, I love with every fiber of my being. And we shall concentrate on the great task we have ahead of us in making the Fournier Foundation not only our legacy, but Monseigneur's and the family's legacy, too.

This will make you chuckle. The midwife prescribed me a herbal medicinal concoction which she says is an aid to fertility. I have no notion if it will be beneficial in the way it is intended or not, but Henri-Antoine insists I at least try it. Secretly, I think he is pleased to not be the only one taking concoctions that taste foul, and which with the best of intentions we tell him to endure for his health. So we take our medicine like good children, together, both resisting the urge to pull a face, not wanting to be the first to give in, and doing our best to appear unaffected by the foul taste. Neither of us wants to be the first to grab for the tumbler of punch within reach to wash out our mouths. So we make the effort not to look at each other while taking our medicine, particularly when the servants are with us. But if we are alone and we dare to glance up and our eyes meet, we lose all sense of decorum and burst into laughter, and sometimes so hard we momentarily stop breathing. We fall about on the cushions, eyes watering. One time a servant entered while we were in this silly state and thought we had both been poisoned, threw the tray in the air and ran out of the room screaming. This only made us laugh harder, particularly when Michel dared to glare at us with a mixture of exasperation and delight, like a parent wishing to scold his children but unable to do so because they are enjoying themselves too much. For his benefit and to save his sanity, we came to our senses and tried our best to appear contrite, though the tears of laughter were still running down our cheeks.

Have you ever seen Henri-Antoine laughing so hard he must hold his sides? It is a joy to behold and a privilege, for you know how stern he is with himself and how in control when he is under the public eye. Did his father ever laugh uncontrollably when alone with you, I wonder? You of course do not have to answer me, Maman-Duchess, for I think he must have at least chuckled and perhaps laughed hard enough in your company to bring tears to his eyes. I thought you would like to know this about your son.

I must away to supper. We are having it on the rooftop, now the sun has set. And because it is so hot, we will take a midnight swim in the plunge pool, and there float and look up at the twinkling night sky. Our time away and our stay here have been magical, but we are both eager to return home, to you, and to our family, to begin this next chapter of our lives, together.

With love,
Lisa
Lady Henri-Antoine Hesham
I write my married name with such wonder, pride, and joy.
xo

AUTHOR NOTE

This work of fiction is populated with real people and places, so if you want to know more, visit the dedicated Pinterest page, where there are loads of pictures, paintings and resources about the people and places mentioned in the book:

www.pinterest.com/lucindabrant/falling-series

Henri-Antoine's inheritance

100,000 pounds/dollars doesn't seem like a lot of money today, but in the 1780s it was equivalent to inheriting around 20 million pounds sterling or 25 million dollars US. But what is more surprising is that the purchasing power, labor value, and income value of such an inheritance was vastly greater. In fact, it was astronomical. The equivalent income value today would be more than 200 million pounds/dollars. That's because labor (people's working hours and skills) and the goods and services they produced, were cheap.

You can learn more about the value of money in the past, and the worth of such a vast inheritance by visiting measuringworth.com.

Falling Sickness (Epilepsy)

I used a great deal of online resources to learn as much as I could about this common neurological disorder. You can too, by visiting your country's Epilepsy Foundation.

For historical detail and the stigma surrounding epilepsy in the past, the following research resources were invaluable:

- *The Falling Sickness: A History of Epilepsy from the Greeks to the Beginnings of Modern Neurology* by Owsei Temkin, Johns Hopkins University Press, Baltimore, 1971
- *Disability in Eighteenth Century England: Imagining Physical Impairment* by David M. Turner, Routledge Studies in Modern British History, London, 2012
- *Swimming with Dr Johnson and Mrs Thrale: Sport, Health and Exercise in eighteenth century England* by Julia Allen, The Lutterworth Press, Cambridge, 2012

Explore real places, objects, and history in *Falling UP* on Pinterest:
www.pinterest.com/lucindabrant/falling-series

Lucinda Brant Author
lucindabrant
22.6k followers   596 following

Falling Trilogy
Falling UP: Book 1

Miss Lisa Crisp

Batoni Brotherhood

Blacklands house did exist!

Toulmin & Gale Bond Street

Chealsea buns

Elsie (Lady Elspeth)

Buying ribbons

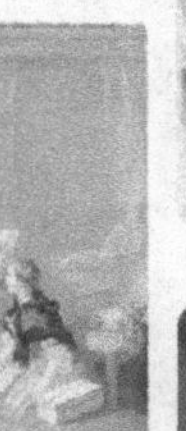

Surgeons Blizard & Willan

Lisa's Rosewood writing box

Chelsea Bun House

Bell Savage Inn

Dancing the Allemande

Elsie's doll

Verjovis Temple Folley & his coin

Swan Inn Alston

Satyr's Son Cover Reveal

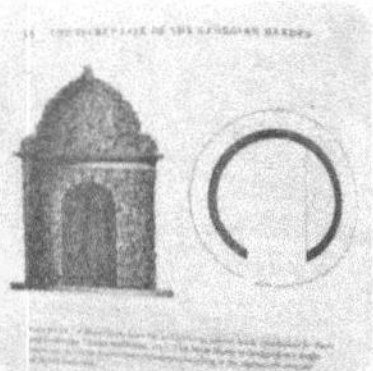
Privy in the grounds of Treat